*published. Most of book one is based on the real life experiences of my family.
Robin Helm
Phil. 4:13*

SoulFire

The Guardian Trilogy, Book 2

ROBIN HELM

Copyright © 2011 Robin Helm

All rights reserved. No part of this publication may be reproduced, stored in a retrieval system, or transmitted in any form or by any means, electronic, mechanical, photocopying, recording, or otherwise, without the prior written permission of the publisher.

The characters and events portrayed in this book are fictitious or are used fictitiously. Any similarity to real persons, living or dead, is purely coincidental and not intended by the author.

Scripture quotations taken from the New American Standard Bible®, Copyright © 1960, 1962, 1963, 1968, 1971, 1972, 1973,1975, 1977, 1995 by The Lockman Foundation.
Used by permission (www.Lockman.org).

ISBN-10:0615536832
ISBN-13:978-061553835

DEDICATION

To my sister and best friend,
Gayle Griffin Mills,
who has given me
her unfailing support
and the benefit of her knowledge,
beginning with teaching me
to read when I was
four years old.

To my father,
Archie Melvin Mills,
who fully believed
that I could do anything
I chose to do
and passed that belief
to me.

ACKNOWLEDGEMENTS

Thank you to Gayle Mills and Stephanie Hamm for editing *SoulFire* and for contributing their ideas and expertise during the development of the story, to Julianne Martin for being a huge source of encouragement, and to Wendi Sotis, for serving as my cold reader and formatting expert. and to Larry Helm, whose help and spiritual leadership has been a stabilizing influence in my life for the past thirty-eight years.

Chapter 1

"Do not neglect to show hospitality to strangers, for by this some have entertained angels without knowing it."
Hebrews 13:2

January, 2008

Xander, Niall, and Roark flew above Lynne's Honda as David drove Elizabeth and his wife to the airport early Friday morning. Since the concert, which unintentionally had become her worldwide debut a few months prior resulting in the creation of her reputation as a widely renowned pianist and vocalist, she had received numerous offers to perform, and she had decided to accept an engagement in Toronto after making it clear that she wished to perform sacred as well as classical music. Lynne would be traveling with her; they planned to spend the weekend as there would be a rehearsal Friday evening and the performance on Saturday night.

David had insisted on leaving well before the time that was necessary. It was an hour's drive to the airport, and he hoped to miss the morning rush hour in Greenville. Any hope of avoiding traffic problems evaporated as a car sped off of a ramp in front of a semi-truck several cars ahead in the lane to the right of them. To their horror, the truck was unable to stop and could not pull into the adjoining lane without hitting other vehicles. The driver had nowhere to go. Everything seemed to move in slow motion as they watched the scene of the accident unfold. The driver of the car realized, too late, that the truck was going to hit her. She attempted to merge with the cars in the next lane, but the truck clipped her from the rear, sending her into a spin across three lanes of traffic. Her Toyota Camry was hit by four cars as the truck jackknifed and slid down the road sideways. The terrible screeching of tires skidding and metal impacting metal seemed to go on and on; then suddenly everything was eerily quiet for a moment. All traffic came to a complete standstill in the wake of the multiple wrecks.

The Camry was crushed and twisted, and several other cars were also badly damaged. The truck driver opened his door and began to walk back down the road to survey the damage and await the police. He was already on his cell phone calling 911. Lynne and Elizabeth bowed their heads to pray for the people involved in the crash as David left the car to see if he could be of assistance to anyone. Roark walked beside him.

Xander already knew that praying for the woman in the Camry was unnecessary. Seconds before the collision, he had seen her guardian flying over the car with a tall, slender angel dressed in flowing, shimmering robes of blinding white. The angel's eyes were large and violet, and his long, white hair was held back with a silken cord. His blue-white wings were not created for speed, unlike those of a guardian or a warrior, but they were large and beautiful. Xander had seen death angels many times before when Jehovah-Shalom was ready to call one of His children home. The presence of such a light being signaled to the protector that the battle was over, and the reward for the saint was at hand. He was always filled with awe and reverence for his Master each time he witnessed the escorting of a child of God to heaven. It was never a time of sadness, for Jehovah-Rohi's timing was always perfect. The believer simply closed his eyes in one world, and opened them in the arms of an angel. Xander watched in peace as the eternal spirit of the woman left her lifeless mortal shell and went to her escort. The death angel held her close in his embrace and spread his wings, lifting her into the air as he flew with her from one world to the next, followed by her guardian.

David had gone directly to the Camry, and, seeing that the woman had not survived the accident, he had hurried to another car to comfort a crying infant whose mother was unconscious. A few other people had also approached the wrecked cars to stay with the injured until the ambulances had time to arrive. Before long, the wailing sirens were heard, signaling the arrival of the police, medical personnel, and wreckers. David returned to the car, but did not tell

Elizabeth and Lynne that the woman had died. He saw no need to further upset his wife and daughter when there was nothing they could do. Roark and Niall knew that he would tell Lynne later, apart from Elizabeth.

Well more than an hour had passed before the road was cleared enough for a single line of cars to begin the painfully slow process of breaking up the traffic jam. Even though the Bennets were near the front of the congestion, by the time they reached the airport, checked their bags at the curb, and wended their way through security, Lynne and Elizabeth had missed boarding their plane. Followed closely by their guardians, they hurried to the ticket counter. Lynne explained what had happened, and they were put on another flight that would be departing in an hour, but, unfortunately, their luggage had already been loaded on their original flight and was on its way to Toronto via Pittsburgh, while they had a layover in Philadelphia before changing to a different airline for the remainder of the trip. Since both flights were to arrive at Toronto International Airport, Lynne thought there would be no problem retrieving their bags. She had been assured by the customer service agent that their luggage would be kept safely for them during the one hour time difference between the flights. Lynne used her cell phone to call their contact in Toronto and apprise him of the problem. Because David had left them at the airport curb thinking that they had made it in time, she also called him to let him know about the delay.

As they sat down to wait, Elizabeth, already upset after witnessing the pileup on the freeway, started to worry that she might miss her rehearsal. *I need that time with the orchestra for my vocal pieces, and I want to be able to spend several hours becoming familiar with the piano I will be playing. We need to do sound checks with the technicians, too.* Xander, behind her, stepped closer, rubbing her shoulders and whispering in her ear. *Be anxious for nothing, my beloved. It will be well. Our Father will supply all your needs according to His riches in glory.* Xander's blue eyes twinkled in merriment. *I will fly you there myself if need be.* Elizabeth pulled a book from her bag and began to read.

Beside him, Niall rolled his eyes. *Xander, being with you now is like enduring a lovesick human male. You have not yet introduced yourself to the lady, you know.*

Xander squirmed a little uncomfortably. *Niall, I have been preparing myself for that by closely observing the ways of men with women, and there were other things I had to accomplish as well. You know that I am now registered at Converse and ready to start my classes when the term resumes. I had to take all those CLEP tests, and qualify for my degree at Liberty. Michael has been helping me by guarding Elizabeth when I have had to be gone and is now prepared to step in when needed. There has been much to arrange, and everything had to be done to my satisfaction. I cannot just appear and start talking to Elizabeth. She will ask questions, and I have had to think about the answers.*

Niall laughed at him. *Admit it. You are afraid. You are as nervous as a moonstruck teenager asking for his first date.*

There was silence between the brothers for a few minutes. Xander, his hands resting on Elizabeth's shoulders, turned his head to look at his brother.

What if she does not ever love me, Niall? Xander's voice was low and strained.

Niall looked at his brother, and his expression was serious. *Of course she will love you.* Then he grinned. *What woman could resist a tall, handsome fellow like you?*

Xander released his breath slowly in obvious frustration. *I know that human women find my physical form to be attractive, Niall, but what if she does not like the way I am? I am not witty, and, even in the angelic realm, I do not converse easily with those whom I do not know well. I fear that I am boring, Niall. Elizabeth loved the human boy, Richard, and I am nothing like him. It is safer to love her from a distance than to reveal myself and risk her rejection.* Xander looked at the floor morosely.

'Faint heart never won fair lady.'. You said that our Master told you that you were formed for each other. As Shakespeare said, 'Screw your courage to the sticking place.' If you accidentally bump into Elizabeth when Lynne is there, I will be with you to whisper hints into your ear if you become tongue-tied. I am fluent in the Song of Solomon.

But you have no more experience with human women than I do! Xander exclaimed aloud. A few guardians passing by with their charges glanced at him in wonder. He took a deep breath and calmed himself.

Niall chuckled. *I am witty and the essence of charm.* He smiled roguishly. *The material point is that I am not in love, and I will be able to think of interesting things to say. I guarded one of Solomon's closest advisors, and you are well aware that Solomon had seven hundred wives and three hundred concubines. I know a few things about wooing a woman.*

I have always wondered about that. Solomon was the wisest human who ever lived. Why did he have so many women? If it is difficult to keep one woman happy, why would he choose to multiply the effort by one thousand? It does not seem very wise to me, Xander interjected.

That is exactly the sort of thing you should not say to a woman. You are definitely going to need me. Niall let out an exaggerated sigh.

I will know when the time is right, insisted Xander, crossing his arms over his broad chest.

Try to make it before her child-bearing years are past, returned Niall with just a hint of sarcasm.

Do not quit your day job. Stand-up comedians have a short shelf life.

Ouch. Niall placed a hand over his heart. *Am I leaking light from that wound?*

Xander snorted, but resumed his usual stoic mien as several more guardians passed by with a group leaving on a mission trip. He was silent as he contemplated Niall's words. As much as he hated to admit it, his brother was correct on two points: he needed to make Elizabeth's acquaintance very soon, and he was gripped by fear at the very thought of it. Elizabeth had reached her full height of five feet nine inches – not short for a human woman, but much smaller than he was. How could such a little person cause such anxiety in him? He knew the answer; she held his heart in her small hands. Her rejection would crush him, and his failure to win her would have far-reaching consequences for the rest of humanity. Xander set his jaw with determination. He must win her love, and he must start that process as soon as possible. He would conquer his fear by facing it.

After what seemed to be an eternity, an airline employee stepped to the counter and announced that boarding would commence for Lynne and Elizabeth's flight. Mother and daughter gathered their belongings and joined the line, Niall and Xander on either side of them. They found their seats in coach, and in due course, they arrived in Pittsburgh and disembarked, crossing the terminal to get to the gates for the other airline. Lynne was mystified to find no one at that desk, and she and Elizabeth went in search of the ticket counter for their original airline. Lynne approached a ticket agent and handed her their tickets.

"Hello. My name is Lynne Bennet. We have just arrived from Greenville, South Carolina, on your airline and were supposed to connect with a flight to Toronto. No one is at that airline counter. Could you possibly help us?"

The woman looked at their tickets with a puzzled expression. "Mrs. Bennet, I'm sorry to have to tell you that the airline you are booked on is not flying today."

Niall and Xander flanked Elizabeth who stood behind her mother.

"Excuse me? There must be some mistake. Your airline booked us on that flight," Lynne said with exasperation.

The ticket agent turned to her computer and typed in some information. "Mrs. Bennet, you are correct. I have no idea why they set it up this way in Greenville."

"You don't understand. We have to be in Toronto tonight. My daughter is performing at Roy Thomson Hall tomorrow night and she has a rehearsal with the orchestra this evening. She has to be there."

The woman looked around Lynne at Elizabeth and recognition lit up her face. "Didn't I see you on YouTube?"

Elizabeth nodded shyly.

SOULFIRE

"Have a seat over there, ladies, and let me see what I can find. It doesn't look very promising, but I'll do my best."

Lynne and Elizabeth trudged to the seats indicated by the agent and sat down heavily. Elizabeth bowed her head. *Father, you know we need to be in Toronto in just a few hours, and it doesn't seem that we have a way to get there. Please help us, dear Lord. In Jesus' name.*

Elizabeth thought, *Amen*, and then opened her eyes to see a pair of feet in low heels directly in front of her. She lifted her head to see the lady from the ticket counter looking at her, smiling.

"It's not wonderful, but it's the best I could do. I have booked you both on an Air Jamaica flight flying stand-by. They're ready to board, so you need to get to that gate as quickly as possible."

"Thank you so much," said Lynne, accepting the tickets from her. The woman quickly gave them directions, and the group of humans and angels jogged to the Air Jamaica terminal and found the correct gate. Lynne approached the agent there and presented their tickets. The last passengers had just finished boarding the plane.

The agent smiled at them. "This is your lucky day. You are in the last row on the flight. We have room for three."

Xander glanced at Niall. *Watch them both for a second. I will be back immediately.*

Niall raised an eyebrow at Xander, and then turned to follow Lynne and Elizabeth.

Xander stepped into the men's room beside the gate, changed to human form, and emerged carrying a small bag and wearing a long-sleeved charcoal Henley, a black sports coat, jeans, and boots. He walked up to the agent and handed her his ticket. She looked up at one of the tallest men she had ever seen, and briefly lost her ability to speak as she took in his angelic face and powerful physique in one up-and-down glance.

"Did I make it in time? I am on stand-by for this flight," he asked, flashing his most devastating smile at her, dimples on full display. He heard her heart accelerate and read her jumbled thoughts. *If only I could be assured of this response from Elizabeth! But Elizabeth looks beyond outward appearance. She is more concerned with the heart.* When the woman made no response, he cleared his throat. *I need to get back to Elizabeth – today if possible.* The sound jolted her back to coherence.

"Uh, yes. There's one more seat. In the back. In the last row." *I sound like a complete fool. I wonder if I could sneak a picture of him with my cell phone. No one will believe me when I describe this man.*

"Thank you. Have a wonderful day." He smiled again, and she stared at him, dumbfounded.

Xander boarded the plane and made his way to the very back of it, heads turning toward him in a wave as he walked. All chatter ceased as he walked down the aisle, the men and women giving him their full attention. He could hear their thoughts – the men noticed his musculature and wondered about his work-out regimen, and the women absorbed his physical beauty while their minds turned to images of intimacy. Xander felt naked, and he was embarrassed as the sound of his boots tapping on the floor seemed to grow louder with each step. *They are all looking at me. I am now a spectacle for humans instead of them being a spectacle for me. I Corinthians 4:9 now applies to me, 'We have become a spectacle to the world, both to angels and to men.'* He tried unsuccessfully to make less noise.

Xander drew no less attention from the few other guardians onboard the flight. The entire angelic realm was aware of their chief's dual nature and of his love for Elizabeth. To see him in his human form approaching the object of his interest raised their curiosity to unheard of heights.

I am a spectacle for the angels, too. Maybe meeting her publicly on a plane was not the best idea, after all. If it goes badly, I will be trapped for the entire flight.

It will be well. You can do this, thought Niall. *You cannot back out now. The course is set.*

Lynne sat by the window, and Elizabeth was in the middle seat. They were probably the only two beings on the plane who had not noticed him. *Perfect,* thought Xander with great relief, smiling at Niall a little smugly.

Niall smirked in response and nodded toward the seat by Elizabeth. Xander's smile rapidly faded, and his muscles bulged as he lifted his bag to put it in the overhead compartment. His head nearly touched the roof of the cabin.

Good thing I am in the aisle seat. Otherwise, there would no place to put my legs. He straightened his shoulders. *This is the time. Now or never.*

He glanced at Niall once more before turning toward Elizabeth and Lynne. Leaning over slightly, he asked, "Do you ladies need for me to put anything up here for you before I take my seat?"

Both Elizabeth and her mother had been looking out of the window. At the sound of a low, masculine voice, they turned their heads toward him. Immediately, Lynne went back in her memory to the time her four-year-old El was lost at Tabernacle. *This young man looks like the same man who brought El back to me, though his hair is shorter. But, it's not possible that they are the same. That was almost fourteen years ago, and this guy can't be older than twenty or twenty-one. The man who found El would be between thirty-five and forty now. I guess it's true that everyone has a doppelganger, even Hercules.* Niall rolled his eyes again.

Elizabeth stared, transfixed, into Xander's eyes. *I've seen those eyes before. There could not be another clear, blue pair like those in the world. Those wonderful, kind eyes reassured me when I was a lost child, and they comforted me when we were in the wreck with Janna.* She looked down to her lap at her hands. *It can't be him. He's not old enough.*

Xander cleared his throat. *I seem to be doing this quite a bit today.* He was pleased that they had come up with their own explanations for his reappearance. His effort to look a little younger by wearing his hair in a modern style and dressing in clothes that were popular with college students had been successful. He was twenty years old according to his identification papers.

Lynne was the first to leave her reverie. "No, thank you. We've already put our things away." She started reading her magazine.

Xander sat down by Elizabeth, trying unsuccessfully not to crowd her. His frame was too big for the seat, even when he scooted as far as he could toward the aisle. *Maybe meeting her on a plane was not the best idea.*

Elizabeth started giggling. *He's trying so hard not to touch me.*

She is laughing at me. I am dying here, Niall.

Give her a moment. It is not every day that a giant appears, you know. It will be well. Relax.

She turned her head to tell him not to be concerned about taking some of her space, but she was struck dumb by his perfect profile. She had been so caught up in his eyes, that she had completely missed seeing the rest of him. *I thought Gregory was beautiful, but even he isn't as gorgeous to me as this guy. There's something . . . a little too smooth about Gregory that makes me uncomfortable sometimes, but I feel completely the opposite about this man. It's almost like I know him, but surely I would remember meeting a guy who looks like this. Everything Gregory does, or says, or wears seems very studied, but this man appears to be genuine.*

Xander, reading her thoughts, could not help but smile. *She already prefers me to Gregory.* He also heard Niall's response. *Humph!*

He slowly turned his face toward hers, and she forgot everything she was going to say. Xander decided that helping her express what she had been thinking about telling him might be a good way to start a conversation. He had spent hours daydreaming of this moment, and the idea of talking to her made his palms sweaty. *That has never happened before*, he thought with surprise. He took a deep breath and forged ahead. *It was easier to close the mouths of the lions in the den with Daniel.*

"I am sorry that I take up so much room. These seats are not made for someone like me."

She bit her bottom lip to keep from laughing. "You are rather, uh, large, but don't worry about it. We were just glad to get on the plane. We were afraid that we'd be stuck in Philadelphia." She smiled a little shyly at him. She had never been so aware of a man's presence before. He seemed to fill the space around her. Even his scent was powerfully appealing to her. *What cologne is he wearing?*

"Me, too. I am flying stand-by. Last minute trip on family business," he said. It was difficult for him to think clearly as she leaned a little closer and breathed in, trying not to be obvious about it.

He smells heavenly, Elizabeth thought.

Lord, please help me not to sound like a blithering idiot. Being human around her has heightened all my senses, and I cannot think well.

The flight attendant's voice came over the speakers instructing them to buckle their seat belts and prepare for take-off. They complied with her request automatically.

His voice is musical. She struggled to think of a response. *This is ridiculous. Stop thinking about the way he sounds, and looks, and smells. That's three of my five senses he has overwhelmed in one shot.*

Xander could not suppress a small smile. *The Acqua Di Gio was a good idea.*

Niall smirked behind him. *You are welcome.*

After another moment's pause, she answered, "So are we. Flying stand-by, I mean. We missed our flight in Greenville, and somehow we were booked onto a connecting flight on an airline that wasn't flying today. It's been crazy."

He looked out the window past Elizabeth and Lynne, spotting two demons riding the wing of the plane. *Niall, do you see them?* he asked with a small frown.

Yes, they have been there a few seconds, observing you and Elizabeth.

With an effort, Xander replaced his slight scowl with a more pleasant mien and returned his attention to his companion.

"May I ask why you are going to Toronto?" he queried.

"I'm giving a concert tomorrow night at Roy Thomson Hall," she answered, lowering her eyes.

She is so beautiful. I would love to touch her face. I remember how soft her skin was when I held her close and flew her to the hospital. Patience, my friend, patience. He forced himself to concentrate on making a sensible reply.

"Really? How interesting. What sort of concert?"

"I play the piano and sing."

"Have I heard of you? What is your name?"

"Probably not. Elizabeth Bennet. Everyone calls me El."

"I have heard of you! I have just enrolled at Converse for the spring semester. I, too, am a pianist and a vocalist, though not of your caliber, I am sure."

"That's amazing! What a small world. What's your name?"

"Xander Darcy."

Niall looked heavenward. *Nobody gives their full name, Xander.*

You are right. He cringed inwardly.

Do not worry. It was a small error.

Elizabeth chuckled, her brown eyes full of amusement. "That's quite a mouthful. What should I call you?"

Whatever you want to. Just call me, please.

Focus, man! Niall thought, smiling behind his hand.

Xander fought his way through his mental fog. "Most of my friends call me Xander or Xander. Do you like Xander?"

"Yes, I do. It's unusual, but it fits you. I'll call you Xander, then." *Maybe I won't be like everyone else to you.*

That would not be possible, Elizabeth.

"May I call you Elizabeth? You seem more like an 'Elizabeth' to me than an 'El.'" *I do not think I could call you anything else. You have consumed my thoughts as 'Elizabeth.'*

"You'll be the only one that calls me that, but that's okay." *Just call me whatever you want to.*

"I would like to come to your concert tomorrow night, if that is all right with you."

"I wish I could invite you, but it's been sold out for a while now. I can't get a ticket for you." *What if I never see him again?*

He smiled widely, showing his dimples. "I am not entirely without connections. I may be able to get a ticket myself. If I can come, would you and your mother like to go to dinner afterwards?"

Dimples! How is it possible that he could be even more breathtaking? Elizabeth tore her eyes away from his face and looked at her mother, a question in her eyes.

Lynne had been following the conversation carefully, though she had not looked up from her magazine. She caught Elizabeth's glance in her peripheral vision and raised her head to see El's eyes pleading with her. Niall whispered to her, *This is a good man. You can trust him.*

Lynne reflected a moment. *She hasn't shown any interest in a boy since Richard broke her heart last year. Perhaps we should get to know this young man a little better.*

"What did you have in mind, Xander?" she asked, directing her gaze toward him.

Niall remembered Lynne's telephone conversations with the booking agent. *They are staying at the InterContinental Toronto Centre which is within walking distance of the Roy Thomson Hall. The Azure Restaurant there has a reputation for being classy and romantic.*

Xander smiled at Lynne. "The Azure Restaurant is located in the InterContinental Toronto Centre near Roy Thomson Hall, and it is very good. I would love to treat you, ladies."

"I think it might be good for you two to be friends, since you'll be going to school together in a couple of weeks, and the location is perfect. We are actually staying in the hotel," Lynne replied.

Thanks for the help, Niall.

Actually, you are doing quite well on your own. I am pleasantly shocked.

"Excellent. I will meet you backstage after the concert."

"But what if you can't get a ticket?" asked Elizabeth.

"I promise you that I will be there. You can trust me on this. I would not miss it for anything," said Xander, looking rather seriously at her.

He is very self-possessed for such a young man. Very mature, Lynne mused.

You have no idea, thought Niall.

Xander, quite pleased with his progress, continued to chat with Elizabeth and Lynne until they landed in Toronto.

After they retrieved their items from the overhead compartment and exited the plane, he joined them as they walked to the baggage claim area. They waited until all the passengers had retrieved their luggage, but there was no sign of theirs. Together they approached the customer service area.

Lynne explained the entire ordeal to the agent, and he checked his computer. "Ah!" he exclaimed. "Air Jamaica passengers are already in Canada when they leave the plane. The flight from Pittsburgh was on a different airline and left your bags in their area. Your bags have not yet cleared customs, and you can't go get them because you are already through. Let me see what I can do."

"But we're in a hurry," Lynne said.

From behind them, Xander had scanned the large area and had seen their luggage, actually sitting some distance away at the other airline's baggage area. He stepped outside the small office. *Niall, get their luggage. I will stay with them.*

Niall flew at flash speed to the men's room on the other side of the customs area. After he had morphed into human form, he walked to the other baggage area and picked up the luggage. Niall telepathed with the guardian standing by a customs agent, and the agent's protector stepped into an office and came back out in human form, dressed as an agent. Niall approached him, produced a passport, and was quickly cleared through customs. Then he casually walked by Xander, left the luggage behind him, and walked rapidly away, returning seconds later in angelic form.

"Mrs. Bennet, Elizabeth," Xander called from the door. "Look what I found."

Lynne was delighted. "How did you do that?"

"I told you that I had a few connections," he replied, winking saucily at Elizabeth.

Elizabeth blinked. *Is he flirting with me?*

Lynne turned back to the office and called to the young man who was still busily typing away at his computer. "Never mind. Everything's fine."

He looked surprised as he glanced up to see the Bennet ladies walking away with a towering man carrying several large pieces of luggage, along with his own small bag, as if they were of no weight at all. *Is there an American pro basketball team in town?*

Xander waited with Lynne and Elizabeth at the curb while Lynne hailed a cab. While the cabbie stowed their bags in the trunk, he had a chance to say a few words privately to Elizabeth.

"I will look forward to your performance tomorrow night, Elizabeth. Do not forget our dinner engagement," he said, smiling into her deep brown eyes.

She looked up at him in wonder. *There are very few boys my age who treat me this way. He's huge, but I like it. Rather than feeling threatened, I feel protected and safe.*

"There is absolutely no chance that I will forget it." She turned from him and slid into the cab with her mother.

He stood watching as the car drove away. *Look back at me. Please, Elizabeth, my love. I want to see your face looking at me.*

As if she had heard him, she turned to look out the rear window at him, and lifted her hand to wave goodbye.

Xander smiled widely and waved back. Then he quickly stepped into a crowd of people and changed into angelic form. In less than a second, he had caught up to the cab and flew over it with Niall.

You are grinning like a lovesick teenager.

Xander could not find it in himself to care whether or not he looked foolish. His heart was light and filled with hope. *This may not be as difficult as I thought it would be.*

Then he remembered the demons on the wing. *There will be complications.*

We will deal with them, answered Niall with confidence.

I look forward to it, said Michael appearing suddenly on Xander's other side, flying with them in formation.

Chapter 2

"And do not get drunk with wine, for that is dissipation, but be filled with the Spirit, speaking to one another in psalms and hymns and spiritual songs, singing and making melody with your heart to the Lord."
Ephesians 5:18-19

Xander, in angelic form, stood to Elizabeth's left as she seated herself at the piano, took a moment to compose herself, and began to play Liszt's *La Campanella*. Her hands flew with such fluid speed over the keys that her audience was left breathless by the artistry of the sound and movement. She followed the playful piece with a lightning rendition of *Valse Oubliée* by the same composer and finished her first set with a virtuoso performance of Igor Stravinsky's Firebird Suite (*Danse Infernale, Berceuse*, Finale) arranged by Guido Agosti. Her skill was such that she was able to mimic the orchestra parts, introducing a bell-like quality to parts of the music, and she brought the cheering audience to its feet with her amazing strength in the final bars.

Elizabeth rose from the instrument, bowed to the audience, and left the stage, closely followed by her guardian, for a brief break as the members of the orchestra took their seats. She thankfully took the water offered to her by a stagehand and sipped it thoughtfully. Though she was focused on her performance, she could not stop herself from scanning the audience from the wings, searching for a tall, incredibly handsome man with wavy dark hair and beautiful blue eyes. *Where is he? I suppose I could possibly miss him in this crowd. Maybe he couldn't get a ticket after all. I wish he had asked for my cell number. But mom was there. Awkward!* She flashed a secret smile. *Maybe I should just grab a microphone and ask if Xander Darcy is in the audience. That would get his attention. Or I may just have to wait for school to start back. Enough! Time to think about the performance, El!*

She is disappointed not to see me! Xander could not suppress a smile as he caught the melancholy edge to her thoughts, followed by her lightheartedness. Several guardians with orchestra members noticed his expression, but were careful to show no response. They had observed their intimidating chief the previous evening at rehearsal, full-well knowing his feelings for Elizabeth, and had seen his love for her displayed on his countenance during unguarded moments. It was a matter of intense interest to them, but an undue show of attention from the ranks he commanded would be unseemly. Now that they could hear her thoughts concerning the imposing guardian, their curiosity was truly piqued.

After the orchestra was seated, the dark-haired young beauty walked confidently back onstage, her trademark white gown flowing behind her as the stage lights caught the rhinestones at her waist and on the straps of the dress. She returned to the bench, nodded to the conductor, and poured her heart into Rachmaninov's Piano Concerto No. 3, Part 1. Afterwards, Elizabeth chose to give the orchestra a short respite by following the demanding piece with a piano solo, Chopin's Etude Op. 25 No. 1, also known as the "Aeolian Harp." The audience was as mesmerized with watching her willowy form moving emotionally with the flowing music as they were by her proficiency at the instrument. She was truly striking – a brunette with long curls flowing artlessly down her back, contrasting sharply with her white gown. Her slender arms moved gently, and her graceful fingers caressed the keys. With each swaying movement, the stage lights caught the rhinestones woven through her hair, holding the shining mass back from her face. She was strong, yet gentle; soft as a whisper and bold as the thunder. The black sheen of the Steinway grand reflected the image of her magnificent hands as her long, slender fingers flew effortlessly over the ivories. Her technical mastery of the instrument was astounding, but her astonishing ability to convey emotion through her music was what set her apart from all other musicians. Elizabeth's performances always left her audiences enthralled and breathlessly wanting more.

As the hall erupted in applause, she stood and walked to the center of the stage, accepting the wireless microphone brought to her by a stagehand while another pianist took her place at the Steinway.

"I hope you have enjoyed the selections thus far," she said, smiling and speaking easily with no signs of nervousness. Her stage presence had matured along with her musical skills.

Further applause signaled the appreciation of those fortunate enough to have obtained a ticket.

"I would like to leave the classical realm now and share with you my own arrangement of a medley of songs taken from one of the few American musical art forms – the Spiritual. I find the words to be poignant and meaningful, and the music to be amazingly powerful in its simplicity. As the slaves sought freedom from physical slavery, many seek spiritual freedom from sin through Christ. These songs equate freedom in the Promised Land, the northern United States and Canada, with heaven. Will you indulge me?"

The crowd applauded their encouragement for her to continue. Elizabeth stood, much as she had at the Fine Arts Festival ten years before, with Xander towering regally behind her. The top of her head now reached his shoulders, but his neck and noble visage were clearly visible to every angel present, and she was again illuminated by his gentle glow.

Niall, in the audience with Lynne, was struck by the similarity of the events. *They truly belong together. Our Master is wise beyond any imagination.*

From beside him, Michael answered, *As He said in Isaiah 55:8-9, 'For My thoughts are not your thoughts, neither are your ways My ways,' declares the Lord. 'For as the heavens are higher than the earth, so are My ways higher than your ways, and My thoughts than your thoughts.'*

Hearing the thoughts of Niall and Michael, Xander gazed directly at them. *We do belong together. Jehovah-Bara formed us for one another.* He knew in that moment that everything would work for their good. He had assurance that whatever they might have to face, and he was sure that it would be terrible at times, God would bring them through it together. He was glad that his Master, in His infinite wisdom, had sent Michael to be with him so that they could guard Elizabeth together. He was beginning to assume human form more and more often, and it was becoming increasingly difficult to ensure that she was never unprotected.

The orchestra began the medley of her symphonic arrangement with the plaintive wails of the violins, playing "Sometimes I Feel Like a Motherless Child" as Elizabeth began to sing softly in the lower part of her range; however, she used the extent of her four-octaves and the full power of her voice as she continued to change keys, going higher and higher, supported by the woodwinds through "Were You There," "I Am a Poor, Wayfaring Stranger," and "Nobody Knows the Trouble I've Seen." As the music became more upbeat, the orchestra shifted into a swing rhythm featuring the brass section in "Swing Low, Sweet Chariot," "Ezekiel Saw the Wheel," and the rousing "Joshua Fit the Battle of Jericho." After she finished the medley, she immediately began singing "Amazing Grace, My Chains Are Gone," by John Newton, Chris Tomlin, and Louie Giglio, with a simple string accompaniment, modulating up a half step on each verse. On the final verse, Elizabeth closed her eyes and sang a cappella, "When we've been there ten thousand years, bright shining as the sun, we've no less days to sing His praise, then when we first begun."

And He was there, in the whirlwind of the Spirituals, and in the still small voice of "Amazing Grace, My Chains Are Gone." The angels felt His presence in that place and raised their palms toward heaven, faces lifted as they hummed in worship. The light grew and multiplied, and souls were touched to seek Him.

John Newton's hymn, written after he had been saved out of the horribly sinful life of the captain of a slave ship, was a fitting end to the medley. As Elizabeth sang the final notes, the crowd was silent. There was no standing ovation or polite applause; no one wanted to destroy the mood she had created. Overwhelmed by the words she had just sung, Elizabeth began to speak to the audience. She told them of how God had shown his mercy to a small-town, Southern girl of humble birth and no importance. For the first time before a large audience, in a few sentences, she shared her personal testimony and her salvation experience. Elizabeth spoke of God's love, forgiveness, and mercy. When she was finished, she handed the microphone to the waiting stage hand, and returned to the piano, closely followed by her protector.

For the finale of the evening, she had decided to do her own original arrangement for piano and symphony orchestra of great hymns of the faith. Elizabeth realized that her choices for the latter part of the evening had been unusual, and that she was very likely changing the course of her career, but she felt led by God to do so. She was serene as she began the opening notes of "Great Is Thy Faithfulness," and continued through "Joyful, Joyful We Adore Thee," "Be Still My Soul," "O, The Sweet, Sweet Love of Jesus," "It Is Well," "What Wondrous Love Is This," "Guide Me, O Thou Great Jehovah," "Be Thou My Vision," "O God Our Help in Ages Past," and ended with Handel's "The Hallelujah Chorus" from *The Messiah*. "Joyful, Joyful We Adore Thee" was entwined with Pachelbel's "Canon in D," "Be Still My Soul" was paired with Debussy's "Clair de Lune," "What Wondrous Love Is This" was woven with Beethoven's "Moonlight Sonata," and "Guide Me, O Thou Great Jehovah" was meshed with Tchaikovsky's "1812 Overture." The music ebbed and flowed with classical themes woven throughout the arrangement, brilliantly joining the genres in a celebration of God's gift of music.

Xander remembered standing by G. F. Handel in 1741 as the fifty-six year old man had composed the music for *The Messiah*, setting to music the Scriptural text, or libretto, written by Charles Jennens. The entire musical score had been completed in an amazing twenty-four days, and Handel had written the letters "SDG," *Soli Deo Gloria*, "To God alone the glory," at the end of his manuscript. The oratorio had been quietly received at the time of completion, but had since become one of the best-known choral works in Western music, as well as one of the most frequently performed. *To God be the glory, indeed, George. You would have loved this performance,* thought Xander.

The audience stood, as was traditional, when they recognized "The Hallelujah Chorus," and they were surprised to see a choir coming down the aisles of the auditorium, singing as they walked. The sound of voices blending together to sing the familiar words filled the hall with His praises, and one hundred seraphim, in addition to the guardians present, flew through the ceiling and filled the upper chambers of the theater. The people felt the air stir with the gentle rush of angel wings as the six-winged light beings swirled and dipped in a choreographed dance of joy as old as creation itself. They glowed with all the colors of the rainbow joining in the center of the auditorium to create a brilliant, white light which chased every demon within a mile radius of the building into hiding, creating a holy circle in the center of the city. Believers in the audience lifted their hands to heaven, knowing that they were in the presence of Jehovah, and their faces shone with His light.

As the singers sang the final "Hallelujah," the angels floated and twirled, finally leaving the building with the human audience stupefied as to what had actually happened. Everyone knew that something momentous had taken place, but only the believers in the crowd knew that God had touched them. They had shivered during those moments of perfect connection with the Almighty, and they had praised him. There was a total oneness with their Creator, and they looked forward to the day when they would meet Him face-to-face.

Even more wonderful things were happening in heaven as thousands of angels repeated the joyous patterns over and over. In every place on the earth, light beings looked to the heavens, seeing the dancing beams, and they listened. Through the spiritual plane, they heard Elizabeth's music, and the whole earth rejoiced.

After a moment of silence, the people erupted into a roar of applause and appreciation for what they had experienced. Some wondered why they suddenly had the urge to go to church, or to pray, or to pull out that old Bible from the closet. Others could not explain what they had felt, but they wanted to know the feeling, that connection with something larger than themselves, again. Still others wanted to think it was foolishness, and denied that it was anything other than emotional trickery. Those who had been before to the auditorium wondered at the light show. They had never seen such a display there in the past, and they could see no equipment that would produce such beautiful, dancing beams. No matter what they said or thought, everyone there knew, in that secret place of the heart, that something supernatural had been there with them. It was a beginning of great things to come.

Elohim received the offering of praise and was well pleased.

~~oo~~

As soon as Elizabeth left the stage for the final time, Michael took his place by her side as Xander ducked quickly behind a curtain and emerged backstage in human form. He leaned his shoulder casually against a wall directly in her path and put his left hand in his pants pocket, keeping her in his line of vision at all times. Knowing that she would be dressed formally, he had opted to wear a black Italian tailored two-button suit with a grey vest over a white shirt. Niall insisted that he wear an ice-blue tie "to bring out his eyes," and black dress shoes. He felt very conspicuous, noting that every human that passed by looked at him from head to toe. *Is that good or bad?* He kept trying to think of things he could say to her, and he desperately hoped that he looked more relaxed than he felt. Something was definitely doing a little dance in his very human stomach, and he fervently wished that he could be assured that it would not work its way down to his legs and feet.

Xander watched Elizabeth, followed closely by Michael who was dressed as a warrior guardian, as she glided towards him, and he knew the exact second she saw him. Her brown eyes lit up with happiness, and the sun seemed to shine from her smile. His heart skipped a beat and glowed as he felt the warmth from that sun. *There is that adorable double-dimple in her right cheek. I know Lynne told her it is where the angels kissed her before they sent her to earth, but it is actually where an angel wants to kiss her.* He returned her smile. *Niall is correct. I am as silly as a teenage boy with his first crush, but I am no longer anxious. This feels right.*

Oh my! she thought. *He cleans up very well. I thought I couldn't possibly be remembering him clearly, but he really is just as beautiful as I pictured him all day long.*

"Hello, Xander. I'm supposed to meet Mom in my dressing room. We're going to get my things so that we can put them in our hotel room before we eat, if that's okay with you."

"The concert was wonderful, Elizabeth. I enjoyed every minute of it. And whatever makes you happy will always suit me."

He opened the door for her, and she was surprised to see a huge vase of sweetheart roses on the dressing table. She went quickly to get the card and smiled broadly as she read silently.

I missed being there with you tonight.

You really shouldn't give concerts without me.

See you soon.

Always yours,

Gregory

Xander felt a distinct chill. *I should have thought of flowers.*

She turned her head and looked up at him. "Gregory Wickham sent the flowers. Do you know him?"

Michael frowned. *Gregory!*

Xander hesitated just a moment – just long enough for her to notice. "We have met a few times."

"Why do I get the feeling that you don't like him?"

Because he is the spawn of Satan? Because he wants to kill you? "I do not think he likes me very much," he replied carefully.

"That's odd. Why wouldn't he like you?" She tilted her head to one side with a puzzled expression.

Careful. He is her friend, thought Michael.

Xander sighed. "I suppose our families have never been particularly close. There was a time when his father worked for mine, and we were like brothers, but that friendship ended years ago. I would rather not open up old wounds." *True. I would rather open new ones. And please forgive me for deliberately leaving the 'we' vague as to whom it is referring.*

Michael grinned, his green eyes twinkling.

"He goes to Converse, you know. You'll be in some music classes with him," Elizabeth said diplomatically.

"I am sure that we will get along well with each other. We have something in common after all. We both think you are wonderful. Should we begin to gather your things? Your mother will be here soon, and it is nearly time for our dinner reservation."

He is avoiding the topic of Gregory. What does he know that I don't know? We'll return to this later.

"You're right, of course. Mom will be here soon. Just let me look around and make sure that I remembered to put everything in my bag before I went on stage." After Elizabeth made a quick check of the room, Xander smiled at her and reached for her bag. She had given it to him and was about to pick up the flowers when Lynne and Niall came into her dressing room followed by a man with his guardian.

Xander recognized his protector, Lexus, a guardian of the upper ranks. He and Lexus had met thousands of years earlier when Xander had been Abraham's guardian and Lexus had guarded Sarah, Abraham's wife. The two of them, along with Gabriel, had shared a meal with Abraham while in human form. Gabriel had told the patriarch that Sarah would bear a son, Isaac, though she was ninety years old. Xander remembered how Sarah had been discovered eavesdropping on their conversation when she had laughed aloud at Gabriel's prophecy. The story had been recorded in Genesis, chapter eighteen. *This man must be important in the Master's plan to have Lexus as a guardian.*

Lexus bent his elbow, palm forward, in salute to Xander, Michael, and Niall. Michael nodded in acknowledgement as Niall returned his salute.

"Hello, Xander. El, this is Jonathan Edwards, an evangelist. Jonathan, this is Xander Darcy. El, Jonathan would like to talk with you a minute."

The young man, who appeared to be in his late twenties, smiled and extended his hand. After he shook hands with Elizabeth and Xander, Jonathan began to speak. "It's great to finally meet you, El. I've been hearing wonderful things about you for a couple of years now, and I bought tickets to this concert months ago so that I could hear you myself. I must say that the praise was not at all exaggerated. God has gifted you phenomenally."

"Thank you, Rev. Edwards. That's very kind of you. Is there anything I can do for you?" She smiled and lifted her brows in question.

"Please call me Jonathan. As your mother said, I am an evangelist. My ministry is growing, but I think that if we work together, we can shake this continent for God. I would like to talk further with you about it, if you're interested."

She thought a few moments before she spoke. "Jonathan, I have actually been looking for a way to use my gifts for God, and I've been praying that He'll show me what He wants me to do. Would you like to meet in the morning before Mom and I fly out?"

Jonathan smiled broadly. "Of course. Could we meet for breakfast in the Azure Restaurant at eight? Lynne told me that you two are staying at the InterContinental tonight. I'm staying there, too, so it would be convenient for all of us."

"That's fine with me. Mom?" Elizabeth asked, deferring to her mother.

"That sounds good. It was nice to meet you, Jonathan. We'll see you again tomorrow morning. I think we have to be leaving now. Xander has dinner reservations for us."

"Until tomorrow, then," Jonathan said, nodding his farewells and leaving the room briskly, followed closely by Lexus.

~~oo~~

Xander held Lynne's chair for her, and then moved to seat Elizabeth. The restaurant was softly lit, with walls of glass that went from floor to ceiling, displaying the beauty of Toronto's city lights at night. Deep blue was the theme color, from the artwork above the bar, *Liquid Veil* by Stuart Reid, to the glasses on the snowy white table cloths.

I am glad that Lynne is with us. This place is so romantic that I need a third person present to remind me that Elizabeth does not know me as I know her. I must remember that, while I love her with my whole body, soul, and spirit, she has just met me. I am a stranger to her.

I am here to remind you of that if you forget, Niall thought.

Michael laughed lightly. *Be mindful that I will guard Elizabeth against you if necessary.*

Xander chuckled as he took his seat.

"Did I miss something funny?" Elizabeth asked him. "I dearly love to laugh. Share it with us." Her smile was so sweet and honest that his mind went blank as he looked at her.

Xander, say something! You are glad to be here with them.

"Oh, I am just happy to be here with the two most interesting, lovely women in the room. Every male in this restaurant is surely jealous of my good fortune," Xander said quickly. *Thanks, Niall. I will do better. I promise.*

I certainly hope so. Focus, man.

Their waiter appeared, introduced himself, and made recommendations from the menu.

As Elizabeth and Lynne ordered the grilled scallops and vegetable tart with water, Xander suddenly realized that he had not eaten in thousands of years. He pretended to study the menu while his mind thought of all the possibilities.

Why did I not think of this before I suggested going out to eat? I do not know if I will like modern food or not. What if it makes me sick? This will not be bread cakes, curds, milk, and veal.

Calm yourself! Niall looked over Lynne's shoulder at her menu. *Order something simple. Try the Azure soup and a Caesar salad with fettucini primavera. Wait until later to try meat.*

That is easy for you to say. You do not have to eat or do anything with the food later.

He looked up at the waiter and smiled. "I think I will have the Azure soup, a Caesar salad, fettuccini primavera, and water."

After the waiter left, Elizabeth looked at Xander curiously. "Are you a vegetarian?"

"No, I just do not like to eat anything too heavy this late in the evening. I will be quite happy to enjoy your company. You must be famished. I know that you did not eat before the concert."

"How do you know that?" Elizabeth asked, her full attention engaged.

Oops! "I just assumed that you would not eat before performing because of pre-program jitters."

Nice recovery. Niall smiled at him.

You are doing well. Michael was encouraging.

"Actually, you're right. I never eat before I perform. I'm too nervous. Have you ever given a recital or a concert? I know that you play and sing, and that you're majoring in music."

"I am fairly new at all this, but I have a request to make of you."

He didn't answer my question. Interesting, she thought. *He is such an enigma.*

Is it good to be an enigma? Xander queried.

She thinks you are interesting. That is good, replied Niall.

Women love mystery. Or so I have heard, added Michael.

"Ask away. It seems to be my night for requests." She laughed lightly.

"May I audition for you?" Xander's blue eyes gazed into hers.

"I would love to hear you play and sing at any time. Why would you want to audition for me?"

"If I am good enough, I would like to play or sing a duet with you. We could do the music at your church sometime."

"My church? How do you know I go to church?" *He seems to know a lot about me somehow.*

His laugh was a low musical sound. "Elizabeth, you gave your testimony at the concert. You sang a medley of Spirituals and played a brilliant original arrangement of sacred songs. It stands to reason that you go to church."

I must be getting paranoid. "You're right, I do. My dad is my pastor. We would love to have you visit our church, and I'm sure that we could get something together for a duet. We live in Bethel and attend Tabernacle Church. Are you familiar with it?"

"I have a townhouse in Spartanburg. I just moved there to attend Converse, and I am looking for a church to attend regularly. Of course, I will not be back in time for services tomorrow, but I would like to come next Sunday, if you do not mind."

Again, he sidestepped my question. Very neatly, too. And he never uses contractions. I have never met anyone so nearly my own age that uses such perfect grammar. 'Curiouser and curiouser.'

Hearing her thoughts, Xander nearly panicked, though his face showed no change in his emotions. *She knows that I am different.*

Elizabeth looked at him thoughtfully. *I think I like the way he speaks. He seems to be a true Southern gentleman – cultured, well-bred, courteous, and charming. He reminds me of the men my grandmother used to talk about. The Judds sang a song about the 'good old days.' People fell in love to stay back then. I want it to be that way for me and whomever God chooses to be my husband.*

He gazed directly into her eyes and smiled his appreciation for her thoughts. *I am so glad that He has chosen me, Elizabeth.*

They were quiet as a waiter poured their water.

Lynne, who had been listening to the conversation with interest, interjected, "Of course we don't mind, Xander. We would be very happy to see you at Tabernacle. If you would let us repay your hospitality for dinner tonight, you are welcomed to have Sunday lunch with us after church. You and El could work on a special for church in our music room after lunch."

He flashed Lynne a full-wattage smile. He was so relieved, he could have hugged her. "How generous of you! Of course I accept your invitation, if Elizabeth agrees," he said, turning to Elizabeth with the same devastating smile. *I have always liked Lynne. Remarkable woman.*

Quite right. Niall chuckled.

Oh, Elizabeth agrees, all right. Elizabeth wants to see those dimples again, thought Elizabeth. She could not suppress her smile of delight. "Never let it be said that the Bennets do not have Southern hospitality. Please come to church with us and stay for lunch next Sunday."

Again with the dimples. Niall rolled his eyes. *Do not forget to get her cell number.*

Her cell number? asked Michael.

Cell phone number. Humans communicate by talking on them or texting messages to each other, answered Niall.

I suppose we warriors miss the day-to-day changes of human life, unlike guardians who are with them all the time. I think I will enjoy this assignment. Michael's eyes sparkled with good humor.

"Would you mind giving me your cell phone number in case I become lost?" Xander asked, striving for an innocent look.

"Tabernacle is on the main street of a town that has a population of three thousand people, but I'll give you my number. I certainly wouldn't want to be responsible for your getting lost. I just couldn't live with that on my conscience," she smiled teasingly. "Why, anything could happen to you in a strange place, all alone." *Like anyone would mess with you. You are the biggest man I've ever seen. There is no doubt that you could protect yourself from an entire gang, if there were such a thing in Bethel.*

She has never seen me. I am a little taller than Xander, thought Michael.

If everything goes well, she never will, replied Niall.

"Do you have anything to write on, Mom?" asked Elizabeth.

Lynne leaned over to get her purse, put it in her lap, and rummaged through it, producing a pen and a slip of paper from her day planner. Elizabeth took the paper and pen from her mother, wrote both her home number and her cell number on it, and handed the paper to Xander and the pen back to her mother. Xander put the paper in his vest pocket.

He looked at Elizabeth mysteriously, with just the hint of a smile. "I must confess something."

Xander had her full attention immediately. *Hmmm. He never volunteers information, and he avoids answering questions. This should be interesting.* "Confess away." She smiled brightly.

He leaned toward her and lowered his voice. "I am not really afraid of getting lost. I would like to call you just to talk," he paused, looked at Lynne, and raised his voice a little, "if that is agreeable with you and your mother, of course."

Lynne was both surprised and amused. "No young man has ever asked my permission to call either of my daughters. I must say that I like it. It's refreshing. It's all right with me; it's up to El." *My antennae are tingling, telling me that El is very much okay with it.*

"Certainly. I'll look forward to it." *He's honest. I find honesty to be very attractive in a man. And he paid respect to my mother; I like that, too.*

I wish I could be completely honest. I do not like avoiding her questions. Xander looked at the table. He felt guilty.

Eventually, you can tell her more. Now is not the time. Niall looked at his brother with an encouraging smile. *It will be well.*

Think of her feelings, Xander. Do you think she is ready to hear the full truth now? asked Michael.

Xander smiled ruefully. *I guess not. She would probably run screaming for the door.*

The conversation came to a close as two waiters came with their first course. From that point on, they talked of the food, music, Converse, and Elizabeth's family. Xander ate very little, and he handled his fork a little awkwardly, which did not escape Elizabeth's notice.

We ate with our hands before. I must practice this. At least my body seems to be accepting the food.

Elizabeth's thoughts were more pleasantly engaged. *Suddenly he is very quiet. I wonder what he is thinking. He shows wonderful breeding and excellent manners. He must have been in a much wider society than I have ever experienced. Maybe he has never had a girlfriend. That would be strange, indeed.*

I am so glad that she cannot read my mind, thought Xander. *I hope she will forgive me for reading hers if she ever finds out.*

Niall caught Xander's eye. *Do not worry about what may never be a problem, Xander. One thing at a time.*

After they finished their meal, and Xander had paid with his credit card, he walked them to their room. He said goodnight to Lynne and Elizabeth at their door and turned to walk down the hallway. Niall and Michael followed them into the room.

As soon as he heard the door close, he looked both ways, and, seeing no one, he quickly changed into angelic form and walked through the wall to join the other two guardians in their hotel room. Niall had been aware for several years that Xander was unable to watch Elizabeth in her private moments, so he was not surprised when his chief turned his back for Elizabeth to prepare for bed. Michael looked at Xander's behavior with curiosity, but kept his thoughts to himself.

How do you think the evening went? asked Xander.

It was not a total train wreck. She did give you her number. How did you like eating modern food?

I guess I will become accustomed to it. I still wonder where it will go.

I suppose you will find out tomorrow, Niall thought with a snicker.

How would you like for your next assignment to be guarding a penguin in Antarctica?

I am not worried. You need me. Niall's thoughts were smug.

True. Thanks.

You are welcome, my chief.

Michael looked at them, amused at their banter.

Something is not right. I am not quite myself, thought Xander.

What do you mean? asked Michael, looking at him with concern.

It is very odd. I almost think that I could sleep. This must be what it feels like to be tired, replied Xander. *I think that I am weary.* He yawned. Then surprised, he put his hand over his mouth. *I am sorry. That was rude.*

Niall stared at him, but Michael smiled. *That is another reason our Master sent me. Elizabeth needs to be guarded when you are human, true, but you are going to need help in another way as well. The more time that you spend in human form, the more you will experience human needs. Right now, you need to rest, Xander.*

How can I do that? I know that you will watch Elizabeth, but what if I am attacked while I sleep?

You always think you can handle everything by yourself, Xander, but you cannot. Elohim has chosen a guardian to watch you while you sleep. As Michael spoke, the third archangel floated through the wall, dressed in a guardian's tunic and full body armor.

I am here, Xander. Do you trust me to protect you?

Gabriel! You will stand guard for me? I am honored. Xander inclined his head.

Let us depart for your bedchamber. You must rest now, said Gabriel.

Can I not sleep here? asked Xander.

Where? There is no bed for you, and you must become human to sleep, answered Michael.

But I have no room, said Xander.

Of course you have a room. Gabriel chuckled and held out a key card. *You will sleep in the room next to this one.*

Of course. Xander looked a little sadly at Elizabeth, sleeping with her hand curled by her face. He would miss watching her sleep, entering her dream world, and waiting while she awakened.

Michael read his thoughts. *Things are not the same now, Xander. She deserves her privacy. You have now entered her life as a suitor. It would be unseemly for you to see her in her private moments. I saw how you turned your back tonight as she changed into her nightclothes. You know that what I say is true.*

I know that you speak the truth, Michael, but I will miss her.

If all goes well, she will be yours in a few short years. Until that time, you can still hear her thoughts and 'see' her dreams if you are awake while she sleeps. That is more than enough. Go rest for now and dream your own dreams.

Gabriel touched Xander's arm. *Let us go through the wall. We do not want to awaken them by opening the door.*

Xander walked to Elizabeth's bed and traced her cheek with his forefinger. He leaned over her, gently kissed her cheek, straightened up, and turned to go. Then he stopped, mid-stride, with a smile on his sleepy face. He had caught the beginnings of a lovely dream, and he saw his own face. *She dreams of me tonight. Are you sure I cannot stay? I can sleep tomorrow while you guard her, Michael.*

No! said the other three angels in unison, laughing.

Gabriel took him firmly by the arm, and they walked through the wall to the adjoining room. Xander took human form and slid between the sheets.

Wonderful! was his last conscious thought before he slipped into his own beautiful dream – the first one of his long existence.

Chapter 3

"And he got up and came to his father. But while he was still a long way off, his father saw him, and felt compassion for him, and ran and embraced him, and kissed him. And the son said to him, 'Father, I have sinned against heaven and in your sight; I am no longer worthy to be called your son.' But the father said to his slaves, 'Quickly bring out the best robe and put it on him, and put a ring on his hand and sandals on his feet; and bring the fattened calf, kill it, and let us eat and be merry; for this son of mine was dead, and has come to life again; he was lost, and has been found.' And they began to be merry."
Luke 15:20-24

The following week sped by in a blur. Xander missed Elizabeth terribly, and he did not like spending time away from her, but there were several things he needed to accomplish before the spring semester started at Converse. He had already taken all of his tests at Liberty and qualified for his bachelor's degree in theology. He was in the process of testing for his master's degree so that he would have the necessary qualifications to join Elizabeth in ministry if all went as he hoped it would. He also had finished nearly all of his bachelor's work for a music degree at Converse. Based on his testing scores and several auditions proving his proficiency in various areas, the chair of the music department had given him credit for many of the courses he had not taken. Xander had spent much of the week flying between the two schools taking tests and getting his spring course work scheduled. The results of his efforts were that he, like Elizabeth, would be able to finish his bachelor's degree at Converse and both of his master's degrees in three more semesters. He would be in classes with her at Converse and would finish most of his classes for Liberty online. If they chose to do so, he and Elizabeth would be able to begin their doctoral work at the same time. She would be nineteen and he would be twenty-two, according to his paperwork. Her birthday was the sixth of July, and his was the seventh. *We can celebrate together this coming summer,* he thought happily.

One obvious advantage to being in her classes was that Gregory would no longer be with Elizabeth without Xander's being present in human form. *No more special lunches with Gregory having food brought in from her favorite restaurants,* he thought with great satisfaction. *I know what she likes even better than he does, and I will be there all the time.*

Xander was looking forward to starting classes and having an excuse to spend time with Elizabeth in human form each day. *Gregory will not be pleased. I wonder how he will react to competition for Elizabeth's attention.*

Xander had called Elizabeth several times during the week mainly to hear her voice. He wanted her to become accustomed to him – to feel comfortable with him. He chatted with her about Converse and Liberty, places to eat and things to do in Spartanburg, and whatever she had done that day. They also discussed what music they could play and sing together after church on Sunday.

He had managed to see her in angelic form for a short while every day as well, though Michael and Gabriel insisted that he return to his own home in Spartanburg to sleep each night. The people in his townhouse community and in the surrounding neighborhood had grown used to seeing the imposing, handsome man regularly. Xander had made a concerted effort to be friendly and non-threatening. It was his aim to blend in as much as was possible, and he had achieved his goal admirably.

Xander also had been learning to cope with all the small trials of being human. The first morning he woke up from sleeping in Toronto, he had been surprised to find a growth of beard and an unpleasant scent about his person. He had showered, using the hotel's amenities, soaps, and shampoos, feeling the sensation of the water running over his body. He played with the knobs, amazed at the difference in the way his skin reacted to hot or cold water.

Humans do this all the time, but do they ever stop to think about it? Do they appreciate the ways their bodies adjust to differences in temperature and water pressure? I could stay in here all day!

You could, but we must go at some point, Xander, thought Gabriel. *You are turning into a prune. Look at yourself.*

Xander turned off the water and stepped out of the shower, wrapping himself in a luxurious towel. He then realized that he needed to buy deodorant, a razor, and other items. Xander had assumed angelic form, and he and Gabriel had flown quickly back to Spartanburg to shop for toiletries as well as clothes and a few furnishings for his apartment, beginning with a bed, since he had to sleep there each night. Finding a suitable bed had proved to be a trial because of his size. They had spent several hours looking in furniture stores before they decided to have it custom-made, along with the bedding.

The internet was proving to be extremely useful for ordering what he needed without spending hours shopping, and he needed to be able to take his online classes, so he bought a laptop and Blackberry. He was not planning to spend a great deal of time in his townhouse, so he did not worry about having it completely furnished. However, it was possible that Elizabeth might see his living arrangements at some point, and everything needed to look as normal as possible. *If I am going to live as a human, I might as well enter into it wholeheartedly,* he thought. *It is a small price to pay in exchange for loving Elizabeth freely, and being able to try to win her love in return.* Then an idea occurred to him. *I wonder if she would help me select the things I need.* He decided not to buy anything else he did not have to have to live as a human. That way, he would have a ready excuse to ask for her assistance and spend more time with her.

~~oo~~

Xander was up early Sunday morning, going through his human routine of showering, shaving, dressing, and eating. He dressed with great care, choosing gray dress pants, a white shirt opened at the neck, a long, black double-breasted coat with rounded lapels, and black dress boots.

He was too large to buy his clothes off the rack, but he had found that his platinum credit card opened doors for having his wardrobe tailor-made quickly by exclusive designers and delivered overnight. His first visit to a tailor had been a less than pleasant experience. He had been measured, enduring with embarrassment their constant exclamations over his size. As the assistants had tried to make his suit fit properly, they had stuck him with the pins several times. Pain was a new and undesirable experience. His taste in nearly everything tended to be conservative, but the perfect fit of each garment spoke of its quality. Xander had observed that well-dressed people commanded respect, so he submitted himself to the humiliation and endured the discomfort. He allowed himself to be touched, though it was vaguely unsettling, because he was willing to use any advantage that he could in order to gain Elizabeth's good opinion. He had never before used his appearance to attract attention, but he knew that Elizabeth noticed Gregory's good looks and stylish clothes. Xander would make certain that he compared favorably to Gregory in both categories.

Getting his driver's license had been a priority, and he was now the proud owner of a South Carolina license and a stratus gray metallic BMW Z4 coupe with black interior. *Driving is one of the best parts of being human so far, but how do people deal with the boring, endless minutiae of day-to-day living?* Filling out paperwork, paying taxes, getting a tag, and buying automobile insurance seemed unnecessarily troublesome to Xander. *Living as an angel is so much simpler. Dealing with mundane matters is exhausting.* He drew the line at cleaning and hired a cleaning service to come to his apartment twice a week. As for cooking, he kept simple food around, such as cereal and milk. Usually, he ate out and was discovering his preferences for certain restaurants and dishes.

After he checked his appearance one last time in a full-length mirror, he splashed on a little Acqua Di Gio, and grabbed his car keys.

Are you finally through preening? asked Gabriel with a smile.

You may think this is vanity, but being attractive is an important part of wooing a woman. Read her mind when she sees me, and then tell me whether or not I have wasted my time. Xander spoke with confidence.

Why have you disguised your natural scent? Gabriel was curious.

I have not 'disguised' my scent. I have chosen a signature scent that Elizabeth will associate with me. Whenever she smells this fragrance, she will think of me, just as I think of her when I breathe in 'Heavenly' by Victoria's Secret. Furthermore, she likes it. I wore it on the plane the first time we met. As much as I am enjoying this inquisition, we must leave now. Driving is much slower than flying, and I do not want to be late. It is rude. Xander locked the door behind him and went to his car. He got in, carefully backed out, and started the half hour drive to Tabernacle Church. Gabriel flew overhead. *It is odd to be guarded,* Xander thought.

It is odd to guard you, laughed Gabriel.

Xander arrived in plenty of time for Elizabeth's Sunday school class. She was standing with her back to him, talking to Charlotte Lucas when he walked into the room. Charlotte stopped in mid-sentence and stared up at him, open-mouthed. *Where are these beautiful men coming from? First Gregory, and now this fine specimen of male magnificence. Is some Hollywood film company secretly shooting a movie here? This must be the mystery man Elizabeth met on the flight to Toronto. Dark wavy hair. Check. Unbelievably light blue eyes with long dark lashes. Check. Makes Michelangelo's* David *seem wimpy in comparison. Check. Perfect nose and full lips with a killer jaw line. And check.* Xander had been around Charlotte so often that he had nearly forgotten she had never met him. Listening to her mentally listing his physical attributes was a little embarrassing, and he fought not to blush.

Noticing Charlotte's expression, Elizabeth turned her head to follow her friend's gaze. Her eyes widened as she took in all six feet nine inches of him. *Every time I see him, he seems to grow even more stunning. How is it possible to have absolutely no physical flaws?*

Xander smiled at her. *Still think I was wasting my time, Gabriel?* "Hello, Elizabeth. It is wonderful to see you again. Would you introduce me to your friend?"

Point taken, thought Gabriel as Michael smiled at his expression.

I am proud of you, Xander. You are making the angels look good, observed Michael.

Edward looked first at Gabriel, and then back at Michael. He was amazed to be in the room with the three most powerful holy angels, and Xander was in human form. *What is happening here?* he asked himself privately. He looked around the room and saw the same puzzled expression he wore mirrored on the faces of the other guardians.

"Charlotte Lucas, this is Xander Darcy. I'm so glad you came, Xander. Char, he'll be attending Converse with us next week, majoring in music. He is a pianist and a vocalist."

I really should have taken piano lessons. I've heard that it's never too late to learn, thought Charlotte. Aloud, she said, "That's great, Xander. I suppose you're another musical genius, like Elizabeth and Gregory."

"Elizabeth is one of a kind. I am fortunate to be able to study with her."

No mention of Gregory, thought Elizabeth. *It should be interesting when they meet for the first time.*

You have already missed that, but it should prove to be entertaining when we meet again. In fact, I think I can promise you many 'interesting' moments in your future when I am there – and I always will be there. Xander smiled as he looked at her.

Elizabeth looked at him speculatively. *And he really didn't comment on Char's statement concerning his musical abilities. He must be a great dancer with all that practice side-stepping. I am SO looking forward to hearing him play and sing this afternoon.*

Charlotte cleared her throat. *There are other people here, guys.*

You are staring at her, Xander, said Michael.

Xander blinked, breaking their gaze.

"I think it's time for me to start the class now," stated Elizabeth, directing Xander to a chair beside hers.

"I'll keep you company, Xander," said Charlotte, sitting on the other side of him. *He even smells heavenly.*

"Thank you, Charlotte," he replied with a smile.

Good thing being around Gregory has given me a measure of comfort with this level of beauty. This man would make Angelina Jolie lose her power of speech. Brad who? thought Charlotte.

Who is Brad Who? asked Gabriel.

Brad Pitt. A film star, Gabriel. Really, have you never been to a movie? answered Xander.

Actually, no. I have not. Archangels do not go to movies.

Elizabeth started her class by asking for prayer requests. After members of the class had shared several concerns, Joshua Lucas led the group in prayer. Elizabeth then opened her Bible and began to teach the lesson from Hebrews chapter eleven, the hall of fame of faith, which named people throughout Biblical times who had exhibited great faith in Jehovah. Xander had been the guardian for many of the great heroes named, and he cautiously contributed to the discussion Elizabeth led.

Following Sunday school, Xander walked with Elizabeth to the sanctuary for worship service. As they entered the auditorium, both of them were amazed to see Caroline Bingley and her mother sitting with Janna and Chance Bingley. Elizabeth took the empty seat to Janna's left, and Xander sat beside her. Chance was on Janna's right, with his mother, Anne, to his right and Caroline beside her. Elizabeth leaned over Janna and Chance to extend her hand, first to Anne and then to Caroline. Anne smiled at her shyly and took her hand, but Caroline looked at the floor, remembering how she had hurt Elizabeth. Elizabeth tapped her arm. When Caroline looked up, Elizabeth smiled at her and reached for her hand again. The older girl tentatively put her hand in Elizabeth's and held it for a moment.

Ros stood in the aisle beside her with an expression of joy that Xander had never before seen on his face. Anne's guardian, Erramun, as well as another protector, stood by his side.

Michael and Gabriel joined Roark, Niall, Alexis, Hector, and the other guardians around the perimeter of the room. The expressions of astonishment worn by the protectors who had not yet seen the archangels that morning were nearly comical. That they were dressed as guardians, though Michael still wore his armor, was not lost on the assembled light beings, and they certainly noticed Xander in human form beside Elizabeth. Angels had been curious about humans since the beginning of the human race, but a duality was an unknown entity. The guardians' interest was boundless, though they kept their countenances under firm control once the initial shock had subsided. The faces of the two powerful angels remained solemn as they listened to David's sermon.

David preached from Luke 15:11-32, the parable of the prodigal son. He told of the young man who had left his father's house and gone to a far country, taking his inheritance and wasting it in riotous living. When all of his money had been spent, his friends left him and he hit rock bottom. It was at that low point in the young man's life that he began to think of his father's love for him, and he decided to return home and beg to be a servant in his father's house. However, the young man's father did far more than forgive him. He took him back as a son and reinstated him to his position in their family. As David spoke the powerful words of restoration and forgiveness, Caroline began to weep under the weight of her conviction for her sins. Her life had radically changed in the past two years, and she thought of all the things that she had done with repugnance. Her many "friends" had deserted her, and, during those evenings Caroline was alone, she had been forced to take a good look at what she had become. Her school work had taken precedence in her new life of assuming responsibility for herself, and she was about to enter her final semester at the local junior college. She had started spending much of her free time with Chance and Janna, and they had begun to have Bible studies together once a week.

As David continued to preach, the Holy Spirit began to speak to Caroline, and she could hardly wait for the invitation. She wanted to make peace with God. Anne Bingley, who had recently joined her children and Janna for the Bible studies, put her arm around her daughter and held her, tears streaming down her cheeks. When David stepped out of the pulpit to the floor in front of the congregation and asked if anyone wanted to come forward for prayer, counseling, or salvation, both Caroline and Anne, followed by Ros and Erramund, left their seats and went to talk with him. The congregation sang a hymn, "Just as I Am," as David talked with mother and daughter. Anne had been coming to the church regularly for six months for marriage counseling, and David had led her to salvation a few weeks prior in his office. He bowed his head to pray with them, and then looked toward the congregation with a broad smile, turning the two women toward the assembled believers.

"Upon her profession of faith in Christ and her request to be baptized, I present Anne Bingley for membership in Tabernacle Church. All in favor, say 'Amen.'" David barely had time to speak the words before a loud chorus of "Amen!" sounded. The angels rejoiced as Erramund took his place by his charge.

David continued, "Many of you know Caroline Bingley. She attended Tabernacle for several years when she was a teenager; Caroline made a profession of faith when she was a child, but she never joined the church. She comes forward today to rededicate her life to Christ and present herself as a candidate for baptism and church membership. If you agree to accept Caroline into our fellowship, say 'Amen.'"

The shouts of "Amen!" filled the building and resounded to heaven as Jehovah-Go'el smiled down upon another sheep returned to the fold. The prodigal had come home, and He was pleased.

"After the closing prayer, Caroline and Anne will remain here at the front. Please come by and welcome them into our church body." Janna and Chance left their seats to stand with their family members and introduce them to the people in the church who lined up to shake their hands.

Jim and Delores Williams struggled with their feelings, as did Joshua Lucas; however, they joined the line and shook hands with Caroline and her mother. *Help me, Lord. Please help me to forgive her. My son is in danger today because of what she did. I need to let it go, Father. I want to give my burden to You,* prayed Delores, valiantly trying to hold back her tears.

Elizabeth and Xander were the last people in line. As Elizabeth reached for Caroline to hug her, Caroline broke down in fresh tears. She whispered to Elizabeth, "Can you ever forgive me for what I did to you and Richard? I am so sorry, El. I want to make a fresh start."

"Caro, you know that I forgive you, and I'm certain that Richard has already forgiven you, too. He's in Afghanistan now, but I have his address. We're still good friends, and we stay in touch. You can write to him and tell him that you have joined the church and are being baptized. He will be so happy. God has truly exchanged beauty for ashes in your life." Elizabeth hugged her again. Releasing her, Elizabeth looked up at Xander. "Caro, this is my good friend, Xander Darcy. Xander, Caro's brother Chance is married to my sister Janna." Xander and Caroline shook hands. Caroline had, of course, already noticed the tall, beautiful man who was with Elizabeth. She was reformed, but she was neither blind nor dead. However, to her credit, she harbored no jealousy toward Elizabeth.

Lynne graciously invited Anne and Caroline to join them for lunch with Chance and Janna, and they happily accepted. When the last of the church members had gone home, the Bennets, the Bingleys, and Xander left under the escort of the most powerful group of guardians ever assembled to go to the Bennets' home.

The surprises for the day had not yet ended, however. Over dessert, Janna shared the joyous news that she and Chance would have an addition to their family in late summer. David, Lynne, and Anne were thrilled to know that they were going to be grandparents as Elizabeth and Caroline laughed at the thought of being aunts. Xander looked at Roark, Niall, Hector, Alexis, Michael, Gabriel, Ros, and Erramund. They welcomed Duarte, the newest guardian, to their group. He would protect Chance and Janna's child; thus, he was already helping Alexis guard Janna.

~~oo~~

Gregory was extremely displeased, but too cunning to destroy those who might prove to be useful to him. He summoned Ryu, Tala, Donovan, and Akuji to a meeting in the strip mall.

They bowed on their knees before the Dark Prince as he stood, arms folded across his chest, sneering at them.

"Do you realize that you have completely lost your influence over the human girl? What have you been doing for the past two years?" he asked coldly.

Ryu spoke without lifting his head. "We thought that she had served her purpose, my liege. She broke the relationship between Elizabeth Bennet and the boy."

"You *thought*? When I need for you to think, I will tell you to do so. It is never acceptable to give up control of a believer. They are always useful. The Bennet family is actually stronger now than it was before I gave all of you your positions of leadership." He continued to speak, contemplatively, "There is something very strange going on with Xander now. He is taking human form far too often."

"Both Michael and Gabriel are regularly seen with Elizabeth and Xander, Prince Gregory," said Ryu.

"I suppose you are useful as spies if nothing else," replied Gregory. "Go from my sight before I change my mind and destroy you. You must develop a relationship with someone else close to Elizabeth. I will expect a progress report very soon. And, Ryu, I want a constant watch placed on Xander. I want to know everywhere he goes and everything he does."

The four demons flew as quickly as they could through the walls, leaving Gregory to plot his next move alone.

So Xander is often with my father's old friends, and in human form. What is going on there? Whatever he is planning, I will discover it. He will not defeat me. I will have Elizabeth. I will gloat in her humiliation as well as his, and I will do it before heaven's most honored. I will succeed where my father has failed. She is mine for the taking. His eyes glittered with excitement. Gregory loved a challenge. It made the game so much more interesting.

Chapter 4

"O magnify the Lord with me, and let us exalt His name together."
Psalm 34:3

Though Xander had been mostly silent during Sunday lunch with the Bennets and the Bingleys, he had enjoyed himself immensely. The conversation had flowed around him and enveloped him. He was comfortable. They were not strangers to him; after all, he had been part of the Bennet family for more than eighteen years, since the moment of Elizabeth's conception.

It is rather strange that I know them so well, and they know me hardly at all, he had thought.

Following the meal, Elizabeth and Janna helped Lynne clear the table. With that task completed, Elizabeth turned to her mother with a smile. "Mom, you and Janna go visit with our guests. I'll load the dishwasher and be with you in a few minutes."

"Thank you, El," Lynne said, kissing her younger daughter on the cheek. "Come, Janna. I think we'll need to fuss over you a little more, now that you're carrying my grandchild."

Janna laughed. "Are you sure, El? I don't mind helping you."

Xander had paused in the doorway to the den, listening to the women talk. "I will help Elizabeth," he offered, surprising the Bennet ladies. As they started to protest, he held up his hand to stop them. "It is the least I can do,

Mrs. Bennet. The meal was superb, and I so appreciate being invited. As I am too large to be decorative, it would be good for me to be useful. Do you not agree?"

He had taken off his coat and hung it on the back of his chair before lunch. His tailored shirt fit his athletic build to perfection as he stood straight and tall, looking toward Lynne for her acquiescence.

Not 'decorative'? He is easily the handsomest man I have ever seen, Lynne thought, amused.

Niall sniffed. *She has not known an extensive number of men, obviously.*

Michael chuckled at Niall's joke.

Xander looked down at the floor to hide his smile. "If you really want to help Elizabeth, I certainly will not stop you," Lynne said lightly. *I think he wants to be alone with Elizabeth. That's what I think. Well, I won't stand in his way.*

I have always liked her. Xander quickly lifted his head a little, turned his face away from Elizabeth, and winked at Niall.

Niall snorted as he, Duarte, and Alexis followed their charges from the room while Gabriel and Michael remained with Xander and Elizabeth.

Elizabeth looked up at him with a teasing smile. "And just how good are you at loading dishes, Xander? You know, I am perfectly capable of doing this all by myself, but I would enjoy talking with you while I work." Xander leaned on the counter, watching her graceful movements as she emptied the food into the garbage disposal, rinsed the dishes, and placed them in the dishwasher in orderly rows. Her hair swung back and forth as she worked. He longed to reach out and touch it.

Could it possibly feel as silky as it looks? I have embraced her in angelic form, but not as a human since she was a child. I must occupy myself before I do something foolish.

That would be wise, thought Gabriel.

"At least give me a wet cloth and let me wipe the table and counters," Xander offered.

"If you insist," she said, handing him a dishcloth.

The kitchen and dining room formed one large area, so Elizabeth was still visible to Xander as she worked. His stomach tightened every time she leaned over to put another item in the machine. *Watching her move does something to me.* He turned his back to her and finished wiping every surface available, making a concerted effort not to look at her. After he finished, he took the cloth back to her and stood behind her, waiting quietly for her to notice that he was there.

Elizabeth was absently humming a worship song they had sung that morning in church, and she did not hear him approach her. She efficiently put the last plate into the washer, squirted the detergent into the compartment and closed it, and then shut the door and started the pre-wash cycle. She turned quickly with the intention of getting Xander to go with her to the music room and nearly bumped into him. Her hands came up in a reflex action and rested on his chest. They stood there for a moment without breathing. Unable to stop himself, he leaned towards her and lowered his face to hers. She closed her eyes, and Michael cleared his throat. Xander caught himself just in time. He straightened up, and they both started talking at once.

Elizabeth's eyes flew open wide. "Oh, excuse me! I didn't see you there," she exclaimed, blushing furiously. *Did he almost kiss me?*

"Here is the dishcloth. I finished wiping the table and the counters, and now I await further instructions," he said quickly, holding the cloth higher so that she could see it. *Actually, yes, I did almost kiss you. Would you have liked that?*

Slow down, Xander, cautioned Gabriel.

Listening from the living room, Niall added, *According to my observations, Christian human males usually wait until at least the third date to kiss a girl. Do not rush her.*

Niall is the expert here, chuckled Michael.

She realized that her hands were still on his chest, and he was holding out the cloth with a quizzical expression on his flawless face.

I could stand here all day, Elizabeth. I will never pull away from your touch. Do not expect me to step back from you.

She dropped one hand by her side and took the cloth from his hand with the other. "Thank you," she said as she put the cloth in the sink to her left. *He smells wonderful. Get a grip on yourself, El.*

"My pleasure," Xander replied with a lazy smile. *She is not unaffected by my presence.*

Michael grinned. *Very good, my friend.*

Do not become overconfident, cautioned Gabriel.

There are at least two too many voices in my head right now, thought Xander a little impatiently. *Guardians should rarely be seen and seldom heard.*

Blessed silence reigned in his mind.

"Shall we go to the music room, Mr. Xander?" Elizabeth asked, her face turned up to his as a small smile played about her lips.

Is that an invitation? If you keep looking up at me like that, you will certainly get what you are asking for.

"I am not afraid of you, Miss Bennet. I am ready for my audition," he said, his blue eyes holding hers in a clear challenge. She did not look away. Instead, a decided twinkle appeared in *her* eyes.

"I'll be the judge of that. I hope you've been practicing. You know you'll never play really well unless you do." She raised one eyebrow and pursed her lips in an effort to keep from smiling.

"Lead the way, fair lady."

"Follow me."

"Anywhere." He breathed the word so softly that she could not be sure she had heard him correctly.

They walked through the den on their way to the music room.

"We're going to go over some music for next Sunday. I'll close the door so that we don't bother you," Elizabeth said, looking from her father to her mother. "Janna, Chance, Mrs. Bingley, Caroline, we'll be back out here soon. I hope you won't leave before we can tell you goodbye."

"We'll be here for a while," answered Chance.

Leave that door open, cracked Niall, looking sternly at Xander. Roark suppressed a smile.

David nodded at Elizabeth, and she and Xander continued down the hall, followed by Michael and Gabriel.

As if Michael and Gabriel would let me get away with anything, thought Xander, grumbling.

Not a chance, little brother. Michael laughed.

Xander rolled his eyes. *Occasionally seen and rarely heard, please.*

Elizabeth opened the door and entered the music room, waiting for Xander to follow her.

She gestured toward the instrument, and Xander went to the piano. Michael and Gabriel stood behind Xander, and Elizabeth took her place to his right. He moved the bench back several feet to accommodate his long legs and allow him room to lean into the keyboard. Then he began to play his own arrangement of Michael W. Smith's *Agnus Dei,* a song based on the Latin phrase meaning "The Lamb of God." After he had played once through the entire song, he began to sing in a rich baritone.

Elizabeth was speechless. Listening to Xander interpret the music was a spiritual experience. *I don't think I've ever heard anything so beautiful before. It's as if Xander is singing of someone he knows personally. Where has he been all this time? How is it that I've never heard of him until now?*

His large hands easily spanned twelve notes, an octave and a half, yet he had such dexterity and delicacy that the piano wept under his masterful fingers. She could easily play runs of parallel thirds with her right hand, but he played them in both hands simultaneously. His hands moved so rapidly that octave runs were like glissandos. Xander did not play with a better technique or more skill than Elizabeth, but his advantages in strength, power, and hand span gave him more options.

Xander finally lifted his hands from the keys, bowed his head for a moment, and then looked up at Elizabeth. She had tears in her eyes, and he was moved by her emotion. It was a moment of perfect communion between their hearts and Jehovah's. The Spirit in him gave witness to the Spirit in her. "You were praying that song," she stated simply.

He exhaled slowly. "Yes. You understand."

"It was an offering."

"All of my music is an offering to Him," Xander stated.

"Do you play classical music?" she asked.

"I play all types of music, but nothing moves me like using my gift in praise to the Almighty. He has been so good to me. He has forgiven me, He has accepted me, and He has changed me. When I stood at the foot of His cross, I did not know that He was suffering that for me, but since He redeemed me, it has all become clear. He died for me. He loves me. When no one else loved me, He did."

Hearing her mind, Xander knew that Elizabeth thought he was speaking figuratively. It was beyond her comprehension to think that he spoke literally of being at the foot of Jesus' cross.

"Xander, do you remember the man who came to meet me after the concert last weekend, Jonathan Edwards?"

"Of course. I have not forgotten any of the time we have spent together." Xander smiled. *Tread lightly, Xander. She will begin to wonder what you mean when you speak in riddles,* thought Michael.

"Jonathan asked me to join with him in ministry. He wants me to play and sing at his evangelistic rallies. I have been considering his proposal very carefully, and I have spent much time in prayer about it. I would travel only on weekends while I'm still in school, and I have prior commitments for concerts that I will not cancel, but I would like to see how God can use me. Would you consider joining with us? You and I could do the music together, and Jonathan could preach."

Xander's face lit up with his excitement. "You would have me with you? To serve God is my heart's desire." His expression became serious as he continued, "I must be honest with you, however."

"I value honesty very highly. What is it that you want to say?"

He moved to the left side of the bench and patted the right side, asking her to sit with him. She sat down and looked up at him with trusting eyes.

"Elizabeth, I want you to know my intentions toward you before I agree to join with you in ministry." His blue eyes were intense as they held hers.

She caught her breath.

He took her left hand and held it with both of his. "Elizabeth, I already have strong feelings for you. I will wait until you get to know me, but you should know from the outset that I am hoping for a relationship with you. To be with you is another desire of my heart."

She laughed a little nervously. "That is certainly direct – and honest. If you are willing to give me time and take this slowly, I think that working together in ministry might show us both if a relationship between us could work."

He smiled his most charming smile. "Then I would consider it a great privilege to be your partner in ministry. First things first, however. What music are we going to do next Sunday for the worship service?"

Elizabeth thought a moment. "I hope you will consent to play and sing *Agnus Dei* just as you did a few minutes ago. There is nothing I could add to improve it."

"Will you at least sing it with me?"

"What did you have in mind?"

He spent a few moments explaining his ideas for a duet, and she consented, agreeing that his arrangement would make the vocal component even better than his solo.

He reluctantly released her hand. When he began to play again, she stood beside him to sing, her high soprano lifting the opening "Alleluia" two octaves above where he had sung it. As she continued to sing, the door opened to reveal David and Lynne smiling at them. Xander stopped playing as he and Elizabeth looked at her parents.

David spoke. "We can hear a little of what you are singing and playing, and I feel as if I'm attending a worship service in heaven before the throne. Do you mind if we leave the door opened so we can hear?"

"Dad, you know how we musicians feel about anyone listening to us practice. It's not polished yet. We haven't worked out all the kinks. Anyway, we're going to do it next Sunday morning in church." Elizabeth made a little grimace.

"It sounds fine to me already, El. I won't mind hearing it twice. Please?" Lynne asked, ruffling her hair.

Xander spoke up. "I do not mind as long as Elizabeth agrees. Could we indulge them this once?" he asked Elizabeth, smiling at her.

"Okay. I'm outnumbered it seems. But you know you're going to hear all of our mistakes," she said with a small frown.

Xander began the instrumental portion again, and Elizabeth began singing alone at the point in the music indicated by Xander. He joined her on "Worthy is the lamb," their voices blending perfectly, swelling throughout the song. They were unaware that the eyes of everyone listening, human and angel alike, had closed, shutting out everything except the music. The guardians knew that no demon could breach that barrier of worship and praise.

Xander and Elizabeth sat quietly as if in prayer for a few moments after they finished.

David looked at them side-by-side, their dark heads bowed together, and thought, *They belong together. It is as if they were made for each other.* Aloud he said, "Thank you for allowing us to share that. I'm really looking forward to hearing it again next Sunday. If it was that wonderful 'unpolished,' I can't wait to hear it after you have actually worked on it."

Everyone laughed at his joke. After a round of farewells, Anne and Caroline took Janna and Chance home with them to spend the remainder of the afternoon. Anne especially wanted to tell Donald that he was going to be a grandfather.

The Bennets invited Xander to spend the afternoon with them so that he would be in town for evening services at Tabernacle. He and Elizabeth spent the time together in the music room, arranging music and playing duets.

Across the street, up in the cover of the pine trees, sat two demons, motionless and quiet. They had watched as Xander and Elizabeth had entered her home followed by Michael and Gabriel, and they had listened to the two of them playing the piano and singing together. As soon as the family left for evening services at Tabernacle, they took flight into the gathering darkness.

~~o~~

Xander hummed to himself as he dressed for his first day of classes at Converse. As he left his townhouse and headed for his car, he noticed that the day was clear and brisk, and he was thankful for his warm jacket as he braved the chilly January weather. He breathed deeply and was exhilarated by the feeling of the cold air in his lungs.

He was optimistic about the direction that his relationship with Elizabeth was taking, and he was delighted to have an excuse to spend part of each day with her. As he drove to the campus with Gabriel flying overhead, he suddenly realized that his guardian had not yet spoken a word.

What are you thinking? Xander asked.

You are happy. You do not need to know what I am thinking, was the short reply.

Xander drew his brows together. *Is there some reason I should not be happy?*

No. Elizabeth enjoys being with you when you are in a good mood. I would not spoil it.

Too late. Tell me why you are silent, said Xander, a little too forcefully.

If you insist. I have been thinking about Gregory. You will meet him today. He is her friend, and you must not forget that. Gabriel was reasonable as usual.

I am not likely to forget it. I have been forced to be in his presence for the past two and a half years, Xander's tone was terse.

You have been in angelic form nearly all of that time. Today, you will meet him as a human. With your dual nature, you are fully human and fully angel. You will be totally human when you are with him.

I know that! What is your point? Xander nearly ran a red light.

Gabriel moderated his tone carefully. *You are more emotional when you are human, Xander. Even now you are losing your temper with me, and I am your friend. He is your enemy and your competition for Elizabeth's affections. You must be in complete control of your feelings. Gregory has lived as a human all of his life. He is well-practiced in deceit and disguise. He will not make an error, and you must not make one either.*

Xander bit back the retort that was on his tongue and took a deep breath. *You are right, as usual, Gabriel. I have had this nature for only a few months. You may have to help me today.*

Would you accept my help?

Xander sighed. He knew he deserved that question. *Yes, I am asking for your help. If I begin to show my feelings for him, tell me so. I do not always know how I am being perceived by others. You are my guardian, and I respect that. I will let you do your job from now on. Speak peace to me when I need it.*

We have made progress. Now watch your driving. I do not want to meet a death angel today.

Xander chuckled. *You are a good friend, Gabriel.*

I am your brother.

They were quiet during the rest of the drive to Converse, but it was the comfortable silence of old friends.

~~oo~~

Xander was put to the test as he walked with Elizabeth to his second class of the day. He saw Gregory walking toward them on the sidewalk, dressed to kill, with a big smile on his face. *If he is surprised, he hides it well.*

Gabriel and Michael seemed unusually large as they stepped up beside their charges, facing down Gregory's guards.

As soon as he was close enough, Gregory reached out his arms for Elizabeth, enveloping her in a bear hug and depositing a kiss on her cheek. Over her shoulder, he smiled maliciously into Xander's glare. He then held her at arm's length by her shoulders, smiling into her eyes.

Gabriel put a hand on Xander's shoulder. *This is the part where I remind you to be calm.*

Then I guess this is also the part where I listen to you. With great effort, Xander relaxed.

"El, it's wonderful to see you. I've really missed you over the break. We must get together and catch up."

Gregory ignored Xander totally. His guards snickered.

"I've been very busy, Gregory. Did you have a good Christmas?" she asked.

"Oh, yes! I just love Christmas. All the decorations, gifts, and Santa Claus – and those parties! How about you?"

Yes, I bet you just love Christmas, thought Xander, narrowing his eyes.

"It was wonderful. The celebration of Christ's birth is my favorite holiday. I made a new friend on the way to Toronto. I think you know Xander Darcy?" she said, looking from Gregory to Xander.

"I do? Well, yes, I guess we've met, though it's been awhile. How have you been, Xander?" asked Gregory smoothly.

"Fine, Gregory, thank you. I told Elizabeth that your father used to work for mine, but that we have been out of touch for many years now." Xander smiled at him.

Michael laughed out loud. Gregory's guards took a step forward, but held their places when they saw Gabriel and Michael rest their hands casually on the hilts of their swords.

Xander saw Gregory's amber eyes flash red with anger, but Elizabeth had been looking at Xander at that instant. Gregory closed his eyes for a moment and breathed deeply. When he reopened his eyes, they were amber again. "I suppose you *would* look at it that way, Xander, though I wouldn't say my father ever *worked* for yours."

Elizabeth, feeling the tension, looked carefully at each of the men. Xander appeared to be relaxed, but Gregory seemed to be having trouble controlling his temper. *What could have made him so upset? There was no insult in Xander's words.*

Gregory plastered a smile on his face. "It is of little importance now. El, will you be my guest at lunch today? I have missed our conversations, and I have a Christmas gift for you." He directed his full attention to Elizabeth.

Xander smiled. His blue eyes were wide and innocent.

Oh, this is good, chortled Michael.

"I'm so sorry, Gregory," said Elizabeth, looking disconcerted. "Xander asked me yesterday to have lunch with him today. We already have plans. Maybe another time?"

"You can count on it," replied Gregory, his charming smile evaporating.

As Elizabeth and Xander hurried to class, he glanced back to see Gregory, still standing stiffly in the same spot, glaring after them. Xander narrowed his eyes as he noticed a shadow of evil pass over Gregory's face; his amber eyes again glowed red as the rage overtook him. Seeing Gregory's face and eyes in Xander's mind, Gabriel and Michael faced the halfling and stepped together, assuming defensive stances, forming a wall of protection between the Dark Prince and their charges.

Xander returned his attention to Elizabeth. In a gesture of intimacy, he raised the hood of Elizabeth's coat over her curls and put his arm around her, speaking to her in a low voice.

"It is really cold out here. Let me take care of you. I do not want you to become ill."

She smiled up at him, her brown eyes trusting his intentions to be exactly as he stated them.

Xander was sure that he heard Gregory swear, but his hearing was much better than the average human's, and Elizabeth did not catch his oath. Gregory and his guards headed toward the parking lot.

Round one goes to Xander, said Michael with satisfaction, turning with Gabriel to follow the couple into the building.

Chapter 5

"You are of your father the devil, and you want to do the desires of your father. He was a murderer from the beginning, and does not stand in the truth, because there is no truth in him. Whenever he speaks a lie, he speaks from his own nature; for he is a liar, and the father of lies."
John 8:44

Gregory was very angry. In fact, he had never before been so enraged as he was now. Watching Xander walk off with Elizabeth after he had put so much effort into developing a relationship with her for himself was too much to be tolerated. He barely contained his wrath long enough to stalk to his car and drive to the house he had recently purchased in Spartanburg. His situation was precarious, and he would no longer chance anyone seeing him change. In the cover of his home, he took demonic form, and, flanked by his guards, winged his way to his father's mansion to apprise him of the situation.

Lucifer, surrounded by his malevolent contingent, looked up from the hardcore pornographic movie scene being filmed before him as his son, accompanied by his guards, flew through the wall. Gregory, eyes blazing red hot, stood before his father as he lounged on a leather couch. The Prince of Darkness rose gracefully and walked into the next room; his son and their guards followed him.

The Dark Lord turned to face his son. "Are you not supposed to be in classes with Elizabeth now, Gregory?" Lucifer asked, his eyebrows raised.

Gregory began to pace in fury before the Dark Lord.

"I am here on a matter that is most pressing, Father. It has the potential to derail all of our plans. The rumors we have heard about Xander are apparently true. He has taken human form and now bears his human name, Alexander Darcy. He has enrolled at Converse and has already been developing an intimate relationship with Elizabeth Bennet. Michael and Gabriel were both with him. It appears that Michael is guarding Elizabeth while Gabriel is with Xander."

"Is there truly a need for such anxiety and wrath, my son? You are far more skilled at being human than Xander could ever be. You are all that is charming and physically attractive to a woman. Xander has no experience in such matters. The idea of his romancing a woman is laughable. I may have to go witness some of his attempts myself. It could prove to be most entertaining – more so than what I have been watching. The world calls that erotic." He casually motioned toward the nude couple before him as he laughed in derision. "They have no idea of the pleasures attainable to those who would avail themselves."

"He was doing very well with her today, right before my eyes. Xander has already been invited to her home, according to my spies, and it appears that our adversary has gifted him in music. They heard him as he played the piano and sang with her yesterday. He attends church with her. I do not wish to go to her home in human form. The very thought is repugnant. I cannot go to her church; I have no entry. Xander will disrupt all of our plans if we do not find a way to stop him."

"What do you propose, Gregory?"

Gregory stopped and looked at Lucifer with calmer, amber eyes. "Elizabeth's best friend, Charlotte Lucas, seems suspicious of me. I need someone on the inside to influence Elizabeth against Charlotte and Xander. I do not want a human who could be swayed by the enemy, as Caroline Bingley has been, or even a human who does our bidding. I know that there are few demons who take the human form of a female, but I require one. There is never a question of where a demon's allegiances lie."

The Prince of Darkness sat up gracefully and crossed his legs. "I know the perfect choice for the job. Cassandra – yes, she will do very well for the job, very well indeed." He turned to one of his guards and commanded, "Duncan, go fetch Cassandra immediately. Bring her to us. We shall be awaiting your return."

Duncan turned on his heel and spread his leathery wings as he flashed through the ceiling, eager to do his master's bidding.

Lucifer turned to his son. "Do you require anything else, Gregory?"

"Yes, Father. There is something that I want. It will be difficult to procure, but I want it by tomorrow, in case Cassandra does not do well. It may take some time for her to gain a place in Elizabeth's confidence, and I must take action myself before Xander worms his way into her affections."

Lucifer's laugh was quiet and unpleasant. "I am the god of this world, Gregory. Anything here is mine for the taking; I own it all. What do you require? You have only to name it, and you shall have it."

~~oo~~

The following day, Xander and Gabriel were approaching Elizabeth and Charlotte as the girls hurried along the sidewalk at school, followed closely by Michael and Edward, when a striking black-haired girl, who was just in front of Xander, called Elizabeth's name. Xander stiffened as he caught the tall, slender girl's scent and realized that she was a demon in human form; he increased his pace to reach Elizabeth and Charlotte. Michael and Edward had already moved to stand beside their charges, ready to defend against an attack. The girl, of course, could see the guardians, but she did not acknowledge them in any way.

The demon's mind was closed to them, but her presence was an indication of a change in Gregory's strategy, and therefore, she was automatically considered to be a grave threat.

As Xander stopped beside the demon, he heard her introduce herself in a melodic voice.

"Hello. Aren't you El Bennet? I'm a friend of Gregory's and a huge fan of yours, so I just had to meet you. My name is Cassandra." She extended her hand. Xander was close behind the girl, and he stepped up beside her to be closer to Elizabeth.

A friend of Gregory's? What a shock.

Xander cringed inwardly at the idea of the fiend touching Elizabeth, but there was nothing he could do to prevent her from shaking hands with the girl.

Elizabeth smiled and returned the greeting. "Thank you so much, Cassandra. This is my friend, Charlotte Lucas. And this is Xander Darcy."

Charlotte nodded and shook Cassandra's hand as Michael and Edward scowled. Xander could not bring himself to make physical contact with the dark one, so he nodded his greeting, making a show of holding his books while reaching for Elizabeth's, and tried to smile.

A bold move. He is sending a spy directly into the enemy's camp. There was a hint of grudging admiration in Michael's thoughts. The warrior could recognize an excellent battle strategy.

"I just started here today, and I don't know my way around yet. Could I tag along with you and your friends for now?" Cassandra asked.

Elizabeth really did not know what to say to the unusual request. "Are you majoring in music? Xander and I are on our way to a master's level theory class. Char is a junior year business major. Are you sure you want to go with any of us?"

Cassandra took a moment to think about it. "You have a point," she laughed. "I'm in freshman courses. Could I meet you for lunch?"

"We'll be in the Gee dining hall at 12:30. Join our table if you're in there at the same time. We really have to go now, or we'll be late." Elizabeth and Char smiled at her, while Xander looked directly into her eyes with no hint of friendliness. After saying their goodbyes, they left for their classes.

~~oo~~

Xander saw Cassandra as soon as she entered the dining hall, promptly at 12:30. After she went through the cafeteria line, making her selections very quickly, she joined Xander, Elizabeth, and Charlotte.

She smiled as she took the only available seat, which happened to be to the right of Xander and across from Elizabeth. He tried not to be obvious while he moved his chair further away from her. Michael, Gabriel, and Edward hovered protectively just behind the shoulders of their charges.

She certainly is beautiful, commented Michael, his green eyes boring holes into her.

But she stinks to high heaven. My nose is burning so much from her foul odor that I do not know how I will be able to eat. She turns my stomach, Xander sniffed.

Evil is always beautiful at first, observed Gabriel calmly. *That is one way Lucifer entraps humans. 'The lust of the eyes' was the first step to Eve's downfall in the Garden of Eden.*

"How was your morning, Cassandra? Did you enjoy your classes?" asked Elizabeth kindly.

"Oh, yes! But I've just moved here from south Florida, and I'm freezing. The most I ever needed in Fort Lauderdale was the occasional sweater or light jacket. I really must buy some heavier winter clothes," Cassandra said with a slight shiver.

"There's a mall not far from here," said Charlotte.

"I live here on campus in a dorm, and I don't have a car." Cassandra left the statement hanging.

Elizabeth's compassionate nature took over.

"I'd be happy to take you shopping tomorrow after classes, if you'd like. I can ask my mom if we can drive separately. She works here as a tutor."

Offer to ride with them, whispered Edward in Charlotte's ear.

Who is this girl? She gives me the chills – just like Gregory does. Elizabeth isn't going anywhere with her alone. For all we know, she could be an ax murderer, thought Charlotte.

Charlotte spoke up quickly. "I'll ride with you, El. I could use a shopping trip, too. I need some new boots."

"I have a better idea – at least I think it is better," interjected Xander. "Ride here in the morning with your mother, Elizabeth, and I can take you girls shopping and then back home afterwards. I need to learn my way around Spartanburg, and you and Charlotte can help me get my bearings while I drive all of you wherever you want to go. I will be your official chauffeur."

Excellent plan, Xander. Michael smiled.

I will have to have my car fumigated, but it cannot be avoided, Xander replied, his eyes never leaving Cassandra's.

Cassandra's eyes glittered at Xander for a moment with just a hint of malice. Elizabeth was looking at Charlotte with a question in her eyes, but Charlotte caught the look that passed between Cassandra and Xander.

*Woah! What was **that** look? She glared at Xander as if she'd like to strangle him. I'm expecting to see her head spin in a complete rotation anytime now. Can we call an exorcist, stat, please? Linda Blair's projectile pea soup can't be far behind.*

"What do you think, Char? Can we stand Xander for a few extra hours tomorrow?" queried Elizabeth, her brown eyes sparkling.

Oh, definitely! Let creepy Cassandra try something with Hercules around.

Hercules? smirked Michael.

I hear that quite often, answered Xander.

"Yes, I think he's just the man for the job. We can get him a chauffeur's hat. Be sure to wear black tomorrow, Xander." Charlotte kept her expression serious.

"Wow! This all sounds great, but tomorrow's not good for me. I'll have to take a rain check. Thanks anyhow, guys," Cassandra said, smiling brightly. "And now I need to rush to make my next class. I'll catch you later." She gathered her things quickly and left.

"Hmmm. Strange," said Charlotte, watching her walk from the room. She turned her head to look at Elizabeth. "El, please don't let her talk you into going anywhere with her by yourself. I have a bad feeling about her. And while I'm being honest, let me add that Gregory gives me that same weird vibe. He is *too* perfect."

"She is a bit odd. I will bow to your superior radar and promise never to go anywhere with her alone. However, I've known Gregory a long time, and he's always been nice to me. Being extraordinarily handsome is not a crime, though he is quite smooth and plausible. I will allow that what seems too good to be true usually is." Elizabeth laughed.

Charlotte smiled at her friend. "I'll take the promise concerning Cassandra for the present. Remember that I've known Gregory as long as you have. We'll discuss him more later. Now, what about our shopping trip? I really do need some winter boots."

Xander entered the discussion. "I still like the idea. Charlotte, let me take you and Elizabeth shopping and then out to dinner on me. I rarely get the opportunity to take two lovely ladies out at the same time," he said easily, bestowing his best smile on them.

Who can refuse the dimples? thought Charlotte, a little dreamily.

The dimples? asked Gabriel as Michael stood by shaking his head and smiling.

I hear that very often as well, thought Xander, a bit smugly.

"Sounds good to me. How about you, El?" asked Charlotte.

Elizabeth smiled brightly, letting her double-dimple show. "Are you sure you don't mind taking us home afterwards, Xander? I think that Mom would let me drive."

"Or I could drive in the morning, El," offered Charlotte.

"I absolutely insist on driving both of you home. I take being a gentleman very seriously, I assure you," Xander replied, a small smile playing about his lips.

Elizabeth bit her lower lip as she thought about the things she should do the next evening instead of going out.

"I promise to have you home by eight." Xander let the smile grow a little wider.

It's as if he can read my mind, thought Elizabeth. *His smile should be registered as a lethal weapon.*

"Well, I suppose I can get my work done if you promise to have us home early. Our last class is over at three. We can shop for a few hours and eat by six."

"Excellent. I will not have to eat alone tomorrow night," answered Xander, with just the right hint of a pout.

Charlotte nearly snorted. *As if you would ever have to eat alone except by your own choice.*

~~oo~~

Xander and Gabriel joined Michael in guarding Elizabeth that afternoon. Xander still felt anxious after the encounter with Cassandra. Gregory was obviously changing his mode of attack.

After returning home with her mother and Charlotte, Elizabeth donned her sweats and athletic shoes to take a run around the block. She had calculated how many times she needed to run the route to make a mile, and she tried to run at least two miles three times per week. It had been a part of her weekly routine since she had graduated from high school. Michael, Gabriel, and Xander flew just above her.

As she passed the church parking lot, she heard a car horn and followed the sound with her eyes. She spotted Gregory in a shiny black sports car at the

McDonald's across the street. He rolled down the window and waved at her with a big smile.

I knew that he was up to something, thought Xander.

I think that the three of us are quite capable of dealing with Gregory, answered Michael drily.

Especially since he has no guards with him, added Gabriel. *He is not here for a battle.*

After looking both ways, Elizabeth, followed by Xander, Michael, and Gabriel, ran across the street to see him. She walked around his car slowly, looking at it from all angles. *He certainly knows how to make an entrance,* she mused.

Gregory got out of the car, closed the door, and leaned against it, arms folded across his broad chest, one ankle crossed over the other. As she finished her circle, she stopped in front of him and smiled, her eyes never leaving the car. Her guardians flanked her, staring at the enemy.

"Hi, Gregory. New wheels? I've never seen a car like this. It is truly awesome! What is it?"

"It's a Lamborghini Cachazo Concept. I just got it yesterday."

"I don't know much about cars, but I do know that concept cars are expensive and hard to acquire. How did you manage to get this?" she asked, still admiring the sleek lines and low-slung body.

He stood up. "I told you that I have connections, El. Don't ever underestimate me. There were only a few of these cars made, and they aren't for sale. I saw it, and I wanted it. If you have the money, and you know the right people, you can have anything you want." His voice was seductive and low.

Xander took a step toward him, and Gabriel put a restraining hand on his arm.

The tone of Gregory's voice shocked her, and she finally looked at him instead of the car. It was as if she were seeing him for the first time. He was wearing a black Ksubi trench coat open over a hooded grey wool sweater bearing an Armani logo. The top of his fitted black T shirt showed under the partially unzipped sweater, and the sweater's hood was flung carelessly over the back of the coat. Black designer jeans and black leather boots finished the outfit. Elizabeth held her breath as she took in Gregory's perfect face, glossy black hair, and honey-golden eyes. He was amazingly sexy and dangerous.

He would look right at home on the cover of GQ, she thought.

Xander was so jealous that he had to look away. *Sometimes, I wish I could not read her mind.*

"Well, what do you think?" Gregory asked, commanding her attention with his eyes.

She released the breath she had been holding. "I want to touch it, but I'm afraid I'll get fingerprint smudges on it. It's so beautiful."

"El, you can touch anything you want of mine, anytime you want to." His voice was pure silk, caressing her with its smoothness. "I thought I had made that clear to you in the past."

He has crossed the boundary! Xander spoke through his clenched jaw. His right hand closed over the hilt of his sword.

He has breached propriety, but he has done nothing to merit drawing your sword. Calm yourself. He is enjoying tormenting you. Would you encourage him to go further just to see your reaction? Gabriel was calm and reasonable.

Gregory took a step toward her. "Would you like to go for a ride?"

Xander took a step toward him. *I will prevent you from coming again if you cannot control yourself,* thought Michael.

He stopped, but took a defensive posture.

She was vaguely uncomfortable. Gregory had never been so forward with her before, and it frightened her. She hesitated.

"I promise that I'll behave. I can be a gentleman, too, you know. I just thought that you should be aware of all your options."

She looked toward her house, and then back at him. "I can't be gone long. I have schoolwork to finish, and my parents will expect me to be home for dinner."

That was not a 'no,' thought Xander.

I am sure that Gregory did not miss that either, added Michael.

Gregory walked to the passenger's side and opened the door. He held out his hand to Elizabeth with a look meant to convey his feelings for her. "Please, El? We won't be gone long. I haven't really seen you since before Christmas. You're always busy with your new friend now." His eyes pleaded with her.

He has been my friend for more than two years now. Have I really been neglecting him?

Gregory has played on her loyal nature perfectly. He knew exactly what to say to make her feel guilty, thought Xander in irritation.

He spoke into her mind, *Do not go with him, Elizabeth.*

She hesitated, but Gregory looked at her, imploring her with his eyes.

"Please?" he asked, still gazing at her, using every ounce of his magnetism.

Please, Elizabeth. Please do not get into his car. Xander was begging her.

She felt so confused. *Gregory is my friend, and I know he will not hurt me. Why do I feel that I should not go? Is it because of what Charlotte said? She has never liked him.*

She walked to the other side of the car and took Gregory's hand, allowing him to help her into the low-slung car.

Gregory closed her door and walked around to the driver's side, pausing a short moment to smile triumphantly at the three angels.

Xander glared at him. Michael and Gabriel maintained neutral expressions.

He opened the door and slid into the bucket seat beside her, reaching across her to get her seatbelt. As he pulled it over her, he managed to lightly graze her body with his knuckles, lingering just a moment longer than necessary before he locked the clasp securely. Her eyes widened as he touched her.

That must have been an accident. Surely he would not have done that on purpose, she thought.

There is such a thing as being too innocent. Xander contemplated having a talk with her later.

Gregory pushed the ignition button, enjoying the raw power of the machine as it jumped to life.

"Where would you like to go?" he asked, turning his head to smile at her.

"It doesn't matter, but remember we can't go very far. I have to get back home soon," she answered. *I'm babbling. I wish I had never agreed to go.*

We are in agreement, thought Xander.

"I haven't seen what she can do yet. Let's take the country road out of town and test her limits," Gregory said, revving the engine.

Before she had a chance to answer, he peeled out of the parking lot and headed toward the open highway, breaking every speed limit on the way.

If he wraps the car around a tree, he could kill her, and he'd probably just walk away – or fly away, thought Xander as he, Michael, and Gabriel flew above the speeding car.

We will not allow that, answered Michael tersely. *The three of us can catch the car before it hits anything.*

Do not worry so, Xander. You will go prematurely gray, added Gabriel.

Remember that I bested his father when we contended over the body of Moses, and I will not be beaten by the son, said Michael, referring to an incident recorded in Jude 1:9. *The Lord will rebuke him.*

Gregory pushed the gas pedal to the floor. He could not resist the smell of Elizabeth's fear. Though he knew it was unwise, he enjoyed it too much to slow down as he glanced at the flashing blue light in the rearview mirror.

When the speedometer hit 200 MPH, she began to whimper. "Gregory, please. I'm afraid. Please slow down."

She is no longer willing. We can interfere. Xander was adamant.

There is no need yet. Let her see him for what he is. Let her be afraid of him, cautioned Michael.

Michael is right. Gregory himself is doing more to push her away than any of your talks could have accomplished, spoke the voice of reason, Gabriel.

Gregory realized his error immediately upon hearing her voice and began to decelerate. "I'm sorry, El. I just got a little carried away. I really love speed, and I've been trained by a professional racecar driver. You were never in any danger."

She huddled back in her seat, fighting tears. "Please take me home now."

"I will. We'll turn around right now, and I'll take you home. I truly am sorry. Can you forgive me?" he asked. He reached for her hand.

"Keep your hands on the wheel, please. I do forgive you, Gregory, but don't ever expect me to get in a car with you again. You are a maniac." Elizabeth crossed her arms and looked out the window with a frown.

Excellent. Xander smiled.

Just as we said it would be, Michael reminded him.

Gregory turned into a driveway, backed out into the road, and headed back toward Bethel.

"I just like to drive fast. That doesn't make me a bad person." His tone was wheedling.

No, driving fast does not make you a bad person, but perhaps being the offspring of the Son of Perdition might qualify you for the appellation. You are referred to as the Dark Prince. Xander's thoughts were edged with sarcasm.

"I'm not saying you're a bad person, but I won't get back in a car with you again if you're going to be driving it." She was firm. "You shouldn't have a sports car. You could kill yourself."

He laughed. "That's not likely."

They rode in silence for a few moments.

"El," he began. "I wanted to tell you something today."

"Oh, so your sole purpose in coming to Bethel wasn't to scare me to death?" She looked at him and arched one eyebrow.

"No, actually I've been very concerned for you since yesterday." Gregory injected just the right amount of sincerity into his voice.

Xander spoke into her mind. *He is the Father of Lies. Do not believe him.*

"I can't imagine why," she returned.

"You seem to have become quite close to Xander Darcy in a very short time," he said quietly.

"Yes, Xander and I are becoming friends. I like him." Elizabeth looked straight ahead.

"Maybe it isn't wise to trust anyone on such a short acquaintance," said Gregory.

"Xander has been a perfect gentleman, and he hasn't tried to kill me yet."

"I haven't tried to kill you either. You're being a little melodramatic, don't you think? At any rate, I've known him for many years, and you've known him a few weeks." Gregory let the statement hang in the air.

"What do you have to accuse him of? I would dearly like to know," Elizabeth said, a little angrily.

"What do you really know of him? Has he talked about his family? Have you met any of his friends?"

Michael, this is getting out of hand. Xander looked the other two angels.

Patience, Xander, cautioned Michael.

"Well, no, but we will talk about those things, I'm sure." Her voice took on a slight hesitation.

"I would love to be a fly on the wall when you do."

By that time, Gregory was pulling into Elizabeth's driveway. She did not think to ask him how he knew where she lived when he had never been there before.

As she opened the door to get out of the car, he leaned over and put his hand on her arm. The trio of powerful angels stood around the open door.

He is touching her again! Xander scowled.

"El, I really care for you, and I would hate to see you hurt in any way. You don't know what he is."

He has planted doubt in her mind. It will grow from that insidious seed. Xander spat the words.

It is what he does best, answered Gabriel calmly.

Elizabeth looked back at Gregory and could see the concern in his eyes. It moved her heart.

"Remember that I'll always be here for you if you ever need me," he said in a husky voice.

"Thank you, Gregory. I won't forget it." She smiled at him. Then she got out of the car and walked to the door. As he backed out of the driveway, he glanced at her. She was standing there with her hand on the knob, looking at him with a faraway expression. She raised her hand to wave goodbye at him, and then opened the door and went inside. Her guardians walked through the closed door, following closely behind her.

Gregory turned the stereo sound system up until the car vibrated and sped away, an evil smile disfiguring his perfect face.

Chapter 6

"Bless the Lord, you His angels, mighty in strength, who perform His word, obeying the voice of His word!"
Psalm 103:20

Immediately after he left Elizabeth's house, Gregory summoned the dark beings of the southeastern dominions to a meeting in the vacant strip mall. As the demons quickly assembled and bowed on their knees before him, the Dark Son stood straight and tall, commanding their attention with his rich, persuasive voice. His expression was haughty as he spoke.

"Look at me."

The dark ones raised their faces to behold their master, and he held their complete attention with his hypnotic eyes.

"Cassandra, come stand before me."

She obeyed instantly. "Yes, my lord?"

"You are having a problem establishing a relationship with Elizabeth Bennet." There was no question in Gregory's tone.

Cassandra inclined her head. "Yes, my lord."

The son of Lucifer looked at her with understanding. "Elizabeth is never alone. She is surrounded by Xander, Michael, and Gabriel, as well as her family and her best friend, Charlotte Lucas. I knew that your assignment was difficult; however, Cassandra, you will not be expected to accomplish your task alone." Gregory spoke gently, and Cassandra looked up at him in surprised adulation.

"Ryu, Tala, approach me." Gregory's voice held an edge of irritation.

The underprince and his captain bowed before the Dark Prince.

Their master spoke coldly and quietly. "I begin to question my own judgment in choosing you to lead this dominion nearly two years ago. However, I will give you an opportunity to redeem yourselves. In order to ruin Elizabeth Bennet, Cassandra and I must have more access to her. We cannot influence her if she is constantly insulated from us by those around her. We are not likely to defeat the three who are guarding her, but we can remove the human element of protection. I want Charlotte Lucas to be eliminated from the equation." His voice rose in pitch and force, and his eyes flashed. "I do not desire for her merely to be discredited; I command that you use any means necessary to keep her from Elizabeth. Jolon, one of my guards, is nearly as good with his darts as was Keegan. Use him – tonight! The guardians assigned to the Lucas family should not pose the formidable problems of those guarding the Bennets; neither do archangels guard Chance and Janna Bingley. Attack those two, and Lynne and David Bennet will fly to their aid taking Roark and Niall with them. Elizabeth and Michael will be alone until Xander and Gabriel hear of it. We must be ever more devious and cunning. Am I understood?"

Without raising his head, Ryu answered, "All that you have commanded shall be done immediately, my prince."

"Go now!" Gregory thundered. He flew so abruptly from the room that his guards were left behind, scrambling to catch up to him.

~~oo~~

The following morning, Xander was surprised to see Elizabeth and Lynne, Michael and Niall flying above the car, driving up to Converse without Charlotte. He, accompanied by Gabriel, had waited for them near Lynne's faculty parking space, and he was looking forward to seeing Elizabeth at school and spending the afternoon with her shopping in Spartanburg. As soon as Lynne stopped the car, Xander walked over to open Elizabeth's door.

His book bag was over his left shoulder, and he reached for her book bag, throwing the strap over his right shoulder while he waited for her to step out of the car.

"Hello, Mrs. Bennet. How are you today?" he asked Lynne courteously.

"Fine, thank you, Xander. Sorry I can't stay to chat. I'm in a little bit of a hurry this morning," Lynne replied with a smile. Looking at her daughter, she added, "You can call me later to let me know what you decide to do. 'Bye!" Lynne nodded at Xander before she and Niall walked quickly down the sidewalk.

Michael and Gabriel stood on either side of Xander. *Where is Charlotte?* Xander asked.

Michael replied solemnly, *She is sick this morning. She is still in bed.*

Elizabeth had gathered the rest of her things while Xander and her mother exchanged greetings. "'Bye, Mom!" she called to her mother's retreating back as she climbed out of the car.

"Good morning, Elizabeth. You are beautiful this morning, as always. Did you have a pleasant evening?" asked Xander, thinking of her ride with Gregory the day before.

"Good morning to you, too, and thanks for the compliment. My evening was… unusual." Her reply was strained.

"Is something wrong?" he asked, his blue eyes reflecting his worry.

"No, I hope not anyway." She avoided looking at him. "Let's get to class."

Xander walked quietly beside her. *Did she sleep well? Was she dreaming of Gregory?*

She did not dream of Gregory, but of you. However, her sleep was not restful, and her dreams were chaotic. He disturbed her with what he said about you, Michael answered.

"Where is Charlotte this morning? I hope she is well."

"She was sick all night and didn't feel up to coming to school this morning. It's probably just a bug. It's January. The flu is going around," Elizabeth said, looking straight ahead.

"Oh. Perhaps it is not too serious, then," he replied, concerned. He well remembered all the times that Elizabeth had been sick. As he thought about her childhood illnesses, a memory of her chicken pox episode was triggered. *Do you think that Charlotte was attacked? Could this have been a dart?*

I do not know. Edward did not mention it, but it is difficult to detect a dart if the demon is well-practiced in the skill. It is possible, Michael mused.

Gregory may have broadened his targeting to include those who stop him and Cassandra from getting too close to Elizabeth, added Gabriel.

Xander was pensive. *That sounds like a plan he would hatch.*

I will send extra warriors to surround the Bennets, as well as Chance and Janna Bingley, this very moment, Michael said, issuing the command with a thought as Captain of the Host.

"Do you still want to go shopping after school today?" Xander asked.

Elizabeth stopped walking and looked up at him. "I think we need to talk, Xander," she said calmly.

"Certainly, if you wish it. Right now?" Xander struggled to keep the anxiety from his face. *How will I answer her questions?*

All that you say must be the truth, but you cannot tell her everything yet, counseled Michael.

"We don't have time now. We'll be late for class if we don't hurry. Can we go somewhere for lunch today? We can go Dutch." She started walking again, and Xander was close beside her.

"I will take you anywhere you want to go, Elizabeth. You know that. However, I must ask that you do not talk of 'going Dutch,' please," he said softly.

"How about the Converse Deli and Coffee Bar on Main Street?" she replied, smiling tentatively up at him.

Finally! A smile. It was a small one, but it was definitely a smile, thought Xander with relief.

"I have been there several times, and I really like it," replied Xander. "Your mother can go as well, if she would like to." *If Lynne is there, Elizabeth will not be able to ask personal questions.*

"No, I think I would like for us to talk alone. I have some questions. You wouldn't be avoiding that, would you, Xander?" she asked archly.

She is far from being stupid, Xander, Michael reminded him.

"No, Elizabeth. I am eager to be interrogated by such a lovely inquisitor. Will I be able to ask questions as well? This would be a good opportunity for us to get to know each other better." *A good offense is the best defense, or so I have heard.*

Good idea, said Gabriel.

"Of course. I'll text Mom and let her know our plans," Elizabeth replied, climbing the steps to their classroom building.

"Be sure to ask her what she would like to eat. We can bring lunch back for her." Xander opened the door and held it for her.

"You know, you are a very thoughtful person, Xander. Mom would love that."

"I try, Elizabeth," he said with a broad, dimpled smile.

I think I'll enjoy looking at that smile during lunch. Gregory can't be right about him, she thought as they arrived at the open door to their classroom.

Xander stood back to allow Elizabeth to enter ahead of him, following her in and taking a seat beside her to her right. Michael and Gabriel stood on either side of Elizabeth. Gregory was already seated to her left, and his two guards were stationed close to him.

Elizabeth glanced at Gregory as she wriggled out of her coat. "Good morning, Gregory."

He gave her a crooked smile. "Hi, El. Sleep well?"

"As always. Did you have a good evening?"

"I had a better late afternoon. How about lunch today?" he asked.

"Actually, I asked Xander to take me to lunch. We're going to have that talk you suggested," she answered, looking directly into his eyes.

He never faltered. "Excellent. I expect that we'll have more time together if he answers you honestly."

Xander had overheard every word. He turned his head and fixed his eyes stonily on Gregory's face. "I would never be anything other than honest with Elizabeth. You certainly cannot say the same."

Elizabeth sighed with relief as the professor called the class to order. *One of them is lying. How will I know which one? Dear Father, please guide me at lunch today and give me discernment to know what is true and what is false.*

And please guide her questions, Father, so that I can answer her. Please give me the right words to say to her, Xander prayed fervently.

'The effective prayer of a righteous man can accomplish much,' thought Gabriel, quoting James 5:16.

~~oo~~

Xander was anxious throughout the long morning, thinking through every possible question he could imagine while trying to formulate plausible, truthful answers. Michael assisted him by telling him the things of which she had thought and dreamed after he had left for the night with Gabriel.

He was so focused on listening to her mind during those hours that he actually failed to hear a professor call on him in one of their classes. Gabriel, hearing his mental confusion, repeated the question for him, and Xander quickly answered aloud.

Finally, their last class before lunch drew to an agonizingly slow close. Xander glanced at Elizabeth with a careful smile.

"Shall we go? I think I am ready for some ham and cheese quiche with the soup of the day," he said, standing, pulling his knee-length, black cashmere coat on over his charcoal, long-sleeved T shirt, slinging his book bag over one shoulder, and then reaching for hers and looping it over his other shoulder.

"Yes, I'm starving. I haven't been chewing my lip all morning like you have, and I skipped breakfast," she said with a laugh, rising and taking her navy pea-coat off the back of her desk. Somehow, even with both of their book bags over his shoulders, Xander still managed to take her coat and hold it for her. After she had turned her back to him and shrugged into the coat, she faced him, looking up to see his expression as he replied to her.

"Chewing my lip? Have you been watching me? And, you know, breakfast is the most important meal of the day. You should always have breakfast." He wore a small frown, worried that she was not resting well or eating as she should because of him.

I would love to smooth that wrinkle between your brows. My gut is telling me that you're the good guy here. You won't lie to me. Impulsively, she reached up and touched the tiny crease on his face with her index finger. He held his breath, not wanting to move lest he cause her to pull away.

Gregory walked by and sneered at the tender scene. "Enjoy your lunch, Xander," he threw over his shoulder, laughing as he exited the room.

I really, truly do not like him. Xander sighed. *However, I am the one that she touched willingly, because she wanted to do so.* He smiled, caught in the beams of light coming through the window.

Elizabeth saw the sunlight illuminating his face and causing his hair to shine. *He looks otherworldly, as if he's a glowing being of light,* she thought in wonder.

~~oo~~

Xander walked Elizabeth to the parking lot and paused before opening the car door for her. "I know that we could walk to the restaurant, but I have a surprise for you in here."

After Xander and Elizabeth were settled in his BMW with their seatbelts on and book bags stowed in the backseat, Xander started the car, and it was filled with the sounds of beautiful piano music. Elizabeth listened for a moment, and then looked at him in surprise.

"Is that me playing on that CD?" she asked, looking at him incredulously.

"Yes, ma'am," he answered, a hint of a smile beginning to play around his lips.

"Where did you get that?" she demanded. "I've never cut a CD, and that sounds professional."

He reached into the backseat, picked up a CD, and handed it to her. "It is professional. I hired the technicians at your concert in Toronto and at several other performances in the last few months. Remember, I was a fan of yours before we ever met. If you like it, you own the rights to it. You can sell it on Amazon. The photograph on the cover is done by a professional I hired to be at those same concerts. I can show you others if you do not like that one. I have several copies for you today, and no one else has a copy but me. If you do not like it, I will destroy all the copies except for mine. I would ask that you let me keep this one."

She stared at him in wonder. "You are unbelievable."

"Is that good or bad?" he asked somberly, gazing back at her.

"That's very good. I should have thought of this myself, but I would have been nervous had I known that I was being professionally recorded. This is wonderful!" She settled back to enjoy her music.

"You do not think it is creepy?" He looked over at her with a question in his eyes.

He is adorable. He looks just like a small boy who has been caught stealing cookies from a cookie jar.

"Not creepy to me. Had you done this and not told me, yes, creepy. However, since you have told me about the photos and recordings, and you have not released them without my permission, it is totally not creepy. By the way, I want the photos," she chuckled.

"Of course, but I would like to keep copies of some of them. They are all beautiful, like you, Elizabeth."

"Xander, you are incorrigible." She reached over and smoothed his hair, which had been tousled by the wind.

Her touch was electrifying to Xander, but he managed to keep a calm demeanor. *If she had the slightest idea what that small gesture meant to me, she would probably stop immediately. And I really do not want her to cease touching me.*

"If you keep rewarding me like that, I will learn to be incorrigible more often." He laughed lightly as he turned to look behind the car, checked the mirrors, and backed out of the parking space; Michael and Gabriel flew overhead.

Elizabeth enjoyed the music during the short drive to the restaurant, talking very little, though she kept playing with his hair for a few minutes, finally resting her hand on his arm which was on the console between their seats. Xander would have been unable to speak in any case. Her touch was so comfortable – so absolutely right. The sensation he felt when she stroked his hair or touched his arm was unlike anything he had ever known before. He felt himself shiver, but caught himself, hoping she did not notice. *I cannot describe this feeling. It is exquisite torture.* He wanted to keep driving forever.

She twirled her own curls around the fingers of her other hand. He held his breath, intensely aware of her smallest movements. *Her hand is so small compared to mine. How can so simple an act give me such pleasure?*

Xander drove carefully, focusing with an iron will, and was rewarded by observing the contrast between her behavior with him and the way she had acted with Gregory on the previous day. She was relaxed, humming along with her CD, watching the city streets, and smiling a secret smile.

This is good, thought Gabriel.

This is very good, added Michael, smiling.

Once they arrived at the restaurant, Xander parked, got out of the car, and came around to open her door. He reached for her hand to help her out of the low-slung sports coupe.

"Thank you, Xander. You always treat me like a lady. You're going to spoil me," she said, smiling with her dark brown eyes and taking his hand.

"No one deserves it more than you do, Elizabeth. You are a very special lady." He kept her hand in his as they walked into the restaurant and waited to be seated. *Her hand is so warm, so soft.*

Michael and Gabriel stood beside their charges.

After the hostess tried unsuccessfully to hide her shock at seeing what appeared to be a film star in Spartanburg, she lead them to a table and a waiter took their orders. Once they were again alone, Elizabeth looked at Xander with serious eyes.

"Are you ready to talk?"

"Are you?" Xander asked reaching across the table to stroke her fingers gently.

She put her hands in her lap and leaned forward. "I can't think straight when you're doing that."

Xander chuckled. *I have not been thinking clearly since we got in the car. It is only by His grace that we arrived in one piece. Interesting and gratifying, however, that I affect her in such a way.* "Then please give me both of your hands. I do not enjoy talking about myself. Holding your hands can serve two purposes. First, I am calmer when I touch you. Second, you will not be as pointed with your questions if you are a bit confused. If I must answer questions, you should allow me the comfort of touching you." His blue eyes were sincere.

Elizabeth sighed and pursed her lips. "You win, but you are forcing me to use all my powers of concentration." Her hands met his in the center of the table.

They were quiet for a moment as the waiter brought their drinks.

Michael and Gabriel smiled at each other from behind Elizabeth and Xander.

"Gregory said some things about you yesterday that made me realize how little I really know about you," she began.

He refrained from making any reply. Being critical of Gregory would make her defend him.

"Where are you from? Do you have any family?" she asked.

"I have lived in many places during my life, and I have brothers who live near here. I suppose that Spartanburg is my home for now. I am not a felon, nor am I being sought for any crime."

She laughed. "I should hope not. What about your parents?"

"Actually, I have no real parents. I was adopted into a large family, and it is my great joy to hear my Father refer to me as His son. I see my Father often, but He prefers to manage His business from afar. He does not live near here, but He is always available whenever I need Him. He has never married. All of His children are adopted, and He cares deeply for us all."

Impressive, commented Michael.

And the absolute truth, added Gabriel.

"You have no mother? That is rather unorthodox."

Xander tilted his head and smiled. "There are all sorts of families, Elizabeth. Many people are adopted. I have been loved all of my life, and I am blessed."

"Do you ever see your brothers?"

He laughed lightly. "Quite often. We are very close."

Gabriel put his hands on Xander's shoulders as Michael smiled at him from across the table.

"Will I ever meet them?"

"It is possible. However, they do not live in Spartanburg as I do, and they travel a great deal."

"Are they... like you?" She smiled shyly.

"Do you mean is there a family resemblance? I am adopted, remember?" He was puzzled.

"No, I mean are they as big as you are? Are they as handsome? Are they as talented and intelligent?" She looked at their hands, entwined on the table.

Xander grinned. "I suppose all of us like to stay in good shape. We are about the same height, though our coloring is different. You might think they are more handsome than I am. As for talent and intelligence, you will have to decide that for yourself, if you ever meet them."

Michael laughed, and Gabriel hit the back of Xander's head lightly, chuckling. *I am taller than you are, and Gabriel is far better looking,* thought Michael.

She looked at him, trying to be objective, but she was distracted by the power of his beauty. She thought about what Gregory had said. *You don't know what he is.*

Elizabeth looked into his kind eyes and saw no malice. She had spent time with him, and she knew that he was godly and compassionate. He was all that was considerate and gentlemanly. Suddenly, she realized that she cared for him because he was good, honest, loyal, and worthy of love.

"Gregory is wrong. I do know what you are, Xander. You are an angel," she said tenderly.

He opened his eyes wide in surprise.

She does not mean that literally, Xander, thought Michael.

"I suppose that I should not argue with a lady." *Thank you, Father. I may speak the absolute truth to her.* Xander's heart was joyful, and his face reflected that joy. "You are right. I am an angel."

Elizabeth was stunned into silence by the brilliance of his smile. She stared at him, forgetting herself for the moment. *If I ever really meet an angel, he will look and act like Xander.*

Michael and Gabriel shook their heads at each other, smiling widely.

Further conversation was delayed by the appearance of a waiter who carried a tray bearing their food. Elizabeth was sufficiently distracted by the arrival of their meal that she did not return to the previous subject.

His timing was impeccable. I will leave him a large tip, Xander thought. Then his mind turned to the fortunate path the conversation had taken. *One day I will have to tell her that I really am an angel. What will she think of me then?*

Chapter 7

"And these signs will accompany those who have believed: in My name they will cast out demons, they will speak with new tongues, they will pick up serpents, and if they drink any deadly poison, it shall not hurt them; they will lay hands on the sick, and they will recover."
Mark 16:17-18

Xander, flanked by Gabriel and Michael, stood waiting patiently for Elizabeth to gather her belongings after their last class ended that afternoon. He had already slipped into his coat and shouldered both of their book bags when Gregory approached her, his two guards following closely behind him. Xander clenched his jaw so tightly that the muscles hardened, giving his face a chiseled appearance. He flared his nostrils once as he breathed deeply, willing himself to relax. His face became calmer, but his eyes were blue ice as he glared at Gregory.

Easy, Xander, thought Michael, though he watched Gregory with narrowed eyes himself.

Gregory glanced at him, his amusement at Xander's discomfort evident in his smirk, as he sauntered confidently to Elizabeth's side.

"Would you like to have dinner tonight? We'll go anywhere you choose. Out of the country is doable, if that's what you want, El." Gregory took her coat from the back of her seat and held it for her.

"I seem to remember telling you that I would never again ride in a car that you were driving, Gregory," she said with determination as she accepted his help with her coat. She lifted her hair as he slid her coat under it, and then she faced him, Xander and the two guardians at her back.

"That's why I arranged for a driver today, El. Where would you like to go? New York? London? Paris? The family jet is waiting." Elizabeth took a step back from him when he began to button her coat for her, and his hands dropped to his sides.

He is touching her, and she does not like it, Xander thought angrily.

Elizabeth can handle this. We should stay out of it, responded Michael, though his hand hovered over his sword's hilt as he and Gabriel widened their stances.

"I left my passport at home; besides, I think my father would probably have a heart attack if I called him and told him I was having dinner in Paris. You might want to check with me first before you make any more elaborate plans for us." She looked down as she buttoned her coat.

Gregory smiled at Xander with malice, but his voice remained smooth and melodic.

"You don't need a passport when you travel with me, El."

"Really? So you know people in high places?" She looked up at him speculatively.

That is an understatement, hissed Xander's mind.

"And in low ones, too, for that matter," Gregory said with a laugh.

*No, **that** is an understatement,* corrected Gabriel calmly.

She laughed lightly. "Somehow, I never doubted that. However, I already have plans for this evening." Elizabeth turned her head and flashed a smile at Xander.

His heart thudded. *I will be happy to play this game, though I did not know we were still going this afternoon since Charlotte is sick.* "Yes, Gregory.

Elizabeth and I made plans several days ago to shop and have dinner together today."

"Xander, you seem to be monopolizing all of El's time lately." He frowned at Xander, and then turned a smiling face to Elizabeth. "Should I make an appointment a week in advance?" he teased.

"The choice has always been up to the lady, Gregory," Xander replied, not quite managing to smile.

"This lady says we need to hurry, Xander. I would like to see Charlotte before it gets too late tonight. 'Bye, Gregory. I'll see you tomorrow." Elizabeth started toward the door, and Xander began to walk down the aisle to join her.

Gregory leaned across the desk and gripped Xander's arm. "This shall not continue. I *will* have her," Gregory muttered harshly, his voice too low for Elizabeth to hear his words.

Instantly, both Gabriel and Michael drew their swords; Crevan and Duglas immediately responded in kind. Gabriel spoke aloud in an authoritative voice so that Gregory and his guards could hear him. *You are touching my charge as well as threatening him. That is grounds for a fight. I am ready if you are.*

Michael added, *My brothers and I will fight together. The battle is evenly matched – three to three.* He looked directly at Gregory with a scowl. *This time, no one will be able to put you back together. You will be in so many pieces that there will be no doubt of your death.*

Xander stopped, dead still, looking at Gregory's hand on his arm with obvious distaste. His voice was quiet and menacing; each word was clipped and distinct. "Remove your arm, or I shall be forced to move it for you. While I would take great satisfaction in removing it completely from your body, that action would draw attention which neither of us wants at this time."

Gregory looked at Michael and Gabriel standing on either side of Xander, glaring at him with swords drawn, and he slowly drew back his hand. "We will continue this later," he said tersely.

"I shall look forward to it. Anytime. Anywhere. Just name the time and place. I will be there." Xander held the halfling's eyes with his as he straightened to his full height and jerked the sleeve of his coat down at his wrist to straighten the wrinkles left there by Gregory.

Michael and Gabriel slowly sheathed their swords, watching without blinking as Gregory's guards stood down and put away their weapons.

Elizabeth had stopped at the door, waiting for Xander, and she noticed the tension between the two men. She saw Gregory grab Xander's arm, and watched them as they exchanged heated words. *My goodness. They look as if they are going to fight. Why are they so angry?* Forcing a cheerfulness into her voice that she did not feel, she called, "Xander, are you coming? I'm getting older by the minute here."

Glancing at Elizabeth, Xander saw the concern in her eyes, and his anger melted away. *She is leaving with me – because she wants to be with me instead of Gregory.* His thought put a genuine smile on his face, and she relaxed in response. He strode to her side and put a protective arm around her shoulders.

Michael and Gabriel followed the couple, backing out of the room and blocking Xander and Elizabeth from the demons' view, never taking their stares from the faces of Gregory and his henchmen until their charges were well beyond the door.

"Are you ready to go, Elizabeth?" His voice was kind and gentle as he steered her from the room.

That's the voice I love, she thought.

His heart jumped in response to the last word she thought. *Then I will be careful to use that voice when I am with you, my Elizabeth.*

"Yes, please. I'll text Mom about our plans when we get to your car, but let's just go now." She took a quick look over her shoulder at Gregory. He smiled and waved, so she smiled, albeit uncertainly, in return.

As they left the building and headed toward the parking lot, Elizabeth lifted her face to his. "What was that all about?"

"Nothing, really," Xander answered, noncommittally.

"It didn't look like nothing." *Don't hide things from me.*

Always be honest with her. Michael was right behind Xander.

She is not a child, and she resents being treated as one, added Gabriel.

Xander had heard her thought as well. "Gregory is jealous of the time you are spending with me. He thought I would stop pursuing you if he threatened me. He was wrong."

"Oh."

"Oh? What does that mean?" Xander looked down at her dark hair shining in the late afternoon sunlight. He knew that he had no right to be so possessive of her – yet.

"I've never taken Gregory seriously. He flirts with anything female."

"He is serious about you, but not in the same way that I am." His statement was calm and deliberate, and he knew that it would provoke a question on her part.

It was her turn to query. She stopped and looked up at him. "What does *that* mean?"

He stopped beside her, took a deep breath, and dropped his arm from around her shoulders, facing her to take her hands in his. *I will always be honest with you.* His eyes were serious as he looked into hers. "My intentions are entirely honorable. I hope to date you, court you, and eventually marry you."

She held his gaze a moment longer, and then began to walk again, leaving one of her hands in one of his. She looked out in front of them at nothing in particular.

"So Gregory's intentions are not honorable, according to you." Her tone held a little resentment.

He sighed deeply. "Elizabeth, I am being entirely truthful with you. I know that he is your friend, and I know that you have known him longer than you have known me. However, I have known his father very well for many years, and I have known Gregory longer and more intimately than you have. He asked you if you had ever met my family. Have you ever met his? Let me ask you something more important. Has he ever made you uncomfortable?" Xander knew the answer to his question, because he had been privy to her thoughts on those occasions.

"Xander, I don't like all this male posturing, and I don't like being made to choose between you. Why can't I be friends with both of you?" *This is ridiculous!*

Careful, Xander, cautioned Michael.

"You can, Elizabeth. I am not asking you to choose. And you do not have to answer my question if you would prefer not to do so, but I would like to hear your answer if you do not mind giving it."

They had arrived at his car, so Xander opened her door, put their book bags in the back seat, and held the door for her. She got in and buckled her seatbelt, obviously pondering his request as he walked around to the driver's side and got in.

Because she had not yet told him where she wished to go, he buckled his seat belt and waited before he started the car. She took her cell phone out of her coat pocket and sent a text message to her mother, telling her that she was with Xander as they had planned previously. When she was finished, she put her phone away and turned her head to look at him.

"Frankly, yes, Gregory has made me uncomfortable several times in different ways, but I am not yet ready to give up my friendship with him. I have always felt safe with you, but I want to get to know you better before we take our relationship any further."

"Please define 'further.' I do not wish to overstep my boundaries with you or pressure you in any way. I want you to tell me if I am ever making you at all uneasy. I would never force you to do anything that you do not want to do." He saw her hesitation. "For instance, I just put my arm around your shoulder, and after that I held your hand. Was that all right with you?"

How does he do that? My objections to the speed this relationship is picking up as it moves along always melt away when I am with him. She spread out her hands on her thighs and looked down at them, taking a deep breath.

She chuckled quietly. "I can hardly object when I have initiated the physical contact several times myself. In fact, I believe that I touched your hair and put my hand on your arm before you put your arm around me." Elizabeth tilted her head while it was still inclined and turned her face partially toward him, looking at him mischievously from the corners of her twinkling eyes.

He laughed aloud; he could not help himself. "You are wholly adorable, Elizabeth. I will try my best not to push you, but you must tell me if I do anything you do not like."

There is little chance of that, I'm afraid, she thought, a little dreamily. *His eyelashes have their own zip code. Richard is the only boy I have ever kissed. What would it be like to kiss this man?*

Would you like to find out?

Xander, do not make her first kiss with you take place in the parking lot of the college, admonished Gabriel, hovering above the car.

This is not how you would have her remember such an important moment, added Michael, rather sternly.

It will be your very first kiss, too. It should be memorable, Gabriel concluded.

Again, two too many voices in my head, even if you are right on this occasion, grumbled Xander. *And thank you both for reminding me that I have never kissed anyone in my entire existence. Let me remind you – neither have you.*

There was blessed silence in his mind.

"My, my. You're so quiet. What are you thinking?" He looked at her to find her amused eyes watching him intently.

He blushed and looked out the windshield. *Too awkward for a conversation.* "At this moment, I am thinking that we should be going. Exactly where do you want to go? I am eagerly awaiting your instructions."

"How about WestGate Mall? I'd like to get some jeans and a couple of new tops, and I really like *Sarku Japan* in their food court. If you don't like Japanese, there are plenty of other choices."

Xander wrinkled his nose the tiniest bit for a second.

"Is there somewhere else you would rather go, Xander?" she asked.

He hesitated, and then spoke diffidently, turning his head to look at her seriously. "I do not usually eat at mall food courts, but we will go wherever you wish."

She smiled in amusement, pursing her lips. "Is there something wrong with food courts?"

He bit his lip, thinking for a moment. "Not really. They are just so – public. There are so many people there. I prefer to dine in more private settings. However, I am open to new experiences."

Elizabeth laughed lightly. "You are such a snob! I understand the tailor-made clothes and the expensive car. Nothing off the rack would fit you, and your knees would be beside your ears in a Honda. But you don't like food courts? No mingling with the masses?"

"You misunderstand me, Elizabeth. I do not look down on people, except in the sense that I am taller than most of them." He broke eye contact and looked out the windshield, unconsciously displaying his perfect profile. It was not lost on her.

"Then what is it about food courts that bothers you? Is the food not up to your standards?" She tilted her head and kept her eyes on his face, smiling playfully. *Some sculptor really should capture that marvelous silhouette before he ages.*

Xander made himself look into her eyes. "That is not what makes me uncomfortable. I eat take-out quite often."

"At home. Alone."

"Yes." *Now she will think I am a freak of some sort.* He listened to her sorting though the information in her thoughts.

"You are shy?" She sounded incredulous. The thought of such an imposing man being shy was slightly ludicrous.

"Not exactly. I am not afraid of anyone. But, Elizabeth – people stare at me, and that makes me uncomfortable."

"Excuse me, Xander, but duh! Of course you get more than your share of attention. You are unusually tall, very well dressed, and extremely handsome. It is natural for people to look at you, especially women. Most men would relish the attention." *He is adorable. There is that little frown between his eyes again.*

Elizabeth could not help herself. She reached over and gently smoothed the wrinkle between his brows with her finger.

He closed his eyes, leaned back on the headrest, and felt all the tension leave his body as she touched him. *We may never leave this parking lot if you keep doing that.*

She spoke softly. "You are not like most men, are you?" She lowered her hand slowly, tracing his strong jawline before she brought her hand back to her lap.

He did not move from the headrest, but turned his head to capture her eyes. His voice was low and musical. "No, I am not. But I will always strive to be what you need. I will adjust to being stared at. Perhaps you can distract me so that I do not notice them?" His lazy smile jolted her senses.

That's the way Richard sometimes looked at me – just before he kissed me. We are in a public parking lot in broad daylight.

She spoke quickly, "I'll do my best. So, are we on for the mall and the food court? I promise to protect you if any women try to pick you up. No one will mess with this." She bent her arm to make a muscle and pointed to it, and he laughed with her.

"Certainly not. I am safe with you by my side to fight the hordes. Besides, no one will look at me when you are there. Your beauty will draw every eye. By the way, have we been on three dates yet?" he asked innocently.

What an odd question. Why is he asking that? she wondered.

"I'm not sure you'd call the times we've been together 'dates,' but I really haven't been counting. Why do you ask? Is there something special about the number three?" Her expression was contemplative.

He chuckled. "Three is special, but I think I prefer the number two."

She shook her head. "So mysterious."

Her CD was playing when he started the car.

"You have wonderful taste in music," she teased as they backed out and headed toward the mall.

"My standards are high, and I always try to surround myself with the best of everything," he returned airily.

"Well, thank you," Elizabeth replied saucily.

~~oo~~

Xander and Elizabeth had finished shopping and were sitting in the food court, nearly through eating their Teriyaki Chicken, when Elizabeth's cell phone sounded.

"It's a text from Mom," she said, retrieving the message.

"Oh, no!" Elizabeth exclaimed, looking worried.

Xander, as well as Gabriel and Michael, had heard her read the message in her mind, but he asked, "What is wrong?"

"Charlotte has taken a turn for the worse. Her parents took her to Mary Black Memorial Hospital here in Spartanburg this morning, and they have admitted her to the ICU. She is really sick. Do you mind if we stop in to see her before you take me home?" she asked anxiously.

He reached across the table and took her hand.

"Of course I do not mind. We can leave immediately if you wish." His voice calmed her.

"Thank you," she answered, standing to take her tray and empty it.

Xander took it from her and spoke gently. "Stay here for a moment. I will take the trays and come back for your packages."

She gathered her things while he was gone, and then followed him with a small frown on her lovely face. He turned to find her behind him, and he reached for her bags, gathering the handles in one hand while he reached for her hand with the other.

"Elizabeth." He spoke her name softly, and she turned her face up to look at him, her brown eyes glistening.

"It will be well. Charlotte will be fine."

They walked hand-in-hand from the mall, and Xander never noticed the people staring.

Elizabeth does indeed distract him, thought Gabriel, walking behind them.

To quote her, 'duh,' replied Michael, his focus never leaving his charge.

~~oo~~

By the time Xander and Elizabeth arrived at the hospital, Charlotte was in a room in the ICU. Elizabeth and Xander joined Charlotte's parents, Joshua, David, and Lynne in the waiting room. Skylar, Roark, Niall, and the other guardians greeted Xander, Michael, and Gabriel somberly.

How is she? What is wrong? asked Xander.

Her temperature is very high, and the doctors do not know what sickens her, answered Roark.

Dr. Walton, an infectious disease specialist who had been called in from Carolinas Medical Center in Charlotte, strode into the room. He had met Timothy and Laura Lucas with David and Lynne earlier in the day. He looked around the room and settled his gaze on the Lucases. "I'm not going to sugar coat this. Charlotte is extremely ill, and we cannot determine what is wrong with her. We have run every test that we can think of for viral and bacterial diseases, fungal infections, or parasites, and everything has come back negative. Her spinal tap, blood work, bone marrow test, and body scan didn't show anything either. If we cannot bring her temperature down very soon, she will become unconscious. In fact, I have never seen an adult with a temperature this high who was still lucid and talking. The six hour window is nearly up, so the next thing will have to be an invasive method. I'm having her airlifted to Carolinas Medical in order to have a team of specialists working with me; the helicopter has already been dispatched to get her, and Charlotte will be there within the hour. I've already ordered critical fever care to be set up and waiting. When she becomes unconscious, you can expect that we will use an IV to circulate cold fluids through her system to bring the fever down to 105° in order to avoid brain damage while we do more testing."

"Why can't you do that now if it will lower her temperature?" asked Timothy.

"We must wait for her to be unconscious. If she were cognizant at the time, the pain would be so great that the shock could kill her."

"Why would you leave her fever at 105°?" questioned Laura.

"Because we don't know what is causing her extremely high temperature. We are hoping that her elevated fever will kill whatever it is." He nodded, and exited the room quickly.

After the doctor left the room, there was complete silence for several seconds while everyone mulled over his words. It was obvious that Dr. Walton's hopes for Charlotte's survival were slim.

Laura took Timothy's hand and looked at Elizabeth's stricken face. "El, you haven't seen Char since she became so ill. Would you like to go in and see her now? Tim and I will be following her to Carolinas Medical Center as soon as she leaves here. We can see her there. Your parents have already been in and spent some time with her."

Xander saw the tears beginning to run down Elizabeth's cheeks, and he put his arm around her. "Mr. and Mrs. Lucas, would you mind if I go in with Elizabeth to see Charlotte?" Michael placed his hand on Elizabeth's back and whispered peace to her.

Timothy replied, "I think that would be good. El will need you."

Xander nodded and left the waiting room with Elizabeth. Michael and Gabriel followed behind them.

As the couple entered Charlotte's room, they noticed that a digital thermometer display by Charlotte's bed read 106.5°, and she looked miserable and frightened. She had been placed between two cooling blankets filled with ice water that was constantly recycling, and plastic bags of ice had been put under her armpits, around her neck, and at her groin. The bags of ice were being changed regularly because her high body temperature quickly melted the ice. Charlotte shivered, but her temperature remained high.

Edward stood at the head of Charlotte's bed, and beside him stood a tall, slender angel with white hair and violet eyes, dressed in a brilliant white robe. The willowy death angel nodded at Xander, Michael, and Gabriel.

Elizabeth stepped to Charlotte's bedside and took her hand.

"El, I'm – afraid. You know – what – happens to – people whose – temperatures stay this – high for too – long." Charlotte's teeth chattered, and her breathing was labored. "I hurt – all over. Have – I died – and gone – to hell? – I'm so – tired. God – can heal – me if it is – His – will. El, pray – for

– me?" Charlotte's voice was weak and hoarse. Her body was stiff, her eyes unfocused.

Elizabeth shook her head. "I have no words; I cannot pray," she choked out. *Father, interpret my heart. It is too heavy for expression.*

The tears rolled silently down Elizabeth's cheeks. She looked up at Xander, her dark eyes imploring him. He moved to the other side of the bed and took Charlotte's other hand.

Xander, prayer is no longer needed for Charlotte. The Father of All is calling her home to her reward, Gabriel said softly.

My Father said in Luke1:27, 'For nothing will be impossible with God,' and in James 4:2, 'You do not have because you do not ask.' I am claiming those verses, Xander answered with conviction. *I feel led of God to pray for her.*

Michael and Gabriel placed their hands on Elizabeth's and Xander's shoulders, while Edward put his hands on either side of Charlotte's face.

In the waiting room, David began to pray aloud while the others bowed their heads, held hands, and joined him silently. The four guardian angels formed a circle around their charges, placing their hands on their shoulders.

Xander prayed quietly, with confidence that his prayer would be answered. "Father, I know that You love Charlotte, and I pray that You would show Yourself in a mighty way in this place today. I pray for her healing, in the name of Jesus, Jehovah-Rophe."

As Xander continued to pray, simply talking to God and imploring Him to restore health to Charlotte, her temperature began to drop. Michael noticed it first. *Amazing. Look at that.* Gabriel and Edward lifted their heads and watched the numbers descend slowly. 106.2°, 106°, 105.8°. The angels began to glow, and the light filled the room as the Spirit touched Charlotte's body. The light beings hummed their praise for the Healer, and the numbers continued to decrease as Xander prayed. 105.6°, 105.5°, 105.4°.

In the waiting room, David sensed the movement of the Spirit and raised his head. He realized that God was working a miracle. The hair stood up on the

SOULFIRE

back of his neck as he gripped Lynne's hand harder. She looked up at him, and he kept praying, his eyes open and his face lifted toward heaven.

Xander continued to talk to the Great Physician, asking for healing, and the numbers kept going down. 105.3°, 105.2°, 105.1°.

The digital display in Charlotte's room showed the numbers going lower and lower. 105°, 104.9°, 104.8°. Still Xander prayed.

"El," Charlotte whispered. Elizabeth lifted her head to look at her friend. Charlotte nodded at the numbers behind Xander and smiled weakly. Elizabeth looked and watched as Xander interceded for her friend. 104.7°, 104.6°, 104.5°.

The nurses stationed in the ICU noticed the temperature numbers dropping on their monitor, and one of them walked to Charlotte's room and looked in. She watched as Elizabeth and Charlotte were being led in prayer by a tall, muscular man, and her first thought was that he was an angel. The room seemed to glow around him, and his face was achingly beautiful. Mesmerized, she watched the numbers in quiet amazement. She had never before seen anything like it. 104.4°, 104.3°, 104.2°.

Xander thought of nothing except the power of the Almighty as he implored the Father for healing on behalf of Charlotte. He could feel the Master's strength coursing through him to the young woman, and he knew that God was doing a wondrous work. He was compelled to keep praying, and the numbers moved steadily downward. 104.1°, 104°, 103.9°.

His prayer began to change as his Father led him. Instead of asking for Charlotte's healing, Xander thanked Jehovah-Mephalti for touching her body and restoring her health. He never raised his voice; nothing was dramatic about the scene except for the numbers. 103.8°, 103.7°, 103.6°.

Xander had been praying for nearly five minutes by the time Charlotte's temperature dipped below 100°. The violet-eyed angel, summoned back to heaven, spread his wings and drifted through the wall, in awe of the unusual events which had transpired this night. Death-bed healings had happened many times during the life of Christ and while the early church was being established, but seldom since then. Edward watched as the death angel departed, then returned his attention to his charge with a smile.

She is healed, Xander. The Great Physician has heard and answered, thought Michael.

Exhilarated, Xander lifted his head and beamed a beautiful smile at Charlotte.

I have never felt such vigor, such a great force, in all my existence, Michael. It was as if the healing power of God Himself flowed directly through me into Charlotte. The excitement in the usually staid Xander's voice was electric.

I could hear the Holy Spirit directing your mind as you prayed, marveled Gabriel. *It was much as it happened with the apostles two thousand years ago after Christ had ascended back into heaven. Are you fatigued?*

Not at all. Quite to the contrary. I have never had such energy before. Xander contained his desire to soar through the walls and fly to the throne room. Instead, he bowed his head and expressed gratitude to his Father for allowing him to be a useful vessel.

Elizabeth bent to kiss Charlotte's cheek. "Thank you, dear Lord, for healing my friend," she whispered through her tears.

The nurse quietly closed the door, stopped by the nurses' station a moment, and went to the waiting room. She hesitated before she approached the Lucases and the Bennets. David saw her enter and stopped praying, looking toward her expectantly. As the pastor fell silent, Charlotte's parents also looked up and noticed the nurse.

"I don't know quite what to say. Charlotte's temperature is down to normal. I actually stood there and watched it drop as the young man prayed. We have called Dr. Walton to ask him what he wants to do. I'm sure that he'll be in to talk with you as soon as he decides." She walked to the door, hesitated, and turned back to the group of believers uncertainly.

"Rev. Bennet, I felt something in that room. It was like nothing I have ever experienced before, but, if anyone asked me, I'd have to say it was God. All of you are different from the other people I know. I want what you have. Could I come and talk to you tomorrow? I have to go back to work now."

David smiled broadly and looked at her name tag. "Certainly, Amanda. I would love to answer your questions and tell you why we are different." He reached into his pocket, took out his wallet, and pulled two cards from it. Handing one to her, he said, "Here are all my numbers. Call me anytime. Do you mind if I get your number as well?" She handed him a pen from her uniform pocket and dictated her cell number as David wrote it on the back of the other card.

She accepted her pen back from him, thanked him, and left the room.

As he turned back to the Lucases and Lynne while pocketing the card, David realized that just as he had witnessed the discovery of Elizabeth's extraordinary gift of music, he had now seen a supernatural gift from God given to Xander.

David quoted I Corinthians 12:8-9, "For to one is given the word of wisdom through the Spirit, and to another the word of knowledge according the same Spirit; to another faith by the same Spirit, and to another gifts of healing by the one Spirit." He looked from one amazed face to another and said, "We have witnessed a miracle here tonight," and he began to sing in a whisper, "I love You, Lord, and I lift my voice to worship You. Oh, my soul, rejoice." The others joined him in softly singing, "Take joy, my King, in what You hear. May it be a sweet, sweet sound in Your ear." [1] And the angels glowed ever brighter as they listened to the grateful praises that rose as incense to the throne of God.

Just as Amanda was opening the door back in ICU, she heard Charlotte speak up in a scratchy voice. "I'm feeling much better now, thank you, Xander. Now could one of you help me lose these cold blankets and ice packs before I freeze to death?"

A chuckle escaped Xander as Elizabeth wiped the tears from her eyes. "The old Char is back," she laughed softly.

Amanda walked quickly to her bedside, smiling. "We'll come in and do that right away. Tell your visitors good night now so that we can make you comfortable. Your parents can stay in the ICU waiting room. Dr. Walton will soon come in to tell you what he's decided."

Elizabeth leaned over and kissed her friend's cheek again and again. "I'll see you tomorrow, Char."

"How can I miss you if you won't go away?" joked Charlotte in a weary voice. Edward smiled.

"Love you, Char," said Elizabeth, turning to leave.

"Love you, too, El. Thanks for praying for me, Xander. I have always been taught that the fervent prayers of a righteous man can accomplish much." replied Charlotte softly, closing her eyes.

Michael spoke aloud to Edward, *You will have two warriors with you from this moment forward. Charlotte has become a target because of her close friendship with Elizabeth.* Edward nodded with a look of relief. Within seconds, two fully armored warriors were on either side of Charlotte's bed.

Together, Xander and Elizabeth told Charlotte good night and quickly left, followed by Michael and Gabriel, stopping in the ICU waiting room to hug the others and talk for a few minutes. Laura Lucas hugged Xander, and Timothy shook his hand, smiling from ear to ear.

David put a hand on his shoulder. "Xander, do you understand what God just did through you?"

"I am not certain whether or not anything like this will ever happen again, Pastor, but it appears that for tonight at least, I have been given the gift of healing. I would ask that this would remain private among us. Others may come asking for healing, and I would not want to give them false hope. God will use me how and when He chooses to do so." Xander spoke with humility.

"I think we could all agree to that, Xander. God will reveal His purpose for you when the time is right." David looked around the room, and everyone nodded in agreement.

"You must be tired, Xander. El could ride home with us and save you the drive to Bethel," David offered.

"Thank you, sir, but it is no trouble at all. Giving Elizabeth a ride home is a pleasure."

David shook his hand and smiled. "I knew you would refuse, but I thought I would offer."

Elizabeth took Xander's hand as they told everyone good night, and the couple walked out together, followed by Michael and Gabriel. As soon as they arrived at the car, Elizabeth turned to Xander, taking his other hand as well. She looked up into his eyes with a look of adoration.

"Xander," she said softly, "I know that God did the healing, but I wanted to thank you for being the sort of man that He could use in such a way. I think that was the most amazing thing that I have ever seen in my life, and I cannot tell you how happy I am to be with you."

"Elizabeth, spending time with you is a miracle every day for me. 'I thank God every time I think of you,' to paraphrase the apostle Paul." He freed her hands and drew her into his arms, holding her tightly. He could feel her body relax into his, releasing all the tension of the last hour. She put her cheek on his chest, and he kissed her hair, breathing in her scent. After a few minutes, he sighed, sorry to let her go.

"I think it is best if I drive you home now. It is getting late," he said with regret obvious in his voice.

"I could always go with Mom and Dad," she returned, laughing at his expression as she stepped out of his embrace.

"Not when I can spend another half hour with you by driving you home. Would you punish me now?" he teased as he opened the car door for her.

"I wouldn't dream of it," she replied, taking her seat and smiling at him.

~~oo~~

The spies inside and outside the hospital had watched and listened to the humans talk as Charlotte's temperature had returned to normal. Jolon's dart had been rendered powerless by the gift given to Xander. They flew away into the night, returning to Gregory to tell him that another weapon had been removed from their arsenal.

~~oo~~

[1] "I Love You, Lord," by Laurie Klein

Chapter 8

"Submit therefore to God. Resist the devil, and he will flee from you."
James 4:7

Spring 2008

Xander stood by his car, waiting impatiently for the police and glancing at his watch every few seconds. *I am already late for class, and Elizabeth must be wondering where I am.* He took out his cell phone and sent her a text message, explaining that he had been rear-ended on his way to Converse and would be there as soon as he could.

Calm yourself, Xander. The authorities will be here shortly, thought Gabriel, standing beside him.

How can I be calm, watching what is in that car with the driver and knowing that Gregory has had a hand in this? There is no telling what mischief he has planned.

The demon in the front seat of the car with the driver who had run into Xander grinned and smirked wickedly at Xander and Gabriel. The dark one continued to whisper into the mind of the human, filling him with anger and hatred.

Michael is there with Elizabeth. Nothing will happen to her. I have already telepathed him, and he is fully aware of the situation. He will summon the entire Host if it is necessary. Gabriel's voice was steady and reasonable, and it irritated Xander to no end.

I am neither a child nor an idiot. I know that Michael will protect her; however, I want to be there to frustrate whatever it is that Gregory has plotted in his evil brain. Can you not understand that?

Silence.

Gabriel?

Yes, Xander?

Silence.

I am being a child as well as an idiot. I am sorry. Xander ran his hand through his hair for the tenth time.

You are human. It is understandable.

Xander gritted his teeth. *Gabriel, sometimes your patience gets on my nerves.*

I know. Should I be impatient?

Xander grinned wryly. *Then you would not be Gabriel.*

Gabriel nodded sagely. *I would be Xander, I suppose.*

I deserved that. Xander saw a flashing blue light as a police car pulled up behind the two cars. *At last!*

I must go. You will not require my help for any of this. Gabriel spread his wings to fly.

Where are you going? asked Xander.

To Converse. There are complications, Gabriel thought as he took quickly to the air. Xander had read Gabriel's mind before he left, and he was anxious to be on his way as he dealt with the policeman filing the accident report.

~~oo~~

Elizabeth, reading while waiting in her mother's car in the parking lot for Xander, was surprised to look out her window and see Gregory and

Cassandra instead. Charlotte had already gone to class, and Lynne had hurried to the tutoring lab. Elizabeth grabbed her back pack, got out of the car, and walked to meet them. Michael stayed close beside her, scowling at the demons and their guards.

"Hello, gorgeous. Short one sidekick?" asked Gregory.

"Hi, guys. I can't imagine what could be keeping Xander. He is never late," Elizabeth replied, looking worried.

"I'm sure he's just caught in traffic or something. Xander can take care of himself. He's a big boy," said Cassandra, smiling.

They seem to be just a little too happy about this, thought Elizabeth.

Very perceptive. Michael was uneasy. The odds were four to one. He considered calling for reinforcements.

"What brings you guys out to the faculty parking lot this morning?" asked Elizabeth. *Surely they couldn't have known Xander wouldn't be here. How could they?*

"I was just hoping to catch you alone so that we could set up a lunch date," answered Gregory, flashing a boyish grin. "Finding you here without Xander was just a stroke of luck, and I have to grab my opportunities when I can. Like you said, he's never late. He's always early, in fact. When I saw that his car wasn't in his usual parking spot yet, Cassandra and I walked over on the chance that he wasn't here today."

"All you have to do is send me a text, Gregory, if you want to have lunch here. Remember I told you I wouldn't go anywhere with you if you were driving, and I still mean that." Elizabeth said, a little curtly.

A shadow of irritation flitted over Gregory's handsome face, but he recovered his smile quickly. "You know I don't like arranging dates of any sort by texting. As far as my driving goes, that, my beautiful friend, is why Cassandra is here. She can drive, or you can drive my car. We have a willing chaperone in our mutual friend."

"Please, El. We almost never have any time together," Cassandra pouted prettily. She had been calling Elizabeth at least twice a week to chat and build a relationship with her, and their friendship had progressed to the point that Elizabeth was comfortable with her.

Elizabeth's cell phone vibrated, and she fished it out of her jacket pocket. "It's a message from Xander. He's been in a fender-bender, and he's waiting for the police. I guess I'll go on to class." She sounded disappointed.

Michael had heard Gabriel's thoughts concerning the accident at the same time Elizabeth was reading her message from Xander. *I do not like this. Gregory and Cassandra are here with two guards,* Michael telepathed back to Gabriel.

"That's too bad about Xander." Gregory managed to look sympathetic. "So are we on for lunch?"

"Your concern is underwhelming." Elizabeth's tone was flat.

"We feel bad for the guy, but he isn't injured, is he?" asked Cassandra.

No thanks to you, said Gabriel, coming to rest on the other side of Elizabeth.

"Well, no, I guess not," answered Elizabeth, uncertainly.

"Then he'll be here in an hour or so, I imagine. We all have to get to class. Are you in for lunch?" Gregory was persuasive and persistent.

They all started walking toward the classrooms together. The two archangels touched Elizabeth at all times. Michael fixed the hellish guards with a burning stare. *Two to four now. I like these odds much better,* he said. They gave him a wide berth.

"I guess so." Elizabeth bit her lip.

"Your enthusiasm is underwhelming," Gregory said, mimicking her earlier statement.

"I'm just worried about Xander. He will expect me to eat with him. He's already had a bad morning."

"I would suggest that you invite him to go with us, but you know how that would go over," he said, chuckling.

"You have a point. I guess he'll understand." Elizabeth looked unhappy.

"I didn't know you two were in a serious relationship," said Cassandra, arching one eyebrow.

"We aren't. We just usually eat lunch together."

"You used to eat with me fairly often," Gregory said in a hurt voice.

"All right. Point taken. I guess we'll see you then, Cassandra. Gregory and I have class together before lunch."

"I know, El. I'll meet you two when your class gets out. 'Bye!" Cassandra hurried off in the opposite direction as Gregory and Elizabeth continued to their first class.

~~oo~~

Xander saw Gregory leaning across the aisle whispering something to Elizabeth as soon as he reached the door of their classroom for the second class of the day. Michael and Gabriel stood at her shoulders, their faces set in stony masks. Knowing that Gregory was responsible for his accident that morning made Xander more suspicious of him than usual, but he was determined not to fall into whatever trap the whelp of the wicked one had set.

Xander took his usual seat on the other side of Elizabeth.

"Good morning, Elizabeth, Gregory," he said, looking at each of them in turn and forcing himself to be pleasant.

He has asked Elizabeth to join him and Cassandra for lunch. She has accepted, though she was not happy about it, thought Michael.

Xander fought to keep the smile on his face, but it did not reach his eyes. *Does he honestly think I will allow him to be alone with her? He is delusional.*

What will you do? asked Gabriel. *You cannot stop her.*

I do not intend to stop her. Trust me. She will like my plan better than his. Xander's entire demeanor changed, and his smile was genuine.

Gregory noticed the difference immediately. "Good morning, Xander. I heard about your little accident. I'm so sorry. How's the Beamer? In the shop?" His words dripped with sarcasm.

Elizabeth looked at him sharply, and then turned to Xander. "I'm really glad that you're okay. I missed you this morning. You can copy my notes from class. I told Dr. Phillips why you were absent."

"Thank you, Elizabeth. I can always trust you to look out for my best interests, just as you can depend on me. Gregory, my car is still drivable, so I will arrange for repairs after school. It is kind of you to take an interest in my affairs."

Conversation ceased as the professor came into the room and closed the door behind him.

~~oo~~

As soon as the class before lunch ended, Xander rose from his seat and slung his book bag over his back.

"Coming, Elizabeth?" he asked, as if he did not know that she had plans.

"She's going to lunch with Cassandra and me," answered Gregory smugly. "I would have invited you, but I was sure that you wouldn't want to come. I thought it would be a good chance to show El my house. I'm having lunch for three delivered there."

Elizabeth turned quickly toward him, eyes narrowed. *I never agreed to go to your house.*

Xander looked surprised. "Really, Gregory? Whatever gave you the impression that I would not enjoy lunch with an old friend such as you? I would love to see your home. Lead the way." He smiled easily at Elizabeth. "Do you want to ride with me? We can follow Gregory and Cassandra. His

Lamborghini is not big enough for all of us." *It actually is not big enough for three people either. Were you going to leave Cassandra behind at the last minute?*

Seriously? We are going to the Little Prince's house? asked Michael with incredulity.

That is what the man said, replied Gabriel glumly.

Can you do that? Michael was disbelieving.

The two fiends with Gregory looked as shocked as Michael did.

Watch me, answered Xander firmly. *You would be going by yourself, Michael, if Gabriel and I did not accompany you. I could go in angelic form and wait outside with Gabriel in case you need us, but I want Elizabeth to see me there so that she will not be afraid. Furthermore, because I am fully human, I can go anywhere a human can go. After all, Gregory himself invited me. Guardians, like you and Gabriel, must go with their charges. Under these circumstances, he cannot refuse us entrance to his house on spiritual grounds.*

Before Gregory could respond with a different plan, Elizabeth spoke quickly, smiling with relief. "That's a wonderful idea, Xander. We'll be right behind you, Gregory." She stood and gave her book bag to Xander as he reached for it.

"I suppose I should call and have that changed to lunch for four," Gregory said smoothly.

"If it is not too much trouble," replied Xander with a broad smile.

"No problem at all. Don't give it a second thought," said Gregory, standing to his feet, his hard eyes belying his words. "Try to keep up. We wouldn't want to lose you."

"Yes, that would be a shame. But have no worries; I will be right on your bumper." *Just like your little friend was on mine this morning.* Xander's clear blue eyes returned Gregory's stare.

~~oo~~

Xander followed Gregory to the outskirts of Spartanburg into a quiet, upscale neighborhood. His home was isolated on a private, tranquil cul-de-sac bordering a lake. They drove up a circular driveway lined with Bradford pear trees to the grand entrance and parked in front of the house. Gregory did not bother with opening the oversized garage. He and Cassandra got out of his car and walked to the front door of the two-story, mottled brick mansion, followed by his ever-present guards, and he paused, turning to smile and motion to Elizabeth and Xander to join them. As Xander got out of the car and went around to open Elizabeth's door, Gabriel and Michael drifted to the ground beside their charges.

"Wow!" exclaimed Elizabeth. "This is an expensive area. Houses in this gated community cost more than three-quarters of a million. I knew he had money, but this is ridiculous." She scanned the landscaping and beautiful view.

"Yes, he is extremely wealthy. Are you impressed?" asked Xander, amused at her expression. Money meant nothing to him because he had never wanted for anything.

She laughed lightly, her brown eyes sparkling. "You know me better than that, I hope." She reached for his hand. "I do feel a little under-dressed for the neighborhood. However, you fit right in." Elizabeth paused to appreciate him fully. His light gray, V necked sweater molded to his sculpted chest, and it was obvious by the perfect fit of his designer jeans that he did not approve of "sagging." *Casual chic looks wonderful on him. What am I thinking? Everything looks wonderful on him.*

He waited for her to complete her appraisal, not the least bit self-conscious about her inspection.

What are you doing? queried Michael.

Giving her time to finish, Xander answered.

You do not feel awkward? Gabriel asked.

Why would I? She likes what she sees. Hearing her thoughts does give me an unfair advantage over most men.

Gregory cleared his throat to no avail. He turned and stalked into the house, leaving Cassandra and the guards to follow him.

"Well?" Xander asked, trying not to smile.

"Well what?" She grinned mischievously.

"Are you quite through? Do you approve?" He lifted one eyebrow and looked at her quizzically.

"Yes. And very much. I think there are very few women who would not approve." Elizabeth's smile faded, replaced by a serious expression. Suddenly, she reached for his hand and tugged him down the sidewalk to the open door.

He becomes stranger every day, commented Gabriel, walking behind the couple.

Definitely. Michael nodded and glanced at Gabriel. *And she is quicksilver, changeable as the wind.*

Elizabeth stopped, her mouth forming an "O" as they entered the two-story foyer which led into the great room with an unobstructed view, through a tall palladium window, of a flagstone patio bordering the lake. She saw a graceful staircase to her right, and to the left was a gourmet kitchen and breakfast area, all bathed in natural light.

Gregory was standing at the table, and he smiled when he saw her reaction.

Elizabeth quickly closed her mouth. "I love your house, Gregory. It's beautiful."

"Thank you. I thought we would eat in here since there are only four of us. The formal dining room seems so large when there are fewer than ten in the party. Come and sit down. The table is already set and everything is ready. I don't want to distress you, Elizabeth, by making you late for your afternoon class." He was every inch the gracious host, stepping aside to hold Elizabeth's chair before Xander could get to it.

Cassandra sat across from Elizabeth, and the two men faced each other at the small table. Their drinks were already in place, and Gregory's housekeeper brought out their plates with quiet efficiency.

Gregory's guards stood behind him, and more demons began to drift slowly into the room, lining the walls. Xander willed himself to be calm as Gregory made polite conversation, enjoying his discomfort.

Michael and Gabriel stood erect, their hands on the shoulders of their charges, their faces showing no signs of unease.

As the room filled with the denizens of hell, Michael looked upward and issued a silent summons which reverberated throughout the heavenly realm and echoed through time and space. Within seconds, the entire lawn and the airspace above the house were crowded with orderly rows of hundreds of holy angels – a Host of warriors, armor gleaming in the sunlight. Their shields and swords were at the ready, waiting for the command from their captain.

Elizabeth noticed a difference in the atmosphere immediately. *Xander was tense; I could feel it even though he didn't show it. Now he is peaceful and calm. Something has changed. The air in the room was oppressive, but it seems fine now.*

Michael looked at Gregory, the Seed of Sedition, with a level stare. *Just give me an excuse. If any one of your malignant servants so much as blinks, the Host will have reason to enter this house and clean the filth that surrounds Xander and Elizabeth.* Michael spoke aloud so that the devilish assembly, as well as Gregory, could hear him.

Gregory did not acknowledge Michael by even the twitch of an eyebrow. He continued to eat and converse with Elizabeth and Cassandra as if nothing were amiss. The four at the table were the only ones in the vicinity that moved a muscle. Evil and good faced each other, motionless, waiting.

Finally the interminable meal was finished, and the group rose to go back to school.

As they walked to the door, the demons stepped aside to make a clear path before them like the Red Sea had parted for the Israelites. Xander had never been so happy to leave a place before in his short, human life.

The group stopped at the front door, and Elizabeth smiled up at Gregory. "Thanks for lunch, Gregory. The meal was wonderful, but it's too far to drive out here for lunch again. We'll have to stick closer to Converse from now on. You know how I hate to miss classes."

Cassandra laughed teasingly. "You really should lighten up just a little, El."

"Yes, everyone knows that you are the prototype for perfect girls everywhere. Surely, missing your one class this afternoon won't completely spoil your record. Nobody should be totally good, you know. It's boring." Gregory reached for her hand and held it as he bent to kiss her cheek softly.

Michael stiffened, but Gabriel reminded him, *She is allowing it willingly.*

Just as Gregory's lips brushed her face, Xander cupped her elbow with his hand. "Thank you, Gregory, but we really do have to leave now." *Relax, everyone. I have this under control.*

Elizabeth looked up at him and smiled. *Thank you for not overreacting – for knowing that his little kiss on my cheek means nothing to me.*

Gregory straightened to his full height. "We'll catch up with you back at school, then." He opened the door for them.

"Goodbye, Cassandra. See you later." Elizabeth turned her head toward the girl as Xander led her through the door.

"I'll call you," Cassandra responded.

Elizabeth looked back over her shoulder and nodded.

She tilted her head up to Xander. "You seem to be in a hurry to leave," she said.

"Do I?"

I am certainly ready to go. Michael's face was stern. His warriors remained in place awaiting his orders.

I am as well, but it could have been much worse, added Gabriel.

Yes. Nobody died, thought Xander grimly as he led Elizabeth through the rows of angelic warriors.

He opened the car door for Elizabeth and held it while she slid into the seat. Then he walked around and got into the driver's side, resting his hands on his thighs and releasing a breath that he felt he had been holding for the past half hour.

"Is everything all right?" she asked, putting her hand over his, looking at him with concern.

"Elizabeth, will you promise me something?" He turned his head to look into her eyes and flipped his hand to hold hers.

"Probably. What do you want me to promise?" she asked, puzzled that he was so serious.

"Promise me that you will never go into that house with Gregory without me."

"Why would you ask me to promise that, Xander? Gregory won't hurt me."

And the moon is made of green cheese, thought Michael.

He released her hand, started the car, drove the remainder of the circular driveway, and turned back toward town.

Michael and Gabriel flew overhead, and at Michael's word, the Host dispersed in a wave. The wind gusted from the concerted movement of so many wings together.

"Elizabeth, I do not want to say anything derogatory about Gregory. I know that he is your friend. Will you just trust me on this? Please?" He glanced at her, his eyes pleading.

She thought about his request a moment, and then spoke deliberately. "Xander, you know that I don't like to be told what to do, but since this seems to be so important to you, and because I don't care to be alone with Gregory anyway, I will promise you not to go to his house without you. Are you happy now?"

He took a deep breath, "Almost."

"Almost?"

"Yes, almost. Will you text your mom and tell her that I will take you home this afternoon?"

"Of course, if that's what you want, but why?"

He drove with his left hand and reached for hers with his right. She held his willingly, and their hands rested on the console between their seats.

"Because I really need to be with you right now. I do not want to go to class this afternoon. I wish to spend the time with you. Just the two of us."

She reached into her book bag and took out her cell phone. After sending a text to her mother, she glanced at his studious profile.

"Will you tell me what this is about? I *am* skipping class for you, you know. I have never done that before." Her voice was low.

"Your GPA will not suffer. I want to take you somewhere beautiful and peaceful. I want to look at God's creation and see things that are green and growing. Have you ever been to Hatcher Garden? It should be in bloom now that it is spring."

She laced her fingers between his. "I think I may have earned a field trip. I haven't been there for years. Will you be my guide?"

He stroked the top of her hand with his thumb. "Can we not walk together? I will guide you when I must and protect you with my life, but today, I need you by my side."

She gently pulled her hand from his and stroked his hair, entwining her fingers in his dark waves.

"I want to be what you need right now," Elizabeth spoke softly.

They rode in companionable silence to the garden. After he parked the car, he came around to help Elizabeth get out, and they joined hands.

"Shall we walk this trail?" he asked.

She nodded her assent. They were quiet as they ambled, admiring the flowers and landscaping.

Under a tree in full bloom, there was a granite bench. Xander gestured toward it. Elizabeth sat down, and he sat beside her, turning his body toward her and taking her hands in both of his. His throat tightened. *I have to get this right.*

"Elizabeth, I have never made a secret of how I feel about you. My feelings have only grown deeper with time. I love you. I want a committed relationship with you. I want everyone to know that you belong to me." He paused. "How do you feel about that?"

She looked down at her hands in his and smiled. Then she turned her head and tilted it to look up at him through her dark lashes. "Xander, I don't know if I love you yet or not, but I do have strong feelings for you."

"Is that a yes?" His voice was gentle and loving.

"Yes." She smiled shyly.

His heart nearly exploded with joy. The contrast between the extreme tension of the past hour and the perfect happiness of the present moment was almost too much for him to bear. Xander reined in his emotions with a great effort and took a calming breath.

He put his hand to her soft cheek and held it gently, drawing her toward him and lifting her chin as he slowly lowered his face to hers, covering her lips with his. He felt his stomach twist in a decidedly pleasant way. *I have wanted to do this for so long. I have dreamed of this moment.*

Xander's breathing accelerated with his heartbeat, and he pulled his face away a few inches, bringing his other hand to her jaw line, holding her lovely face between his hands. *Her skin is like silk, but warm and alive.*

He leaned back a little further to look into her sparkling eyes, still holding her face in his hands. "Elizabeth, that was my first kiss."

"Ever?" she said, wide-eyed and a little shocked.

"Yes, ever. And I am glad that you are the only woman I will ever kiss." He put his forehead to hers, stroking her cheeks with his thumbs and breathing her scent deeply, slowing the racing of his heart. She leaned into him and put her palms on his chest.

He kissed her again, tenderly. His stomach clenched. *My physical reaction to her is so powerful. Gentle. I must be gentle.*

She broke the kiss, looking at him skeptically, her face still close to his. "You have never kissed anyone else?"

"Never." His voice was husky, and his expression was solemn, though his blue eyes twinkled. He could read her thoughts, and they were explicit in expressing her appreciation.

"I must say, you do it very well."

"Not like a beginner?"

"Not at all like a beginner. Kiss me again."

Xander chuckled, and did as his lady commanded, drawing her into an embrace and kissing her more deeply. His insides twisted into knots, and his entire consciousness focused on her. Briefly, he wondered if he might pass out from the sheer pleasure of having her in his arms at last, where she belonged. After a few seconds, he knew that if he died from the joy of it, he would die a happy man.

Michael and Gabriel had the grace to remain silent, though Xander knew that they were there.

They sat together on the bench in silent companionship. Finally she looked at him with merry eyes and stated, "I suppose that makes you my boyfriend."

"And you are my first and only girlfriend."

"And you don't find me boring? I am a good girl, you know," she teased, smiling and showing her double dimple.

"You could never bore me, and I love you because you are a good girl." Xander leaned over and kissed her dimple. "You know, that's where the angels kissed you before they sent you down from heaven to your parents."

She tilted her head, looking at him with surprise. "That's what my mother has always told me. How did you know that?"

"You said I was an angel. Remember?" *Please understand me. I wish that I could tell you.*

Elizabeth gazed at him with eyes full of love. She knew of no other man who was so patient and kind, so godly and good.

"I remember. If anyone ever was an angel, Xander, you are."

He sighed as he stood and pulled her to her feet. "I could sit here and kiss you for the rest of the day, Elizabeth, and I would never tire of it. But it is probably for the best that we walk for a while before I take you to eat and then back to your house. And, you may think it is silly, but there is something I want to do when I take you home."

Her curiosity shone from her eyes. "What? I could not imagine ever thinking you are silly."

"I want to make this Facebook official. I want everyone who knows us to see that we are a couple. I want every human male out there to know that you are taken; you are mine." *And every non-human male as well.*

His expression was so full of happiness and love that she could not help but smile. "I don't go on Facebook very often, but if you send me the invitation, I will certainly accept it."

And just for that moment, there were no demons or battles, no Gregory or Lucifer. All was very right in Xander's world.

Chapter 9

"He makes the winds His messengers, flaming fire His ministers."
Psalm 104:4

June, 2008

Xander and Elizabeth had been providing the music for local evangelistic meetings led by Jonathan Edwards for several months, and the response had been enthusiastic. The rallies had so far been on Saturday evenings in towns within a two hundred mile radius; however, with the approach of summer break from college, they had agreed to more extensive travel and longer meetings. Praying that he would have an evangelistic team together in time, Jonathan and his manager, Dave Branard, in the previous year had arranged with churches in metropolitan areas to have camps, called SoulFire, set up for teenagers in colleges throughout the United States. The teens would be housed in the college dormitories and have morning group devotions followed by Bible study on the college campuses. After breaking for lunch, they would work on supervised mission projects throughout the cities during the afternoons and then would come together for evening worship. The first such event was to be held in Atlanta, Georgia, during the second week of June and would last Monday morning through Friday evening. Students from throughout Georgia and South Carolina were staying in dorms across the city and were going to be bused to one of the city's major arenas each evening. With a seating capacity of 21,000, it was the largest venue in which Xander and Elizabeth had ever led worship or played before an audience.

The couple had developed a unique style of worship music that was original and appealing. They were each proficient in several instruments as well as various vocal styles, and they had classical and traditional sacred backgrounds from which to draw. The music they had written for the upcoming summer rallies was contemporary but drew from classical themes and great hymns of the faith. Elizabeth had written a piece called "Embrace Me," based on her experience the previous year when she had felt the presence of evil in her room. The song spoke of surviving an ordeal while feeling the arms of the Savior holding her in His embrace, and she sang it while Xander played the piano and harmonized, while other musicians provided an acoustical guitar and a violin in the background. They also used a full band for several songs, including "Watching You," written by Xander from God's point of view, revealing the way God watches over His children throughout their lives. They collaborated on "Healed," inspired by Charlotte's recent brush with death, which compared physical and spiritual healing. There were new songs for each evening, themed with Jonathan's messages in mind, and some of their songs, such as "Forgiveness," were taken directly from Scripture. Each night, they would begin by singing the same rousing opening number, "Life on Fire," featuring Elizabeth on the piano and Xander surrounded by three sets of stacked keyboards backed by bass guitar, electric guitar, drums, acoustical guitar, and a quartet of backup vocalists. They had already used some of the songs in the local meetings, and their music touched every heart, regardless of background, religion, or ethnicity; it broke cultural barriers. Xander and Elizabeth could not be associated with one style or genre, because they borrowed from across the wide spectrum of music. There simply was no music that they could not perform well. Their style was to avoid having a style.

Elizabeth was already nationally known through YouTube, national and international concerts, as well as the sale of her CD's on the internet, but Xander's reputation was confined to the Carolinas. These meetings would constitute his national debut. When Elizabeth had first approached Jonathan about including Xander in their travels, he was skeptical; however, after hearing them together the first time, he was an ardent fan. The evangelist had feared that Xander's talents would be no match for Elizabeth's, but he was soon amazed at how they complemented each other in every way.

In preparation for the series of summer meetings, the couple had hired a photographer for publicity stills and had cut a professional CD of their music to be available to those at the camps and online. Xander and Elizabeth had assisted Dave in hiring musicians; sound, lighting, and video technicians; and a stage crew, and they had rehearsed extensively between the time Converse had dismissed for the summer and the tour started. Each night of the crusade was professionally, carefully planned for the greatest impact, using the most current technology. The week was a visual and auditory feast designed to lift up and encourage believers, and to invite non-believers into God's family.

The Sunday afternoon before the camp was to start on Monday, Xander drove to Elizabeth's house to pick her up for the trip. They were meeting Jonathan in Atlanta that night at the hotel in which they all would stay for the week. He parked, went to the door, and rang the doorbell. Gabriel stood beside him.

Elizabeth smiled happily as she opened the door. "Good. You're wearing jeans, too. Well, your version of jeans, anyway." Xander had never mastered "sloppy." He always looked well-dressed, no matter if he wore jeans, shorts, or khakis. All of his clothes were tailor-made for his unusually large frame, and they fit perfectly.

Behind her, Michael looked huge.

"Elizabeth, you look beautiful, as always." He leaned down to kiss the dimple in her upturned cheek.

When he straightened again, she looked past him out the door.

"Did you get a new car?"

"I thought we needed something bigger for our luggage and all the traveling this summer. Do you like it?"

She squeezed past Xander and ran out to look at his new white Cadillac Escalade. "I love it!" she announced, looking back at him. "Do you still have the BMW?"

He followed her back out to the SUV. "No, I traded it in. I have not really liked it since the accident. Though it was repaired, it always seemed damaged to me. If I want something different when we go back to school in the fall, you can help me shop." *I can get something we both like.*

Xander looked forward to the summer with great anticipation, and he had bought the Escalade to make the arduous traveling easier for her. He would be with Elizabeth every day, and he hoped that they would grow even closer over the two months of touring. She would be eighteen and he would be twenty-one in July, and they had only one more year of college before they finished their master's degrees. He knew that most people did not marry any longer when they were nineteen, but he wondered if Elizabeth would be different in that way as well. She certainly did not conform to all the other norms of teenagers. He never pushed her physically, but privately he wondered how he would wait another two or three years to marry and consummate their marriage. He also missed being with her while she slept; he missed her every minute they were apart. When he was away from her, there was an Elizabeth-shaped hole in his heart, and it ached for her.

"I may be shopping for a car myself," she said with a huge grin. "Mom and Dad might let me buy a car for my birthday. I've been saving nearly all of my money from concerts and CD sales, and I have a healthy bank account now. Mom could stay home, or go back to her job at Peniel. Char and I could still ride together for our last year."

"That is interesting," Xander managed to say with a slight upturn to his lips, though it took more than a little effort. He liked for Elizabeth to have Niall with Michael and Edward guarding her on her way to school, and he liked being able to drive her home. *We could fly over here and help guard them. But then, how would I get my car to school?*

Do not worry about it right now, Xander, thought Gabriel.

I am sure that Edward, the warriors, and I can manage to guard her during a short drive to Converse. You are going to go prematurely gray, added Michael.

"I know that look and tone of voice, Xander," Elizabeth replied, arching an eyebrow. "What's wrong with my getting a car? I'll be eighteen by then.

Most of my friends had cars with they were fifteen." She had a stubborn set to her chin.

"Nothing is wrong with it, Elizabeth. You are very responsible and mature. I just worry about others who are not as good at driving as you are, like the man who rear-ended me in the spring. *And Gregory's playmate who was with him.* And, I like to drive you home sometimes. If we went out to dinner, you would have to drive home from Spartanburg alone if Charlotte drove herself. If she did not drive, we would all three be together for dinner. I like Charlotte a great deal, however…" His voice trailed off.

She stood on her tiptoes and put her arms around his neck, pulling his face down to hers for a kiss. "You are very sweet and overly protective, but I'll be fine, and we can work out all those details later. Charlotte and I could take turns driving. She has her own car. If I'm going out with you, she could drive us to school, and then you could bring me back home. You're going to go prematurely gray, you know."

Michael laughed. *I think I have heard that before. Smart girl. I knew I liked her.*

Not seen and not heard, Xander reminded him as he bent his head for another kiss.

You really should write down all these rules for us, thought Gabriel. *Do you have a handbook for guardians?*

David cleared his throat from the porch. "You guys need some help with El's luggage? It's a good thing you bought a bigger car, Xander. I don't think all she has packed up would have fit into that BMW."

Roark grinned from behind him.

Elizabeth and Xander stepped apart, smiling sheepishly, and she headed for the steps followed by Xander. He shook David's hand, spoke to him, and went into the house after Elizabeth. Her bags were waiting in the living room.

"We're about to leave, Mom," she called up the stairs. Lynne hurried down, Niall close on her heels, and gave Elizabeth a hug.

"Call me when you get to Atlanta. Love you. Take care, Xander. Precious cargo, there." Lynne smiled at him.

David and Xander took Elizabeth's suitcases to the car and put them in the rear with Xander's luggage. Lynne followed them outside to tell the couple goodbye. Elizabeth gave each of her parents a last hug and a kiss on the cheek, and then slid into her seat while Xander held the car door for her. After he was seated in the driver's seat, he waved at David and Lynne through the windshield. They, along with their guardians, waved back.

Xander backed out of the driveway, and they were on their way, being led by a GPS and escorted by two archangels.

~~oo~~

After Xander and Elizabeth had been driving for a couple of hours, her stomach began to grumble.

"Feed me! Feed me! Feed me! Feed me, Seymour! Feed me all night long," she began singing gruffly, mimicking the voice of Audrey II from *The Little Shop of Horrors*.

Xander laughed, pulling back his hand as she began to nibble on his fingers.

"I already have the Cadillac, so you do not have to get me that, but 'I would like a Harley machine, toolin' around like I was James Dean, makin' all the guys on the corner turn green.'" She giggled in delight at his portrayal of Seymour. "Where would you like to eat, my little carnivore?"

"Any place is okay with me. How about a cheeseburger and fries? There are places all up and down the interstate." She looked longingly at a sign advertising a fast food restaurant on the next exit.

Xander grimaced. "Elizabeth, I would do nearly anything for you, but the idea of eating in any restaurant of that sort makes me slightly queasy. There are just too many people handling money that also handle the food in those places for my comfort level. Money is filthy, and, besides that, the idea of greasy burgers and fries never has appealed to me."

Elizabeth laughed at him. "Xander, I wouldn't be as fastidious as you are for a million dollars."

"Make fun of me if you will, but I will not have *e coli*, food poisoning, high cholesterol, or anything else caused by a virus, parasite, or improper handling of the food. Eating at those places is so unhealthy that it is insupportable. Our bodies are temples of God, you know." He fell silent for a few minutes.

Since Niall is not here to roll his eyes, I will do it for him, interjected Michael, looking skyward as promised.

Xander may be a bit stiff, but he is correct, thought Gabriel with total sincerity.

A bit stiff? He makes Herod the Great look positively cuddly! exclaimed Michael.

Do not go there, warned Xander. *I know you too well, Michael. I was there when you contended with Lucifer for the body of Moses, and I remember when you fought him for twenty-one days to deliver the answer to Daniel's prayer. The incidents are recorded in Jude, verse nine, and in Daniel, chapter ten, if you need to refresh your memory. You were right in both instances, but you do not back down either. Standing for what is right is admirable. The food that I eat may not be as important an issue as the ownership of Moses' body or the answer to Daniel's prayer, but the principle is the same. And do not forget that Daniel also refused to eat food that was unhealthy in the first chapter of Daniel. I was his guardian, and I well recall that you cheered his decision because it honored God. Will you not support me?*

Michael was quiet for a moment, and then replied, *You are right, my brother, to consider Jehovah Elohim's desires for you in all things. I will always stand with you when you do what pleases Him. I apologize.*

It was not often that the warrior displayed such humility, except to his Master. Xander was moved.

I accept your apology, and I am grateful to know that you are with me, even in small things.

Excellent! Hine ma Tov u'ma nayim sheveth ah-iym gamy a-hadh, beamed Gabriel quoting Psalm 133:1, "Behold, how good and pleasant it is for brothers to dwell together in unity!"

During Xander's silence, Elizabeth had been listening to their CD and thinking about what Xander had said.

After reflecting on his words, she turned her head toward him. He was looking straight through the windshield as if he was concentrating on something.

"Xander, are you upset with me?" she asked tentatively, reaching over to brush his hair back from his forehead and stroke his cheek.

He turned his face to kiss her fingers and glanced at her with a smile before returning his eyes to the road. She massaged his neck. "Elizabeth, I have never been angry with you. You have elicited many emotions in me, but never that one."

She tilted her head, trying to look at his face with an impish smile. "Now, you know that I can't resist that. Which emotions do I rouse in you?" She brought her hand back to her lap.

"This will have to be a two-way street, Elizabeth. If I must bare my soul for you, I will expect something in return." His voice was gentle and lyrical.

"My spirit always rises with every attempt to intimidate me, as you well know. To quote what you once said to me, 'I am not afraid of you.'" Her tone was playful. She loved any sort of banter, and Xander did not usually disappoint her in verbal swordplay; however, in this instance he chose to surrender before the battle even started.

"All right. I have never loved anyone else the way I love you, and I have never loved any other woman at all. After God, I love you more than anything or anyone else. Are you certain you want to have this conversation while we are driving down the interstate?" His blue eyes were intense as he glanced at her.

"I'm not sure." She bit her lip, and then grinned. "Maybe it is better to have this conversation while your hands and eyes are busy. You don't intimidate me – that is certainly true, but sometimes I scare myself. While your attention is partially turned away from me, I think I can say something to you that I haven't said before. Do you want to continue this while you're driving?"

His heart turned over and his breath caught in his chest. *Could she truly love me enough to tell me rather than just think it? Do I want to hear her actually say those words aloud while I am occupied and cannot respond to her?*

Maybe she is wise, Xander, thought Gabriel.

Or perhaps she is afraid of your response, Michael amended. *Just be careful not to frighten her.*

Xander reached for her hand and wove his fingers through hers.

"Yes, I want to hear whatever you have to say, although I would rather see your beautiful face while you say it."

"Then pull off at the next exit. We just passed a sign that advertised an Olive Garden restaurant a mile from here. Is that sufficiently healthy for you?" Her voice held a teasing note.

"Of course, as you well know since I have taken you to the Olive Garden in Spartanburg several times. I see it up ahead."

He changed lanes and took the exit to the right, following the directions to the restaurant. After he parked, he turned to her as much as was possible within the confines of the bucket seats. Because it was summer, it was still light outside even though it was evening. Xander took a deep breath and waited for her to speak.

His blue eyes fringed with long dark lashes were totally fixed on her, and she lowered her eyes. *He is so intense. He is like my sun, and I orbit him.*

No, Elizabeth, my love. You have it backwards. My every move is calculated by what you do and what you think.

Elizabeth freed her hand to pick up the CD case that was in the console. A wonderful picture of the two of them graced the front. Xander sat on the granite bench in Hatcher Garden with Elizabeth behind him and slightly to his left, her right hand resting lightly on his shoulder. The trees and bushes were in full bloom, and they were both smiling in obvious contentment. She flipped it over to another picture of them on the back – a black and white shot featuring the two of them playing a duet at a Steinway grand. The picture was taken from slightly above them and displayed the couple in a three-quarter profile. Elizabeth was nearest the camera, playing the treble keys, and Xander's height allowed his neck and head to show above her as he played the bass. They laughed in easy camaraderie.

She traced his face in the picture with her index finger.

She is so lovely in every way. Thank you, Lord, for letting me love her and be with her. He held his breath and waited for her to speak.

Elizabeth looked up at him through her lashes, and her brown eyes were serious. She touched the two of them in the picture as it rested in her left hand. "Do you know what this is?" she asked, lifting her face to his.

He waited, silent and motionless, for her to answer her own question.

"This is love frozen in time." Her voice was quiet and full of emotion.

She laid the CD back in her lap and reached for his face with both of her hands. He leaned over to meet her, letting his hands rest at her waist.

The sun was setting, and it was growing darker.

Holding his face between her hands, she looked directly into his eyes in the fading light. "I love you, Xander. I have never loved anyone else the way that I love you, either. I thought I was in love before, but it was nothing compared to the way I feel about you."

His heart rejoiced and sang. He thought of verses from the Song of Solomon and spoke them to her. "How beautiful and how delightful you are, my love, with all your charms! Put me like a seal over your heart, like a seal on your arm. For love is as strong as death, jealousy is as severe as Sheol; its flashes are flashes of fire, the very flame of the Lord. Many waters cannot quench love, nor will rivers overflow it. If a man were to give all the riches of his house for love, it would be utterly despised."

Elizabeth recognized the verses and leaned even nearer to him. She initiated the kiss, and he followed her lead. When she indicated she wanted to be closer to him, he drew her into an embrace. She parted her lips, and he responded in kind, tasting her softly.

Michael, from beside the car, cleared his throat.

Gabriel, by Michael's side, thought, *Perhaps this is not the best place for a display of affection, Xander.*

Though he did not like it, Xander realized they were right. It was the public parking lot of a family restaurant. *We will be together for the next two months.* He comforted himself with the thought.

She broke the kiss to breathe, and he spoke quietly, almost reverently, "Elizabeth, my love, should we not go in to eat now? We must get to Atlanta to meet Jonathan and the others. I would gladly stay here like this with you for hours, but I can still hear your stomach saying, 'Feed me. Feed me.'"

She sighed, still holding his face close, and nuzzled his nose with hers. Pecking his lips quickly, she drew back and replied, "Yes, Seymour, it's time to feed me. And we have 'miles to go before we sleep.'"

~~oo~~

Xander pulled up to the hotel around ten o'clock that night. He left Elizabeth in the car, texting her mother that they had arrived safely, while he went to the front desk to check in. Jonathan had the rooms reserved, and a bellhop came out to the car with a cart to get their luggage.

After their bags had been stacked on the cart, Elizabeth and Xander followed the bellhop to the elevator, and Xander texted Jonathan to let him know that they had arrived safely. The evangelist met them in the hallway when they got off the elevator, smiling and extending his hand. Lexus was behind him and exchanged greetings with Michael and Gabriel.

As they walked to their rooms which were beside each other, Jonathan talked excitedly. "I'm so glad to see you both again. We have all the rooms on this floor, so it's fairly private. The crew members, techs, and other musicians are already here, and we'll set up at the stadium first thing in the morning. It will probably take most of the day to make certain that everything is ready for tomorrow night. I want to run through everything several times to work all the bugs out. Would you like to meet for breakfast in the morning around eight?" he asked.

Xander looked at Elizabeth for her answer. "It sounds good to me," she said.

"Here in the hotel restaurant?" asked Xander.

"Yes, they have a breakfast buffet. I've stayed here before, and it's really good. So eight is okay with you two?"

They both nodded. "Eight it is," replied Xander.

Jonathan, followed by Lexus, headed for his room, calling a quick, "Good night!" over his shoulder.

When his door closed, Xander pulled Elizabeth to him for a fast kiss. "Elizabeth, I have a surprise for you tomorrow."

"Really? I love surprises. Give me a hint."

"If you guess correctly, it will not be a surprise anymore. Good night, Elizabeth. I love you," he said, smiling and kissing her again. "I will be saying that every night for the next two months. I am a happy man."

She opened her door and stood just inside her room. Looking at him with mischief in her eyes, she exclaimed, "Yes, but I love you more!" She laughed, reverting to the childhood game she had played with her parents, rapidly closing the door before he could reply.

He smiled broadly. *Good night, Michael. Be ready to meet Elizabeth tomorrow. I have met her family; now she needs to meet some of mine,* he thought as he walked to his door, opened it, and went in.

What are you babbling about, Xander? I cannot meet her. I do not know what to wear or what to say. Michael's thoughts had a distinct edge of nervousness. Xander grinned.

It will be nothing, Michael. Think of the things that Xander has worn and copy him. It will be simple, Gabriel replied reassuringly.

I am glad that you think so, Gabriel, because you, my brother, will be meeting Elizabeth as well. Xander chuckled.

Is that truly necessary? asked Gabriel.

Of course it is. I cannot continue to be a man with no past. Gregory has already planted a seed of doubt in her mind concerning my family. You can just casually drop by the arena tomorrow, meet her, and be on your way. I do not wish for you to stay long. Say that you have business in Atlanta and took the opportunity to drop by and see me. I will introduce you to her. Chat a few minutes, say that you can tell that we are busy, and leave. That way, she will know you if I ever need for you to be present in human form, answered Xander.

Gabriel considered his words. *I do not particularly like it, but I see your logic. It is sound. We will do it. Will we not, Michael?*

Do not bother me further. I am occupied in selecting my wardrobe for tomorrow, and you know that I have nothing to wear. Good night, Xander and Gabriel, returned the warrior from inside Elizabeth's room.

Tomorrow night will begin the unfolding of the Master's plan. Gabriel's normally calm tone was edged with excitement.

Where there are so many gathered to worship, and the possibility of thousands becoming believers, there will always be evil ready to attack, thought Xander.

That has already been taken care of. Michael's voice was confident.

You are looking forward to it? asked Gabriel.

Absolutely, replied Michael.

Xander was busy getting ready for bed. He wanted to sleep so that he could dream of a lovely dark-haired girl telling him what his heart had longed to hear from her lips. He did not worry about the next day. As Jesus Himself had said in Matthew 6:34, "Therefore do not be anxious for tomorrow; for tomorrow will take care for itself. Each day has enough trouble of its own."

~~oo~~

In an empty department store located in a rough section of Atlanta, Lucifer called an evil assembly to order in the middle of the night. He and Gregory stood before most of the demons of the southeastern dominion.

The Lord of the Demons, his eyes as bright red and hard as rubies, issued terse commands to his bowed servants in a voice that would not brook failure while Dark Spirit coiled at his feet.

"The battle begins anew tonight. We have ruled this city for many decades, and we will not lose it this week. Use every resource available. Wake the people you rule if they are asleep; possess them body and soul. SoulFire, indeed! They are playing with fire, and they have no idea of the repercussions. If Jehovah wants flames, we will oblige Him."

"Rouse everyone who does your bidding – all of those under your influence – and target the churches and homes of the few believers in the area," added Gregory. "We will show them that there is a price for defying us. That territory is ours, and we will not relinquish it." His eyes glowed crimson as his anger flared.

The demons jumped to their feet and cheered the words of the Dark Lord and his son. They screamed and howled and worked themselves into a writhing mass of frenzy at the thought of Jonathan Edwards, Xander, and Elizabeth taking people whom they had controlled for many years and leading them to Elohim. Atlanta was theirs, and they certainly would not give it up without a fight.

And the darkness grew and swelled; the anger and hatred crept from the abandoned store and sought destruction. The demons blanketed the area following the commands of their masters, waking the people of south Atlanta and filling their minds with evil. Lucifer's dark forces filled them with wicked desires and urged them to act. Murder and mayhem broke out in that section of the city, and the riot police were called in to quell the burning and looting.

After nearly one hundred fifty years, Atlanta was burning again.

Chapter 10

"But if I say, 'I will not remember Him or speak any more in His name,' then in my heart it becomes like a burning fire shut up in my bones; and I am weary of holding it in, and I cannot endure it. But the Lord is with me like a dread champion; therefore my persecutors will stumble and not prevail. They will be utterly ashamed, because they have failed, with an everlasting disgrace that will not be forgotten."
Jeremiah 20:9,11

Xander was awakened from a sound sleep by Michael shaking his shoulders and calling his name.

Xander! You must get up now. The southern part of the city is burning. We must leave immediately. There is no time to sleep now. Michael's voice was commanding and urgent.

Xander sat up, trying to remember why he was in a strange room. In a few seconds, he realized that Michael was in full warrior mode.

What time is it? asked Xander, rising from the bed.

It is four in the morning, not that it matters. We must leave this instant. I have already summoned one thousand of the host, and they are even now engaging the enemy, protecting churches as well as believers and their homes. Change into angelic form.

The Captain of the Host was issuing an order, and Xander obeyed without question. When Xander took angelic form, Michael saw that his armor included a helmet as well as a special covering for his feet.

Your armor is now different from mine, Michael observed.

Xander had noticed the change as well. *Jehovah-Naheh said that I now had the helmet of salvation and my feet were shod with the preparation of the gospel of peace. This is the first time since my conversion that I have gone into battle. Perhaps I have these extra safeguards as His child when I fight the evil ones.*

Interesting, commented Michael, spreading his wings.

As they flew through the wall, Xander remembered Elizabeth.

Who is guarding Elizabeth in your stead? Xander asked, concern evident in his voice.

Jehovah-Gador Milchamah instructed that Gabriel was to guard Elizabeth while you fight Lucifer's forces with me. Elizabeth and Jonathan will have their own assignments from Jehovah-Saboath.

~~oo~~

Elizabeth's eyes flew open as Gabriel leaned over her, speaking into her ear, *Elizabeth, wake up. You must pray for the believers of Atlanta and for rain. Turn on the television. They are under attack by Satan and his followers. Pray, Elizabeth. Make intercession for them.*

Elizabeth sat up in bed, turned on her bedside lamp, and picked up the remote control. The display on her clock radio read 4:15. She stretched and yawned, turned on the television, and scrolled through the channels until she found a local news program. After a few minutes of watching the graphic violence and listening to the reports, she got out of the bed and walked to the table and chair by the window in her room. Sitting with her elbows on the table, she put her face in her hands and began to pray aloud for the people who lived in the troubled area. Gabriel stood behind her, resting his hands on her shoulders. She began to pray for protection for the believers who lived in the midst of the bedlam, and for God to send rain to quench the fires that raged out of control.

A few doors down the hall from her, Lexus was rousing Jonathan with a similar message. Jonathan also switched on his light, got up, and turned on the television, selecting a cable news channel. The images of the flaming buildings and looting were already filling the screen, and the riot police were struggling to get the situation under control. Hundreds of people were screaming and running for safety; others were fighting. There appeared to be organized gangs terrorizing anyone in their paths. Store alarms sounded, piercing the night as windows were broken and doors were kicked open, and sirens wailed as dozens of fire trucks sped to the scene. He watched, stunned as the fires seemingly erupted by spontaneous combustion. From the aerial shots, he could see buildings in blocks unaffected by the fires suddenly start to burn, but he could not see anyone starting the fires or leaving the scenes of the blazes. The evangelist knelt beside the bed, bowed his head, and began to pray for the people of Atlanta who lived in that area. He prayed both that God would preserve the churches and show His might and glory and for non-believers to be spared so that they might have the opportunity to know God. Jonathan was to sleep no more that night.

In the room next to his, the scene replayed as Hector, another guardian of the higher ranks, awakened Dave. Several hundred miles away in South Carolina, Roark and Niall were also relaying the message to pray for the people of Atlanta to Elizabeth's parents. Believers across the country were on their knees with their guardians whispering into their minds.

~~oo~~

Xander and Michael raced to the densely populated, low-income section of Atlanta that was just beginning to burn as Michael quickly issued orders. *Double the numbers of warriors on every church and sanctified dwelling. I want four warriors on the roof of every church and ten others surrounding the buildings. Two warriors are to be on the roof of each house that shelters a believer, with two others on the ground. Take solid, visible angelic form if you are on a roof. Humans bent on mischief approaching churches and houses should be able to see you with your sword at the ready. Warriors who are not guarding churches or the homes of the Master's followers should search the area for believers who are outside their homes or churches and help their guardians keep them safe. No church or believer's home is to burn. We will lose no one who belongs to the Master to the schemes of Satan this night.*

Xander spoke authoritatively. *Guardians, tell your charges to remain indoors and pray. No believer who stays in his home or in a church will be harmed. Non-believers who remain in dwellings with believers will also be protected because of the warriors. If your charges are already outdoors, tell them to return home. Guardians of those servants who will not listen, warriors are here to help you defend your charges. Do all that you can to keep them safe, even from themselves.*

Suddenly, in front of them, Xander and Michael saw a strip mall begin to burn, but there seemed to be no source for the fire. Xander thought that the roof burst into flames before the rest of the building, so he looked at the trees, buildings, and utility poles near the point where the fire originated, seeking to track the source.

Michael, look on the roof of the neighboring building. That is Gregory, is it not?

It is, indeed, and he has four guards around him, replied Michael. He and Xander hovered for a moment and watched as Gregory, in demonic form, gathered a ball of fire in his hands and threw it at another business. The store exploded, and the flames continued to spread to the next building. Gregory laughed, looking directly at Michael and Xander as looters fled from the building, scattering like rats on a sinking ship.

Gregory saw the thieves running and grinned wickedly at the Captain of the Host and the Chief Guardian, his hands gesturing toward his handiwork. "What do you think of my pyrotechnic display? Father and I like your SoulFire idea so much that we decided to expand upon the theme." He laughed as he conjured another fireball and flung it at a nearby church.

A warrior on the church roof batted the flaming orb with his sword and directed it into a building which was already burning.

Gregory began to throw the flames with both hands, moving faster than human eyes could see. Trees and shrubbery caught fire, houses went up in flames, and fireballs landed in the crowds thronging the streets. People ran in all directions, trying to escape the rain of fire. The Son of Perdition tossed a ring of fire just beyond his feet to the roof on which he stood as he spun in a circle, dancing in the center of the hell fire and filling the air with the sounds of crackling flames and his hideous laughter. The tar of the roof scorched and sizzled.

Michael and Xander landed on the rooftop where Gregory and his guards had established their point of attack. Crevan, Jolon, Braeden, and Duglas formed a wall of evil between the holy angels and Gregory.

Gregory smirked at them. "What are your grounds for attack? This is our territory. You have no right to be here."

"We are commissioned by the Lord of Hosts to protect the churches and believers who are under attack in this section of the city. You just tried to burn a church. That alone is justification for our presence," replied Michael, his voice ringing with authority.

"And you, Xander? You are a guardian. I have not attacked your charge. El is not in this area. What gives you the right to be here?" Gregory sneered at him as he tossed a ball of fire from one hand to the other.

"Gregory, you astonish me. Have your spies failed you? I have been a guardian warrior for three years."

"What is that to me? You are wearing *shiny* armor," he mocked. "That changes nothing. A guardian cannot use force against my father's forces unless we directly attack his charge." He made a show of looking around. "I still do not see any sign of your little girlfriend. I would be very happy if you would bring her here, however. She must grow weary of your pathetic attempts at making love to her. I could educate her in those pleasures and have her begging me for more. She is a luscious little piece, and she would make a good plaything for me." Gregory leered, licking his lips as he spoke the last words.

"You will *not* speak of Elizabeth in that manner." Xander spat the words, and Gregory snickered.

Michael put a hand on his arm. *Do not allow him to bait you. You must keep a clear head.*

Xander calmed before he spoke again. His voice was soft and menacing.

"Again your information is lacking. Though I am still Chief of the Guardians, Michael has been Elizabeth's guardian since January. However, for tonight, that duty has shifted to Gabriel. Michael is the Captain of the Host, and I became a warrior under his command when I assumed angelic form this night. My orders were issued by Elohim Himself. Take your arguments to Him." Xander allowed a smile to play around his lips. "Are you afraid of me, Gregory? Is that why you wish for me to leave? I remember just last year that I bested you in battle. You were carried from the room, like the spoiled little brat that you are, nearly cleaved in half." Xander's eyes hardened as his deep voice resounded, "Come out from behind your guards, you coward, and this time I will make certain that you do not survive."

Gregory's eyes glowed bright red, betraying his anger, and he drew his sword. "One day soon my father and I will rule all the universes, though you will not live to see it."

Michael, in reaction to Gregory's display of his sword, unsheathed his weapon and flew as quickly as the blink of an eye between Crevan and Jolon with his sword in his right hand and his shield in his left. As the demons turned to strike at the warrior, he flew straight up and they struck at each other. Howling in fury and pain while screaming curses, Crevan, minus his right arm, and Jolon, missing most of his right wing, took refuge behind Braeden and Duglas.

Xander's sword hissed as he ripped it from its sheath. Holding the attention of Braeden and Duglas while Michael fought their fellow guards, Xander advanced slowly toward them. The demons came to meet him, leaving their backs unprotected, as well as opening a large gap between them and the other two guards. Xander immediately took the tactical advantage and flipped over and behind them. Turning with blinding speed, Xander grasped his sword with both hands and swung it with all his might. He caught Braeden's torso, slicing into it deeply, but Duglas leaped out of the path of his weapon.

Michael dove swiftly into the space between the two demons he had injured and their fellow guards. With his blade extended and his shield protecting his midsection from attack, Michael slashed the demons in two as he flew by them, and they dissolved, spiraling and screaming into the fiery pit. He scanned the rooftop for Gregory but could find no trace of him.

Duglas charged at Xander and took flight, aiming for the guardian warrior's neck. Just before Duglas reached him, Xander flipped again, landing to Duglas's right. The fiend spun to get into position to use his sword, and Xander took his shield in his hands, holding it flat horizontally and grasping the edges of it as he turned. He slung the shield, spinning the weapon at the perfect moment so that it struck the demon in the throat, knocking him to the roof. Xander flew straight at him and severed his head as he struggled to rise. He vanished in a cloud of foul-smelling smoke. Calmly, Xander leaned over and retrieved his shield.

Michael stood over Braeden who was fatally wounded but not yet unbodied. *Shall I finish him, or do you want to end what you started?* asked Michael.

Braeden groaned and tried to crawl away, but his life was ebbing and he was too weak.

Xander walked to the demon and stood over him for a moment. He looked into Braeden's eyes and saw the hatred there. *Even this foul creature should not be left to suffer and die a slow death. He will know torment in hell, but not by my hand. I am no fit judge.* Xander used his sword to quickly banish the dark one from the earth.

Where is Gregory? Xander asked, glancing around the top of the building.

He is gone. The little prince left his guards to fend for themselves and ran, probably following Lucifer's orders. I notice that Lucifer does not show himself. I suppose he is too far above this company to soil his hands. Michael saw a flash of lightning split the night sky and heard the roar of thunder instantaneously. Within seconds, they were standing in a torrential downpour.

Xander and Michael laughed aloud. *Gregory's fireballs will not be nearly as effective in this storm,* commented Xander.

I would say that the Master has rendered that particular weapon virtually useless at this time. Let us scout the area.

As they flew, they saw all the churches and houses that were being protected by angelic warriors. The buildings were clearly delineated by the light glowing around and over them, enveloping them. The darkness receded as the light grew.

Xander and Michael spent the next two hours patrolling the area, joining the occasional skirmish, until the troubled area was quiet again and there was no longer any danger to the churches or the homes of servants of Jehovah. The rain continued, quenching the fires and sending people running for shelter.

No church or dwelling of a believer had burned, and the presence of those untouched buildings was a testimony as they stood in sharp contrast to the burned-out shells around them.

As the sun began to rise, the reporters and television news people began to knock on the doors of the unburned houses. At one such home, an elderly African American lady answered the door, her Bible in her hand, no sign of fear on her face. She stepped out onto her small porch, and her guardian took his place beside her. Xander and Michael landed in her front yard to listen to the exchange.

A television newsman shoved a microphone in her face, asking, "Hello. My name is Mark Goodman with WAGA news. Ma'am, would you give us your name please?"

She smiled, unruffled. "Certainly, young man. My name is Eileen Watts. Can I help you with something?"

"Yes, ma'am. Your house is one of the few on this block that hasn't burned to the ground. Can you explain that?"

"Son, I don't pretend to know everything about the Almighty's ways, but I did receive a phone call a couple of hours ago. I was already awake because of all the noise outside; I was up reading my Bible and praying. I answered the phone, and it was my neighbor, Louis, across the way there on his cell phone. His house had already burned, and he was standing in the street. I could see him from my window. Louis asked me who the two big men on my roof were. He said that they were glowing and waving swords at anyone who tried to come to my door. Louis said that no one bothered me because they were afraid of those men."

Mark looked interested. "Mrs. Watts, do you have any explanation for that? Do you know who those men were?"

Eileen Watts face was wreathed by a beautiful smile. She opened her Bible. "I have an idea or two about that, young man. I'm a Christian, and God promised right here in Romans 8:35-39 that He would take care of me." She pointed at a passage and began to read. "He said, 'Who shall separate us from the love of Christ? Shall tribulation, or distress, or persecution, or famine, or nakedness, or peril, or sword? Just as it is written, For Thy sake we are being put to death all day long; we were considered as sheep to be slaughtered. But in all these things we overwhelmingly conquer through Him who loved us. For I am convinced that neither death, nor life, nor angels, nor principalities, nor things present, nor things to come, nor powers, nor height, nor depth, nor any other created thing, shall be able to separate us from the love of God, which is in Christ Jesus our Lord.'"

The newsman was incredulous. "You think that Jesus was on your roof?" *She's a nut job.*

She spoke patiently and kindly. "I think His angels were on my roof defending me from evil, and I'll bet if you ask around at the other unburned houses, you'll find that I'm not the only one who had big, glowing men with swords on their housetops."

"That's a very interesting concept, Mrs. Watts, *and a great angle for a story*. I think I'll do that. I notice that none of the churches were burned either."

"Of course they weren't, son. If God would send His angels to protect me, don't you think He would have more angels on those churches? Would you like some coffee? I have some made in the kitchen."

"No, thank you, ma'am. I think I have some legwork to do. You've given me some ideas. Look for yourself on the news today." The young newsman and his crew headed back out to their van ready to speed away to find more unburned houses. However, when he got into the van with all the equipment, something else occurred to him.

Mark looked at his cameraman. "Do you have any footage of churches or unburned houses from last night?" he asked.

"Tons of the stuff," was the answer. He began to scan through the images on a screen in the van. When he saw a church, he paused the feed.

"Wow! Look at that!" Mark exclaimed.

"What is it?" asked the cameraman. Clearly visible on the roof were two faintly shining, white images. They were not clear enough to have a defined shape, but there was no mistaking that something was there.

The newsman replied, "If Mrs. Watts is right, we are looking at two angels. Let's go. There's definitely a story here." The van pulled away from the curb.

I must get back to the hotel before Elizabeth and the others miss me, thought Xander. *I am going to be tired today, I think, but it was well worth it.*

You will not be the only one who is fatigued, my brother. Elizabeth, Jonathan, and many others were awakened to pray just as we left your room last night. They have been praying for hours.

Maybe we can fit in a nap before tonight. Otherwise, it is going to be a very long day.

Before he and Xander rose to the sky and took flight back to the hotel, Michael issued an order for his warriors to spend the rest of the day in the burned area of south Atlanta.

SoulFire

Chapter 11

"But now, thus says the Lord, your creator, 'O Jacob, and He who formed you, O Israel, do not fear, for I have redeemed you; I have called you by name; you are Mine! When you pass through the waters, I will be with you; and through the rivers, they will not overflow you. When you walk through the fire, you will not be scorched, nor will the flame burn you. For I am the Lord your God, the Holy One of Israel, your Savior.'"
Isaiah 43:1-3

The next morning, Xander knocked on Elizabeth's door fifteen minutes before the appointed time they were to be at breakfast.

"Just a minute!" he heard her call, so he leaned on the wall by her door, resting as he waited.

True to her word, Elizabeth opened her door and peeked out at him with a tired smile.

"Hello, Xander. Are you as sleepy as I am this morning?" she asked as she came out of the room, closing the door behind her.

Xander saw the dark circles under her eyes and was tempted to tell her to go to back to bed. However, he knew that Elizabeth would not appreciate being told what to do; therefore, he held his tongue.

"I am indeed in need of more rest. Did you hear about the fires in south Atlanta last night?" he queried, though he already knew that Gabriel had awakened her to pray about the situation.

"Yes, I was up about half the night watching the TV news and praying. I woke up with such a strong impression that I needed to pray that I could not sleep. How did you know about it?" she asked, looking up at him.

"Much the same thing happened to me. I, too, was awakened in the night because of the fires. According to this morning's news, torrential rains that were not forecast earlier put out the blazes, and the area is relatively quiet now. Order has been restored, though many people are now homeless and in need. Most of the businesses in that section were burned out or looted, and those businessmen are hurting, as well."

I wish we had caught Gregory, thought Michael. *He is still free to wreak havoc on another unsuspecting community. He will probably follow us all summer as we travel across the country.*

That sounded dangerously close to a whine. Someone must have been up all night. I think Michael needs a nap. Gabriel deadpanned from beside Xander.

Michael groaned. *If you must make jokes, at least they should be good ones.*

Xander reached for Elizabeth's hand as they walked toward the elevator. She was quiet and thoughtful as she pushed the button.

Be grumpy now if you like, but you had better put on your happy face when you meet Elizabeth later today, Mikey, thought Xander.

Mikey? That will not do! replied Michael, affronted.

I do not think that 'Bertram' fits well with this century. 'Mike' is much more modern, answered Xander.

Gabriel laughed at Michael.

Do not laugh at your brother's expense, Gabe, warned Xander.

Gabe? I sort of like it. Very twenty-first century. I suppose it is better to use those names than our names that we have normally used in human form. I have used 'Norris,' but it really does not belong in this time period. Gabriel smiled.

I thought not, answered Xander.

May I at least have a surname of dignity? queried Michael, a bit testily.

You are my adopted brothers. Your surname is 'Xander,' he replied with satisfaction.

I suppose it must be so, grumbled Michael.

"You are very quiet this morning, Mr. Xander," said Elizabeth as the elevator doors opened.

"Not at all, Miss Bennet. I am meditating on the very great pleasure I have received from seeing your fine eyes so early in the day, and I am looking forward to a summer spent with you in ministry. Two of my brothers are in the area today, and I told them to come by the arena later to meet you. Would you like that?" he asked as they walked to the smaller dining area used for breakfast, followed by a scowling Michael and a smiling Gabriel.

"Really?" Her eyes sparkled. "I'm going to meet some of the mysterious Xander clan? Do I look all right?" She looked down at her outfit – skinny jeans with a turquoise sleeveless top and sandals – with a small frown. "I know I must look exhausted, and I wish I had dressed up a little more. Maybe I can go back to my room and change after breakfast."

"You are beautiful as always, Elizabeth. There is no need to dress to impress my family. They will certainly love you just as you are." *In fact, they already love you.*

Jonathan saw them as they entered the dining area and stood to get their attention. Lexus loomed behind his weary charge, actively examining the room.

Xander and Elizabeth saw him and went to the table he had reserved for them; Dave Branard was already seated there, and Dave's guardian, Hector, was beside Lexus.

Five of the largest, most powerful angels ever created are here. Jehovah has provided great protection for this team, thought Xander. He looked around at the guardians with the musicians, back-up singers, and crew, noting that there were many of the middle and upper ranks among them as well. He also noticed with trepidation that a few crew members had no protectors. Dave,

Jonathan's manager, had not hired all of the crew personally, and this was the first time that he, Xander, and the others had seen some of them. Dave had interviewed the crew leaders and allowed them to choose who would work on their teams.

Lucifer has an inroad with these few people. We will have to watch them carefully. Xander telepathed so that all angels present could hear.

Michael, Gabriel, Lexus, and Hector had also noticed that some members of the crew were not believers. *We will be vigilant,* said Michael as the others nodded solemnly in agreement.

Perhaps they will accept Jehovah-Yasha during these camp meetings, offered Gabriel, the hope evident in his voice.

It is possible, replied Lexus. *Jonathan is strong in the Spirit. He has not yet realized himself the power that has been given to him by the Almighty, but I have seen it.*

The same is true of Elizabeth, said Michael.

After wishing Xander and Elizabeth a good morning, Jonathan suggested that they get their food from the buffet and return to begin the day together with devotions. They led the way to the serving line, and the rest of the large party followed them, talking about the events of the night before.

Once they were again seated, Jonathan led his table in thanking God for the food as well as praying for the troubled area of the city, and they began to eat.

Xander was facing the television which was tuned to a cable news channel. The sound was muted, but as he noticed the footage of looting and burning, he paid closer attention and was interested when he read the scroll across the bottom of the screen.

"Jonathan, look at the news." Xander nodded toward the screen. "I could tell from your prayer that you already know a large portion of south Atlanta burned last night." Xander kept his eyes on the images as the others at his table turned to the monitor. The entire room quieted as all heads turned to the riveting video feed from the night before of people thronging the streets, breaking into stores, and carrying away merchandise. Riot police dressed in black uniforms and black helmets were shown patrolling the area, arresting looters, and trying to restore order. Several people had died in the confusion. According to the news, the area was still considered to be unstable, though the fires had been put out by the unexpected thunderstorms and the looting had stopped. The police presence had remained to maintain the peace.

Lucifer and Gregory are trying to stop SoulFire by using physical fire and violence, Xander, thought Michael. *They will not be successful.*

"How far is that from the arena? Will we be able to continue with our nightly rallies?" asked Elizabeth.

Jonathan was quiet for a moment, and then answered, "I don't think we are close enough to that area of Atlanta for it to affect us; I am more concerned about the kids doing mission work in the city. I need to make a few phone calls to the camp leaders at each college and to my contact at the arena. Please excuse me. I'll be back as soon as I can."

Jonathan left the room, already pulling up numbers on his cell phone as Lexus walked beside him.

The others ate in silence, watching the news and waiting for Jonathan's return.

"I've just thought of something," said Elizabeth after she had finished her breakfast. "I need to text Mom and tell her and Dad that we're okay. I'm sure this news is spreading quickly, and I don't want them to worry." She took her cell phone from her pocket and sent a text message to her mother.

After Jonathan had been gone about half an hour, Xander took Jonathan's Bible from the table by his plate and opened it to the passage he had studied in his own quiet time that morning. He stood with Gabriel behind him, held the open Bible in his left hand, and began to speak. Xander was friendly, but was known to be a man of few words. He had not yet spoken in any sort of evangelistic meeting except to introduce the music. Upon hearing his rich, deep voice, every head turned in his direction, curious to hear what the imposing young man had to say.

"In preparing for these weeks of ministry in SoulFire, I began to search the Scriptures for references to fire, and I found that there are a great many. This morning, I focused on Deuteronomy 4:23 and 24, 'So watch yourselves, lest you forget the covenant of the Lord your God, which He made with you, and make for yourselves a graven image in the form of anything against which the Lord your God has commanded you. For the Lord your God is a consuming fire, a jealous God.' We are not to put anything in our lives before our relationship with God. Whatever stands between us and the Father becomes an idol, and often, God will remove it. Search your hearts. Is anything standing between you and God? Before we begin this summer of reaching people, make sure that God is first in your own life.

"Now, think of what has taken place here in Atlanta over the past few hours. As a teacher I know would say, God was not shocked off His throne this morning by the news of the riots in south Atlanta. Nothing that is happening here has surprised Him. Fire can certainly be destructive, but it is also cleansing. Fire purifies and sanctifies. The people who live in the affected area need to be ministered to at this time. They need our prayers, and they need the message that we have – that God loves them and He wants to draw them to Himself. They need to know that their lives are not hopeless, and this is a time when they will be open to listen. Rather than backing away from our purpose, we should put our shoulders to the grindstone and work even harder. This is an opportunity for us to turn this city around for God. As Joseph said to his brothers who had sold him into slavery in Genesis 50:20, 'And as for you, you meant evil against me, but God meant it for good in order to bring about this present result, to preserve many people alive.' Do not allow Satan to have the victory here. You can be certain that he caused these riots to try to stop us, but God can use it for good. He can take this tragedy and turn it into a victory. Hearts that were hardened in south Atlanta yesterday are tender today from grief and suffering. People who were not reachable for the Lord before the fires are now looking for something to believe in. They are seeking answers to their questions. Let us not grow weary in the work that God has laid out for us."

Xander bowed his head and prayed for strength of purpose for those in the room and for everyone else involved in SoulFire throughout Atlanta. He prayed that God would show them what to do and give them the words to say. As he continued to pray, Jonathan returned and paused in the entrance to the room, bowing his head with the others. Already he had been aware of a depth of spirituality in Xander and had been waiting for it to be expressed more openly, apart from his music. Rather than feeling threatened by Xander's leadership, he rejoiced that God had sent him another partner in addition to Elizabeth.

When Xander had finished praying, Jonathan walked to his side smiling broadly. Lexus and Gabriel stood behind them.

"I have good news," said Jonathan. "All of our leaders here in Atlanta feel that we should continue as planned. As soon as it is safe, we will send youth teams into the burned-out area to help with the cleanup. This afternoon, those of us who want to go will have a police escort into the area. We will have bottled water and food to hand out, and we will assess the needs of the people who live there. We will also send buses to the area each evening to pick up anyone who wants to come to the evening rallies. Several area churches are already opening their doors to be shelters to those whose homes were burned, and money is being collected to take the people shopping for clothes and toiletries. The Red Cross and other agencies will be on the ground there as well. SoulFire Ministries will spread the word of what is needed for those people throughout the country as we travel. One night during each week this summer, we will take up an offering for the people of Atlanta, and they will know that God is showing His love for them through the generosity of His people. There will be no triumph for Satan here. The rest of you get loaded up to go to the arena and set up. I'll just grab a bite, and we'll head out of here in about fifteen minutes."

As the others scattered to gather what they needed for the day, Jonathan went back through the buffet line for hot food. Elizabeth, Xander, and Dave remained at the table with him while he ate, ironing out some last minute details connected with the afternoon trip into the burned-out area. Michael, Gabriel, Hector, and Lexus stood at the four corners of the table, forming a protective shield around their charges.

~~oo~~

The trailers and vans carrying the equipment were already at the arena when Jonathan, Dave, Xander, and Elizabeth arrived, shadowed by their guardians. Crews were busily unloading the transporting vehicles and setting up the stage area, the sound equipment, and the video screens. It was a hive of activity.

Now would probably be the best time for your appearance, Michael and Gabriel. Keep it short and sweet. Remember that you are in Atlanta on family business, and you have a schedule to keep. That is the truth. And remember that humans shake hands. No angel salutes, thought Xander as he and Elizabeth stood near the stage area, occasionally directing members of the crew concerning the placement of the instruments. Jonathan and Dave stood close by.

We are Xander's 'brothers' and need to meet the future sister-in-law, Michael explained to the amazed Lexus and Hector.

You are choosing to appear in human form before all these people without an emergency of any sort? asked Lexus, his surprise evident.

Yes, answered Gabriel. *We are Xander's family. Elizabeth will have to see us from time to time in order for things to appear normal. It is in the Master's plan. Watch them for a moment. We will return in a minute or so.*

Lexus and Hector nodded. They knew that Elohim had chosen to make Xander a duality in order that he might love and marry Elizabeth.

Michael and Gabriel flew at flash speed into an empty men's room, changed into human form, and walked across the arena and up to Xander and Elizabeth.

Xander saw them approaching and nudged Elizabeth, looking toward them and nodding. "There come my brothers now."

One by one, the crew members and technicians stopped to stare at the regal men striding toward the group of ministers.

Elizabeth's mouth dropped open, and she closed it quickly. "What did your father feed you guys? One of your brothers is even taller than you are, and the other is your same size. And, though they don't have your coloring, they certainly resemble you in masculine beauty. Char would love to be here." *I wish that I had asked her to come. She would have loved it, and I would have enjoyed having her with us this summer. We could have shared a room. I always have two double beds or a king-sized one. I should have thought of this earlier.*

That is an excellent idea, Elizabeth. I would like to have Charlotte here, as well, so that we could make certain she is protected, thought Xander.

Michael and Gabriel smiled, hearing Elizabeth's thoughts even while they were halfway across the arena.

Jonathan, with Lexus, walked up beside Xander. "Who are those young men?" he asked.

"Two of my brothers. We were all adopted by the same Father," Xander explained.

Jonathan stroked his chin thoughtfully. "Interesting. You aren't related by blood?"

"No. We just had the good fortune to be loved by the same wonderful Person. Actually, we are closer than most biological brothers, I think."

By that time, Gabriel and Michael were within a few feet of the group. Xander went to Michael and embraced him with a huge smile; then turned to Gabriel and hugged him as well.

Love the clothes. You both very much look the part of successful young businessmen. The short hair is better, too.

Thank you. I can pick out a suit and hairstyle with the best of them. I have helped you shop and gone with you to the stylist, you know, answered Gabriel. His honey-blond hair shone in the lights, and his deep blue eyes twinkled merrily.

Does this outfit make me look fat? asked Michael, grinning.

Xander turned to Elizabeth and Jonathan with a dimple-popping smile. "Elizabeth, Jonathan, I want to introduce my brothers, Mike and Gabe Xander. Mike is the tall fellow."

"I have looked forward to meeting both of you for quite some time now. I was beginning to think that Xander had just imagined you," Elizabeth said, smiling as she extended her hand first to Michael and then to Gabriel.

"We are quite real, as you can see," said Michael, winking at Xander.

"We were starting to think that he was exaggerating your beauty, Elizabeth, but I am relieved to know that Xander is truthful. I am so pleased to meet you at last." Gabriel was as gallant as he was handsome.

"Will you be staying in the area long? We would love to have you at our rallies this week," interjected Jonathan.

"No, I am afraid that we must be off in a few minutes. We are on family business for our Father and can stay only a few minutes," Michael replied, his green eyes becoming serious for a few seconds.

Elizabeth had been watching them closely. "Are you musically talented like Xander? He is amazing."

"We hum rather well," answered Gabriel, smiling at her as Michael and Xander laughed aloud.

You finally told a good joke! Impressive! thought Michael.

"You know," said Elizabeth, looking at the brothers thoughtfully while the laughter had died down, "you seem to be more of a 'Gabriel' than a 'Gabe,' and you are more like a 'Michael' than a 'Mike.'"

Michael raised an eyebrow. "Very astute of you, Elizabeth. I actually prefer to be called Michael, but most people seem to shorten my name automatically."

"Michael it is then. How about you, Gabe?" she asked.

"Like Michael, I prefer the old-fashioned form of my name as well. You may call me Gabriel if it pleases you."

Whoever reared these men certainly knew their grammar. It's as if they're all from another century. All of the angels in the arena heard Elizabeth's thoughts.

And on that note, I think we should exit, stage left, thought Michael.

Excellent idea, replied Gabriel.

I concur. You did very well, my brothers. Thank you. Xander turned to Jonathan. "I am pleased that you were here to meet some of my family."

"So am I," answered Jonathan. "Will we ever meet your father?"

"I expect so, though it may be years from now." Xander took Elizabeth's hand as a chilling thought occurred to him. *It will be after you are dead.* Sadness washed over him. *One day, Elizabeth will die. What will happen to me? Am I mortal enough to die?*

Do not think of that now. Michael's voice was kind, and his green eyes were somber.

If you die, Xander, you will go to heaven, added Gabriel.

What an odd thought – never to be an angel again, mused Xander pensively.

"I enjoyed meeting you very much, Elizabeth," said Gabriel, reaching out to shake her hand, and then Jonathan's. "And you, too, Jonathan."

"Take care of our little brother," Michael said as he shook hands with Jonathan and Elizabeth.

"Only you would call Xander *little*," chuckled Elizabeth.

Michael flashed her a smile that was as bright as his shining, blond hair.

I heard your earlier thought about Charlotte, and I agree. Gregory may go after her while we are gone. I have sent extra guards, warriors, for Elizabeth's parents, for Charlotte, and for Janna and Chance, but I think it is better to have Charlotte with us. She is very good about coming between Elizabeth and Gregory, should he choose to take human form, thought Michael.

I will arrange it, replied Xander.

Michael and Gabriel turned and walked away from them, stopping to wave just before they left the arena. Within a few seconds, they were back with Xander and Elizabeth, again wearing the garb of warrior guardians.

~~oo~~

After Xander and Elizabeth had spent the morning rehearsing all of their music for the evening, they grabbed a quick lunch from the catered buffet in the arena while their opening band, Thorncrown, practiced and did their sound check with the tech crew. The couple then joined Jonathan, Dave, and other members of the SoulFire team in visiting the south Atlanta area with a police escort. Jonathan had arranged to have tables set up with water, food, and hygiene items. SoulFire Ministries had sent people ahead to train two hundred counselors from area churches to be available at the arena every night, and most of those people also joined the evangelistic team in the burned-out neighborhoods for the afternoon.

The big story of the day was breaking as they prepared to leave the area. Jonathan's van had a television, and the group with him gathered around when he called them over to hear the news. A young newsman, Mark Goodman, was reporting that none of the churches in the area had been so much as scorched. Furthermore, all of the houses that had not burned were inhabited by Christians. His interviews of Eileen Watts and other Christians were shown, as well footage of several churches and houses with brilliantly glowing forms on their roofs.

"It appears, my friends, that we are seeing our God at work in a mighty and miraculous way here in Atlanta," said Jonathan with a big smile. He took his cell phone from his pocket and made a few calls. "We will have a special guest this evening at SoulFire. You're going to love her."

We love her already. Am I right, Michael? asked Xander.

You are, indeed, brother, answered Michael with a smile.

And, later this evening, we may have more guests that will surprise Elizabeth even more, added Gabriel.

Chapter 12

"As for me, I baptize you in water for repentance, but he who is coming after me is mightier than I, and I am not even fit to remove His sandals; He Himself will baptize you with the Holy Spirit and fire."
Matthew 3:4

June, 2008

Xander and Elizabeth waited with their guardians in their separate dressing rooms that evening as the arena filled to a full capacity crowd of 21,000. People were waiting outside an hour before the doors opened, forming a constantly moving line of humanity. Jonathan had arranged for buses to run to all the college campuses to pick up the campers, as well as to the troubled area of Atlanta, to transport all who wanted to attend. In addition, he had decided several months earlier to open the rallies to the public, holding the number of seats necessary to seat the teenagers; consequently, SoulFire would be packed every evening. Churches from all over Atlanta were bringing their young people, and adults of all ages were coming as well. Families had bought tickets together, and Life Groups from area churches were using the conference as a summer retreat, planning their own activities for their morning and afternoon hours and coming to the rallies in the evenings. SoulFire had been well-publicized across the country and was a main event of the summer for many people. There were eight week-long events planned in different major cities across the United States, and thousands of people who did not live in those cities traveled for several hours to attend. Some stayed in hotels, and others found housing with friends who lived in the chosen metropolitan areas.

The rallies were advertised as "come as you are," both in dress and in life circumstances. The masses of people wore everything from jeans and flip-flops to shorts and T shirts making a collage of color as they poured into the arena, laughing and greeting each other. All throughout the areas surrounding the halls and entryways, huge screens were set up, showing videos and pictures of the ministry activities in which the teens had been involved during the day. Crowds gathered, inspired by the images of the young people landscaping, painting, and doing construction for people in impoverished areas of Atlanta. There were films of teens working in soup kitchens; mowing lawns; conducting day camps with children; visiting in nursing homes, reading Bibles and singing with the elderly; washing cars; and participating in many other ministries. The images were filled with laughter and joy as the teenagers put feet to the message of God's love.

Local church leaders were behind tables at each video area, signing up people to participate the next day. Helpers handed out flyers with schedules and locations, directing workers to areas of need. There were also signs telling participants what they could bring the next evening if they were unable to leave their jobs for the week of ministry. Areas were set up to take clothes, canned food, water, and other needed items to be distributed throughout the economically depressed areas of Atlanta in addition to the neighborhoods affected by the fires.

Those leading the rallies also dressed down. Xander wore black jeans and a white, collared shirt, with the sleeves rolled up to his elbows. His muscled forearms and large, beautiful hands always drew more attention than he wanted, but that was something he could not help. He had purposely tried to avoid wearing anything that would cause anyone in the audience to look at him rather than to listen to the message of the music he would be playing and singing.

Elizabeth's white, sleeveless top flowed over her black jeans, fluttering softly about her form as she moved. Her jewelry was simple – silver loop earrings, an over-sized turquoise ring her mother had given her, and several chains of varying weights and thicknesses with gold and silver beads randomly scattered on the necklaces. From one chain hung an antique cross her aunt Grace had brought her from Italy and on another was a delicate sand dollar charm that had been given to her mother by her grandfather, affectionately known as "Papa." Her garnet cross, a gift from her father, was on a shorter, finer chain. She always kept her family close to her by wearing jewelry or clothing that they had given her. Unlike Xander, who could hear the thoughts of those around him, Elizabeth did not worry about what people thought of her appearance. She had never thought of herself as particularly attractive, and it did not occur to her that people might focus on her beauty rather than on the words she sang. Her choices in clothing, although fashionable, were modest rather than showy, and they suited her personality.

Shortly before Xander and Elizabeth were to go on stage, crew members came to alert them, and they made their way backstage, followed closely by Gabriel and Michael. As Elizabeth came into his view, Xander smiled.

"You look wonderful, Elizabeth. More than that, your inner beauty shines from your face." He quoted Proverbs 31:30 to her. "'Many daughters have done nobly, but you excel them all. Charm is deceitful and beauty is vain, but a woman who fears the Lord, she shall be praised.' I am so glad that you asked me to come with you and share this summer in ministry." He reached for her hand.

"I'm so happy that you accepted the invitation, Xander." She looked down at their joined hands. "'O magnify the Lord with me, and let us exalt His name together.'" She looked into his eyes and returned his smile.

He held her eyes with his gaze. "Psalm 34:3 has always been a favorite verse of mine, but I never thought I would have someone like you to share it with me, Elizabeth. I thank God every day for bringing you into my life. There are ways in which this journey to bring us together has put me through the fire, and one day I will tell you all about it, but right now I want you to know that it has all been worth it, and I would gladly do it all again."

She looked a little puzzled by his statement, but she accepted it. *We don't have time to talk now. He'll tell me what he meant later.*

He took both of her hands in his. "Shall we pray together before we open the conference?"

She nodded, and they bowed their heads. Michael and Gabriel put their hands on the shoulders of their charges as they spoke to God and asked for His blessings on their offerings to Him.

As they raised their heads, crew members were motioning to them. Thorncrown, the opening band, had been playing for the past hour as the people filled the arena, and they were preparing to leave the stage. When they stopped playing, the house lights went down and videos of various ministries which had been ongoing during the day played on the screens around the platform.

Xander thought through the words and music of their first song as sound technicians gave Elizabeth and him ear buds so that they could hear the other musicians. The wireless microphones were already on the stage on stands.

Elizabeth quickly put in her ear bud and reached up to pull his head down for a quick kiss. She held his face between her hands, mere inches from hers. "I love you, Alexander Darcy. You are everything I've ever dreamed of in a man." Then she kissed the tip of his nose, turned, and ran onto the stage with Michael right behind her.

He was momentarily struck dumb. *She chooses this time and place to tell me that I am all she has ever desired in a man? And then she runs away? How am I supposed to think straight after that?* Xander's blank expression lasted only a second before it was replaced with one of sheer joy. He turned his head to look at Gabriel who stood beside him. *She loves me as much as I love her! Gabriel, she knows me well, and she still loves me!*

Gabriel laughed aloud at him and the lightning speed at which his emotions could change.

Go, man! Do not leave her alone out there. Gabriel gave Xander a little push.

Xander headed toward the stage, but stopped as a familiar, loving Voice spoke into his mind. *I Am well-pleased with you. You have shown yourself to be worthy of her love, and she has given it freely. Now feed My sheep together.*

Breathless with happiness, Xander raced after Elizabeth; every trace of fatigue from the long night and day had vanished with her declaration followed by God's affirmation. Xander felt the same exultation that he had known the night that Jehovah had given him a dual nature. The Almighty had freed him to love Elizabeth, and her love had liberated him to be all that God intended for him to be. His Father was pleased with him. All was right in Xander's world for that wonderful moment.

Elizabeth was already at the piano, playing the opening song with the band, when Xander hurried into the stacked keyboards. He faced the audience with stands of keys in front of him as well as to both his left and his right and immediately joined the other musicians on the introduction, riffing as the audience began to clap. Gabriel, Michael, and the other guardians stood behind their charges, emitting a soft glow that grew as people joined with Elizabeth and Xander in singing "Life on Fire." Before they had reached the end of the first verse, everyone was on their feet, waving their hands in the air, singing as they read the words from the giant screens on the sides of the stage. Cameramen focused on Xander and Elizabeth, showing them on screens across the top of the stage.

After the first song, Xander strapped on an acoustic guitar and Elizabeth picked up her flute before they came to the mikes at the front of the stage. He played the opening bars of "Watching You," setting the tempo for the rest of the band before a few of them joined him in playing the quieter song. As he began to sing of the way God watches over His children throughout their lives, Elizabeth played a countermelody that wove through his words, bringing to mind the gentle laughter and quiet sobs that people experienced during their happiest and darkest moments. Parents held their children a little closer to their chests, and tears trickled down the cheeks of those who had recently experienced life-changing events, such as losing loved ones to sickness or tragedy. Many were present whose homes had burned the night before; some had even lost family members in the fires. They were hungry for the message imparted by the song. Xander sang as one who really knew what it meant to be cared for and loved by God. His face reflected his Father's glory, and all over the arena, people knelt to pray with him as he led them after he finished singing.

The thousands of guardians present knew that there were many hundreds of humans there who had never accepted Christ. One man had even come in who was indwelt by demons, and he began to mutter as God's name was lifted up. The man who was possessed got progressively louder during the hour that the singing continued. Michael dispatched warriors to stand around him, protecting the people who were in seats near the large, disruptive man. Eventually, he drew so much attention that security personnel for the arena came to lead him to a quieter place so that he could calm down. He fought with them, and five guards had to carry him out, kicking and screaming, to a secure area containing monitors with several different views of the stage via a closed circuit feed. They searched the man, but they missed the knife he had secreted in his boot. He sat with the security guards and seemed to become quieter away from the crowd, watching the monitors in front of him and scratching his own arms until they bled.

The last song before Jonathan spoke was "I Burn for You, Lord," sung as a duet by Xander and Elizabeth with only their acoustic guitars as accompaniment. He sat on a stool at the front of the stage with one long leg extended and the other bent in order to rest his guitar on his thigh. Elizabeth stood beside him, her guitar supported by a shoulder strap. The building was darkened except for a spotlight focusing all eyes on the two of them. The song was based on Psalm 66:8-12, and before they began to sing, Elizabeth quoted the passage. "Bless our God, O peoples, and sound His praise abroad, Who keeps us in life, and does not allow our feet to slip. For Thou has tried us, O God; Thou hast refined us as silver is refined. Thou didst bring us into the net; Thou didst lay an oppressive burden upon our loins. Thou didst make men ride over our heads; we went through fire and through water; yet Thou didst bring us out into a place of abundance." The chorus of the song was simple. "You have refined us as silver, Lord. We went through the fire, and You delivered us." As they repeated the chorus several times, the crowded arena filled with the voices of God's people raised in song, thanking God for the trials that had refined them into useful vessels, and praising Him for His deliverance from those dark times. Both angels and humans lifted their hands in praise to God, and the angels hummed the melody as their chief sang.

And God received the worship of both humans and angels with a smile.

When the last strains of the music faded away, there was a hush throughout the huge building. Jonathan, shadowed by Lexus, walked onto the stage, holding the hand of an elderly African-American lady as they approached a microphone. Xander and Elizabeth, followed by Michael and Gabriel, left the stage as Jonathan introduced his guest. Stagehands removed the stools and replaced them with a clear stand.

"Hello, Atlanta. We are so glad to be here with you for SoulFire 2008, and I want to introduce you to a new, very special friend of ours. You may have seen her on the news earlier today. Mrs. Eileen Watts has agreed to tell you what happened at her house and in her neighborhood last night as a large portion of this city burned. Welcome her now."

The young preacher began to clap and the audience joined him as Mrs. Watts smiled and took the microphone he offered to her. As her guardian stood beside her, Mrs. Watts told of God's protection throughout the long night as the riots and fires surrounded her house. She held her worn Bible and quoted Romans 8:35-39, emphasizing that nothing had been able to separate her from the love of God. She told of her neighbor's call in the night, alerting her to the fires and telling her about the glowing men on her roof who had stopped anyone from harming her. Her faith was so strong and real that every Christian present wanted a faith like hers, and every unbeliever who heard her testimony felt God's power flowing from her. When she finished, Xander, who was waiting in the wings with Elizabeth, came back onstage to escort her off. After he made sure that Mrs. Watts was comfortable, he returned to the wings to listen to the sermon with Elizabeth. Stagehands handed them bottles of water which they accepted gratefully.

Jonathan moved to center stage and rested his Bible on the plexiglass stand. Lexus stood to his right as he opened the Word to I Peter 1:6-7 and began to read. "In this you greatly rejoice, even though now for a little while, if necessary, you have been distressed by various trials, that the proof of our faith, being more precious than gold which is perishable, even though tested by fire, may be found to result in praise and glory and honor at the revelation of Jesus Christ."

Jonathan looked up, his earnest face shown on the giant screens across the top of the stage while the Bible verses were displayed on the two screens flanking the platform. He continued to speak, talking to the people as if he was having a conversation with them. "Atlanta, you have been tested by fire in the last twenty-four hours. You have been tested, and you have come through the fire. Now it is time for the results: the praise and honor that is to be given to Jesus Christ who has revealed Himself to you. Christians, we have a unique opportunity to share His love by helping those who have been left homeless. We can minister to a city that is still in shock. We can be His hands and His feet on this earth, in this city. This is a time for action; but first, you must examine yourself. Is He first in your life? Do you burn for Him?"

He continued to speak, using Scripture after Scripture pointing out that Almighty God wanted first place in their lives, that He promised salvation and comfort to those who belonged to Him, and that the only protection from evil was to be found in Him.

When he was finished, he bowed his head to pray, and Xander and Elizabeth came back onstage with their guardians. She seated herself at the piano while he stood surrounded by the keyboards. They looked at each other to coordinate their timing and began to play and sing softly.

Jonathan raised his head and opened the altar for any who needed to talk or pray with a counselor. Several hundred trained men and women came forward and stood facing the audience at the foot of the stage in front of the platform. As people streamed down the aisles, each of them was directed to a counselor who took them aside to designated counseling areas.

Suddenly the quiet was destroyed by a man, covered in blood and screeching as he ran down the middle aisle, fighting his way through the people in an attempt to reach Jonathan. He had escaped from the guards, leaving one severely wounded, and they ran behind him, trying futilely to catch him. He seemed to possess superhuman strength and stamina as he pushed people out of his path, climbing up onto the stage and finally standing before Jonathan. Lexus moved to stand between Jonathan and the man who was possessed by seven demons, but Jonathan was willing to face him. His guardian could not intervene because Jonathan's mind showed that he had decided to confront the man. Lexus returned to Jonathan's right side.

Xander and the other angels could see the demons crawling in the man, gripping him inside and out. They could hear his tortured mind with its jumbled, incoherent thoughts, cursing and blaspheming God. Xander and Gabriel moved quickly to the front of the stage, and Xander grabbed the man from the back, pinning his arms to his sides with an iron grip. He continued to fight, kicking his feet and finally freeing one arm to reach for Jonathan with his hand, grasping for the preacher's neck. Xander held him back, but the man struggled to be free. The hatred of the demons shone from his eyes which were red-rimmed and as wild as those of a rabid animal. The security guards had finally reached the stage, but Jonathan waved them away, facing the crazed man calmly. "Let him go, Xander."

One guard spoke up in agitation. "You don't want to release that crazy lunatic, mister. It took seven of us to pull him off Frank after he stabbed him – and Frank's nearly dead now. I don't know how this man is holding him by himself, but I wouldn't let him go if I were you."

Jonathan repeated firmly with no sign of doubt in his hazel eyes, "Let him go."

Xander looked at Jonathan as the man flailed in his arms. "Are you sure about this, Jonathan? He is very strong."

"'Greater is He that is in me than He that is in the world,'" quoted Jonathan. "Set him free. He cannot hurt me. I claim the name of Jesus."

At Jonathan's words, Michael planted himself to Jonathan's left.

Xander released the man who then ran at Jonathan, his hands grasping like claws and the sinews of his arms straining as he tried to put his fingers around Jonathan's neck to strangle him. The man's face was contorted, and he shrieked with frustration, but he was unable to touch Jonathan. The veins in his neck stood out like cords, and his hands hovered inches from the young man's throat, but he could go no closer. Michael held one of his wrists in a vise-like grip, and Lexus firmly held his other wrist.

"Let me go!" the man growled at Michael in an unearthly screech. Then, in a high, sing-song voice, he said softly, "Where's Elizabeth? Where's Elizabeth?"

Guard her, Gabriel! Xander's mind shouted.

Gabriel flashed from his place beside Xander to stand protectively in front of a wide-eyed, frightened Elizabeth. She had heard the implied threat.

She is safe. They will not get through me, answered the archangel. He spoke into Elizabeth's mind, *It will be well, Elizabeth. Do not fear.*

Jonathan looked the possessed man squarely in the eyes. "What is your name?"

"My name is Legion, for we are many," the man replied in a hoarse, flat voice, dropping his hands to his sides and starting to back away.

"Legion!" exclaimed Jonathan with authority. The man stopped, dropping to his knees, covering his face, and cowering before the young preacher.

"I command you in the name of Jesus Christ to come out of this man."

The man immediately fell to the floor, convulsing and jerking seven distinct times as each demon left him, flying through the air and out of the building, chased by warriors, as the demons sought another body to inhabit. As the last fiend left the man, he lay quiet, exhausted and limp. Security personnel immediately moved in to stand around him.

The crowd was hushed. Everything that had happened had been caught by the cameras and witnessed by everyone in the arena. Stage mikes had picked up the sounds, and the scene had played out on the screens throughout the building.

One of the security guards walked up to Jonathan and Xander, saying, "We've already called the police to come get that lunatic. He pulled a knife from his boot and attacked one of us while we were watching the monitors. He was able to get away and out of the room in the confusion, but he'll pay dearly for this. An ambulance is on its way here to take the wounded man, Frank, to the hospital."

Elizabeth, followed by Gabriel, walked up beside Xander as he spoke to the security guard. "You do not need the police or an ambulance. The man is

SOULFIRE

fine now; we will take care of him." Xander heard the Holy Spirit speak into his mind, and he obeyed. "Where is the wounded guard? Bring him to me."

"There's no choice about the police. He attacked Frank and nearly killed him. He will go to jail and stand trial for attempted murder, but I will tell them to bring Frank to you. After what I've seen here tonight, I think you may be the only ones who can save his life," answered the security guard.

The security guard then used his radio to call his co-worker who had stayed with the wounded guard. The ambulance had arrived, and the EMT's had put the man on a gurney. They were on their way out of the room with him, but one of them was a Christian, and his guardian spoke into his mind. *Take Frank to the young minister who is asking for him.* When the EMT heard Xander's request over the radio, he told the others that they should do as Xander asked. The rest of the team protested, but he said that he would take full responsibility. Because he was in charge of the group, the others did as he said.

The crowd parted to let the men and the gurney through, and they rolled it all the way up to the stage. Xander jumped down from the stage and turned to catch Elizabeth as she followed him. Together they went to the gurney, looking at the bloody sheets covering the bandages around the man's abdomen. His shredded shirt had been pulled away from the multiple stab wounds, his face was ashen, and his eyes were closed. Elizabeth began to pray quietly while she held the guard's cold hand. Jonathan joined them, praying on the other side of the gurney, and their guardians formed a shield behind them.

Xander lifted the sheet gently and began to pull away the bandages. One of the EMT's tried to stop him. "His torso is badly injured, and he's bleeding heavily. If you remove the bandages, he may bleed out before we can get him to a hospital."

Jonathan put a hand on the EMT's arm. He had long suspected that both Xander and Elizabeth had been especially gifted by God. "Do not interfere. He will be well."

Xander exposed the wound and placed his hands over it, bowing his head and praying to Jehovah-Rapha for healing. The blood ran through his fingers and down the guard's sides for a moment, and then stopped. Xander reached for the sheet that had been covering the guard and wiped his hands on it. He took a clean cloth from another EMT and cleaned the blood from the injured man's abdomen. As Xander gently rubbed the blood away, the man opened his eyes. He was confused to see a crowd around him, and he sat up. Xander, Elizabeth, and Jonathan stepped back as the rest of the EMT crew gathered closer to the gurney, their faces reflecting their shock.

"I don't see a gash anymore. Where was he hurt?" asked one.

"How do you feel?" asked another, seeing that there was no longer any wound at all.

Frank looked at them with surprise. "I feel fine." He looked around. "Where did all this blood come from?"

"It came from you."

They all looked at Xander with amazement.

The Christian in the group smiled at Xander. "Thank you. Something told me that you could help this man."

"I did not heal him; God restored him through me. He told me what to do, and I obeyed." Xander was firm. He would not take credit for that which his Master had done.

The others wanted to know if they could come to the rallies on the nights they did not have to work. Jonathan assured them that he would find a place for them all.

Frank, the security guard who had been healed, asked to talk to Xander, and they went to the side to talk privately, away from the crowd, while Jonathan returned to the stage to check on the man who had been delivered from demonic possession. He was sitting up and looking around in confusion. When he saw Jonathan, he smiled. As they talked, Jonathan realized that the man's last memory was from at least five years prior. The police arrived as the man accepted Christ as his savior. They started to handcuff him, but turned to look at Xander as he walked up with Frank smiling beside him, a guardian close by his side.

"Can you arrest him if this man has no wound?" Xander asked.

"He's covered in blood. Where did it all come from?"

Frank, in his bloody, tattered shirt, said, "It came from me, but this man healed me. I no longer am hurt, so I don't see how you can charge him with anything if I refuse to press charges for assault."

"You refuse to press charges after he attacked you?" asked one of the policemen as if he could not believe what he was hearing.

"Yes, I do. Had he not attacked me, I would never have met this man of God or my Savior. He meant to hurt me, but he helped me instead."

The man who had been possessed turned to look at Frank and Xander. Xander noticed that he now had a guardian with him.

"You forgive me?" he asked Frank.

"If God can forgive me for the many years I lived for the Devil, I can certainly forgive you." Frank reached out his hand with a smile. "What is your name?"

"It's been so long since anyone has used my name that I barely remember it. It was Bobby before I became a drunk and a drug addict, lost my home and family, and sank into darkness. This man," he said, pointing to Jonathan, "has showed me the way to a new life. He's going to help me get back on my feet and make something of myself. I guess I'm Bobby again." He extended his hand to Frank, and the men shook hands, and then embraced.

One of the policemen reached to shake Xander's hand. "I guess our work here is finished. I hope there are still seats available here. I want to bring my family tomorrow night."

Xander and Elizabeth smiled at him. "I think something can be arranged," she said, looking back up at Xander.

After talking a few more minutes, the EMT's and policemen left to finish their shifts. Many of them had received tickets from Jonathan to attend the conference on the nights they did not have to work.

Jonathan had been told earlier that day that the seating arrangements could be changed to hold another thousand people, and he had told the arena managers to go with the new set-up for the rest of the week. An unnamed benefactor had wired the money needed into the SoulFire Ministries bank account to pay for adjusting the seating layout in order to allow more people to come. The anonymous donor had contributed large amounts several times since Xander had joined the ministry team, and Jonathan privately wondered if Xander himself was supplying the funds.

Again, it was all caught on camera, and boom mikes on the floor in front of the stage had picked up the sound. The people had watched everything unfold. Some had prayed throughout the exorcism and healing. Others had watched in fascination. Still others had quietly praised God for the mighty works being done through His servants. A few people left, but most stayed, waiting to see what other miracles God had in store.

And the angels raised their hands toward heaven, rejoicing that God had added more than five hundred believers to the fold.

Chapter 13

"Blessed be the Lord, my rock, Who trains my hands for war, and my fingers for battle; my lovingkindness and my fortress, my stronghold and my deliverer; my shield and He in Whom I take refuge; Who subdues my people under me."
Psalm 144:1-2

Xander, Elizabeth, Jonathan, and Dave were late getting back to the hotel. They had ridden together in Jonathan's van, and the bus carrying the crew was close behind them. Most of them seemed to want nothing more than to go to their rooms and rest. Jonathan had extended their meeting time for the next morning until 9:30, thinking that everyone needed time to unwind and sleep in.

It had been a long day, certainly, but Xander was energized by all the things that had happened at the rally; he knew that sleep would not find him for an hour or two at least. When Jonathan and Dave, followed by Lexus and Hector, told Elizabeth and him good night and headed for the elevator, Xander took Elizabeth's hand in his and led her to the window at the end of the hall. In comparative privacy, he leaned down to whisper, "Would you like to indulge in a little adventure with me?"

Michael and Gabriel stood on either side of them, arms folded. *Elizabeth needs to rest, Xander,* remonstrated Michael.

Once her surprise arrives, we will not have as much time together, answered Xander.

Elizabeth looked at him mischievously. "An adventure? I love adventures."

"Neither of us has had adequate exercise in several days. There is a gym in this complex, but I have another idea which will serve the purpose. It is rather unusual, but I think it would be useful and enjoyable for you. Would you like to work out with me?" Xander smiled in invitation.

"What kind of a workout?" asked Elizabeth, her curiosity evident.

Are you sure about this? queried Gabriel, hearing Xander's thoughts.

Absolutely, answered Xander.

"You will like it, and I think you will be very surprised at how quickly you learn. I want to teach you how to defend yourself, Elizabeth."

Are you serious? Michael inquired. *She could be hurt. You are a full foot taller than she is, and you must outweigh her by one hundred pounds.*

I would never hurt her. You are her guardian, not her mother. Xander was firm.

Elizabeth had often wondered how Xander maintained his physique, and she was curious to learn more about his regimen.

"Let's go change, then. What should I wear? Shorts and a T shirt?" she asked, as they walked toward the elevator.

He pressed the button. "After a few sessions, I recommend sweat pants or pajama bottoms and a long-sleeved T if you have them with you. As you learn more about what I am going to teach you, protective clothing may become necessary. At any rate, tonight will be introductory. You will not receive so much as a scratch."

The doors opened, and they entered the elevator. She bit her lip as she mentally catalogued the clothes she had with her.

"Should I go for loose or fitted? I have no idea what we'll be doing. Give me a clue." Elizabeth looked up at him, suddenly thinking about how big and muscular he was. *I'm going to look like an idiot next to this man. I've never seen him have to defend himself, but I have no doubt that he could take out a small army all alone.* She thought about how he moved fluidly, with controlled strength and catlike grace. She remembered how he had showed no fear at all earlier in the evening, grabbing the possessed man and holding him by himself when it had taken five large security guards to subdue him and even more to pull him off of his victim. *All I know how to do is run. I should have played sports or taken dance lessons, but I was always playing the piano.*

The doors opened, and he walked her to her room.

"Do not worry about what clothing you wear now. We will adjust to whatever you have. Perhaps tomorrow we can stop by a mall and pick up something more suitable, provided you want to keep training with me after tonight. I will be back at your door in ten minutes."

"Okay," she said, opening her door with her key card.

Just as he had promised, he was waiting by her door, Gabriel behind him, when she opened it ten minutes later. She was wearing gray flannel pajama bottoms, a red SoulFire T shirt, and Adidas sneakers. Her hair was pulled up in a pony tail. Michael's grim face was clearly visible behind her.

Xander nodded with approval. "Are you ready?"

"Uh...sure." Elizabeth's eyes were round, and she swallowed in a gulp. She had never seen so *much* of him before. *I thought he looked good in his fitted sweaters and T shirts, but this is ridiculous.*

Xander was surprised at her reaction. He had dressed in what he usually wore to train without thinking about it – a white tank top and black pajama bottoms. *There may be more benefits to this idea than I expected. I just wanted to spend time with her doing something we would both enjoy, and I wanted to teach her self-defense so that she would no longer be afraid the way she was tonight. If her opinion of me is raised in the process, that is even better.*

He took her hand as they walked to the elevator, followed by Michael and Gabriel.

"Where are we going?" Elizabeth asked.

"I asked the hotel manager if we could use an empty meeting room at night, and he agreed. We need plenty of open space."

Her curiosity was piqued. After they entered the elevator and he pushed the button for the ground floor, she looked up at him with a question in her eyes. "Are you sure you want to do this together? I'll probably just slow you down in whatever it is you do."

Michael and Gabriel stepped back as Xander moved behind her and rubbed her shoulders. "I do not have any expectations at all, Elizabeth. I will be happy to work with you at whatever level or speed is comfortable for you. Do not worry so; I have heard that it will make you turn gray prematurely."

Michael snorted, and Xander smiled at the sound.

By the time the doors of the elevator opened, Elizabeth was relaxed. "Are you sure you wouldn't rather just continue the back rub for a few more hours instead?" she asked.

Xander chuckled and took her hand, leading her into the hallway. "I thought your courage rose with every attempt to intimidate you. Come with me now; I will rub your back for you after the lesson if you need it."

He opened the door to the room, taking note of the locations of the chairs stacked against the walls and the tables folded on handcarts. The center of the room was empty and the carpet was an industrial grade, closely-cropped, nondescript brown. *It will do,* he thought.

She remained in the doorway as he went to the middle of the room and held out his hand to her. "Come."

Michael and Gabriel took up positions near the wall to Xander's left.

"Remind me again," she said uncertainly as she went to him. "Why are we doing this?"

He leaned over and held her face between his hands. "Because I love you, Elizabeth, and I will not have you afraid. You must feel comfortable in the ability to protect yourself. I will be there to guard you nearly all the time, but I could tell that Bobby frightened you when the Legion within him said your name. You are strong in faith, but you need to develop confidence in your physical abilities. No one would ever expect you to fight demons, Elizabeth. That is one reason that God put me into your life; I will fight for you. However, you should not fear the evil ones. Your fear gives them too much control over you. They will use it against you."

Her surprise was evident. "You were thinking of me when all that was happening? How is that possible?"

Xander laughed softly and kissed her forehead, drinking in her scent. He turned his head, resting his cheek on her hair as he spoke in a low voice. "Elizabeth, I am nearly always thinking of you. God has first place in my life, but you are a strong second. You complete me. If anything happened to you, I would not want to live. Can you not understand what I have been telling you for the past six months? Am I that inept at expressing myself?" He enveloped her in his arms.

I must have done something right at some point in my life for God to give me this man. I do not deserve him, she thought. *I will do whatever he wants me to do if it will help him to have peace of mind.*

He held her at arm's length and sighed. "This would be a pleasant way to spend several hours, but we both need to rest, and I want to begin your training. Are you ready?"

With only the slightest hesitation, she raised her chin and answered firmly. "Bring it on."

He rewarded her with a full-dimples smile. "Excellent."

Remember that you are not training with me now. Neither of us has ever taught a human. Michael was still unhappy with the idea, though he now understood Xander's reasoning.

Michael, Xander has shown many times that he is mindful of his own strength when he is with Elizabeth. Besides, she is a part of him. He would not cut off his own arm. Gabriel spoke gently.

Xander focused on the task before him. Elizabeth watched with fascination as his expression changed from one of love to a look of total concentration.

"Let us begin with defensive and offensive stances," he said, illustrating the most basic one, a low crouch with fists up and elbows pulled against the body, used by warriors and guardians.

"Are you teaching me martial arts?" Elizabeth asked.

"My methods are similar to those used in the different schools of martial arts, but they are ancient and unique. I have learned from masters. Try to copy my body position."

Thank you for the compliment, thought Michael with a nod. *I suppose that teaching her stances will not hurt her. I just do not want her to have false confidence that she can fight someone like Legion. She could be badly hurt if she ever tried such a thing.*

I will never encourage her to fight, Michael. I want her to learn the basic moves in case she is attacked and for some reason we are unable to help her quickly enough. I am trying to buy a few seconds – time that could make a difference. I feel led to do this, and you cannot dissuade me. I am positive that I am right. Xander was adamant. The Captain of the Host silently deferred to the Chief of the Guardians.

While she did her best to imitate him, Xander walked around her, correcting her posture and giving her further instructions about the position of her feet, arms, and hips. He touched her lightly when necessary, careful to avoid taking liberties with his physical contact under the guise of showing her how to move her body.

It is as I thought it would be. Elizabeth learns this as quickly as she does everything else, thought Xander, well-pleased with her rapid progress.

Before it was over, Michael was speaking into her mind, reinforcing Xander's verbal commands.

By the end of an hour, Elizabeth was able to assume eight different stances as Xander called out the names of them.

They are here, said Michael, hearing his subordinate's telepathed thought. *We should go to the lobby now.*

"You have done remarkably well. I think that will be enough for tonight," said Xander proudly.

"But I'm really getting into it now. I want to learn more," Elizabeth said eagerly. "Please?"

It was difficult for Xander to refuse her anything, but he knew that she needed to rest, and with the excitement that was awaiting her, she would probably be up for another hour at least.

"We can practice every night, precious. By the end of the summer, you will be a formidable opponent," he replied, pulling her ponytail playfully.

He hardly ever tells me 'no.' Something's up. Elizabeth looked at him sharply. Xander was smiling in anticipation. *It must be good. His surprises always are.*

She is beginning to know me very well, thought Xander.

"Come. I have something I want to show you." He smiled at her, taking her hand in his.

She peppered Xander with questions as they walked down the corridor to the lobby. He just kept smiling enigmatically and refused to say a word in response. Gabriel and Michael were amused by her persistence.

As they came out of the hallway into the lobby area, Elizabeth saw her parents and Charlotte standing at the front desk. Her parents heard her squeal of delight and turned toward her.

"Here she is now," said David, catching her in a hug as she flung herself at him. Roark, Niall, and Edward stood to the side, nodding their greetings to Xander, Michael, and Gabriel. From beside the guardians, six strong warriors saluted the Captain of the Host. He acknowledged them, and they stood at ease.

"Is everything okay? We saw the fires on television. Your text was a little short on details," added Lynne as Elizabeth left her father's arms and went to her mother's.

"It seems like we've been gone a month. I can't believe it's just Monday night. I have so much to tell you!" exclaimed Elizabeth.

Looking over her mother's shoulder, she saw Charlotte's luggage and noted that there were several large pieces.

"Char! Are you coming on tour with us?" asked Elizabeth, leaving her mother's arms to hug her friend.

"If you want me to. Xander called yesterday and said that he had cleared it with Jonathan. If you can put up with having me as a roomie this summer, I'll try to make myself useful," Charlotte replied, laughing.

Elizabeth stepped back to look at her. "Are you kidding? I'd love to have you with me." *I wish for it, and it comes true. What are the odds?*

Xander had been at the front desk getting a room key card for Charlotte. David had already picked up the one that Xander had left for him there. There had been no rooms available on their floor, but Xander had been able to get the Bennets a room on the floor directly under theirs. Elizabeth walked over and surprised him by standing on her tiptoes to kiss his cheek. "Thank you, Xander. This is such a wonderful surprise. You really are the best!"

"How long are you and Mom staying, Daddy?" she asked looking back at her father, knowing that he would not leave Tabernacle without a pastor for very long.

"We've planned to stay the rest of the week for the SoulFire conference and head back on Saturday. What have you two been up to this evening? Do you normally walk around in pajamas?" asked David, looking at Xander. *That's one big boy. I'll never have to worry about Elizabeth when he's around.*

"Daddy, everybody wears pajama bottoms casually now. Anyway, we've been working out." Elizabeth looked up at Xander with justifiable pride. "Xander has been teaching me some self-defense moves."

Xander and Elizabeth walked back over to the group, and Xander handed Lynne and Charlotte their key cards. "Charlotte, you are welcomed to join us if you wish to do so. We plan to practice each evening to stay in shape this summer. I want Elizabeth to know how to protect herself."

Charlotte laughed aloud. "I'm not big on working out, especially at night. While you guys rehearse, I'll probably just walk around the arena. I brought my Pilates DVD, too, so I can work out in the room. Don't worry about keeping me busy. I have my laptop with me for online courses I'm taking this summer, and I brought a few really good books to read." *Though seeing you in your workout clothes just might make it all worth it, Xander.*

Michael, Gabriel, and Niall snickered upon hearing Charlotte's thought, while Edward and Roark smiled. The warriors remained stoic, watching the scene.

Elizabeth prodded Charlotte, teasing her. "Char, you definitely should join us. Xander really knows his stuff. It's a sort of amalgamation of martial arts styles. You should see him move. I can't wait for my next session."

Elizabeth's parents smiled indulgently at her enthusiasm, but Charlotte arched an eyebrow at her friend. "I'm trying to be good. You should not tempt me to break the tenth commandment."

That comment elicited a snort from Michael and chuckles from the other guardians. Even the warriors fought smiles.

Elizabeth understood immediately, thinking of the tenth commandment recorded in Exodus 20:17, *'You shall not covet your neighbor's house; you shall not covet your neighbor's wife or his male servant or his female servant or his ox or his donkey or anything that belongs to your neighbor.'*

Xander blushed and looked at the floor as David and Lynne tried unsuccessfully not to smile. *I should have thought to take a shirt to our training session. I should not have come down here uncovered.* He was mortified.

Charlotte is joking, Xander, thought Gabriel. *You have not caused her to sin.*

Seeing Xander's expression, Elizabeth bit her lip to keep from laughing. "Char, we certainly don't want to lead you into temptation, but I'm a little confused. I know Xander isn't the house, so is he the wife, the servant, the ox, or the donkey?"

Charlotte was not at all embarrassed to admit the obvious. "Now, Elizabeth, you know that he is none of those things, but it is quite plain to anyone who is around the two of you for more than ten minutes that he belongs to you."

David broke into the conversation to give Xander some relief. "If you folks don't mind, I'm really tired and want to go to bed. It's a long drive from Bethel to Atlanta."

"I agree. We have all week to talk. I'm just glad to see the two of you safe," said Lynne, hugging Elizabeth again, and then reaching up to hug an astonished Xander. He did not know what to do at first, but after a moment, he gently returned her embrace.

"I'm a hugger, Xander. You'll just have to get used to it if you plan to stay around our family," said Lynne, releasing him.

"I confess that I am not accustomed to displays of affection, but I do not object to them. In fact, I find that I rather like it," Xander said, smiling shyly at her.

"That's good," said Elizabeth, her eyes merrily shining. "I think you might be considered by my mom to be one of the family at this point. We have you now, and there's no getting away." She gave an evil laugh and grabbed him around his waist. "And Char," she said, looking at her friend, "wait until you meet his brothers. They aren't as handsome as Xander, but they come very close."

Hah! thought Xander.

She is obviously blinded by love, replied Michael.

Of course it only stands to reason. Yours is a match made in heaven, added Gabriel.

I like that, Gabriel. May I borrow it? queried Xander.

Be my guest.

"Really? Brothers, plural? If you tell me they play the piano, I may actually kill myself." Charlotte hit her head with her palm dramatically.

The expression on your face is priceless, Xander said to Michael, who looked truly stunned. *Do not be anxious. I shall protect you from Charlotte.*

"Bed! Now!" said Lynne emphatically, pointing at the elevator.

Xander grabbed Charlotte's luggage while David carried his and Lynne's. They crowded into the elevator talking and laughing until the doors parted once again and, after agreeing to meet with the rest of the SoulFire team at 9:30 in the morning, they went to their rooms for the night.

Chapter 14

"But the Lord is faithful, and He will strengthen and protect you from the evil one."
II Thessalonians 3:3

Lucifer was absolutely livid; his eyes glowed a bright crimson. The only sounds in the deserted department store serving as a meeting place for him in Atlanta were his staccato footsteps as he stalked to and fro before his bowed, hushed assembly. He had limited his summons to the underprinces and captains of the United States, fully aware that the situation in Atlanta was spinning out of his control. He realized that the humiliation of his son's failure to stop the SoulFire meetings must not be displayed for the rank and file of his forces, and that a strategy to prevent the loss of more territory must be devised immediately. Had his vanity not required an audience at all times, he would have refrained from calling even the higher ranked among his minions.

He walked angrily back and forth on the dais, his black satin robes swishing quickly around his legs, for fully twenty minutes while Gregory sat at ease, legs crossed, on his throne to the right of the Dark Lord's. Lucifer finally glanced at his son's face, and the sardonic expression he saw there raised Beelzebub's ire to new heights.

The Anointed Cherub halted in front of the Dark Prince, barely concealing the depth of his wrath, and took a deliberate, deep breath before he spoke.

SOULFIRE

"Why do you smile so, Gregory? I see nothing humorous in this situation. Yesterday, Atlanta was under our control, and tonight, our grasp slips more by the moment. Please share your joke with me, for I find nothing amusing in the events of the past twenty-four hours."

Dark Spirit raised his head from where it had rested upon his coiled body on the throne to Lucifer's left and hissed his agreement with Lucifer's statements. His eyes glowed as he turned his evil face toward Gregory and fixed his cold stare upon him.

Gregory looked up at his father with calm, amber eyes. "Father, Atlanta is not lost. All we need is a damage control specialist, someone who has connections in the news media. The reporter, Mark Goodman, who broke the story about the Watts woman and the unburned churches and houses, would be an excellent choice. He has not yet become a believer, so he is available for our use. He already has the attention of the public. If he were to cast doubt on all that has occurred by accusing the SoulFire team of trickery, people would believe him."

Gregory stood to his feet, totally relaxed in the midst of all the tension, and walked gracefully past Satan to Dark Spirit's throne, draping his arm across the back of the huge chair. Lucifer followed his progress across the dais with his flaming eyes, turning his head and his body in synchronization with the movements of his son.

Gregory spoke softly. "I think it is time for us to fully utilize the power at our disposal. Jonathan Edwards may be able to cast out the lower demons, but he would have no success against Dark Spirit."

Lucifer rubbed his chin thoughtfully with his beautiful, tapered fingers as his eyes returned to the color of honey. "This Mark Goodman you speak of – is he addicted to drugs or alcohol? Has he given up control of himself so that we may use him? If he does not surrender himself, we cannot possess him without his permission to do so."

"He does not appear to use drugs or drink to excess, but can we not offer him money, success, fame, and fortune? Perhaps he lusts after a promotion – a TV network news anchor position or his own cable news show? A prestigious, lucrative job for him, more influence and favorable coverage for us. Those are in your power to give, Father. Who would turn those down?" Gregory's eyes glittered with wickedness.

Lucifer considered his words, and then began to smile an evil, twisted smirk. "I think you may be right, my son. What say you, Dark Spirit? Are you ready to inhabit a human body again?"

As Lucifer reached out to stroke the huge animal, the snake looked steadily into the Dark Lord's eyes and lifted the rattles at the end of its body, shaking them as if in warning of what was to come. Suddenly, the rattler slithered from the throne to the floor. The assembled demons silently crept back from the serpent's path as it wound its way through the crowd toward a broken window in a back office. The reptile pushed itself from the window and slipped into the humid Southern night, headed for an apartment in the suburbs where a young man slept peacefully, unaware of the heinous beast stalking him in the thick darkness.

~~oo~~

Xander was up by eight Tuesday morning, looking forward to another day. After greeting Gabriel, he began his morning with a short study of Ezekiel 28:14-19, opening his mind to whatever the Holy Spirit would reveal to him concerning the passage. As he sat at the table reading the passage, he was struck by its relevance to recent events. "'You were the anointed cherub who covers, and I placed you there. You were on the holy mountain of God; you walked in the midst of the stones of fire. You were blameless in your ways from the day you were created, until unrighteousness was found in you. By the abundance of your trade you were internally filled with violence, and you sinned; therefore I have cast you as profane from the mountain of God. And I have destroyed you, O covering cherub, from the midst of the stones of fire. Your heart was lifted up because of your beauty; you corrupted your wisdom by reason of your splendor. I cast you to the ground; I put you before kings, that they may see you. By the multitude of your iniquities, in the unrighteousness of your trade, you profaned your sanctuaries. Therefore I have brought fire from the midst of you; it has consumed you, and I have turned you to ashes on the earth in the eyes of all who see you. All who know you among the peoples are appalled at you; you have become terrified, and you will be no more.'"

As Xander meditated on the passage, he thought of Lucifer, the anointed cherub, whose forces had burned a large section of Atlanta on Sunday night. The very weapon of choice of Lucifer and Gregory, fire, would eventually consume them with everlasting torment. He read the passage again, noting that time seemed to shift in those few verses. To Jehovah, it was as if Lucifer's demise had already happened. The prophecy concerning Lucifer's defeat spoken by Ezekiel from God thousands of years ago would certainly happen, just as Satan's fall from heaven had taken place thousands of years before Ezekiel wrote about it. He rested his chin against his knuckles as he thought, *My Father does not wear a watch. The past, the present, and the future are all the same to Him.* The idea fascinated him. *He has no beginning nor will He ever end. He has always existed, and He always will be. The great I Am is infinite, omnipotent, omniscient, omnipresent, and immutable.* Xander bowed his head and offered praise to his Maker, giving thanks for his Father's love and protection during the past two days, expressing his gratitude for the gift of salvation given to so many during those days.

When he finished praying, his mind reached out for Elizabeth in the room next door, and he heard her thoughts as she threw a pillow at Charlotte's head, waking her to get ready for their late breakfast. *I'm so glad that Char is here. How like Xander to think of me and to know what would make me happy. He arranged all of this for me because he loves me. In some ways, I think he is constantly protecting me and those whom I love. I really think he would storm the very gates of hell for me.*

Gabriel heard her as well. *She is very astute, Xander. Her mind comprehends much on a subconscious level. She knows more than she realizes.*

I hope that she will think of those things when I tell her what I really am. Xander's thoughts were somber. *If only she knew already. This knowledge is the only thing keeping us from perfect communion.*

When will you tell her? asked Gabriel gently.

After the summer meetings end. I cannot chance alienating her during these weeks of ministry. Xander was quiet for a moment. *I am praying that God will show me the right time and give me the words. I wish that I could tell her now. I am afraid that the longer I wait, the more betrayed she will feel.*

Gabriel made no response, and Xander knew by his silence that Gabriel agreed with him. He was caught in a terrible predicament. Waiting to tell her would make her feel that he had been deceiving her from the beginning, while telling her now might affect their usefulness during this important summer.

I cannot tell her at this time. She may refuse to work with me after she knows, and I know that our Father wishes for us to minister together this summer. Many lives will be changed through SoulFire. I cannot do anything that might upset all the plans that have been made. Yet, I may lose her by waiting to tell her. His insides twisted into knots at the painful thought.

I do not know how it will be accomplished, thought Gabriel, *but I do know that all will be well in the end.*

I think you are right, Gabriel, but I do not look forward to the agony of being separated from her while she comes to terms with the knowledge. I do not know what she will do when she is told. I would desire that God would make a way in which we would not have to go through this fire; however, I submit to His will. Xander spoke with resignation.

He shook his head as if to clear his mind. *Enough! I will not dwell on this further and allow the uncertain future to spoil the present. We are together now.* Xander thought of Jesus' words in Matthew 6:34, *Therefore do not be anxious for tomorrow; for tomorrow will care for itself. Each day has enough trouble of its own.*

He closed his Bible, rose from the table, and headed for the bathroom to shower, shave, and dress.

~~oo~~

At Jonathan's request, the hotel restaurant manager had extended the breakfast buffet hours so that the SoulFire team and crew could come down later. A private banqueting room had been set up for them with rectangular tables set end-to-end, and more substantial fare had been added to the normally light breakfast offering.

Xander, Elizabeth, and Charlotte arrived at 9:30 and joined David and Lynne in the buffet line. Their guardians walked beside them as the warriors took up positions along the perimeter of the room. Jonathan and Dave were already seated, waiting for Xander and the others to eat with them.

Xander held Elizabeth's chair, and Jonathan stood, moving to seat Charlotte while David did the honors for his wife. Jonathan had met Charlotte several times during the spring when she had come with Elizabeth to some of their weekend rallies.

"Good morning, Charlotte," the young man said with a smile, holding the chair by his own for her, and then sitting beside her. "I'm so glad that you will be traveling with us this summer. I am hoping that you will agree to be a counselor. So many people came forward last night that several counselors had to speak with groups of ten people or more. I have asked many of the local pastors to volunteer and bring church leaders with them, and the response has been good, but I'm hoping that we'll need more each night."

Charlotte replied, "El has been telling me about all that has happened since you and the team have been here, and I must say that you've had quite an exciting time. While I hope that we will not have fires in every city we visit, I am prepared for whatever may come and looking forward to being a part of this ministry for the rest of the summer. I would be happy to be a counselor, and I'd like to help in any other way I'm needed. Just tell me what you want me to do."

Jonathan nodded his assent and stood to bless the food. After they had finished eating, he opened the Bible he had brought with him, led the group in a short devotional and outlined the schedule for the day with them. When he was finished, the crew left the room to make final preparations before they left for the arena to have rehearsals. Jonathan, Charlotte, Xander, and the Bennets remained at their table, talking and laughing for a few more minutes, surrounded by their guardians. The warriors remained stationed around the room.

The young evangelist looked at Elizabeth and Xander seated across the table from him. "I have been thinking. Perhaps the band that plays before the rally starts could handle the music for the invitation time so that you two could help with counseling. What do you think of the idea?"

Elizabeth thought for a moment before replying. "I am open to whatever you need me to do, Jonathan. Xander do you agree?" she asked, glancing in his direction.

He nodded at her, and then turned his head to address Jonathan. "Of course. We will help Thorncrown to prepare for tonight so that we can help you. Do you not think that Rev. and Mrs. Bennet would be a great help this week as well?"

"An excellent suggestion, Xander. Are you two in agreement?" Jonathan asked, looking at David and Lynne.

As they nodded their assent, the front desk manager, Mr. King, entered the room, came to Jonathan, and tapped him on the shoulder. "Rev. Edwards, there's a young man here to see you, and he seems to be very upset. Actually, he's been here, sitting in the lobby since seven this morning. His name is Mark Goodman. He's the reporter who broke the story about the churches and houses that weren't burned Sunday night. I told him that you were very busy, but he insists that I ask you to see him."

Jonathan looked up and saw the reporter in the doorway wearing a look of abject fear. Glancing back up at Mr. King, Jonathan asked, "I know that you probably want to have this area cleaned. Do you have an empty room where we could talk for a little while?"

"Certainly. The room next to this one will be vacant all morning. The chairs are stacked. Should I call for someone to help you?" answered Mr. King.

"No, that won't be necessary. The other men and I can handle it. Thank you." Jonathan shook the man's hand, stood, and walked to the doorway.

"Hello, Mr. Goodman. I'm Jonathan Edwards," he said, extending his hand to the rumpled young man. "I'm sorry you had to wait for such a long time. I would have come down earlier to see you had I known you wanted to talk to me. Do you mind if these people with me sit in on our meeting? I'm sure you recognize El Bennet and Xander Darcy. Dave Branard is my manager, and the others are Elizabeth's parents and her friend, Charlotte Lucas. Her father is a pastor, David Bennet." Jonathan gestured toward each of them as he said their names.

"No, I don't mind at all," he replied looking behind him nervously. He looked at Jonathan again. "I'm beginning to think there might be strength in numbers. Please call me Mark."

"My thinking exactly, Mark. These people will be able to help me with whatever your problem might be. I would appreciate their counsel, and I'd rather they would hear your story from you instead of second-hand from me." Jonathan glanced back at the group looking at him expectantly from the table.

"Let's go next door," said the young minister. "Xander, you, Dave, and David can help me set chairs in a circle for everyone. Mark has something he wants to tell us."

The group assembled in the next room, followed by the guardians and warriors, and the men placed the chairs in a circle as Jonathan had requested. Mark sat between Jonathan and Xander, agitated and twisting his hands in his lap.

Mark looked apprehensively around the room, and David spoke to calm him. "Mark, you are safe here with us. You seem to be distressed, and there is a reason you came to Jonathan. Tell us what is wrong. Perhaps we can help you."

The words burst out, flooding from the young man as if a dam had been breached. "I think I must be losing my mind! Last night, I heard about all that went on at your rally, and at the time, I didn't believe it. But something happened to me last night, and I don't know where else to go for help. If you can't help me, I don't know what I'll do." Tears began to flood his cheeks as he struggled to speak. Xander reached over and placed his hand over Mark's hands. He could hear his thoughts, and he knew that Mark had every reason to be terrified.

Gabriel moved to stand at the shoulders of both men, placing one hand on Xander's shoulder and the other on Mark's. Another guardian flew slowly through the walls and stood by Gabriel.

Xander spoke calmly in a reassuring voice, "Mark, nothing you can say will surprise me. I will believe whatever you tell me, and I think that the rest of the group will believe you, too. We can help you. We want to help you." Xander moved his hand to Mark's arm.

Mark gulped and accepted the tissues that Lynne had pulled from her purse and offered him. He wiped his face and took a deep breath.

"I don't know if I dreamed it or not. It seemed so real. I was asleep in my apartment, and there was a hissing sound beside my bed. I looked, and I saw a huge rattlesnake coiled there. His head was as big as my two hands together, and he rose up above me. He must have been as big as an anaconda, but he had rattles. I could hear them. When he looked at me, I couldn't look away from his eyes. I could hear him talking, but his mouth wasn't moving. Did you hear what I just said? I could hear a snake talking. He was evil, and his voice slithered around in my brain. I *am* crazy." He put his head in his hands, and the tears ran through his fingers. Xander laid his hand on the man's knee as Jonathan put his arm around him. Lexus stepped up closely behind his charge.

Dark Spirit, said Michael ominously from behind Elizabeth. The other angels nodded, their faces grave.

"You are not crazy, Mark." Jonathan spoke gently. "What did the snake say?"

Mark put his hands back in his lap, gripping them together so tightly that his knuckles were white.

"It sounds like a story from mythology, or literature. It made me think of *Doctor Faustus* or 'The Devil and Daniel Webster.' I know it sounds like I'm making this up, but I swear that I'm not."

"It's okay, Mark. Nobody thinks you're making anything up. Tell us what the snake said." Jonathan looked at him with trusting, peaceful eyes, and the reporter believed him.

Mark looked behind him, turned back to them, and then whispered, getting louder with each sentence, "He said that if I would give myself to him, he would make me rich and famous and successful. And – he said that if I didn't, I would die. Oh, my God. He wanted my soul! He was the devil, and he wanted my soul!"

Jonathan kept his voice very soft and even. "What was your answer, Mark?"

"I told him – I said I needed to think about it. The snake said he wants my answer tonight. He's coming back, and he'll kill me!" Mark began to sob again.

Xander patted his shoulder. "That was very good, Mark. You gave yourself time to get away. I know this question will sound strange, but you have to answer it before we can help you. Do you want to accept his offer?"

"No! I don't want to give myself to him! My grandmother took me to church with her every Sunday when I was a child. I know what it means to sell your soul to Satan. What good is money or success if I spend eternity in hell? Only God can help me now. I want what you all have. I want Jesus in my life, but I don't know how to ask Him. Can you help me?" The young man was begging, pulling on Xander's arm, and then turning to Jonathan.

"Yes, we can. You came to the perfect place for help, Mark," replied Jonathan, smiling at him. The evangelist led the newsman down the familiar Roman road, turning in his Bible to Romans 3:23 and reading the familiar words. "Mark, this verse says, 'For all have sinned and come short of the glory of God.' Do you believe that you have sinned?"

Mark nodded and answered, "Of course. I have lied, cheated, and done many other things that are wrong."

Jonathan smiled at him and turned to Romans 6:23. "The Bible says here, 'For the wages of sin is death, but the free gift of God is eternal life in Christ

Jesus our Lord.' Do you believe that you have earned spiritual death, eternal separation from God for those sins?"

"That's what my grandmother taught me. I do believe it, though it never bothered me until last night," Mark replied.

Jonathan turned to Romans 10:9-10 and read, "'That if you confess with your mouth Jesus as Lord, and believe in your heart that God raised Him from the dead, you shall be saved; for with the heart man believes, resulting in righteousness, and with the mouth he confesses, resulting in salvation.' Mark, do you believe that God took human form, died on the cross, and rose from the dead in payment for your sins?"

"Yes. I know that He did."

Jonathan flipped back through the pages in his Bible. "Mark, probably the most well-known Scripture verse is John 3:16. Did you learn that verse in your childhood when you went to church with your grandmother?"

Mark nodded mutely.

"Let's all say it together," Jonathan said, looking around the circle. Together, the group recited, "'For God so loved the world, that He gave His only begotten Son, that whoever believes in Him should not perish, but have eternal life.'"

Jonathan continued, "Mark, God wants you to be in His family. He loves you so much that He sacrificed His Son for you. His Son willingly died in your place because He loves you so much. Do you want to accept His free gift of salvation?"

"Yes. What do I have to do?" he asked.

Jonathan laughed gently. "You have already done it. You have believed, accepted, and confessed Him. Would you like to kneel with us and pray, thanking Him for your salvation?"

Mark went immediately to his knees, and everyone in the circle joined him. His guardian, Custodio, took his position behind his charge as he prayed.

Mark looked at Jonathan who knelt beside him. "I don't know how to pray."

"Just talk to God as if He were here, because He is, Mark."

Mark took a deep breath. "Dear God, I believe in You, and I want to be saved. Thank you for sending Your Son to die for me. Thank You for saving me. Amen."

There was complete human silence for a moment as the assembled angels rejoiced, humming and glowing brightly in praise to the Jehovah-Yasha.

Mark looked up at the circle of smiling faces. "Is that all?"

Xander patted his back, chuckling. "Yes, that is all. It is so simple that it confounds the wise. There is nothing you can do to earn salvation. It is a free gift that needs only to be accepted."

Mark smiled, though he was still anxious. "I belong to God now. There is nothing to fear?"

Elizabeth spoke up, remembering the night of terror she spent in her room a couple of years before. "There may be things that frighten you now, but you can always trust God to take care of you, Mark."

They all stood, remaining in the circle.

Xander, hearing his thoughts and knowing that he still fought with his fear, spoke again. "Mark, if you do not want to stay alone at your apartment, you can stay here. There are two double beds in my room, and you are welcomed to use one of them for the rest of the week if you wish to do so. I can promise you that you will be safe. The snake will not come here." His voice was confident and strong.

I wish he would, thought Michael. There was a rumbling chorus of agreement from the warriors present.

Mark eagerly accepted his offer. "Are you serious? You don't know me, but you would let me stay here with you? I'm taking you up on your invitation before you have a chance to change your mind."

The others laughed.

"Xander is nearly always serious, Mark," said Elizabeth, leaning out a little to look past Xander at the newsman.

Xander took her hand, saying, "Elizabeth, would you like to go with Mark and me to his apartment after rehearsal to pick up whatever he will need for the rest of the week?"

Excellent plan, Xander. That would give us four angels: you, Michael, Custodio, and me, should Dark Spirit choose to make an early appearance, thought Gabriel.

I like the idea as well, although I feel certain that he will wait for the cover of darkness before he crawls from whatever rock he is under, said Michael. *I will leave two warriors there tonight, though I am sure that Lucifer's spies will already have reported Mark's decision. I would love to be there when the unholy trinity hears that they lost their spokesman. I suppose they will have to choose another.*

"Of course," answered Elizabeth. "We can go after rehearsal. Mark, do you want to come with us to the arena? You can call your workplace and tell them that you are covering the rally tonight. It would make a good story, don't you think?"

Mark's eyes brightened. "That is a wonderful suggestion, El. The station should have someone covering the conference, and since I broke the big story yesterday, I can join it with everything happening at the rallies. I can do live interviews with the security personnel and some of the people who were there last night. I'll call for a crew to meet me at the arena this evening. By then, I'll have all my background work prepared. The station manager will love it!" He stopped for a moment, thinking. "Is that all right with you, Jonathan?" he asked, looking at the evangelist.

"It's more than all right. I think it's providential. The man that was chosen by Lucifer to be his spokesman will be doing stories for SoulFire Ministries instead. I love the irony. Perhaps we might talk later in the week about the possibility of your joining us for the rest of the summer tour. Don't give me an answer now. Just think about it." Jonathan, as well as everyone else in the room, was smiling broadly.

"I don't have to think about anything," answered Mark quickly. "If you still want me by the end of the week, I'm on your team for as long as you'll have me."

Xander, you have never lived with a human before. This should be interesting, chuckled Michael, as the humans continued to converse, unaware of the angelic conversation taking place around them.

I just hope he does not snore, replied Xander.

I wish for the same thing, said Gabriel. *It is bad enough to listen to you all night. Stereo would be much worse.*

I do not snore! Xander was highly insulted.

He cannot take a joke, commented Michael.

And it is unfortunate, because I am becoming quite adept at humor, added Gabriel, with great gravity.

Michael snorted.

Xander refrained from rolling his eyes only by using all of his self control.

Even the warriors smiled.

The more interesting thing is that Xander talks in his sleep, said Gabriel with total sincerity.

Keeping a shocked expression from crossing his face took a truly Herculean effort on Xander's part. *Please tell me that you are joking. This is not funny.*

It was not intended to be, answered Gabriel.

Why have you not told me before? queried Xander.

We have not mentioned it because we always knew what you were thinking and dreaming. That you said it aloud while sleeping never revealed anything which we did not already know. There was no reason to disturb you with the information, answered Michael.

Gabriel, you must awaken me if I start talking while Mark is not asleep. Xander's thoughts were desperate. *This is too embarrassing. What if I talk of Elizabeth? And I could talk about being an angel. That is even worse. I must never sleep around Elizabeth until she knows.*

You may rely on me, my brother, said Gabriel gravely. *Let us hope that Mark is a sound sleeper. Otherwise, I will be rousing you every half hour.*

I talk that much? Xander was having difficulty hiding his agitation.

It appears that while you are reticent when awake and in control, you become quite garrulous as you relinquish that aspect of your personality in sleep. Most of the time you mutter rather than talk. Do not worry yourself, brother. Custodio will speak peace to Mark's mind, and he will sleep deeply. All will be well. Michael's voice was soothing.

Custodio nodded at Xander, indicating that he understood the responsibilities of his position.

No one was smiling when the conversation ended.

Elizabeth touched Xander's arm, and he startled. She laughed a little at his expression. "My, you have been lost in thought," she whispered as she leaned toward him.

He forced himself to relax and smile, and then lowered his voice to reply into her ear, "I think I am just a little preoccupied with all that has been happening."

"Is everything truly all right, Xander? You really were a million miles away." She betrayed her anxiety with the small wrinkle which appeared between her brows.

Unable to stop himself, he smoothed the spot with his finger, using the same gesture she had employed with him so many times. "As long as you love me, Elizabeth, all is right with me."

She glanced around at the others to make certain that no one was watching them, and then she quietly replied, "If that is your main criterion for happiness, I believe that I can say with confidence that you should be a happy man for a very long time."

His world was back in balance and the skies were blue again.

Chapter 15

> *"And suddenly there came from heaven a noise like a violent, rushing wind, and it filled the whole house where they were sitting. And there appeared to them tongues as of fire distributing themselves, and they rested on each one of them. And they were all filled with the Holy Spirit and began to speak with other tongues, as the Spirit was giving them utterance. Now there were Jews living in Jerusalem, devout men, from every nation under heaven. And when this sound occurred, the multitude came together, and were bewildered, because they were each one hearing them speak in his own language."*
> Acts 2:2-6

Rehearsals for the Tuesday night rally took the entire morning. After practicing all of their own music, Xander and Elizabeth broke for lunch with everyone else, and then spent a couple of hours working with Thorncrown, their opening band, to prepare for the commitment time. Because Thorncrown used only contemporary Christian rock for the pre-rally music, Xander and Elizabeth listened to some of their more reflective numbers and made suggestions as to the selection and style of their choices. The less experienced band was glad to have their input as well as the opportunity to have feedback from two of the best known artists in Christian and classical music circles. The couple had invited several bands to audition during the past spring for the summer tour, and the band members of Thorncrown had been excited to be chosen to travel with SoulFire Ministries.

Mark had phoned his station manager from the arena, explaining his ideas for a series of stories, and had been promised a camera crew for the rally that night. After receiving the "go ahead," the young newsman had stayed busy on his phone, using the contact cards filled out by those who had come forward the previous evening to set up interviews. He had managed to secure both Bobby and Frank, along with several of the EMT personnel and arena security staff. Mark had remained within view of Xander or Jonathan at all times, unwilling to be alone after his horrifying experience the previous night at his apartment. He tried to keep his mind occupied so that he could not dwell on the terror he had felt just a few hours before. Instead, he made a concerted effort to think of his salvation, God's promises, and the protection He had provided through the SoulFire team.

Xander had noticed during rehearsals that both Jonathan and Charlotte, with Lexus and Edward standing behind them and the two warriors back against the wall, had out their laptops, busily working away at a table in one of the private rooms with large windows bordering the arena. Listening to their thoughts, he heard Jonathan developing his messages for the week, adding to the outlines he had already prepared, and Charlotte reading a chapter for an online course she was taking during the summer. Eventually, Jonathan was satisfied with his preparations, and he began to glance at Charlotte occasionally, attempting unsuccessfully to concentrate on checking his e-mail. When she felt his eyes on her, she looked over at him, smiled, and then turned back to her work. Jonathan flushed at being caught watching her and studiously kept his eyes on his computer screen.

Interesting, mused Xander. *Perhaps I was not really the One who thought of bringing Charlotte to travel with us.*

They would make a good couple, thought Gabriel.

Michael nodded his agreement.

Xander had driven his Escalade, bringing Elizabeth, Charlotte, and Mark with him, so that they could take Mark back to his apartment when they broke for the afternoon. Elizabeth's parents had decided to spend the day at the hotel, resting from their long drive. As soon as Xander and Elizabeth were finished practicing with Thorncrown, Xander texted the young man, telling him they were finished rehearsing and could leave anytime. Elizabeth sent a message to Charlotte at the same time.

Within a few minutes, Mark, Jonathan, and Charlotte joined Xander and Elizabeth in front of the stage, surrounded by their guardians and warriors.

"Are you ready to go?" asked Xander, looking at Mark and Charlotte.

Jonathan cleared his throat. "I would be happy to give Charlotte a ride back to the hotel if she still has work to do. You and Elizabeth could take Mark to his apartment."

The man is actually blushing, thought Xander. *He casts out demons without flinching, but he cannot talk to Charlotte directly about her wishes? She causes him to be nervous?*

You have to ask that? questioned Michael, vastly amused.

It was not so long ago that you could hardly form a coherent sentence around Elizabeth, Gabriel interjected.

I still have trouble with that at times, admitted Xander, sheepishly.

Elizabeth looked at her friend quizzically. "Char?"

"I am a little tired. I think I'll take Jonathan up on his kind offer," answered Charlotte, smiling at Jonathan with just a hint of teasing in her brown eyes.

Jonathan's face lit up as he reached for her laptop case. "Wonderful! Let me help you with that."

"I'll see you back at the hotel, roomie," Charlotte said over her shoulder to Elizabeth with a wink as they walked away.

"I'll meet you guys at the car. I forgot to get my laptop." Mark, followed by Custodio, hurried away.

Elizabeth bit her bottom lip in an attempt to stop her smile as she watched Jonathan and Charlotte walk across the arena together, but she could not stop her dimples from making an appearance, and Xander could not stop himself from giving them a quick kiss.

"That's where the angels kissed me, you know," she said looking up at him, her eyes sparkling with good humor.

"I know. Just before they sent you down to me," he replied quietly.

"I thought *you* were the angel." Elizabeth took his hand as they started walking to the exit.

"Well, yes, but I was already here waiting for you. Sending babies was never in my job description." He could not stop himself.

This is a dangerous conversation, thought Michael.

"Angels have job descriptions? What is yours?" she asked.

Be careful, cautioned Gabriel.

"You cannot tell? I am your guardian angel, Elizabeth." She looked up at him and stopped walking, surprised at his serious tone.

The smile left her face as she considered his words. She thought of how he had been there several times recently when she had needed him and of her feelings of complete safety whenever he was with her. *He always thinks of me first.*

"A guardian angel. That fits you perfectly, Xander. You are my own personal guardian angel." She smiled up at him, a beautiful, heartbreaking smile. "Will you always be my protector?"

"Always. You will never be alone, and I will always keep you safe," he said, his voice husky as he pulled her into the relative privacy of the hallway leading to the exits. "I will love you for eternity. God made us for each other and put us together." He pulled her into his arms and kissed her fiercely, as if joining with her could keep all of the demons at bay. Xander wanted her to understand; he wanted her to know what he was. He could not bear the thought that she might think he had deceived her and be angry with him.

The passion of his kiss surprised her. *He is always so gentle with me. Why is he reacting this way? Does he fear losing me?*

Xander, what are you doing? Think. Gabriel's mental nudge was quiet.

Xander broke the kiss, whispering, "I am sorry, Elizabeth. I did not mean to frighten you."

She pulled his face back down to hers and looked into his eyes. "Do not apologize for loving me. I could never be afraid of you, Xander. I love it when you are gentle, but I also like to see this side of you."

Xander smiled at her admission. He drew her closer to him and rested his cheek against her hair. "I look forward to a time when I will not have to be so careful with you. Sometimes, it is…difficult to regulate myself when I kiss you. Do not ever think that my self-control means that I do not want you. However, I respect you in every way, and I would not risk compromising your reputation or damaging your testimony." Xander closed his eyes, and a shadow of pain passed across his face. When he opened his eyes again, his expression was calm. He released her and took her hand.

"Mark is waiting. We had better go," he said with regret.

"I know." She stood on her tiptoes to kiss him quickly before she took his hand. "We don't have much time alone, do we?"

As they began to walk together to the exit, he replied ruefully, "That is probably a good thing."

I agree, thought Michael soberly.

She laughed, and he chuckled with her in spite of himself.

After they were gone, a demonic spy stepped from the shadows and flew through the ceiling.

~~oo~~

After Mark unlocked the door to his apartment, Xander touched his arm. "Let me go in first."

Elizabeth waited in the hallway, behind the men.

Mark stepped back to allow Xander to go past him. The room was empty, but Xander, Gabriel, and Michael could smell the lingering, putrid odor of the demons who had been there recently, as well as Gregory's distinct halfling scent. Custodio noticed the difference and looked at the other angels with a question in his eyes.

Gregory has been here. He is Nephilim. Michael spoke tersely.

Custodio was, of course, aware of Gregory and his origins, but he had never smelled Nephilim before. He wrinkled his nose with distaste at the stench.

Mark and Elizabeth followed Xander into the apartment and stood just inside the door, both of them looking around in amazement. The living room was destroyed, as if a giant child had thrown a temper tantrum and broken everything within reach. The carpet was soaked, and more water seemed to be flooding in by the minute. Mark stared in astonishment as he looked around him at the shambles of everything he owned. As they walked from room to room, they discovered that the destruction and water damage worsened. The kitchen appliances and the bathroom fixtures had been demolished, along with furniture, lighting fixtures, his clothing, the television, and all of his personal belongings. Mark had lost everything from his apartment except the clothes he was wearing. Nothing was salvageable.

I guess it is safe to assume that Gregory, Dark Spirit, and Lucifer know that Mark is with us now. Michael's remark was curt. *They must have done this while he was at the hotel or the arena this morning.*

I am just glad that he was not here when they came. They do not take rejection well, stated Gabriel.

Elizabeth touched Mark's arm. "Mark, you should call your landlord or apartment manager. They need to come see this and call the police."

Mark nodded numbly, taking out his cell phone and calling the manager. "My apartment has been vandalized and is flooded. Could you call the police and come immediately?" After he finished his call, he looked at Xander. "Did that snake have anything to do with this? Could this have been the work of the devil?"

"Yes, demons have been here. I can sense it," Xander answered. "Mark, you belong to God now. Satan can destroy your belongings, but God is sovereign. He will protect you."

Mark nodded. He so much wanted to believe what Xander said.

After the manager turned off the water to the apartment, the next two hours were spent filing a police report and cataloguing the damage. There were no fingerprints except for Mark's in the apartment, and there was no evidence indicating a forced entry. Fortunately, Mark had renter's insurance and could recoup most of his losses. He also remembered that he had left some of his clothing at his parent's house a short distance away.

Mark told the apartment manager that he no longer felt safe there and wanted to break the lease. Under the circumstances, the manager agreed, though he refused to return Mark's deposit. Too tired and dispirited to argue with the man, Mark decided to shut the door on his past life in Atlanta, and he left with Xander and Elizabeth. He had called his mother while the police were dusting for prints in his apartment to tell her about the break-in, and she had offered to gather his clothes together for him and have them ready for him to pick up on the way back to the hotel. He had gratefully accepted her offer, and Xander and Elizabeth had agreed to stop by his mother's house with him. Though the clothes were not his best, at least he would have a few things to wear until he could find the time to go shopping.

~~oo~~

Xander could sense the electricity in the air as he and Elizabeth, accompanied by Gabriel and Michael, arrived at the arena that night. Her parents had ridden with them and followed an usher to the seating reserved for the counselors. The space around that section was thick with guardians and warriors, including Niall and Roark.

Thorncrown was beginning their hour-long set, and the people were already starting to fill the arena. Listening to the thoughts of those in the crowd, Xander detected several ethnic groups – Chinese, Korean, and Hispanic in large numbers among them.

After they had arrived back at the hotel earlier, Mark had moved his pitifully few articles of clothing into the room he was sharing with Xander, showered, and dressed in the best that he had. When he had come out of the bathroom looking unhappy, Xander would have loaned him some of his clothes, but he knew that they were all much too big for the six-foot tall newsman.

Knowing that Mark would be on-camera and seeing his dilemma, Xander had called Dave Branard, who was about Mark's size, and Dave had graciously offered the use of his wardrobe. Mark had gratefully accepted at once and had changed clothes before he caught a ride to the arena with Jonathan, Charlotte, and Dave, their guardians flying above the van. He had driven his own car to the hotel that morning to see the SoulFire team; therefore, his Toyota Rav4 had not been at his apartment when it had been vandalized. However, he still preferred to ride with Jonathan or Xander for the moment. He did not feel safe when he was alone, and though he hated that feeling, he had not yet been able to overcome it.

The camera crew met Mark at the arena, and they began to work immediately. Bobby and Frank were already there, and he began his interviews with them, first separately and then together, outside of the main arena in the hallway area which circled the building. He worked in a roped-off area to reduce the noise level and used the people streaming in and the workers at the tables as a backdrop. His interview technique was friendly and low-key, and the men opened up to him, following the lead of his pre-planned questions. Mark was very good at his job, and his professionalism propelled him past the anguish of the past twenty-four hours. His excitement rose as he continued to work, talking with the security personnel and EMT's he had lined up. He also made impromptu stops at the ministry tables and video areas which were showing the different work tracks of the camp teens in Atlanta, as well as footage from the rally held the previous night. His film was a collage of color and activity, showing people joyously sharing their faith in many different ways.

Mark had already arranged interviews with Jonathan, Elizabeth, and Xander for the following day. Updates would be running all week on WAGA; he would do his on-camera spot with Jonathan at the hotel after breakfast, and then spend hours in the editing room while the couple rehearsed in the morning. He hoped that he could catch Xander and Elizabeth while they broke for lunch, and he knew he had to shop for clothes after that. He would not take advantage of Dave's generosity any longer than was absolutely necessary. Mark was a handsome twenty-five year old blue-eyed blond whose good looks had always been an advantage in his work; he was aware that a poor appearance on his part would detract from the story, and he was determined that his SoulFire reports would be his best work. He knew that Xander and Jonathan could not babysit him forever; if he had to shop alone, he would do so. Mark had always been confident in his ability to take care of himself. He did not like to feel incapable of defending himself or helplessly dependent on others for protection.

Before coming to the arena, Xander and Elizabeth had decided to try to encourage Mark. Together they had chosen Scriptures and written them on a card which Xander then had given him as they all left the hotel. Xander had chosen II Samuel 22:2-3, "The Lord is my rock and my fortress and my deliverer; my God my rock, in whom I take refuge; my shield and the horn of my salvation, my stronghold and my refuge; my savior, Thou dost save me from violence." On the opposite side of the card, Elizabeth had written Psalm 27:1-3, "The Lord is my light and my salvation; whom shall I fear? The Lord is the defense of my life; whom shall I dread? When evildoers came upon me to devour my flesh, my adversaries and my enemies, they stumbled and fell. Though a host encamp against me, my heart will not fear; though war arise against me, in spite of this I shall be confident." Mark kept the card in his pants pocket, pulling it out from time to time and repeating the verses until he had nearly memorized them. He had also downloaded a complete Bible onto his iPhone that afternoon, and he read at every opportunity. He knew instinctively that his fear could be conquered only with help from God; he had to trust in God's protection.

~~oo~~

The service had been truly amazing. From the time Thorncrown had started the pre-service music, the packed house had been completely engaged. They had come to their feet as Xander and Elizabeth played and sang the opening song and remained standing throughout their music. As the house lights dimmed for the final song before the message, the band left the stage, leaving the couple in a spotlight at the front center stage, close enough to touch the people in the front row. They both sat on stools, Michael and Gabriel behind them, each playing a guitar plaintively enough to quiet the crowd of 22,000 people, weaving countermelodies and harmonies with the instruments. Before they began to sing the duet that Elizabeth had written during those hours that she had prayed all night for Atlanta, she spoke to the people from her heart, sharing with them how God had given her the song telling of His great love for the people of that city. The words of the song were based on Zechariah 13:9, "And I will bring the third part through the fire, refine them as silver is refined, and test them as gold is tested. They will call on My name, and I will answer them; I will say, 'They are My people,' and they will say 'The Lord is my God.'"

As she and Xander continued to play softly, Elizabeth looked over the audience and talked to them in a clear voice which was full of emotion. "God did not send the fire that destroyed so many homes and businesses, and even took lives Sunday night, but He used it to draw many of you to Himself. As John the Baptist said in Matthew 3:11, 'As for me, I baptize you in water for repentance, but He who is coming after me is mightier than I, and I am not even fit to remove His sandals; He Himself will baptize you with the Holy Spirit and with fire.' Satan sought to destroy you with fire, but God used it to baptize you with the Holy Spirit. God never sends us anything evil, but He always uses that evil for our good when we allow it. Many of you would never have turned to God had Satan not attacked you. He was defeated with his own weapon."

When she was finished speaking, she nodded at Xander and they began to sing "They Are My People" together. The simple song was even more powerful because of its simplicity. By the end of their duet, when Elizabeth would sing, "They are my people," the crowd would join Xander in answering, "The Lord is my God." In the stillness of the moment, a sound like a mighty wind filled the building as hundreds of six-winged angels flew in through the ceiling and the walls, and the light around Elizabeth and Xander turned red and danced like fire. The couple remained in the center, their faces bathed in pure white, brilliant light, radiating the joy of the Lord, singing the words over and over while the seraphim spun and twirled like the spokes on hundreds of wheels, flooding the arena with every color of the rainbow, chasing every shadow into oblivion. People raised their hands in worship alongside thousands of guardians and warriors who lifted their faces toward heaven, humming to Elohim.

The puzzled light technicians could no more control the light than they could make the sun rise or the waves of the ocean still. One by one, they stood with the people and the angels as the light continued to shimmer, settling first in one place and then in another.

When Xander and Elizabeth stopped singing, the light faded and the technicians scrambled to make certain that the stage remained properly lit. The angels who had entered the arena during the song hovered in the air above the people, knowing that the full glory of their Master had not yet been displayed. They waited in silence and stillness.

Jonathan had watched from the wings, fully aware that what he was witnessing had not been created by man. It reminded him of what had happened at Elizabeth's concert in Toronto during "The Hallelujah Chorus." His spirit told him what his mind did not comprehend; he was seeing glimmers of angels. He shivered and shook himself before he strode onto the stage, Bible in hand, ready to speak from I Kings 18, a chapter detailing the battle of the prophet Elijah with the prophets of Baal on Mount Carmel. Lexus followed and remained behind him.

Xander and Elizabeth left the stage in the opposite direction of Jonathan's entrance as stagehands removed their stools and placed Jonathan's plexiglass podium where he had told them earlier that he wanted it. They, along with Michael and Gabriel, sat in the wings sipping water and listening to Jonathan.

His message was riveting, detailing how a single prophet of God, Elijah, had withstood 450 prophets of Baal, challenging the false prophets of Jezebel to pray for Baal to send fire to devour a sacrifice. Elijah had mocked them as they had leaped around for hours, cutting themselves until the blood gushed from their wounds, loudly calling on their god, yet no one answered. He told how Elijah had then requested that his sacrifice be doused with water though it was a time of drought, prayed, and "then the fire of God fell, and consumed the burnt offering and the word and the stones and the dust, and licked up the water that was in the trenches." The people who had been watching all day had fallen on their faces, declaring that "The Lord, He is God." Afterward, they had slain Baal's prophets and God had sent rain in abundance in answer to Elijah's prayer.

After that great display of God's power, Elijah had run, frightened by the threats of Jezebel, King Ahab's wife, who sought to slay him because her prophets had been killed. He had felt sorry for himself, even as God had sent an angel to care for him. Elijah had complained loudly, outlining all that he had done for God, finishing his tale of woe with, "And I alone am left; and they seek my life, to take it away." And God had answered, "'Go forth, and stand on the mountain before the Lord.' And behold, the Lord was passing by! And a great and strong wind was rending the mountains and breaking in pieces the rocks before the Lord; but the Lord was not in the wind. And after the wind an earthquake, but the Lord was not in the earthquake. And after the earthquake a fire, but the Lord was not in the fire; and after the fire a sound of a gentle blowing. And it came about when Elijah heard it, that he wrapped his face in his mantle, and went out and stood in the entrance of the cave. And behold, a voice came to him and said, 'What are you doing here, Elijah?'"

Jonathan continued to speak, "Elijah had seen all the pageantry of God's might shown through creation, his prayers had been answered miraculously, God had sent an angel to minister to him, and still he whined that he had done so much for God, and he was the only one left who served him. God finally answered, 'Yet I will leave seven thousand in Israel, all the knees that have not bowed to Baal and every mouth that has not kissed him.'

"Do you ever think that you are alone? No one else around you at school or at work or in your family serves God – except for you? You are wrong if you think that. God always preserves a remnant. Satan will try and try until time ends, but he will never win; he will never defeat God. He did not defeat God Sunday night in Atlanta; he did not win last night here in the rally; he will never win this war. If you are not a child of God, there is a battle being fought for your soul. It is your choice. Who will you choose? Satan, who hates you and will ultimately be defeated, or Jehovah God, Who loves you and cannot lose?"

As Jonathan prayed, Thorncrown came onstage and began playing softly behind him. He then lifted his head and asked the hundreds of counselors to come forward. While they formed a line on the floor in front of the stage, Jonathan invited the people to come if they wanted to make a decision or ask for prayer. The counselors stood several lines deep, and Charlotte, Elizabeth, and Xander were with Jonathan at the back of them, close to the stage. As the people streamed to the front, counselors met them and led them to an area that had been designated earlier.

Finally, a Korean woman came with her elderly mother and stopped in front of Charlotte, talking to Charlotte in her native tongue. Charlotte looked at Elizabeth beside her, remembering the day at Converse when Elizabeth had spoken to the Indian students in Hindi.

"El, can you tell me what this lady is saying?" asked Charlotte, touching Elizabeth on the arm.

"Yes, she says that she and her mother want to know about God," Elizabeth answered, perplexed that Charlotte could not understand her.

Jonathan, on the other side of Charlotte, had long suspected that Elizabeth had the gift of tongues, but he had not seen it manifested before. He had heard rumors, but he had not witnessed it himself. He smiled at Elizabeth. "She is speaking Korean, and not only can you understand her, but also you are understood by her. Go with them and talk to them, El. God is using you in a mighty way."

Elizabeth hesitated a moment to take in what Jonathan had said, and then she took the Korean woman's hand, turning to lead her and her mother to the counseling area. As they were walking away, a Chinese boy came to Xander, and began to speak with him. Charlotte heard Xander answer the boy in his own language.

"Xander, do you speak Chinese?" Charlotte was amazed, as was Jonathan.

Xander considered for a moment before answering, "Yes. I am able to speak any language that I try. I am something of a linguist. Languages are easy for me to learn. However, I do not have the gift of tongues that was given to Elizabeth by God. I actually learn the different languages and speak them. With her, everyone understands what she says at the same time, no matter what language they speak. She also understands everyone. If five people speaking different languages were speaking to her at the same time, she would understand them all."

Jonathan stared at him. "You already knew this?"

Xander replied, "I have known it for quite a while now."

"Why didn't you tell us?" asked Charlotte.

"I knew that God would reveal it when He was ready to do so."

"And why didn't you tell us that you could speak multitudes of languages?" queried Jonathan.

"I saw no need to do so. I knew that God would use me if He needed me. I have been waiting for Him to send someone to me who required me to use my talent. We do not want to be a sideshow that people attend for entertainment." Xander took the boy by the hand and walked with him toward the counseling area. Gabriel walked by his side. Xander saw Elizabeth and wondered if she had been listening. Her thoughts had been quiet. From beside her, Michael looked at Xander and lifted an eyebrow.

Elizabeth, who had stopped walking when she heard Xander speak to the boy in Chinese, had indeed overheard the entire exchange. She had asked the lady to wait a moment while she listened, and she was astounded. Xander had known about her gift before she had, and he possessed a monumental talent as well. The implications for their ministry were staggering. After a moment, she recovered and smiled at the lady, asking her to continue walking with her to a place where they could talk.

He and I will discuss this later, Elizabeth thought.

Reading her mind, Xander wondered, *Will she wonder what else I have kept from her?*

Gabriel held his peace as did Michael. They had no answers for him.

The angels who had awaited the revelation of Elizabeth's gift and Xander's talent rejoiced as the harvest of more than a thousand souls was gathered for Jehovah-Yasha that night. The holy ones radiated warm, glowing light, humming as they danced, joyous in the knowledge that the combined gifts and talents of the couple, along with those of Jonathan Edwards, would lead to the gathering of masses of souls for His kingdom. All of heaven then knew that the Third Great Awakening would bring more people to their Master than the first two combined.

After the final person had accepted his place in the family of God in the arena that evening, the seraphim positioned their wings for rapid flight and soared through the roof of the building, back to the throne room of Elohim, to offer praise and worship to the Creator of All Things.

Chapter 16

"If I speak with the tongues of men and of angels, but do not have love, I have become a noisy gong or a clanging cymbal. And if I have the gift of prophecy, and know all mysteries and all knowledge; and if I have all faith, so as to remove mountains, but do not have love, I am nothing."
I Corinthians 13:1-2

Just as Xander had suspected she would, Elizabeth was contemplating the questions she wished to ask him while they rode back to the hotel from the rally that evening. David and Lynne Bennet had ridden with them to the arena, and, after the rally had ended, Xander had made certain to invite them to ride back to their lodgings with them, pre-empting her inquisition and allowing him time to hear her thoughts and think of appropriate answers. She was not at all fooled by the subterfuge, though she had no way of knowing the full extent of it. *Maybe if she hears the facts a few at a time, she will not be as hurt when she knows it all,* he thought.

Perhaps, but you are playing a dangerous game, cautioned Gabriel, flying above the SUV with Michael, Roark, Niall, and four warriors.

David leaned forward in his seat to speak to Xander. "I've never been a part of anything like that before. It was absolutely amazing! How many people came forward?"

"There will be no final number until the decision cards are counted, but I would estimate that there were over one thousand. It was exciting, was it not?" Xander replied.

"Yes, simply unbelievable. I'm thankful that we came. I wish we could travel with SoulFire all summer, but someone has to keep the home fires burning, no pun intended," said David, looking out his window at the city flashing by. *So many people who need the Lord, rushing around, but missing the most important thing in life. The big cities never sleep.*

"Mr. and Mrs. Bennet, are you hungry? Would you like to stop for dessert?" Xander asked, looking in the rearview mirror. *If we are late enough getting back, perhaps she will forget her questions for now.*

You risk angering her by putting her off, warned Michael.

Elizabeth looked at him sharply. *Does he think I will forget if he avoids being alone with me long enough? Surely he knows me better than that.*

Xander bit his lip. Michael was beginning to know her very well indeed.

David spoke. "I don't want anything. How about you, Lynne?"

"All I want is to put on my pajamas and go to bed. Tonight was very exciting, and tomorrow is sure to be just as overwhelming. I'm exhausted," Lynne replied.

"Elizabeth?" asked Xander, glancing at her.

"I've been looking forward to another training session all day, Xander. I hope you aren't going to disappoint me by calling it off." She met his eyes with a clear challenge in her look.

No way out of that one, Xander, thought Niall.

Xander reached for her hand, and she met him halfway. They rested their clasped hands on the console between them.

"I would never willingly do anything to make you unhappy, Elizabeth. You know that." His voice was gentle and sincere.

"Training session? That's what you two were doing last night just before we arrived, right?" asked David.

"Yes, Dad. Xander is teaching me self-defense, and he's a very good instructor. Did you know he's something of a martial arts expert?" Elizabeth looked between the bucket seats at her father.

"Really? I can't say that I'm surprised. He seems to be a man of many talents and abilities. I have a feeling that we don't know the half of the matter," replied David with a smile.

I would put that fraction a little higher, thought Niall.

"I think that it's an excellent idea, Xander. Is there any chance that we might be able to observe?" Lynne, her previous fatigue forgotten, was frankly curious about the young man. Each time she found out something else about him, she realized that there were many more sides to him than any of them had suspected.

"I would not mind at all," replied Xander. *In fact, I would welcome you and Mr. Bennet.*

Elizabeth spoke quickly. "We just started last night, Mom. Could we give you a demonstration later in the week? All I know how to do right now are stances."

There is nothing slow about Elizabeth. I hope you are ready for this. Michael's voice was not pleased. *You should never have said that you already knew she was gifted with tongues. Now she wants to know how you knew.*

I am tired of hiding things from her, Michael. I love her, and I do not wish to have secrets from her. Xander was firm. *A good relationship must be built on honesty and trust. I may not be looking forward to answering her questions, but I am confident that this is the correct course of action.*

You said you would wait until the summer is over before you tell her what you are, Gabriel reminded him. *That was a good decision. If she becomes upset with you, it could negatively impact this ministry.*

Trust me? Please? I will be careful. I will not tell her everything now, but I will not avoid answering what she asks. An oppressive silence hung above the vehicle; Xander could feel the disapproval of his brothers, and it hurt him. *Have I not proven that I have good judgment? What have I done to deserve your censure?*

Niall spoke quietly. *You have always done what pleases our Master, Xander, and you have done nothing to give anyone just cause to doubt you.*

"I suppose we can rest tonight and watch you train when you are more comfortable with the idea, El," answered Lynne.

"Thanks, Mom," Elizabeth replied, turning to smile at her mother between the seats. "How is Janna doing? I've been talking to her on the phone every few days, and she says she's fine, but you know she always says that. Is she taking good care of herself and my nephew?"

"I talked to her this morning, and she's doing really well, though she misses seeing her feet. She said to tell you she's sorry she wasn't there to see you off Sunday," said Lynne, launching into a favorite subject of hers, her daughter and her soon-to-be born grandson. "She and Chance are getting the nursery ready in boy colors. They haven't picked out a name yet."

Lynne and Elizabeth kept the conversation going until Xander pulled up in front of the hotel. Mother and daughter got out and went inside to wait in the lobby while David rode with Xander to park the car. Niall, Michael, and two warriors stayed with the ladies.

As the men walked back to the hotel entrance, trailed by Gabriel, Roark and two warriors, David looked over at Xander. "You know, trying to avoid whatever it is you don't want to talk about won't work with El."

Xander glanced at the older man in surprise, and then he looked down at the pavement. "It was that obvious?"

David chuckled. "I know El like the back of my hand. She's like a dog with a bone if you try to distract her. Just tell her what she wants to know and get it over with. It can't be that bad, can it?"

"That depends on your point of view, I suppose. I have not done anything wrong, and I do not wish to keep secrets from her; it is only that the timing is not good. There are things she does not know about my background, and I do not want to upset her during our work with SoulFire this summer." Xander's voice was low and strained.

"Do you love her?" asked David.

Xander looked at the man he hoped would be his father-in-law some day. "With all that I am."

"Then trust her. She may surprise you."

"She always does," said Xander.

David put his hand on Xander's shoulder. "I'll be praying for you."

Xander sighed. "I appreciate that."

The automatic doors opened, and the men walked through together. David patted Xander's shoulder in a fatherly manner, and then dropped his hand to his side.

Lynne stood in the lobby with Niall and the warriors. "Xander, El said to tell you that she's gone upstairs to change clothes. She'll be ready whenever you are."

"I must go then. It is rude to keep a lady waiting," Xander replied, smiling. He squared his shoulders and headed for the elevator. Behind him, Lynne raised an eyebrow as she looked at David. He shrugged, and together they followed Xander.

~~oo~~

Xander, dressed in his usual workout clothes, waited outside Elizabeth's door. He hesitated for a moment, and then knocked. She opened the door quickly, as if she had been waiting for him.

"My, my. So serious," she said, pulling his head down for a quick kiss.

Xander wanted more than a peck on the lips and placed his hands on either side of her face, holding her for a deeper kiss, trying to convey his love for her, hoping that she would still have the same feelings for him when an hour had passed. When he finished, he kept his face close to hers, touching her forehead with his.

Please, Father, help her to understand. Help her to forgive me, he pleaded. *I cannot bear to lose her now. Please lead my mind, guide my words, and put a guard upon my mouth.*

Michael and Gabriel knew better than to make any comments.

She drew back a few inches and looked up into his face. "Are you ready to teach me some more?"

"Are you ready to learn?" he asked.

"Of course."

He took her hand and led her to the elevator. He pushed the button for the lobby, and then put his arms around her, clasping her to his chest. She heard the hammering of his heart through his tank top.

Elizabeth pushed away from him just far enough to look up into his face. "Xander, this has gone on long enough. Just tell me how you knew I had the gift of tongues. That's all I want to know. Surely the answer isn't worth all this angst you're suffering."

Xander swallowed the lump that had formed in his throat, and the doors of the elevator opened on the lobby floor.

"Come. I do not wish to talk in this public area." He reached for her hand and led her down the hall to the same room they had used the previous night. Xander opened the door and held it for her without releasing her hand. After he had closed it, they went to the center of the room. She sat cross-legged on the floor, pulling him down to sit facing her. Michael and Gabriel stood against the wall, their expressions carefully neutral.

"Okay. Just spit it out. Remember that I love you." Her smile was encouraging.

He looked into her eyes, begging her to understand.

"Elizabeth, you already know that I am different from other people."

"Yes, you are exceptionally talented in music, have prayed and healed dying people through the power of the Holy Spirit, have the strength of at least five men, are extremely tall, have devastatingly good looks, and are the godliest man I know. You surprise me all the time with your hidden abilities – like your being a martial arts pro and speaking who knows how many languages. I know that you aren't like everyone else. I know how that feels, too, Xander. I have always been different from the other people around me. Now I find that I am stranger than even I knew."

She took both of his large hands into hers and held them on her crossed legs.

"If we are comparing abnormalities, we can stop now. I definitely win this category." Xander attempted a smile.

She waited, holding his eyes with hers so that he could not look away.

"Elizabeth, no one else can know this." She nodded her agreement. He took a deep breath and released it. "I can read the minds of nearly everyone around me. I have 'heard' people around you thinking in foreign languages, and I 'heard' you understand them in your mind. When you sing in other languages, everyone 'hears' you in their own tongue. Charlotte has thought of the incident at Converse around me. I know the Indian students understood you, and you understood them." Xander spoke softly and watched her, his eyes riveted to her face, trying to gauge her response past her jumbled thoughts.

Elizabeth was stunned speechless. *I don't know what I expected, but it certainly wasn't this.* She drew her eyebrows together and closed her eyes, breathing deeply as she tried to absorb what he had said. Images began to race through her mind, and thoughts flooded her consciousness. She had wished for Char to come, and the very next day she had arrived. There had been times that he had answered questions before she had asked them. He always seemed to know when she was afraid, or sad, or happy. He responded to situations so quickly, before anyone else even had time to think about what to do. She knew that he was telling the truth.

She opened her eyes to find his gaze fixed intently on her.

"Are you reading my mind now?" she asked.

"I cannot help it, Elizabeth. I am not trying to do so. I would stop if I could." His voice was gentle, pleading.

No, you would not. Gabriel spoke softly. *If you are going to tell her these things, be completely honest.*

You are right, thought Xander.

"Would you really?" she demanded, eyes blazing. "Because I know that I would read your mind if I could."

"I suppose to be completely honest, I should say that I want to make you happy. If my ability makes you unhappy, I hope that I would want to stop. But, to tell the absolute truth, most of the time I am glad that I can hear your thoughts."

Elizabeth immediately heard the exception in his statement. "Most of the time?"

He looked away, uncomfortable. "I have heard you admire Gregory's looks, and I was jealous. Also, there have been a few times that you believed him instead of me."

She reached for his chin and turned his face back toward her. "That's all?"

"You met me on a plane in January. Apart from your amusement at my clumsy attempts at conversation on that flight, that is all you have thought since then that made me wish I could not hear you. Elizabeth, you have a kind, beautiful, godly mind. I hear so many terrible things in the minds of other people that it is a pleasure to listen to you." His eyes were sincere. She dropped her hand back onto her legs, covering his hands.

"You said that you can hear the minds of 'nearly' everyone around you. Who can't you hear?" she asked.

"I cannot hear Gregory, Cassandra, and a few others."

"Why not?" She was curious.

"My answer will make you angry," Xander said in a somber tone.

"Just tell me. You'll know if I'm angry." Her voiced was edged with sarcasm, and he winced at her meaning.

"My gift is from God. The farther away from God someone is, the harder it is for me to read their minds. When they are completely turned against God and given over to Satan with no hope of redemption, it is very difficult and sometimes impossible to 'hear' their thoughts."

He thinks Gregory and Cassandra are evil past any chance of salvation, she thought.

"Yes, I do," he answered.

"Does Gregory have the same ability that you have? Can he read my mind?" she asked, a little frightened.

"No, Elizabeth. God has not given Gregory that ability. He would abuse it."

"That's probably true." She was quiet a moment. "Can you hear me all the time?" Her mind was whirring again, thinking of her reactions to his kisses and his body. He could hear her trying to stop her thoughts.

"My gift is limited by distance. If you are more than a few miles away, I cannot hear you." Xander's voice was low and quiet.

"This is too much to process. You know what I think when we're kissing, when I see you, when you touch me? You cannot imagine how I feel," she said blushing, remembering her reaction to him the night before when she had first seen him in his workout clothes. "What about when I am sleeping?"

"Most of that time I am sleeping, too. However, if I am awake and close by, I can 'see' your dreams. They are like your thoughts." He looked at the floor. "I am sorry you are embarrassed. You do not understand the joy you give me." He raised his face to hers and looked earnestly into her eyes. "To see myself in your mind and to know that you love me – it humbles me. I try to deserve your love, and it makes me a better man."

"You know, Xander, all of that is easy for you to say. I can't read *your* mind. I can never hide anything from you, but you can choose to tell me what you wish for me to know." She frowned.

"If I could give you that gift, I would. I have never lied to you, though I have not said everything I was thinking from time to time. If you will allow me, I will point out one advantage to my 'freak' gift," he said, looking at her with a small smile.

"Please do. I could use a little cheering up about now." She lifted her chin and tilted her head, still unsmiling.

"From now on, since you know that I can 'hear' you, if there is something you want to tell me that you do not want others to hear, you can just think it. You now know that you do not have to wait for privacy. I will find a way to respond to you." He smiled at her again, more broadly.

She considered his words. "That's true." Her expression became mischievous as she said, "I don't even have to ever say 'I love you' again or call your name. I can just think it."

Xander offered a silent prayer of thanksgiving. *Thank you, Lord. She has accepted it, though she did not like it.*

He took her hands in his and stood, pulling her up with him. "No, love. That will not do. Hearing you think those words is wonderful, but nothing compares to hearing you say them aloud."

"You are fond of telling me that I have to give something to get what I want. Now the situation is reversed. If you want to hear me say certain things, you will have to promise to tell me what you are thinking," she said adamantly. "After all, I can't read your mind. Fair is fair."

"Be reasonable, Elizabeth. I cannot tell you everything I am thinking. I would be talking nonstop, and most of what I would say would be very banal. I will promise to tell you what I am thinking when it concerns you, and if we are in private. Furthermore, I will tell you what I am thinking whenever you ask me. I cannot do more than that without causing extreme embarrassment to both of us as well as to those around us. Agreed?" His smile reached his eyes.

"I suppose so," she said grudgingly. "You know, we are sort of perfect for each other. We're both freaks."

Xander laughed aloud. "I love the way your mind works. Now let us begin to train your body to be just as agile." He kissed her nose, becoming playful. His face grew somber again as another thought passed through his mind. *I have not finished, have I, Father? Please help me.*

"There is one more thing about my ability," he said, wishing that he did not have to tell her, but knowing that if he did not, she would throw it back at him later.

"There's more?" She was incredulous.

"Yes. Remember when I said that I would find a way to respond to you if you 'thought' something to me?" Xander asked, holding both of her shoulders and looking directly into her eyes.

"Yes. I'm guessing this has to do with the way you would respond. Am I right?" she asked, her eyes wide.

"You are correct, as usual. Elizabeth, not only can I hear what you are thinking, but I can speak into your mind, and you can hear me." He waited for the inevitable question.

After a short silence, she asked, "Have you ever done that before?"

"Yes. I have spoken comfort and peace to you at times when you were upset. I also tried to get you not to get into the car with Gregory that day you rode with him." He knew what she would say next.

"You weren't there that day. How do you know about that?" Her face betrayed her suspicion. "Have you been watching me?"

"Sometimes I miss you, and I watch you from places where you cannot see me. I worry about you, too, and I want to know that you are well. I guess that makes me a crazed stalker." He lowered his head. When the silence became oppressive, he looked at her from under his lashes. "Elizabeth, please say something."

Why don't you just read my mind, Xander? I seem to have no rights to my own personal thoughts or space.

That is not true. I try to stay away from you, and I have struggled against invading your privacy.

Elizabeth suddenly pulled her hands from his and turned her back, putting her face in her hands. "I recognize your voice! I have heard that voice in my head! It *was* you telling me not to go with Gregory that day." She lifted her head and dropped her hands to her sides. "And I have heard you telling me that everything would be all right, but there is another voice that I hear more than yours."

Xander was grateful that she had not remembered his voice from her childhood. *Could my voice sound a little different in her mind since the Almighty gave me a dual nature? It must be so. However, she did not recognize Michael's voice when she met him. It could be that our angelic voices do not sound the same in human minds as they do aloud. Both things could be true. My Father must have realized that this time would come. He must have prepared for it. Thank you, Abba, Father.*

He tentatively placed his hands on her shoulders, ready for her to pull away again. "God speaks to us in many ways, Elizabeth. There are voices in my head as well." *I expect them to erupt any time now to tell me how badly I am handling this.*

The silence from the wall was telling.

Xander waited in agony for her to speak. He could hear her analyzing all that he had said. Finally, she faced him and spoke with resignation.

"I suppose that the worst thing of which I can accuse you is loving me too much." She was not smiling, but she was at least looking at him without disgust.

"Thank you for being gracious, Elizabeth. You are probably the only woman in the world who would handle this information with such kindness. I should be silent now before I begin to babble in gratitude." Xander nervously raked his hand through his hair.

"Xander, I cannot bear knowing that you are watching me when I cannot see you. You must promise me not to do that anymore," she said firmly.

I cannot be around her in angelic form again until she knows everything, he thought. *So be it.*

"Elizabeth, you could ask me for anything right now, and I would agree to it if you would just forgive me and smile at me again." He reached for her hands, imploring her with his eyes.

After a moment's hesitation, she put her hands in his, though she did not smile.

"I do forgive you, but you know this isn't over. I will have more questions," she said, arching a brow.

"I know, love. You have always been inquisitive, and this revelation is too much for your curious mind to lay to rest in such a short time. I will expect more questions," he answered, kissing her cheek lightly. She allowed his kiss, and he could feel the tension begin to leave her body.

"Shall we begin our training now?" he asked, trying not to sound giddy in his relief.

"You will hear my questions before I ask them," she stated with a little resentment. "Your answers will be ready. This is all so unfair." Her pout was adorable.

Xander chuckled. "That is true, but I cannot help it." His expression became serious. "Your consolation will have to be that you have the ability to surprise me as no one else ever has, and my happiness rests with your approval. I have known every time you doubted me and believed Gregory, and it has cut me to the heart. This gift is a double-edged sword."

His extreme vulnerability displayed before her so openly touched her deeply, and she could not maintain any sort of anger toward him.

Elizabeth took a deep breath and exhaled slowly, releasing her discontent as she breathed out. "I think an hour of hard training will help to settle my mind before I try to sleep. Let's get to work. I don't want to think about this anymore now. Show no mercy."

"I am your servant," Xander said, bowing.

That went amazingly well, thought Gabriel.

True. It is fortunate, although very sad, that Elizabeth would understand the concept of being a 'freak,' answered Michael.

For the next hour, Xander reviewed stances with Elizabeth, and then advanced to several ways to block an attack or break a hold. As he played the part of the attacker, he imagined himself to be Gregory, devious and cunning in his methods.

It was a very intense session.

Chapter 17

"He will cover you with His pinions, and under His wings you may seek refuge; His faithfulness is a shield and bulwark. You will not be afraid of the terror by night, or of the arrow that flies by day; of the pestilence that stalks in darkness, or of the destruction that lays waste at noon."
Psalm 91:4-6

Lucifer's eyes narrowed as he fixed a blazing glare on his son. "Tell me again how we lost the stronghold of Atlanta. Whose brilliant idea was it to burn the city?" His voice was icy.

"Well, it was not mine. You were the first to bring up flames, if I remember correctly." Gregory stood his ground, facing his father with his fists clenched by his side, eyes glowing with rage.

"You were the one on the roof, throwing fireballs and losing your entire force of guards to Michael and Xander as you ran from them. It was humiliating. Our enemies are laughing at us because of you."

Lucifer spat the words, turning abruptly on his heel to pace the length of Gregory's living room in Spartanburg.

"At least I was there," muttered Gregory darkly, scowling at his father's back.

Lucifer whipped his head around and roared, "What did you say?" He strode across the room and grabbed Gregory roughly by his shoulders. The Dark Prince brought his hands together and raised his arms with lightning speed, breaking his father's hold on him. He retained just enough coherent thought to keep silent.

Dark Spirit slithered between them. *Enough!* he thought into their minds as he rose up and turned his cold gaze from one to the other. *Fighting among ourselves causes us to lose sight of our goals. Instead of casting blame on one other for this fiasco, we should be coming up with a workable plan. Obviously, burning Atlanta brought people together to help each other, and their fear sent them running to those meetings where they became believers. Attacking the cities will not work. The church always grows during times of persecution.*

The Dark Lord looked into the serpent's eyes speculatively. "I sense that you have a better idea. Share it with us."

Dark Spirit's forked tongue darted out several times, and his eyes sparkled, as hard and cold as diamonds. He hissed, *Rather than attack the cities, we should divide and conquer the SoulFire team itself. My spies tell me that Elizabeth and Xander grow more involved with one another every day. It appears that he has admitted to her that he has been hearing her thoughts and speaking into her mind since she met him in January. He has not, however, told her the entire story.*

Gregory's eyes lightened, glittering with sudden understanding. "Just since January? She still does not know that he was her guardian angel. She has no idea that he has always been watching her and listening to her."

He will eventually tell her that himself. She has forgiven him for invading her mind, and she will forgive him for being her guardian as well – if she does not find out for herself first.

Lucifer's face twisted in a sneer. "She will feel betrayed that he did not tell her the entire truth himself. She will think he deceived her."

"I will be happy to tell her. I can run into her at their next stop in Washington, D.C., and be her sympathetic friend," offered Gregory, smiling devilishly.

No, Gregory. She will think that you are lying. He has undermined her trust in you. The girl needs to see Xander's treachery for herself, and the longer he waits to tell her, the better it is for us, because the stronger she will feel about his betrayal. I have several ideas concerning the best ways to accomplish this, and the beauty of it is, if the first try is not successful, we can keep trying until she knows. None of these things will destroy our territories or drive any more people to the meetings. If we split the two of them apart, we kill SoulFire. Rumors and innuendo about a quarrel between them will destroy that ministry. The sooner we can do this, the sooner SoulFire will end.

Dark Spirit had the undivided attention of both Lucifer and Gregory.

"Tell us your ideas…" said Lucifer, his eyes calming as he stroked the beast.

~~oo~~

After the extreme tension of the first few days in Atlanta had passed, Xander had enjoyed the rest of the week immensely. Thousands of people of varying ages had surrendered their lives to Christ, revival had continued to spread through the city, God's love was being shown through the compassion and service of His people to those who were in need, and he had taken the first step toward revealing the entire truth about himself to Elizabeth. More than that, she had accepted it and had forgiven him for his secrecy. He felt that they had grown even closer to each other; she had begun to play games with him using their mental telepathy. For the first time, Xander had begun to feel glimmers of confidence that Elizabeth would understand and continue to love him even when she was in full possession of all the facts, and he was anxious to tell her everything. He wanted nothing to come between them, and, even though the rallies were a joy to him, he counted the days until the SoulFire tour was finished so he could confess all to her.

Mark's series of reports concerning all that had happened in Atlanta, from the fires to the miraculous events which took place at the SoulFire rallies, had been picked up by a cable news channel, and they had offered him a short term job following SoulFire with a small camera crew for the rest of the summer. He had gratefully accepted and submitted his resignation to WAGA, leaving that station in good standing. The station manager had appreciated the national attention Mark had garnered, and he had assured the young man that he would always have a job waiting for him in Atlanta if he ever cared to return. Jonathan and Mark had talked, and Jonathan had invited Mark to travel with SoulFire Ministries for the rest of the tour. He left his car in Atlanta at his parents' house for the summer, using the oversized van provided by his new employers and taking turns driving with the other three young men on his crew. The young men also shared hotel accommodations, booking two rooms in the hotel used by the SoulFire team in each city.

Jonathan and Dave rotated driving shifts in his van, and Charlotte split her time between Elizabeth and Jonathan, sometimes riding with one and sometimes with the other.

The itinerary was grueling; as soon as the rallies were over on Friday night in one city, all of the equipment was dismantled, packed up, and loaded into vans and semi-trucks. The caravan of vans, trucks, and Xander's Escalade, escorted by a mighty band of guardians, archangels, and warriors, would begin traveling early Saturday morning and usually drive all day, depending on the distance to the next conference. From Atlanta, the trip to Washington, D.C., took eleven hours of driving, not including stops for meals and bathroom breaks. The following week ended with a wonderfully short three hour trip to Philadelphia, and the next stop was six hours away in Boston. After the fourth week, the fatigue was beginning to set in, and the twelve hour drive to Chicago seemed to go on forever.

In each city, God's glory had shone like a brilliant Bethlehem star, attracting capacity crowds. The news of the spiritual births of tens of thousands of new believers spread like wildfire throughout Christendom and the excitement building in the country was palpable. Jehovah continued to use the gifts and talents of Xander, Elizabeth, and Jonathan in mighty ways, adding thousands to His kingdom each day. Though Jonathan had not cast out any more demons during the meetings themselves, he had done so while visiting the ministry sites of the campers in each city, and Mark was there to capture each exorcism on film. The images were compelling; only the eye witness testimonies of those who were there stopped people from thinking it was all a hoax, a trick played by experts manipulating the camera footage. Even then, there were many doubting Thomases who would not believe unless they saw with their own eyes.

Recognizing the usefulness of Elizabeth's gift of tongues, Jonathan had begun to give her larger speaking roles in the conferences. Though he still ended each rally by bringing the final message, she had started giving short talks, relating the Bible to current situations and real life dilemmas, in between music sets.

During the decision time at the end of the services, it was not unusual for Xander to feel the Spirit leading him to pray for specific people who had come forward for counseling, and through him, they were healed of terminal diseases as well as their spiritual sicknesses and addictions.

It was a time of perpetual celebration in heaven.

Apart from occasionally finding flat tires and spray paint on their vehicles on the Saturdays they were to travel, the SoulFire crew had not been bothered by demon attacks after Atlanta. Michael, realizing that Lucifer often lulled people into a sense of complacency by ceasing warfare only to catch them off guard later with an unexpected assault, did not allow his forces to rest. The Captain of the Host ordered warriors to do battle training on a daily basis. As an extra precaution, Xander also commanded guardians to train in shifts while warriors protected their charges.

~~oo~~

After the long drive to Chicago on Saturday, the SoulFire team had slept in on Sunday and met for lunch in the hotel restaurant. They made their way through the buffet line and carried their plates to rectangular tables set for eight. Xander, tired because he insisted on driving the entire time so that Elizabeth could rest, sat across from Jonathan at the meal with Elizabeth seated to his right. Charlotte was beside Jonathan facing Elizabeth; Dave, Mark, and a couple of members of Mark's crew joined them. A waiter came and took their drink orders, returning swiftly with their preferences. The rest of the crew and Thorncrown filled up most of the available seating, and the atmosphere was noisy and friendly.

Michael and Gabriel, along with all the other angels, stood around the perimeter of the room, building a hedge of protection for their charges.

Because it was Elizabeth's birthday, Xander made an extra effort to hide his fatigue, but she noticed the faint circles under his blue eyes. She reached for his hand and squeezed it, thinking, *I love you, my angel. You look tired. Char and I have a suite this week with a nice big couch and a television. Do you want to nap on the couch this afternoon? You can sleep with your head in my lap as I watch a movie.*

But it is your birthday, today, Elizabeth. You are eighteen, and we should do something to celebrate. I want to take you out for a nice dinner – just the two of us.

Your birthday is tomorrow – the big two-one. You are officially an adult. That's what should be celebrated. All I want for my birthday is to hold you and stroke your hair while you nap this afternoon. I'll rub your shoulders, too, if you want.

Let us compromise. Elizabeth smiled at that. Xander returned her smile and continued, *I will take a nap, and I will gladly accept your offer of a massage, if you will go out with me tonight. I love for the others to be with us, but I want to be with you alone for just a few hours. That is what I wish for my birthday – a special evening with you.*

She entwined her fingers with his and gently stroked his wrist with her thumb. *I accept with great anticipation. Dress up?*

I want to take you out for a very special evening, so, yes. Be sure to bring your dancing shoes. Xander caught her thumb with his and squeezed her hand before letting it go to pick up his fork. Charlotte was looking from him to Elizabeth with altogether too much interest.

Xander cleared his throat, and Jonathan glanced at him. "It is Elizabeth's eighteenth birthday today, and we are planning an evening out tonight alone. I hope that will be agreeable with everyone else."

Elizabeth laughed. "He's not telling you that his twenty-first birthday will be tomorrow, so our celebration will be a joint one."

Charlotte smiled at her friend. "Fortunately, Xander is not the only one who knows the date of your birthday, El, and it's a good thing that you told me last week that he'll be twenty-one tomorrow." She nodded toward the door where a waiter stood with a large birthday cake, candles blazing. "I'm not a great singer, but here goes anyway." Charlotte started singing "Happy Birthday," and everyone in the room joined her in serenading the couple as the waiter brought the cake to their table. There were eighteen yellow candles and three blue ones above a musical staff with the words "Happy Birthday, Elizabeth and Xander."

To Xander's utter astonishment, the cake was set before him and Elizabeth with cries of, "Make a wish!"

If I do make a wish, you'll hear it. I think I'll just keep it to myself. Help me blow out the candles. She chuckled aloud.

He smiled and did as she requested. He knew what his fondest wish was, and he hoped that it was her wish as well. However, it would have to wait until she knew everything about him.

I hope you get your wish, Xander, said Michael, smiling at his brother.

Happy first birthday, brother. I wish I had gotten you a gift. Dancing shoes would have been just the thing, added Gabriel.

~~oo~~

After lunch, Xander had confirmed the arrangements for everything he had previously set up for their special evening when he had gone to his room to change into his workout clothes. He and Elizabeth had done their training session early, having missed working out the previous day because they were traveling, and knowing that they would be out late on their date during the upcoming evening. Xander had been so pleased with her progress in the past few weeks that he had begun to teach her different kicks and other offensive moves. He and Michael had discussed her training and decided that she was ready to learn more aggressive techniques. The Captain of the Host had given Xander a bo staff, blessed by God especially for Elizabeth, and using his own bo staff, Xander had added working with the weapons to their regimen.

Following their workout, the couple had returned to Elizabeth's suite to enjoy their long afternoon together.

Because Jonathan and Charlotte had gone out together after lunch, they were alone in the suite, except for Michael and Gabriel who stood a few feet away. Michael's arms were folded across his massive chest, and he looked ready to go to battle for Elizabeth's honor at any moment. Xander did his best to ignore both of them.

Xander lay belly-down on the floor in the living area of Elizabeth's suite still dressed in his workout clothes, though barefooted, appreciating Elizabeth's vigorous attention to his back. She had put a small pillow on the floor for him, and he had his head turned, resting on the pillow with his eyes closed, thinking contently about the paradox of the slight pain of her hands kneading his sore muscles being such a pleasure. She straddled his back and sang Martina McBride's "Valentine" to him as she worked the knots out of his muscles.

Her beautiful voice singing words of love washed over him like a gentle wave, and he was totally relaxed. Xander had nearly fallen asleep when she stopped singing, and he heard her thoughts. Unable to resist, he kept his eyes closed.

Finally, he's asleep. I can stop singing because he does not hear my thoughts while he sleeps. I knew when I started this massage and felt his muscles under my hands that I would give myself away if I didn't find a way to hide what was in my mind.

He really wanted to keep listening, but he remembered his promise to her. Opening his eyes, he smiled and said, "Elizabeth, I am not asleep."

"Great! Now I'm embarrassed." She moved off his back to the floor by his side, covering her face with her hands.

He turned on his side, bending his elbow, resting his dark head in his left hand, and looked at her with a tender expression. Reaching up, he gently pulled her hands down with his right hand and held them.

"I thought you were singing that song to me because you love me. Imagine how I feel knowing that you were doing it only to hide from me." He smiled, teasing her.

"Oh, I meant every word of the song, and I love you so much that I'm afraid of it. I love you in every way possible."

He drew his brows together. "Afraid? Why? I love you to distraction, and you know it."

She looked away. "You could leave me."

Xander sat up facing her, cross-legged, still holding her hands. "Elizabeth, I promise you that I will never leave you." He reached out to turn her face toward his with two fingers and held her brown eyes with his. "I will never love anyone else the way I love you. You cannot understand what you mean to me." She was quiet, but her thoughts were not. "Do you fear something else? You just said, 'I love you in every way possible.' Are you afraid of your physical attraction for me?" He stroked her cheek gently with his hand.

Her eyes filled with tears, but with great effort, she held them. "You already know how much I am attracted to you. It's as if you are a magnet, and I am iron. You have heard my thoughts over and over, yet you have never tried to do anything the least bit inappropriate. I do appreciate your respect, but I wonder if perhaps my attraction for you is greater than yours is for me."

Xander moved his hand to cover hers and sighed. He looked at the floor, and then peeked from under his lashes at her face. "It is perhaps a very good thing that you cannot read my mind, love. I have struggled against my physical responses to you from the earliest moments of our acquaintance."

"Then why does it seem so easy for you to resist me?" One tear escaped and rolled down her cheek. She quickly wiped it away and looked at him, hoping that he had not seen it.

Xander saw her rapid movement and was pierced to the heart. He pulled her onto his lap and held her close, burying his face in her hair. "If you think that, then I truly deserve an Oscar. *Te amo, te quiero, te necessito, y te deseo, mi querida.*" He laughed quietly. "I am a fool for you, Elizabeth. What am I thinking, speaking words of love in Spanish to a woman who has the gift of tongues? Did you even know I was speaking Spanish?" Xander put his hand under her chin and lifted her face so that he could see her eyes. There was an unmistakable sparkle there.

"Since I am fluent in Spanish, I did recognize it. I suppose if you had spoken in a language unfamiliar to me, I would have heard it in English. I'm not sure exactly how this 'gift' works all the time. At any rate, I understood your meaning."

He bent his head and met her lips in a kiss, enveloping her with his arms.

Michael coughed.

Anyone looking in the window would think we were unchaperoned. They would be very wrong, thought Xander impatiently. *However, Gabriel, I do have an idea about that gift you could give me for my birthday. Some privacy possibly?*

I am sorry, but I think not at this time. You have made your point to Elizabeth. Perhaps it is time to move on? suggested Gabriel calmly.

On my wedding night, you will both turn your backs and remain silent. Xander's thoughts were loud.

Agreed. After you are married, replied Michael.

Xander broke the kiss and stood to his feet effortlessly, holding Elizabeth cradled in his arms, her head on his shoulder. He walked over to the couch and set her at one end of it, picking up the remote control from the end table and handing it to her.

"I believe you promised to hold my head in your lap while you watch a movie and I take a nap. And there was something else – stroking my hair? I am claiming my present."

Elizabeth turned on the television and flipped through the channels while he padded to the window and closed the curtains so that he could sleep in the semi-darkness. As he pulled the drapes closed, he noticed a demonic spy on the roof of a neighboring building, watching them through the window. *No surprise there,* he thought.

He has been there the entire time, commented Gabriel.

Elizabeth soon found a movie on HBO, *The Bourne Ultimatum*, and snuggled down in the cushions to watch it. Xander walked back and stretched out on the couch as much as he could; his calves were propped on the arm of the sofa while his feet hung off the end. He turned on his side with his head in her lap, trying to find a comfortable position.

Elizabeth frowned slightly. "You can't sleep like that, Xander. This is a sofa bed. Get up and help me pull it out."

Michael glared at Xander. Gabriel frowned at Michael.

"Elizabeth, I do not think that is a good idea." *I am not made of stone.*

"I promise I will not try to seduce you," she teased. "Your virtue is safe with me."

"I am not worried about you."

She wound her fingers through his hair. "Well, I have no reason not to trust you. You have an iron will and supernatural self-control."

"I have never been with you before…in such a position." He hesitated, keeping his face averted from hers.

She leaned forward so that she could see him. "Why, Alexander Darcy! I do believe that you are blushing. I should not have said this is a sofa bed. It isn't. It's a large, flat couch. Now get up so that we can pull it out. I'd hate to have to use some of my new moves on you and possibly hurt you." She punched his arm lightly for emphasis.

Sighing, he rolled off the couch and stood, holding out his hands to her to pull her upright. Together they opened the couch, and she was pleased to see that it was made up with sheets and a blanket tucked around the mattress.

Elizabeth hopped up on the mattress, putting cushions at her back and patting her lap, smiling encouragingly at him. He lay diagonally with his head in her lap. "Isn't this better?" she crooned, gently rubbing his forehead and playing with his hair. "Now you have room to stretch out and sleep."

Yes, go to sleep. Now, thought Michael.

Michael, he has not done anything wrong, and this was your charge's idea. Gabriel's voice sounded mildly irritated.

Xander yawned in spite of himself, and then smiled up at her self-consciously. "Sorry. I guess I do need a nap, but please wake me when the movie ends. I need a shower before we go out, and we have reservations." *You must wake me if I talk in my sleep, Gabriel.*

Do not be anxious. I will rouse you if your dreams cause you to become talkative, answered Gabriel.

Elizabeth watched him as his beautiful face relaxed, and his dark lashes rested on his cheeks; his breathing gradually became steady and deeper while his chest rose and fell rhythmically. She leaned down and lightly kissed the lips of her angel, and afterwards she looked at Matt Damon on the television screen. There was no comparison. Elizabeth rested her head on the back of the couch, and, lulled by the noise from the television, fell asleep.

She slept so deeply that she did not hear when Xander murmured her name.

~~oo~~

Xander, rejuvenated by his nap, had a spring in his step as he walked to Elizabeth's door and rapped on it. Charlotte opened the door, smiled, and invited him in. *Holy moly! Happy birthday, El!* she thought, admiring the fit of his beige Irish linen suit and black V-necked T.

Gabriel smiled at Xander's discomfort and nodded at Edward who returned his greeting.

As he walked to the living room, Xander spoke quickly to prevent Charlotte from thinking any further. "Hello, Charlotte. Is Elizabeth ready?"

"Almost. Rome wasn't built in a day, you know." She laughed lightly.

Xander spotted sunflowers, her favorite flowers, on the table by the couch. *Surely not from Gregory.* Following his line of sight and noticing the small frown between his eyes, Charlotte said, "The Bennets sent El flowers for her birthday. Beautiful, aren't they?" Xander rewarded her with a fully dimpled smile.

He heard the bedroom door open and close, and turning, he silently admired the vision that was Elizabeth. The summer dress she wore was cobalt blue with thin straps and a flirty skirt featuring a layered hem that flared a few inches above her knees. Her taupe high-heeled sandals, he noted with satisfaction, were perfect for dancing, and her hair was loose, hanging in curls down her back. She twirled before him, modeling her outfit. Michael stood beside her.

Do you approve, birthday boy?

Oh, yes. Definitely. I think there are few men who would not approve, love. You are beautiful.

Charlotte watched the exchange curiously. "Why do I always feel that you two are having a private conversation that no one else can hear?"

Edward tried unsuccessfully not to smile.

"We're just on the same wavelength, Char. How was your afternoon – your entire six hours of free time – with Jonathan?" asked Elizabeth innocently.

"Point taken. I'll just shuffle on into the bedroom and mind my own business now," Charlotte answered. "I have a dinner engagement to dress for. You two aren't the only ones who can have a night out occasionally, you know," she said airily over her shoulder as she left the room.

"I really like, Charlotte," said Xander. "She knows when to gracefully exit a room." *Unlike some friends of mine.*

Just doing my job, answered Michael.

You will not even know that we are with you, thought Gabriel.

Now that would be a wonderful birthday present. Xander smiled at the idea.

He reached for her, and she came to him, wrapping her arms around his waist, looking up at him with her luminous dark eyes. Xander bent his head to her face and kissed her, almost reverently.

As he drew back a few inches, she smiled sweetly and said, "I wish we could just stay here and cuddle. We never do that – at least not for very long."

She has no idea how tempting she is. She would not ask for that if she knew how difficult it is for me. He kissed her dimple. "I promise you that one day, we will cuddle all day and night if you want to do so. But right now, we have birthday plans."

She made a little moue, and then quickly replaced it with a smile for him. "Let the celebrations begin. Lead the way."

~~oo~~

Xander had engaged a car and driver for the night so that he would not have to worry about parking, and their first stop was at Grant Park for SummerDance where people were dressed in everything from shorts and T shirts to dinner attire. He left his jacket in the car because the night was warm.

While planning for her birthday in May before they left on tour, Xander had Googled nighttime entertainment for weekends in Chicago. After looking at the schedule, much to Gabriel's amusement, Xander had bought instructional DVD's and taught himself to do the Latin dances being featured that particular weekend. Elizabeth was amazed and pleasantly surprised when he was able to teach her to salsa and meringue. There was a featured instructor, but the park was too crowded to see him or the video screens well, and a group formed around the beautiful couple, following the handsome Xander for the hour-long lesson. He had grown more comfortable in crowds during the SoulFire tour, and he had determined in himself that he would not limit Elizabeth's enjoyment of her birthday to avoid the stares he invariably attracted. He willed himself to dance, looking only at Elizabeth, and not worrying about the throngs of people.

"You've been holding out on me," she said breathlessly. "I didn't know you could dance."

"You never asked me," he replied, winking at her.

"What other hidden talents are you hiding, Mr. Xander?" she asked saucily.

"You will just have to stay with me to find out the answer to that question," he answered, teasing her in return.

Michael and Gabriel hovered above them, constantly scanning the moving crowd.

The car was back promptly to pick them up and deliver them to the Everest restaurant on the fortieth floor of the Chicago Stock Exchange on time for their dinner reservations. Their view of western Chicago at night was magical, and the wonderful art and sculpture displayed added to the ambiance.

Gabriel and Michael took their places behind their charges after Xander had seated Elizabeth.

Knowing her preferences, he had pre-ordered for them both, and as soon as they were seated, their waiter brought them their drinks and Maine crab, followed by salads with apples and walnuts, Maine lobster, and steak. For dessert, he had chosen the selection of five chocolate tastes.

They took their time, conversing quietly and holding hands over the table between courses.

When they were finished, Xander leaned over to Elizabeth and whispered, "I must agree with the *Chicago Tribune* concerning this restaurant."

She raised an eyebrow delicately in question.

"This is indeed Chicago's most romantic restaurant," he answered. His eyes said more to her. *If you already knew everything about me, love, I would be asking you to marry me now,* he thought privately.

"As in most things, my opinion matches yours. I love you, Xander."

"And I love you." *One day very soon you will know just how much. Just four more weeks.* He fervently hoped that they would be husband and wife by the next summer.

Chapter 18

"The Lord will deliver me from every evil deed, and will bring me safely to His heavenly kingdom; to Him be the glory forever and ever. Amen."
II Timothy 4:18

At breakfast the following morning, Xander learned that one of the crew members, Lance Miller, had gone to the ER during the night with severe stomach pain and gastrointestinal problems. He had eaten at a street festival and had developed food poisoning. After treatment, the young man was doing much better and would be returning to the hotel soon, but the incident had made Xander consider several possible scenarios which he needed to discuss with Jonathan and Elizabeth; he had already made the necessary arrangements with Asim, Michael, and Gabriel through telepathy. His brothers agreed that the possibility of a demonic attack or illness might make it necessary for them to appear in human form, and there had to be a reasonable explanation for how such an event could occur.

After they were seated, their guardians behind each of them, Xander addressed them. "Jonathan, Elizabeth, I think there is a matter which we need to address. After hearing that Lance was taken to the hospital last night, I realized that we need to exchange personal information with each other. Jonathan, you have the applications of everyone hired to go on this tour, and you have the information for Elizabeth and Dave. Elizabeth, you know all of Charlotte's family and could contact them if we needed to do so. And, Jonathan, Dave probably has the numbers for your parents, correct?"

Elizabeth nodded, looking puzzled.

"Yes, Xander. What am I missing?" Jonathan smiled, amused at his supremely organized friend.

"Who would you call if I became ill or was injured? No one here could check me into a hospital, and none of you know how to contact my family. I have written my land line number for my townhouse in Spartanburg on a card for you as well as one for Elizabeth. Call there if the need arises and leave a message. Knowing that we are touring, my brothers check the voicemail constantly, and they would get the message. I have also included their cell phone numbers, though you would probably have a difficult time reaching them. Just leave messages. Mike and Gabe are usually traveling, and cell service is unavailable on flights. They could be wherever we are very quickly." Xander handed the cards to Jonathan and Elizabeth, and she put the card in her purse, frowning a little at the thought of anything bad happening to him.

Jonathan looked at him quizzically. "We are driving all over the United States right now. How could you guarantee that your brothers would find us in time? Perhaps you should sign a medical power of attorney over to me or Elizabeth."

"I would not wish to burden either of you with possibly serious decisions concerning my welfare. I had not mentioned it before, but in my family, all of us fly, and we have our own means of transportation."

Awareness dawned in Jonathan's eyes as well as Elizabeth's. She asked, "You all fly? You are all pilots? My, my. Yet another surprise. And you have your own means of transportation. A family jet, I suppose?"

Xander remained silent, looking at his plate and allowing them to draw their own conclusions.

Jonathan mistook his silence for embarrassment, pocketed the card he had been holding, and spoke quickly. "Thank you, Xander. I will be sure to keep the card in my wallet in case we ever need it."

Xander looked up at him gratefully. "If I am injured and you do not have your card, there is another one in my own wallet, and all of the numbers are programmed into my cell phone. Elizabeth has my password."

Sensing that Xander was not finished, Jonathan asked, "Is that all you wanted to talk about, Xander?"

"Actually, no. I have been thinking about our schedule. Jonathan, you, Elizabeth, and I are already tiring, and we are only halfway through the tour. If we decide to travel this much again, a tour bus driven by a professional with cots in the back would be better for us. Since it is inconvenient to purchase one now, as well as having the additional concern of what we would do with my car and your van, I think that we should consider flying to the last three cities. It is at least a sixteen hour drive from here to Denver, seventeen hours from Denver to San Diego, and twenty-two hours from there to the Dallas-Fort Worth area, not allowing stops for meals and bathroom breaks. Crew members could drive our personal vehicles. The trucks are handled by professional drivers, and crew members could drive the vans and other vehicles in shifts so that they could sleep on the way. Charlotte could fly with us, and Dave could stay with the caravan to handle any problems. What is your opinion?" Xander asked.

"I have been thinking along the same lines, though not in as much detail. The drive back from Texas to Spartanburg is sixteen hours, but we'll be finished then and can take our time. We might split that drive into two days. If you agree, I'll have Dave arrange for the tickets today. He can drive us to the airports, and we can share a taxi from the airports to the hotels when we arrive in each city. Dave, what do you think?" asked Jonathan, looking at his manager.

"I think it's a good plan. I was beginning to think we might have been a bit too ambitious in spanning the whole country this summer. If you guys can preserve your energy in this way, we should be fine."

Xander looked at Elizabeth, and then at Charlotte. "Are you in agreement, ladies?"

"Definitely," said Charlotte quickly. She had been dreading the sixteen hour drive on the coming Saturday.

"Let's see. A few hours on a plane, or every weekend spent driving in a car? Um. Yes, Xander, I like your idea, as usual." She smiled as he squeezed her hand under the table. "If we fly out on Friday nights, we could sleep on the plane and have Saturdays and Sundays free."

Dave thought a moment and replied, "That could probably be arranged. I'll get right on it this morning while we're at the arena."

Michael and Gabriel, as well as Lexus and Edward were pleased. It would be easier to guard their charges on a plane rather than the interstate. The warriors remained stoic, as usual.

~~oo~~

Xander, thinking ahead as always, had arranged an outing for Elizabeth and him the following Saturday in Denver. Jonathan and Charlotte had made other plans. The four of them had been unable to make the night flight because the rallies had ended after departure time of the last non-stop flight for the day, so they had flown out of Chicago just after seven on Saturday morning and had arrived in Denver by ten. After they had taken a taxi, guardians flying overhead, to the hotel and checked in, they had a late breakfast together and discussed their itineraries for the day.

Xander had already checked with Elizabeth before he had proceeded with their plans, and she was very excited to be spending an active day outside with him. There had not been much time for outdoor exercise and sightseeing during the past month, and she was looking forward to spending the afternoon riding the South Platte River Trail, especially since it connected with several other trails allowing for off-road biking. Coffee shops, restaurants, bookstores, and other places to shop were accessible from the main trail, so there was no need to pack a lunch, and they could park the bikes and relax whenever they tired.

After Elizabeth and Xander had changed their clothes, they took a taxi to a bike rental shop located adjacent to the trail. There, they chose bicycles for the day after listening to the advice of the proprietor.

Gabriel and Michael flew above them as they began their outing. They had been riding intermittently for about two hours when Michael spied a child-sized demon in a park to their right. The demon was playing tag with a human child, and ran toward the bike path with the little boy in hot pursuit. Thinking that Elizabeth was the target, Michael flew in front of her bicycle and Gabriel took a position behind it. Xander, looking to see that Elizabeth was properly protected, misjudged the speed of the human child as the demon passed harmlessly in front of him. He jammed on the brakes, swerving to avoid hitting the child, and skidded on some loose gravel, sending himself headfirst into a tree to the left of the path.

He could not morph into angelic form with the entire park watching, so, in front of Elizabeth's horrified eyes, he took the fall as a human. As she watched, everything seemed to slow to a crawl; time stood still. Xander felt himself sliding until he stopped suddenly, striking his head on something very hard. He heard Elizabeth calling his name in anguish, but it seemed far away. He felt great pain, saw a flash of light, and then there was blackness.

Elizabeth, watching the accident from across the road, saw Xander glimmer for a moment, seeming to change shapes. She supposed that the bright sunlight was causing her to see an optical illusion, and she squinted her eyes. When she fully opened them again, he no longer glowed.

He returned to consciousness a few minutes later, and Elizabeth's tear-streaked face was the first thing he saw. His world was upside down, and in his confusion, he did not understand why the sky was above and behind her. People had gathered in a circle around them, and he could hear a siren in the distance. He saw Michael and Gabriel behind Elizabeth, looking down at him with grim expressions, and he thought with wonder how beautiful they were, shining in the bright sunlight. Xander dimly remembered Elizabeth, but he could not think of the names of the two glowing men.

"My head hurts. What happened?" he asked in a whisper. His pupils were fully dilated, making his eyes look nearly black.

"You slid on the gravel while we were riding bicycles and hit your head on a tree," Elizabeth answered, trying to calm herself for his sake.

"Who are those men?" His eyes were directed past her face, behind her.

She looked behind her but saw only family groups, mainly women and children.

"I don't see any men, Xander," she answered gently, rubbing his forehead.

Gabriel spoke into his mind, *We are your brothers. I am Gabriel and he is Michael.*

We are angels, Xander. You are an angel, too, added Michael.

Xander became agitated and struggled vainly to sit up. "Have I told you that I am an angel?"

Elizabeth smiled tremulously, "Yes, you have. You are my angel."

"They are angels, too."

"Who, Xander? Who are angels?" She tried to understand him so that he would calm down, and she fought the fear rising in her mind. *He's seeing angels. Dear Lord, please don't take him from me.*

Michael put his hands on Elizabeth's shoulders, but did not speak to her. *She hears Xander's voice and knows that he can put his thoughts into her mind. What will she think if she hears me now?* he asked Gabriel.

Xander heard Michael's thoughts and looked at him, puzzled. He tried again to get up, but she put her hands on his shoulders. "Do not move, love. Someone called 911, and the ambulance is coming."

"The light hurts my eyes. What happened?" he asked her, his blue eyes tormented.

She patiently answered him again.

Gabriel feared that approaching Xander might make him say more about their being angels, so he stood back. *What should we do, Michael? We cannot speak to him again, and you should not speak to her. Elizabeth has not called us, and we cannot simply appear. We must limit our thoughts; he can hear us even now.*

Michael saw a guardian with a woman who stood near them. He nodded to the angel and spoke. *Tell your charge to ask Elizabeth if she has contacted his family.*

Xander looked past Elizabeth again. "They are talking to me in my head. Can you hear them, too?"

"Xander, no one is talking to you except for me." She leaned to his ear and whispered, "Remember that you can hear my thoughts and those of everyone else? That's all you're hearing – the thoughts of all these people."

"I see another one," said Xander, looking at the woman's protector.

Elizabeth quickly wiped away the tears that spilled down her cheeks. *Please, Father. Please don't take him from me.*

The guardian immediately did as Michael had commanded, and his charge approached Elizabeth.

"Miss, are you his wife, or have you contacted the young man's family?" asked the woman, touching Elizabeth's shoulder.

Elizabeth looked up into her kind face, smiled through her tears, and answered, "No, we are not married. Thank you for reminding me to call his brothers. Do you know which hospital is the closest? I need to tell them where he will be."

The lady answered her question as Elizabeth reached into her pocket for her cell phone. Xander had programmed in all the numbers for her the week before. *It's a good thing he thought of giving me these numbers. It's almost as if he saw this coming.* She quickly called all three numbers, leaving a message in each place.

The crowd moved back as the ambulance pulled up. As soon as the vehicle had stopped, paramedics got out and came to Xander to examine him. After noting his dilated pupils, sensitivity to light, and disorientation, one of the paramedics put a neck brace on Xander and told Elizabeth that it seemed to be a severe concussion, while another one called it into the hospital and two others went to get the gurney.

Xander's feet hung off the end of the gurney, and it took four men to lift him into the ambulance. When Elizabeth started to climb in after them, one of the paramedics stopped her. "No one can ride with him, ma'am. Sorry."

"But I have no way to travel, and I'm alone. We're here with SoulFire Ministries for the rallies at the arena."

The driver turned upon hearing what she said. "You're El Bennet? Is that Xander Darcy? My kids are in the SoulFire camp this week." The man's guardian stood by the ambulance, ready to fly over the vehicle.

She nodded, "Yes, I'm El. I'm his girlfriend."

"Let her in, guys. He would want her to be with him."

Xander looked from one to the other, his eyes wide. The men helped Elizabeth get into the back of the ambulance, and she sat beside the gurney, holding Xander's hand. She watched the paramedics closely, answering their questions to the best of her ability and moving out of their way as they cleaned and bandaged his abrasions. The background noise of the men communicating with the hospital was constant.

Xander could hear the thoughts of the EMT's, Elizabeth, and the people in the crowd; he had heard Gabriel and Michael earlier. Normally, he selected voices to hear and knew the difference between angelic and human voices; however, his mental impairment kept him from remembering how to separate and categorize the thoughts he heard, adding to his general confusion.

"Do you know that I am an angel?" he asked her.

"Yes. You're my angel," she answered.

"I was not supposed to tell you," he wailed, becoming agitated.

"It's all right, Xander. Everything is fine," she said in a soothing voice, trying to hold her tears.

"What happened?" Xander asked.

She repeated the story, telling him how he hit a tree.

He was quiet a moment, looking around the ambulance, confused by the noise of the siren.

He looked back at Elizabeth.

"Have I told you that I am an angel?"

Not wishing to upset him again, she thought, *Please forgive me for lying, Lord.* "No, you haven't."

"You are lying to me? Why would you do that? I wanted to tell you." His eyes filled with tears.

"I know, love. You are an angel. It's okay," she whispered, holding his hand and stroking it.

Above the ambulance, Michael and Gabriel flew with the other guardian, their faces somber. *They have never attacked Xander before. I supposed that they were trying to harm Elizabeth,* Gabriel telepathed to Michael so that others could not hear. *He is my charge. I have failed him and our Master.*

Gabriel, he will be well. There is no death angel here. I never imagined that the target was Xander either. You have failed no one. Xander would have expected you to protect Elizabeth. He would have been livid if you had not done so. Michael replied privately, trying to reassure his brother.

I will make no more assumptions. He is my charge, and I will protect him, declared Gabriel.

There is a more serious problem right now, thought Michael. *He changed forms briefly when he was hurt. What if he does that again? We must get Elizabeth away from him somehow.*

I doubt that she will leave him willingly. We may have to insist upon it as Xander's brothers. I do not wish to hurt her. Gabriel was grieved, and his expression showed his anguish.

Michael was silent.

"I hear them again," said Xander, looking at Elizabeth. She stroked his head and tried to ignore the look of confusion in his eyes. It unsettled her to see him less than strong and confident.

As Xander leaned over the rail of the gurney to vomit, the paramedic was ready with a basin.

Elizabeth took out her cell phone and called Jonathan to tell him what had happened. Jonathan promised to meet her at the hospital as soon as he could.

Xander leaned back and allowed the paramedic to wipe his mouth while he stared at Elizabeth with a baffled expression. "Are we dating?" he asked.

She took his hand to hold it. "Yes."

"How long have we been dating?"

"About four months." Elizabeth smiled at him tremulously.

"Have I told you that I love you?" he asked.

"Yes, and I love you, too." She put her hand on his head, running her fingers through his curls and pushing his hair back from his forehead. Then she leaned over and kissed his brow tenderly, keeping her face close to his.

"Do you know that I am an angel?" Xander's eyes were tormented.

"Yes, you are my angel, Xander," she said evenly.

"Have you forgiven me?" Xander's voice rose in pitch.

"Of course." She glanced at the paramedic and saw that he was occupied with cleaning up the vomit. "It is our secret." She tapped her head to indicate that she knew about the mind reading and made a conscious effort to think into his mind. *I love you.*

He heard her, and his eyes widened. "You really know, and you still love me?"

She nodded and kissed his cheek.

"My head hurts. What happened?"

As she told him about his accident again, the ambulance pulled up to the ER entrance. One of the paramedics opened the back door and hopped out, turning back to Elizabeth to help her out.

The crew lowered the gurney to the pavement and rolled it into the ER entrance, giving all their information to a nurse who met them at the sliding doors. An orderly took the gurney into an examination room, followed closely by Elizabeth, Gabriel, and Michael.

The nurse asked Elizabeth for Xander's insurance card and helped her roll Xander to his side so that she could get his wallet from his back pocket. Her picture was the first thing Elizabeth saw when she opened it, and then she found his credit cards, personal information, and insurance cards neatly filed in the leather slots. Xander watched in confusion as Elizabeth pulled the card from his wallet and gave it to the nurse.

"My head hurts. What happened?" he asked.

Elizabeth told him about the accident while the nurse left to copy his insurance card. A doctor came in to examine him while she was talking.

You go change while I stay with Elizabeth and Xander, Gabriel said to Michael.

Michael went through a curtain and into a closet, transformed into his human form, and walked to the front desk. He gave the startled clerk his name and told her he was there to see his brother. When she had recovered her power of speech, she told him how to find Xander.

The imposing angel walked through the curtain and extended his hand to the doctor. "I am Michael Xander, Xander's brother." He nodded at Elizabeth in greeting, and then focused his attention on Xander. *Xander, you can hear my thoughts. That is as is should be. Do not speak of it. Gabriel, you can go change forms now.*

I will not leave him again. Gabriel was adamant.

Xander looked from Michael to Gabriel and back again. *Can you hear me?* Xander asked.

We can, my brother. Gabriel looked into Xander's eyes. *Do not talk of it.*

Some part of Xander's mind heard and understood. He remained silent.

You must, Gabriel. My warriors will arrive with Charlotte when she and Jonathan come, and they will be with Xander. Charlotte should meet both of us in case we need to be around her in the future, Michael thought reasonably.

He is my responsibility. I will not leave him again. Gabriel's face was anguished.

My brother, none of this was your fault. You must go now and return in human form. Michael issued the command as Captain of the Host, and Gabriel could not go against it. He did as he was ordered to do.

The doctor introduced himself and told Michael that they were taking Xander to have a CT scan, X-rays, and a neurological exam. He left the room to order the tests, telling them he would return after he had reviewed the results.

Michael stood beside the bed across from Elizabeth and put his hand on Xander's shoulder.

"What have you gotten yourself into this time, little brother?" he asked, smiling.

Xander looked at him, wrinkling his brow. "You are my brother?"

"I am Michael. Gabriel is right behind me. When we got the message, we were already in Denver on business. We had planned to see you tonight or tomorrow." Michael gazed straight into his eyes, willing him to understand.

"He has been so confused, Michael," said Elizabeth, looking at Xander anxiously.

"Were you there? At the accident?" asked Xander. "I thought I saw you."

"No, Xander. He wasn't there. I was there with you," answered Elizabeth, stroking his forehead.

Xander looked from one to the other, trying to think through the mental fog.

"Are you feeling any better, brother?" asked Michael. Gabriel came through the curtain and joined them, moving to stand beside Michael, the worry clearly marked on his face.

Xander looked at the new face, and he remembered the conversation between the two men. "Gabriel?"

"Yes, brother. I am sorry that you were hurt." Gabriel took Xander's hand.

Xander's mind had slowly begun to clear, and he thought of Michael's words. "It was not your fault, Gabriel. I cannot remember what happened, but I know that you could not have prevented it."

"I wish that I had been there for you, my brother. I feel responsible. Father told me to look after you."

Elizabeth looked at him compassionately. "No, Gabriel. A child ran in front of Xander. It wasn't anyone's fault; it was an accident. Besides, Xander is a grown man now. You can't be with him every minute. I'm sure your father will understand that."

"Elizabeth is right, Gabriel," said Michael kindly. "Our Father will understand."

Are you truly all right, Xander? Are you yourself again, or do we need to send Elizabeth away? asked Gabriel.

What do you mean? Xander replied.

You briefly changed into angelic form when you were injured. She saw but thought it was her eyes playing tricks on her. Can you hold your form now? Gabriel looked unblinking into Xander's eyes.

Xander's eyes widened at the information, but his facial expression remained neutral. *I am not as confused as I was at first. I think I will be fine now. Do not send her away. She would be upset at that.*

You mean you would be upset. Michael smiled.

Xander looked up at Elizabeth. *Yes, I would.* "Thank you for staying with me. I hope it was not too terrible for you. I do not like being a burden."

She bent over and kissed his lips quickly. "You could never be a burden, and just try to get rid of me. I will not leave you until you are well again."

His smile was so beautiful, despite the darkening bruise on his forehead, that she held her breath and closed her eyes. *He still has the power to stun me into silence. Father, thank you for sparing him today. Help him to be whole again quickly. He loves You so much, Lord, and He wants to serve You this week. Heal him, please. Thank You for giving him to me. He completes me.*

She opened her eyes to see Xander looking at her, smiling.

She looked at him, a question in her eyes. *You heard me?*

Yes, my love. Thank you.

She kissed him again on the cheek, softly. When she straightened up, she looked full into the smiling eyes of Michael and Gabriel.

Turning her eyes back to Xander, she teased, "So you call them Michael and Gabriel now instead of 'Mike' and 'Gabe'? Are you copying me?"

"I heard them tell you that they prefer the more formal versions of their names, and I decided to humor them. Occasionally, I do what they want me to do," he answered.

Gabriel and I should stay with Elizabeth when you are taken for further examination, Xander. It will seem odd if either of us disappears, and we also need to meet Charlotte. I have heard from the warriors assigned to her that she and Jonathan are in the waiting area. I will send those two warriors with you if you and Gabriel agree. They will be in contact with me at all times. If I am required, I can be with you in seconds, thought Michael.

The plan is sound, answered Xander.

Agreed, added Gabriel, though he did not like it.

Two huge warriors walked through the curtain as an orderly came in to take Xander for his tests, and Elizabeth, Michael, and Gabriel went to the waiting area. Jonathan and Charlotte were there and came to meet them.

Charlotte's eyes were round as she took in all seven feet of Michael's fiercely masculine beauty, and then turned to absorb the peaceful, angelic face of Gabriel.

Elizabeth chuckled lightly. "Charlotte, these are Xander's brothers, Michael and Gabriel. They were already in Denver on business and were able to be here quickly when they got my messages. Michael and Gabriel, this is my best girl friend, Charlotte Lucas."

She extended her hand for a handshake, but Gabriel took it and bowed over it formally. Straightening, he smiled at her and said, "I am very pleased to meet you, Charlotte. I truly appreciate the friendship you have with my brother and Elizabeth." She caught her breath audibly.

"I am happy to meet you, too, Gabriel. Nice to meet you, Michael," she added, reaching for his hand. He shook her hand and smiled widely, adding to her mental disorder.

"I am always happy to meet any of the friends of my family," he said in his rich, deep voice.

Jonathan cleared his throat, drawing the men's attention to himself. "It's good to see you again, Michael and Gabriel, though I'm sorry it's under these circumstances. What happened?"

Elizabeth again related the story of the accident – how they had rented bicycles for the afternoon to ride the trail, and the child had run in front of Xander, causing him to skid in a tree.

Jonathan put his hand on Elizabeth's arm and looked from her face to Michael's. "What can I do to help?"

Michael thought a moment. "We will wait here until the doctor tells us if our brother must stay the night or not. We want to know his prognosis. Could you call the bicycle rental store and tell them what happened? Then we would know what they want us to do about the bikes." Jonathan nodded.

"Do you have their number, Elizabeth?" asked Jonathan.

"Yes, I do." She fished the card from her pocket and handed it to him. As he took his cell phone from his pocket, he walked to the ER entrance to make the call.

In a few minutes, Jonathan returned to the group. "Someone had already called them. The store name and number is on their bicycles. I suppose they have had other incidents in the past. At any rate, they said they would go pick up the bikes themselves. If there is any difficulty, they have my number and will call me."

"Jonathan, would you mind taking Xander back to the hotel when he is released? We will meet you there. Our vehicle cannot accommodate all three of us."

Jonathan laughed. "I can well believe that, and I'll be happy to do as you ask."

Gabriel added, "If you could take Elizabeth as well, that would be helpful."

Charlotte replied, "We rented a car for the next two days, so I'm sure it won't be a problem."

"Excellent," said Michael.

"By the way," said Charlotte, looking from Michael to Gabriel with a gleam of good humor in her eyes. "Do either of you gentlemen play the piano?"

Elizabeth just smiled and shook her head.

Chapter 19

"For now we see in a mirror dimly, but then face to face; now I know in part, but then I shall know fully just as I also have been fully known. But now abide faith, hope, love, these three; but the greatest of these is love."
I Corinthians 13:14

Lucifer swore and slammed his fist into the coffee table of Gregory's living room, reducing the sturdy decorative piece to splinters. "He actually tells her over and over that he is an angel, and she is too stupid to understand!"

"I have always thought that human intelligence was highly overrated, particularly in women," agreed Gregory, sighing in disgust, sitting heavily and crossing his legs.

Dark Spirit hissed. *You both miss the point entirely.*

Lucifer frowned and glared at him with flaming eyes. "How so? What have we missed?"

Xander did indeed tell her that he was an angel while he was confused and injured, but did he continue to tell her once he had his wits about him? The gargantuan serpent laid his head on the arm of the sofa and fixed his cold stare on the Dark Lord.

Gregory thought a moment, and then an evil smile slowly played around his lips. "No, he did not. When she finally does find out, she will feel even more betrayed."

"It was the perfect opportunity to tell her, and yet he held his peace." Lucifer rubbed his palms together in fiendish glee. "This is too good."

Exactly. The thought slithered through their minds.

~~oo~~

The doctor had come to the waiting room after viewing Xander's test results and talked to Elizabeth, Charlotte, Jonathan, Michael, and Gabriel. Xander had been diagnosed with a severe concussion and had been required to stay in the hospital overnight. To no one's surprise, Elizabeth had refused to leave him and had stated emphatically that she would sleep on a recliner in his room. She had already called her parents and apprised them of Xander's injury, and that she would be staying with him in the hospital.

Charlotte and Jonathan had left as a frustrated Xander was being admitted, and Michael, Gabriel, and Elizabeth had gone to Xander's room with him. Michael had summoned two warriors to guard the couple for a few minutes so that he and Gabriel could leave after promising to keep in touch with Xander by telephone. The archangels had left the room, ducked into a men's restroom, and changed into angelic form before returning to Xander's room. Michael had dismissed the warriors, and he and Gabriel had taken up their positions as guardians once more.

Charlotte and Jonathan returned some time later with toiletries and fresh clothing both for Xander and Elizabeth, as well as Chinese take-out for their dinner. He brightened considerably at the sight of clean clothes and the aroma of the cartons of one of his favorite foods.

Jonathan put their overnight bags by Elizabeth's recliner as Charlotte deposited the food on Xander's tray table with a smile. He went to the other side of Xander's bed; Charlotte remained beside Elizabeth across from him. She said, "I hope you can eat some of this, Xander. I know the hospital food is atrocious, and I've heard that you can be a bit picky about what you eat. El said your stomach was a little …unsettled in the ambulance. Do you feel well enough to eat bourbon chicken? We also bought some wonton soup in case you want something lighter."

"Charlotte, I knew there was a reason I adored you beyond your amazing good sense, beauty, and discernment. I am starving, and I know that Elizabeth must be hungry as well. We have not eaten anything since breakfast."

Elizabeth's stomach growled in response, and they all laughed.

"Xander knows he has to 'Feed me! Feed me! Feed me, Seymour! Feed me all night long,'" she sang.

"Have you been doing your Audrey II impression for him?" Charlotte said, grinning at her friend's antics.

Michael, Gabriel, and Edward smiled, and Lexus wore an amused expression, but the warriors' faces remained somber.

"Seriously, Char, it was wonderful of you and Jonathan to go to the hotel and get clothes and other things for us. Thanks so much." Elizabeth hugged her friend. "And thanks for the Chinese. I owe you."

"Yes, you do. I'll just put it on your tab," replied Charlotte airily.

"Charlotte, are you ready to go? We should probably let them eat while the food's still hot," Jonathan said as he checked his watch.

Elizabeth noticed his movement and returned her attention to Charlotte. "You look wonderful, Char. What are you guys doing for dinner? We could share the take-out."

"Not me," said Xander, shaking his head. "I am not sharing any of my food."

"No worries, Xander. Jon and I have dinner reservations."

Jon? thought Xander.

Yes, answered Edward. *It is her special name for him.*

Is he serious about her? Xander's thoughts had a protective edge.

Yes, his admiration for her grows daily. Tonight he plans to ask her to be his girlfriend, replied Lexus.

And, since she has already figured that out, of course, she intends to accept him, added Edward.

Excellent, thought Michael.

They will be a strong team together for the Master. Gabriel's thoughts were content.

Jonathan smiled at the sound of his "pet" name coming from her lips in front of the others. "Xander, would you like for us to pray with you before we leave?"

Xander reached for Jonathan's hand to his left and Elizabeth's to his right. She took Charlotte's hand, and Charlotte reached across the bed for Jonathan, forming a circle. Their guardians stepped up behind them, placing their hands on the shoulders of their charges.

They bowed their heads, and Jonathan began to pray. "Dear Father, thank you for preserving our brother-in-Christ, Xander. We pray that You will continue to heal him so that he can continue in Your work. Give him a good night's rest and hold him in Your hands. In Jesus' name. Amen."

Only Xander and Elizabeth continued to hold hands. Charlotte walked to the other side of the bed to stand beside Jonathan.

"Thanks for the clothes, Jonathan," Xander said gratefully, looking at his friend.

Jonathan raised his eyebrows in mock surprise. "What? You don't like the hospital gown? It's air conditioned in the back."

"I like it as much as you would, I suppose," answered Xander ruefully. "It is not large enough, and the nurse said that I must wear it until I leave tomorrow morning. The thing does not even reach my knees. It is embarrassing."

Jonathan laughed at his friend. "We'll be back to get you around ten. The nurse said that you would probably be discharged by then. You can rest all day at the hotel tomorrow, and then see if you feel well enough to sing Monday night."

"I will be. I am only a little lightheaded. The doctor said that I may have some dizziness and memory loss, but otherwise I will be fine." Xander was firm.

Elizabeth looked at him sternly. "We will see how you're doing after tomorrow, Xander. There is no need to risk your falling off the stage and further injuring yourself."

Michael chuckled. *She will not let you overexert yourself. I am glad.*

Having her with me all night will keep me awake and raise my heart rate, teased Xander.

Shall I put a suggestion into her mind that she should go back to the hotel? asked Michael innocently.

Only if you want to be on the losing end of a training session. I beat you in the throne room, and I can do it again, 'big' brother, answered Xander.

Jonathan and Charlotte said their goodbyes and left hand-in-hand for their evening out, followed by Lexus, Edward, and the two warriors. Elizabeth went into the bathroom and changed into sweatpants, socks, and a T shirt; she then busied herself with setting out their food and drinks on his bed table.

Well, that cleared the room considerably, thought Michael.

Yes, though it is still a little crowded for my taste, replied Xander, smiling.

Get used to it, answered Gabriel tersely. *I am here for the duration, and you will not be rid of me as long as you draw breath.*

At least stand on the other side of the room. I am in no danger of attack from Elizabeth. Even in my weakened state, I believe that I could fight her off, Xander joked.

Do not make light of it. I find no humor in my failure, and I assure you that it will not happen again. Gabriel's words were spoken quietly but with absolute conviction.

I am human, Gabriel. Humans have accidents and get hurt. Elizabeth was attacked and suffered a concussion while I guarded her. Sometimes things are beyond our control. I do not blame you for what happened, so please stop blaming yourself. If you do not stop worrying so, you will go prematurely gray, Xander thought.

Thank you for trying to make me feel better. It almost worked, Gabriel replied.

Michael thought, *Come, brother,* and he and Gabriel moved to stand against the wall of the small room.

"Are you ready to eat, Mr. Strong and Silent?" asked Elizabeth. "I could feed you, you know."

"Did Jonathan pack my pajama bottoms or sweats?" he asked, eyeing her comfortable clothes with envy.

She looked in his bag and pulled out his black pajama bottoms. "These?"

"Yes. Wonderful! I will continue to wear the gown, but I am going to wear those under it." She handed him the pants and turned her back.

"Is this good enough, or do you want me to leave the room?" she asked shyly, singing "Amazing Grace" in her mind to block her thoughts from him.

Xander grinned, recognizing her ploy. "I am finished, though I enjoyed your rendition of 'Amazing Grace.' You could sing the second verse."

Elizabeth blushed and changed the subject. "Are you ready to eat now?"

"Can you raise the back of the bed so that I am sitting up? I would not want to spill food on my lovely gown." His eyes twinkled as he looked at her.

She was still for a long moment, caught in his gaze. *I know you can hear this, but I don't care. When I thought that you might leave me, I could not bear it. I knew I loved you, but I did not know how much until today.*

Xander answered her with a quote from the book of Ruth. *'For where you go, I will go, and where you lodge, I will lodge. Your people shall be my people, and your God my God. Where you die, I will die, and there I will be buried. Thus may the Lord do to me, and worse, if anything but death parts you and me.'*

Unable to speak, she leaned over and kissed him. Then she stood back up, pushed the bed control buttons until he was sitting up satisfactorily, and opened the cartons of Chinese food. She situated the table over his lap and handed him his chopsticks and a napkin. Xander pulled her down with his free hand for another kiss, and then he began to eat. Elizabeth picked up her container and stood beside him, holding it carefully, trying not to drop any food.

"There is a problem," Xander said, tilting his head to look at her.

"Really?" she asked, concerned, putting her container on the table. "What do you need? Do you have enough napkins? Do you want something else to drink?"

"None of those things are the problem. I do not need any*thing*," he said calmly.

She drew her brows together, confused.

"You are much too far away." He moved over as much as he could and patted the small area beside him.

"You will actually let me sit on the bed with you?" Elizabeth asked, shocked. "You never let me get that close."

"Tonight I will. I think I will be able to control myself in a crowded, busy hospital while I am wearing this ridiculous gown. This is not exactly the most romantic moment of our lives. Besides, I am sick," he frowned slightly, pouting a little. "I need a little more attention than I normally do. However, if you do not wish to…" Xander managed to look disappointed. He hung his head, but looked up at her face through his lashes, judging the effect of his words.

You are doing this for her – not for you, thought Gabriel, surprised.

Yes, she needs the reassurance that I am well, answered Xander.

Well, do not get too healthy. Watch yourself, admonished Michael.

You know that I would never disrespect or compromise Elizabeth in any way, thought Xander, a little sharply.

Elizabeth immediately lowered the guardrail and hopped up beside him. She leaned into him happily and kissed his cheek. Her trust in him was implicit.

"Thank you for letting me do this. Do you have enough room?" she asked.

"Do not worry so, Elizabeth. Being in a small space with you is certainly not a hardship," he answered, kissing her forehead. "We should eat so that we can rid ourselves of this bed table. This is like a sleepover. I have never been to one, so you will have to tell me what we should do."

"Oh!" she giggled. "I don't have any nail polish with me, but we could do each other's hair and watch chick flicks. I suppose talking about boys is out. I know! We can play games, like Truth or Dare and Hangman. I saw some paper in the drawer over there."

"How about just watching the movies and going to sleep early? I do want a promise from you before I go to sleep, though," Xander said, with just the hint of a smile.

"Really? What do I have to promise? Not to steal your virtue?" she asked.

"I am more concerned about waking up with red nails and a new hairstyle," he replied in jest.

Elizabeth laughed at him. "I am making no promises of the sort. Besides, what if I fall asleep first? What are you promising?"

"I promise not to tease you or take pictures with my phone if you snore or drool in your sleep," Xander said, very seriously.

"Well, since I don't do either of those things, I have nothing to worry about," she huffed.

"I would love you even if you did," he whispered, immediately redeeming himself in the lady's eyes.

~~oo~~

The next morning, Xander awakened before Elizabeth and lay still, careful not to rouse her. She had turned toward him in the night and slept with her shoulder under his arm and her arm thrown across his torso. Her head was on his chest, and her hair streamed over his forearm. He had embraced her in his sleep and held her close. It was as natural as breathing in and out.

For the first time in many months, he was "seeing" her dreams and was very pleased that he was featured prominently in them. Her dream ended, and her eyelids fluttered open slowly. Her eyes widened as she saw his face close to hers, smiling in contentment. Xander leaned over to kiss her.

"Did you sleep well?" she asked.

"Very well," he answered. "I hope to wake up like this every day in the not-so-distant future."

She smiled and kissed his nose. "If my dad finds out, you'll *have* to marry me, you know, even though nothing happened," she teased.

"I would not mind being a Boaz to your Ruth," Xander replied seriously. "I would happily be your kinsman redeemer. 'And now my daughter, do not fear. I will do for you whatever you ask, for all my people in the city know that you are a woman of excellence,'" he said, quoting Ruth 3:11.

Elizabeth smiled, and then changed the subject abruptly. "Did the nurse wake you up, checking on you in the night?"

"She came in three or four times, but she did not disturb me."

"She saw me?" Elizabeth asked, a little alarmed.

"She did, but she was unconcerned. My injuries are minor compared to most of the people here. You were not hindering my recovery." He smiled widely at her. "In fact, I think you may have speeded the process. I feel very well this morning."

She sat up and stretched. "You are altogether too satisfied with yourself, Mr. Xander. Were you watching my dreams?"

"I saw one just before you awoke. It was lovely." He pulled her down for another kiss.

"Fortunately, I don't remember it. I'm sure that I would be embarrassed judging by the look on your face. I'm guessing that you played a starring role in it."

"I admit that I was in it, but there was nothing about it that should make you uncomfortable, love." He stroked her hair.

"I think I'd better get up and get ready. They will be here with breakfast soon. I ordered for both of us last night. Oatmeal. Yummy!" She grimaced as she climbed out of the bed, grabbed her overnight bag, and headed for the bathroom.

He watched her close the bathroom door, contemplating what she had said earlier. "It would be no sacrifice to marry you, Elizabeth. I only hope that you will still want me after you know everything," he whispered.

Michael and Gabriel stood at the corners of the room, as silent and inscrutable as sphinxes.

~~oo~~

Xander recovered rapidly and acted true to form by insisting on taking part in the Monday night rally. Gabriel plastered himself to Xander's side, concerned that his charge was taking on too much without giving himself time to heal properly. Xander still felt a little lightheaded from time to time, but he hid it well by moving more carefully and slowly than was usual for him. Within a few days' time, he was fully recovered.

The week turned out to be a stellar one; more than five thousand souls were added to the kingdom, and many more decisions about life changes were made. The spiritual fire that had blazed through Atlanta at the beginning of the summer was still burning across the country, purifying the body of Christ and building the church.

Before anyone could believe it, the final weeks in San Diego and the Dallas-Fort Worth area were over. Fifty thousand known salvations were recorded, and many more were made privately or as a direct result of the ministry of

SoulFire in those areas. A true revival was sweeping the nation, reawakening dead churches and electrifying others. Jonathan was already planning weekend fall retreats in Charlotte and Jacksonville, as well as an international tour for the summer of 2009, and Elizabeth and Xander had agreed to continue in ministry with him as a part of the SoulFire team. Mark Goodman had also signed on as the publicist for SoulFire, though he planned to continue accepting freelance work as a reporter.

As they were traveling home from the Dallas-Fort Worth rallies with Michael and Gabriel flying overhead, Lynne called Elizabeth with the news that Jane was in labor, and that she and Chance were at the hospital in Spartanburg. Because they were only a few hours away, Xander and Elizabeth decided to drive straight to the hospital, hoping to get there before the baby was born. Elizabeth called Charlotte, who was riding with Jonathan, to tell her of their change in plans.

They arrived just in time to join the rest of the family in welcoming eight pound Matthew Chance Bingley. David and Lynne, as well as Chance's family, had already seen Jane and Matthew, so after hugging her parents fiercely, Elizabeth, accompanied by Xander, went to meet her nephew. His guardian, Duarte, stood by Hector and Alexis, and they all saluted Xander, Michael, and Gabriel as they entered Jane's room.

Xander looked at the happy little family and wondered if a son was in his future. He had decided that he would tell Elizabeth everything in the coming week, and if she accepted his confession and forgave him, he would propose to her. He had already planned everything out, and he knew the perfect place to take her. In a few days, he would be freed of his secret, and he would know his fate. The guardian warrior bowed his head and prayed, placing the entire situation in his Father's hands.

Chapter 20

"Therefore, laying aside falsehood, speak truth, each one of you, with his neighbor, for we are members of one another. Be angry, and yet do not sin; do not let the sun go down on your anger, and do not give the devil an opportunity."
Ephesians 4:25-27

Xander knew that Elizabeth would need several days to visit with her family and her new nephew, as well as to rest from the frantic pace of the past two months. With that in mind, he had asked her if they could spend the following Saturday together, and she agreed happily.

He spent the entire week arranging the perfect setting in which to reveal his true self to her and ask her to marry him. Though he made time to see Elizabeth every day, the majority of his time was spent with Gabriel in the majestic Blue Ridge Mountains, building a beautiful swinging rope foot bridge across a narrow gorge with a stream running through it. He and Gabriel had constructed the bridge on land owned by a wealthy supporter of SoulFire Ministries, Howard Mills. He had offered the use of his mountain retreat at any time to the SoulFire team members, and Xander had contacted him privately to obtain his permission to build the structure. The site was on an ATV trail which connected to both the house and the main highway as well as running back through the woods in a maze; Mr. Mills's children and grandchildren rode the trails regularly.

The bridge was a short hike from the main house, yet it was secluded enough to be completely hidden from prying eyes. As he worked, Xander imagined himself telling her that he was an angel, rehearsing the words he would use, and finally flying from the bridge in solid angelic form. He hoped that she would be comfortable enough with him after the initial shock that she would allow him to carry her while he flew. Xander wanted her to embrace the idea of what he was so completely that she would allow him to assume either form around her without any concern of frightening her.

The bridge itself was about thirty yards long and five feet wide with thick, latticed rope handrails. It was quite sturdy and safe, and the wood of the walkway itself was laid very closely so that there were no spaces in between the boards. Xander had arranged for all the building materials to be delivered to the retreat on Monday. The ATV trail was professionally graded, graveled, and wide enough for two four-wheelers side-by-side, so the deliveries had been made directly to the building site. Normally, the entrance to the main highway was blocked with a locked gate, but the gate had stood open all week to allow the delivery trucks access to the area. With no one around to see them, it had been a simple matter for the angels to fly the heavy rope and cut-to-order wood back and forth across the one hundred fifty foot drop.

Xander had offered to dismantle the bridge during the following week if Mr. Mills wished it; however, the gentleman had seen the beautifully situated edifice on Friday after it was completed and had admired it so much that he had decided only to block access to it with locking metal gates. He wanted to use the bridge himself in the fall, as it would afford the best view of the colorful leaves throughout the valley.

The day he had both anticipated and dreaded dawned with a glorious sunrise, clear and cloudless. Though Xander had slept very little, he nearly sprang from the bed, eager to be with Elizabeth in full honesty. She had accepted everything else about him so well that he had little doubt that she would assimilate this last revelation about him with her usual aplomb.

Gabriel stood beside Xander as he read his morning devotions and prayed, asking his Father to guide his words and open Elizabeth's heart.

This is it, thought Xander as he dressed after his shower. He dressed for hiking – jeans, sneakers, a T shirt, and a shirt with the sleeves rolled up to his elbows. Xander walked back to his bedroom and took a small box from his night table. He opened it and looked lovingly at the ring he had designed for her himself. It was as special and unique as his Elizabeth, and he badly wanted to see it on her finger. The band was platinum, made of three delicate vines woven together and sprinkled with small diamonds. Nestled in the tendrils was an oval, brilliant-cut, perfect one-carat diamond. Xander knew that Elizabeth would prefer a stone that was not ostentatious, and he had chosen what he thought she would like. He bought the highest quality, but it was not large enough to be showy. *It is like her – precious and beautiful, rare, of great value, and with hidden depths.* Xander wrapped the ring in tissue paper and put it in his shirt pocket, buttoning the pocket so that he would not lose it.

Gabriel smiled beatifically, *It is indeed an important day for you, my brother. All things are ready.*

Xander was blissful. *Gabriel, I can hardly wait to tell her. There will be nothing standing between us any longer. I will not have to hide anything from her again.*

She will know about all of us after she hears what you have to say. She is intelligent, and she will realize that you are not the only angel she has met. Remember that it may take her some time to absorb so much information, Xander. Do not overwhelm her. Go slowly, if you are able. Gabriel's voice was gentle.

Knowing her mind will be helpful. I will be careful. Thank you, my brother. Xander felt the tinge of concern in Gabriel's mind and knew that Gabriel wished only the best for him and Elizabeth. He was impatient to have the ordeal behind them, but he was not offended by Gabriel's words of caution.

As he drove to Elizabeth's house, Xander ate a breakfast bar and played her first CD of piano music. *How is it possible that she has known me only seven months? I have loved her for so many years. Dear Lord, please let this go right today. Please help her to understand.*

The door to her house opened as he parked the Escalade, and she stood in the doorway, smiling at him with Michael standing behind her. Xander had told her that they would be hiking, so she also had on jeans with a tank top, open shirt, and sneakers. Her mother had French-braided her dark hair, and it hung in a thick plait down her back.

He quickly left the SUV, followed by Gabriel, and went to her, surprising her by drawing her to himself and kissing her soundly. She put her arms around his neck, enjoying his method of greeting her. When he broke the kiss, he held her face between his hands.

Smiling mischievously, she asked, "Have you missed me?"

"Yes, definitely." His blue eyes were serious, and he stroked her cheeks with his thumbs.

"You have seen me every day, Xander, but I understand what you mean. I've missed you, too. It was so different from this summer when I saw you all the time."

"I miss you all the time you are not with me." He dropped his hands to hers and held them. Looking past her into the kitchen, he asked, "Where are your parents?"

"They've already left for Spartanburg. Mom is helping Janna by cleaning her house and doing her laundry while Janna takes care of Matthew. Dad and Chance are going to get groceries and cook Dad's famous potato soup. The Bingleys are joining them later. They said we could come for supper if we wanted to," said Elizabeth.

"We probably will not be back in time. It will take us several hours to drive each way. Have you eaten breakfast?" he asked.

"Yes, I had cereal, so I'm good until lunch. You?" She tilted her head up at him.

"I had a breakfast bar on the way over. If you are ready, we should leave now. It will take about three hours to get there."

Elizabeth sensed his excitement and anxiety, so she released his hands and went to the living room, returning with her purse and two bottles of water she had grabbed from the pantry. She threw one of the bottles to him, and they headed out the door, pausing for her to lock it after them.

Michael and Gabriel flew overhead while Xander and Elizabeth chatted easily, catching up on everything they had missed during the past week. Elizabeth regaled Xander with all of little Matthew's activities and the joys of being an aunt. She had spent most of the week at Janna's, holding the baby at every opportunity and talking to her sister. Xander knew that he had been a frequent topic of conversation between the sisters, and that Elizabeth's entire family approved of their relationship. Every time he had been there, he had been treated as one of the family.

Within two hours they were driving the winding roads of the Blue Ridge Mountains, and the scenery was beautiful. She knew that he had spent much of his time during the past week working on a project of some sort, and she wondered if his activities had anything to do with their plans for the day. *He will tell me when he is ready and not before,* she thought.

He chuckled. "You are right, love. Some things should not be rushed, and many surprises are improved by the anticipation of them. I hope you will like what I have in mind for today." Her hand rested in his on the console, and he squeezed it with gentle pressure.

"But I want to know now!" she said, faking a pout.

"We will be there very soon," he replied, kissing her knuckles. *I hope there will be a ring on that finger on the ride back.*

One thing at a time, brother, thought Michael. Like Gabriel, he knew that once Elizabeth was aware of Xander's true nature, she would realize that his brothers were angels as well. It was unsettling.

Xander saw the turn off to the left and slowed to make the turn onto the narrow road. He smiled as he saw Elizabeth lean forward, looking around curiously. They emerged through the trees to see the main lodge; it was rustic, fitting perfectly into its surroundings. A porch wrapped around the front and one side of the house.

"Here we are," said Xander, leaning over to kiss her quickly before he got out and opened her door.

"It's wonderful, Xander. Is this the surprise?" she asked, her brown eyes shining, envisioning a day of hiking in the mountains.

"This is part of it. Come with me." He reached for her hand and led her to the front door, unlocking it and drawing her inside. Michael and Gabriel walked behind them.

"Are you hungry?" he asked.

"I could eat something, especially if we're going to be out hiking after this," she answered.

"We will probably be out for a few hours. I have lunch ready. You can just sit and let me serve you," he replied, smiling.

"I'll be right back," she said, walking down the hallway, opening doors until she found a bathroom. Michael followed her, and Gabriel remained with Xander.

Xander went into the kitchen and got out the chicken salad he had bought and stored in the refrigerator the day before. He put plates, glasses, napkins, and utensils on the bar along with the salad, fruit, croissants, and tea. Elizabeth came back and sat on a stool as he filled their glasses with ice and poured the tea.

"Wow! I'm impressed. A girl could get used to being pampered like this. Watch out, Xander, or you will spoil me," she said, smiling at him.

"Elizabeth, I would love to have the privilege of spoiling you for the rest of your life. I have never made any secret of that." He kissed her cheek and took her hand, saying grace before they ate.

When they were finished, he bagged the trash to take with them on the trip home and washed the few dishes, allowing her to dry them and replace them in the cabinets. Then he reached for her hand again and led her out the back door and down the ATV trail. The weather was perfect, in the 70's, and the day seemed to be made for outdoor activities. Elizabeth hummed happily as they walked hand-in-hand.

Michael and Gabriel flew above them, trying unsuccessfully to scan the area for enemies. Michael grumbled, *He could not have chosen a worse place to defend if he had tried. An entire phalanx could be hiding in those trees.*

He was thinking of the beauty and romance of the area – not of having a tactical advantage in a battle, replied Gabriel.

The trail ended in a clearing with a spectacular view of the bridge. Elizabeth gasped audibly when she saw it, and she turned to Xander.

"This is such an amazing place! How did you find it?" she asked.

"Do you remember Howard Mills?" She nodded. "This is his land and his lodge. He offered it to any of the SoulFire team who wanted to use it, and I took him up on his offer. Do you like the bridge?" Xander searched her face for her approval.

"I love it. Can we walk over it? Is it safe?" she queried.

"Yes, it is safe. I examined it thoroughly this past week. Does the height frighten you?"

They walked toward the bridge as she answered with a laugh. "No, I have no fear of high places. Besides, I know that there is no danger if you approve of it. You are always overly cautious when I am concerned."

He led her by her hand to the bridge's entrance, and they began to walk slowly to the center, adjusting to the sense of the slightly swaying movement. Gabriel and Michael hovered above them.

Elizabeth let go of his hand to grasp the thick rope handrails and steady herself, looking out at the mountains, and then down the steep drop to the water flowing over the rocks below her.

"Elizabeth," Xander said from behind her, in a voice just above a whisper. She turned to face him, looking up into his steady gaze.

He put his hands over hers on the rails and continued to speak, his voice a low melody. "I love you with all of my heart, body, and soul. Only God could love you more than I do. This is a beautiful place, but it can never be as beautiful to me as you are. The more I know you, the more I love you, and you are beyond precious to me. Every time I kiss you, it is just as if it were the first time. I feel that now familiar twist inside, and I want to make you my own. I brought you here to ask you something, Elizabeth, but before I do, there is something you must know – "

As the words left his mouth Xander felt an odd sensation. He looked quickly behind him, and his heart sank as he watched the ropes which held the bridge in place begin to disintegrate, and then they disappeared completely. Michael and Gabriel saw the bridge start to waver and fall in the same instant. In desperation, Xander reached with one hand for Elizabeth as he grabbed the rope handrail with his other. However, she had already fallen beyond his reach, so he let go and fell with her. Gabriel and Michael remained with Xander and Elizabeth, but they could do nothing to stop Elizabeth from plummeting to the rocks in the stream at the bottom of the gorge. At that moment, a death angel tentatively approached, awaiting Xander's decision.

Elizabeth screamed as she fell, clutching at the air, swimming in nothing. Her screams echoed back from the sheer rock faces on either side of them and seemed to go on forever. The options flew through Xander's mind with fearsome speed, and he knew with deadly certainly that he had but one choice. Gabriel could not catch her and remain invisible without a plausible explanation, and neither could Michael reveal himself under these conditions.

Xander had realized that Gregory was somehow responsible for their predicament, but he did the only thing he could do, knowing all the while that he was doing exactly what Gregory had hoped that he would do. Gregory would win either way – whether Elizabeth died or Xander revealed himself, Gregory still would have achieved his goal. He would separate them and destroy their ministry together.

Xander morphed into visible angelic form and flew straight down, wings streamlined behind him, flying beneath Elizabeth. He caught her in his arms just before she reached the sharp rocks, hugged her to himself, and stretched his wings wide, using his powerful musculature to carry both of them back up to the clearing. He held her close and slowed a little, hoping that it would not be the last time she would allow his touch. As soon as he touched the ground he felt her fighting against him, and he released her, gently placing her on her feet.

Gabriel and Michael checked the fallen bridge and found that at least five feet of rope had simply disappeared.

Gregory must have been hiding close by, employing his dark arts, thought Michael.

Gabriel nodded his agreement.

The two of them, still invisible, flew to stand on either side of Xander.

She backed away from Xander, her eyes wide with fright as she looked at him gleaming in his golden armor and glowing with the light of God. He was so beautiful that it was surreal; she did not trust her eyes. He folded his wings, let his hands drop to his sides, and waited for her to calm. Xander could hear her mind reeling, going through the possibilities and remembering the things he had said. *He is my Xander, and yet he is not.* His chest clenched in pain as he heard her. *He is no different from Richard. He has lied to me, over and over. Even when he was telling the truth, he was lying to me.*

Xander reached out to touch her, and she jerked away as if he were a poisonous snake.

"Don't touch me. Don't you dare touch me! What are you?" she demanded as her fright turned to anger.

His voice was gentle and persuasive. "I am an angel. You have said it many times, and I have said it as well."

"You knew that I did not believe that in a literal sense. You let me babble on and on, and told yourself that you were telling me the truth, all the while knowing that you were deceiving me." The tears flowed down her cheeks and her chin quivered. Her lovely face contorted in agony.

He stepped toward her. "Elizabeth, I was going to tell you. I was saying the words when we fell. I had to take this form to save your life. Please do not back away from me."

She stood still, considering his words.

The roar of an engine broke the silence, and Cassandra drove from the trees in a Jeep Liberty. She was in human form, as was Gregory who sat in the front passenger seat. They stopped behind Elizabeth, and Gregory hopped out, going around and standing beside her. Cassandra remained in the Jeep with the motor running.

Michael bristled, placing his hand over his sword as Gabriel fixed Gregory with an unblinking stare.

"He still hasn't told you all of it, Elizabeth. He still holds back the full truth from you." Gregory sneered at Xander and ignored the archangels.

Elizabeth did not trust Gregory, but in that moment, she knew he spoke the truth. Her expression hardened as she faced Xander.

"What does he mean, Xander? What else is there?" she demanded.

Xander was quiet, knowing that anything he said would make the situation worse. His mouth was set in a tight line as he waited for Gregory to speak the words that would ruin his life.

"He is your guardian angel, Elizabeth. He was present at your conception, and has watched you all of your life. Xander has known all of your most private moments since you were born. Isn't that true, *Xander*?" asked Gregory, looking at him in challenge.

Elizabeth's eyes widened in shock as she thought of Gregory's words. She knew by Xander's silence that what Gregory said was true because he did not deny it. "How could you do that, Xander? How could you watch me bathe, and see me with Richard, and know everything about me, but not tell me? That isn't love. I am a fool." She covered her face and wept into her hands.

"And what of you, Gregory? Will you tell her what you are?" spat Xander.

"You have already told her that Cassandra and I are evil and beyond redemption. You have poisoned her mind against me. What else is there I can say? She will have to choose whom she can trust, Xander. I have never lied to her," said Gregory with confidence. He put his arm around Elizabeth and drew her to his chest, rubbing her back.

"Do not touch her, halfling," Xander said in a menacing voice.

Elizabeth looked back at him, eyes blazing. "You have no right to decide who can touch me. We are finished. I can't trust you anymore."

"Elizabeth, let me explain. Please. You would understand if you would let me talk to you," he pleaded with her, imploring her with his eyes.

She turned to face him. "You probably could talk me into believing anything you wanted me to believe, Xander – if that is even your real name. I don't want to talk to you. Don't call me, and don't come to my house. If I ever want to talk to you again, I'll call you, but don't hold your breath." She laughed a little hysterically, "If you even have to breathe." She threw her hands up in the air and lowered her head in a gesture of finality. "I don't want to love you or anyone else. I wish you had let me die. Stay away from me."

Xander knew that she meant it, and he felt a knife twist in his heart. He bore the full, crushing weight of her rejection.

"At least let me take you home, Elizabeth. Or you can take my car if you want." *Just please do not go with Gregory.*

She laughed bitterly. "Obviously, you don't need a car. You can just fly wherever you want to go, can't you?"

Gregory touched her arm. "El, let Cassandra and me take you home." His voice was friendly, non-threatening.

"Gregory, what are you doing here anyway? How did you know we would be here?" asked Xander desperately, trying to get Elizabeth to think rationally.

Elizabeth looked at Gregory expectantly.

"I saw the birth announcement for her nephew in last week's paper, and I texted El to congratulate her. We chatted, and I asked her if I could see her today. She replied that she was going to be with you. I had a good idea that you would ask her to marry you today, and I wanted to be certain that she knew what you were before she accepted you, so I watched you this week, Xander. I followed you up here several times, and I knew that you would bring her here today. Cassandra and I have been waiting for you all morning. El has been my friend for a long time, and I wanted to protect her." His eyes were sincere; he was a practiced liar.

I did not mention the texts because there was nothing unusual or suspicious in them. He sends her messages from time to time, and she always answers him, thought Michael. *I am sorry.*

Gregory set up everything ahead of time. He was expecting my question, and he was prepared for it. Xander's thoughts were chagrined. He had walked right into another trap set by Gregory.

No guards with him. He is being careful not to provoke a fight. He has put much thought into this, added Gabriel.

"Do you believe me, El? Will you let us take you home now?" Gregory asked, looking into her eyes.

She nodded and turned to walk to the Jeep with him.

Xander grabbed her arm. "Please, Elizabeth. Do not go with him. Let me call you a taxi, or take my car. You are not safe with them." He did not tell her what Gregory and Cassandra really were because he was unsure how much more she could stand to know at that moment, and, furthermore, he doubted that she would believe him under the circumstances.

Michael spoke into her mind, *Do not go with them.*

"You, get your hand off of my arm, and, you, whoever you are, stay out of my head," she said with quiet determination, jerking her arm away from his touch.

"Elizabeth, listen to God. Pray about this. What is He telling your heart?" Xander tried to reach her one last time.

"God? I don't know what I believe anymore, and I don't want to pray. Leave me alone." Her voice was deadly calm, devoid of emotion, and her words dropped like stones.

She walked to the Jeep with Gregory and climbed into the backseat as he got into the front. Cassandra began to drive the trail toward the highway, and none of them looked back.

Xander took invisible form, and he, Michael, and Gabriel flew above the speeding vehicle. There was nothing they could do as long as Elizabeth went with them willingly, and Gregory knew it. Xander could only pray that she would ask for help when she needed it.

Chapter 21

All day long they distort my words; all their thoughts are against me for evil. They attack, they lurk, they watch my steps, as they have waited to take my life. Thou hast taken account of my wanderings; put my tears in Thy bottle; are they not in Thy book? For Thou hast delivered my soul from death, indeed my feet from stumbling, so that I may walk before God in the light of the living."
Psalm 56:5,6,8,13

August 2008

Xander dropped from flying above the Jeep Liberty and lay in abject misery on the top of the vehicle as it turned onto the highway, pulling his wings closely against his body and winding his fingers through the metal attachments on the roof. He was as near as he could get to Elizabeth, who was lying in the backseat sobbing quietly. Each of her tears stabbed his heart and her every gasp for breath pierced his soul. He heard her thoughts, crying for her lost love, weeping at his betrayal, and the pain of it was nearly more than he could bear. The only thing that kept him sane was the knowledge that he had to be ready to defend her, for he was certain that she would need him soon, though she would not want him. *She will never want me again.*

In that moment, he hated what he was. He envied the people coming toward them in the other lane of traffic; he wanted to be like them – normal, mortal, and human with no trace of supernatural abilities. *What good is it to have these powers if Elizabeth does not love me anymore? My spirit is ripped in two. I have nothing.* With that thought, he decided that he would protect her even if she did not want it, whether or not she asked for it. If he could not be with her, he could at least make certain that she was safe.

Michael spoke to Xander, not unkindly. *You cannot intervene if she does not ask for help, Xander. You must be Xander, the Chief of the Guardians. You must obey the regulations which our Creator has set for us. We act within His limitations on our power.*

Why should I adhere to the rules when Gregory never has? Xander snapped.

Gabriel's reply was gentle. *Because you are not like Gregory, and you must not become like him. He has won this skirmish, but we will win both the battle and the war. Do not let him destroy you. Do not give him what he desires. We will help you, our brother and friend. We will be with Elizabeth and you.*

Xander could hold it in no longer. His pain burst from his mind. *There is no Elizabeth and me. She does not love me anymore! She no longer wants me!* His screams tore through the heavens and resounded through the halls. The raw agony of his cry was felt by every angel, and they trembled for their brother, covering their faces with their wings.

A comforting Voice carried on the breeze and whispered through the trees. *Xander, My son, Elizabeth cries because she loves you. She has not stopped loving you, but she has lost her way at this time. She will soon require your strength and courage for the battle ahead. You must not give in to despair. She has also turned from Me, but I know her. She is My child, as surely as you are. She will desire the relationships with both you and Me again. You must keep her safe until the scales of Gregory's deceit fall from her eyes. I want you to go with her for Me. Will you do that, Xander? Will you go for Me?*

Xander lifted his tear-stained face at the sound of the Voice that he knew so well. *My Abba, Father. Here am I. Send me, Lord.*

Will you obey Me? Can I trust you to follow My commands? The question was quiet and solemn.

Please forgive me, my Adonai. You are so good to me, even when I am rebellious. I love you, Lord. I will obey You, even unto death. Xander's voice was constrained and apologetic.

I am pleased, My child. I love you more than you can comprehend, and I will always love you. Nothing shall ever separate you from My love. Do not give up hope. I have not stopped working in your life nor in Elizabeth's. I have counted your tears and saved them in My bottle. I have heard your cries. You are so precious to Me. The Voice wrapped Xander in comfort like a blanket. It soothed and refreshed him; the Voice gave him strength and direction.

Let it be according to Your will. Xander rejoined his brothers, flying just above the Jeep. He would no longer wallow in self-pity and grief, and he set his face forward with a steely glint in his eyes.

I must go back for the car, thought Xander.

What? Why do you want the car? asked Michael, unwilling to leave Xander alone.

We do not know where Gregory is taking her. If she allows us to help her, she will need a way of escape when the battle is over. We will not have time to call any of her family to come, and I doubt that she will agree to go with me. We have not come very far yet. I can fly back, retrieve the car, and rejoin you within half an hour, Xander answered.

I will go, offered Gabriel. *You want to stay with Elizabeth.*

Can you drive? asked Xander skeptically.

I have never done so before, but I have watched you many times, answered Gabriel.

I appreciate your willingness, Gabriel, but this is not a good time to learn the skill. I will be back very soon. Anyway, I think she will feel better if she sees me in human form. Michael, your telepathy is not limited by distance. You must stay in contact with me in case he turns off this road. I think he is taking her to his house in Spartanburg, but I cannot be certain of that.

Michael thought, *Elizabeth promised you that she would not go there alone with him.*

She probably will not worry about honoring a promise to me, and, at any rate, they are not alone. Cassandra is with them. He will probably have reinforcements there. You may want to summon the Host.

Michael nodded his agreement, and Xander left them, flying so fast that he was a streak of light, headed back toward the lodge.

~~oo~~

Xander was back behind them within twenty-five minutes. He could tell by Elizabeth's hazy thoughts that she had cried herself to sleep. *Good. She will not see me behind them, and she will not be afraid of Cassandra's excessive speed.* Even so, her dreams were disturbed.

Cassandra must have spotted Xander in her rearview mirror, because the Jeep, already traveling over the speed limit, suddenly shot ahead, traveling much too fast for the winding mountain roads. Xander was apprehensive until he saw Gabriel and Michael dip to fly on either side of the vehicle, placing their hands on the doors. They would not allow it to crash or drive off the road as long as Elizabeth was in it. He matched their speed, knowing that he could fly from his car if he had to do so. Cassandra was practically airborne, passing unsafely, and obviously trying to lose him. *She should know that I will never allow that to happen. Is she trying to frighten us away? Is her message that we should back away or they will kill Elizabeth? Surely Cassandra and Gregory know that Gabriel, Michael, and I would never abandon her.*

Just as Xander had thought, they took the I-26 exit, headed toward Spartanburg. He was relieved to be off the smaller roads and on a safer highway. Cassandra still drove like the demon she was, but they were not as likely to endanger Elizabeth or anyone else on the interstate.

Elizabeth awakened as they were pulling into Spartanburg. Xander dropped back in traffic as he heard her come to consciousness. She sat up and looked around, disoriented, and then huddled back into her seat as her memories came crashing back into her mind. A few minutes passed, and she noticed a familiar building.

"Where are we going, Gregory?" she asked in a raspy voice, leaning forward and looking out the window.

He turned and smiled in a platonic way, as if he wished only to be her friend. "We're going to my house so that you can calm down in private. Your sister lives only a few miles from me, and you can call her if you want to."

Elizabeth sat back and thought for a few minutes. Her parents were at Janna's house, and she did not want them to see her for a while. They would know that she had been crying; they would ask questions she was not ready to answer.

"I hoped that you would take me home," she said tremulously.

"We will, Elizabeth. Just come with me for a little while, relax, and we can talk. Cassandra and I will take you home later – anytime you want to go." His voice was smooth and persuasive, and his amber eyes were full of sympathy for her.

His gaze was magnetic, hypnotic. She had forgotten how beautiful Gregory was. *Xander could be wrong about him. Gregory has never hurt me, and he hasn't lied to me. He's my friend. Besides, Cassandra is with us; we won't be alone. I wonder if Xander was just jealous of him.*

"Okay. Fine." Elizabeth leaned her head back on the headrest and closed her eyes. *My head hurts.* She rubbed her temples with her fingers as Gregory watched her in the side mirror.

"Ah! Here we are," Gregory said as Cassandra pulled the Jeep into the open garage. She pushed the remote button and closed the garage door. While it closed, she opened her own car door and stepped out, walking toward the steps that led into the house. Gregory got out and opened Elizabeth's door, reaching for her hand. Together, the three of them went in the side entrance, through a mudroom, and into the kitchen.

Michael followed Elizabeth into the house as Gabriel hovered over Xander's car, parked on the side of the road a few houses down from Gregory's.

Xander got out of his car and walked to Gregory's yard. He leaned against a tree and listened intently to Elizabeth's thoughts. Gabriel alit and stood beside him, ready for any opportunity to enter the house.

Xander listened as Michael spoke to them from inside the house. *Gregory has only two guards with him. He must be trying to avoid my calling in reinforcements. I am sure that he also knows that you two will not enter unless Elizabeth asks for help. Xander, you could enter on technical grounds as you are still considered to be one of her guardians with me, but I think it best that we wait to see what he has planned. I do not wish to push him into escalating this into a full-out attack unless it is necessary. Elizabeth does not need to see Gregory killed before her eyes.*

I do not like this, thought Xander. *However, I will wait.*

He listened to Elizabeth's thoughts, and "saw" through her mind.

"Are you thirsty, El? It's been a long ride," Gregory commented, stopping and taking three glasses out of a kitchen cabinet.

His brawny guards, Keir and Delano, stood against the wall, watching Michael intently. He ignored them, keeping his eyes on Elizabeth and Gregory.

"I guess," she said with disinterest.

"Cassandra, what can I get for you?" asked Gregory.

"A soda would be good," she answered.

"The same for you, El?" Gregory looked toward her.

"Sure."

"Go in the family room and have a seat. I'll bring our drinks," Gregory said.

Michael went with Elizabeth and Cassandra to the den, though he did not like leaving Gregory unattended. He would not call for reinforcements when his charge had not been threatened, but he took his shield from his belt and put his arm through the bindings, holding the straps securely. Elizabeth curled up on the couch and Michael stood behind her, glowering and dominating the room. Delano and Keir followed them into the room and stood at either end of the sofa.

Cassandra turned on the television and sat in an overstuffed chair, making a show of watching a movie.

Gregory soon joined them with their drinks on a tray, handing Cassandra and Elizabeth their glasses and sitting next to Elizabeth on the couch with his soda.

Elizabeth sat up, took several sips, and made a face. "This tastes a little salty."

"Really?" asked Cassandra. "Mine's good."

"Maybe you're not used to that brand of cola, El. Would you like something else?" Gregory was solicitous and concerned for her welfare.

"No, this is fine. Don't go to any bother," Elizabeth replied, taking another drink. She drank about half of it before setting her glass on a coaster on the coffee table. She leaned over on her side and rested her head on the arm of the couch, pulling her knees up to her chest.

After a few minutes had passed, Xander could hear the confusion in her mind. She was not asleep, but it was as if she were drunk. *She said the drink tasted salty. Could he have drugged her? She did not drink it all, so perhaps she will be alert enough to know what is happening to her.*

Michael had also noticed her mental haze. He frowned at Gregory. *I did not see him put anything in her drink; I cannot prove a threat. She is still awake, though she is groggy. So far, she has participated willingly, but if she even thinks a cry for help, we will respond.*

Gregory leaned over her, talking softly. "El, you are so beautiful. You deserve so much more than a life of drudgery, earning pennies when you could be wealthy beyond imagination. I love you, El. I have always loved you. I know that you feel abandoned and alone, but you aren't. I am here for you just like I've always been here for you. You are the only woman I've ever loved. Let me give you everything you want, all that you deserve. I can make you feel good in ways that you have never felt before."

Xander gritted his teeth and clenched his fists. Gregory's face was blurred in her mind. She was hearing his words as if he were far away.

Gabriel put his hand on Xander's arm. *She will call for you, brother. She loves you.*

What if she does not want my help, Gabriel? Will we stand out here while he seduces her? Xander was terse.

Gregory slipped off his shirt quickly, and she looked at him in wonder. *Why did he do that?*

Cassandra and the guards turned to watch, their lust plain on their faces.

Michael thought into her mind, *Elizabeth, wake up. Think about what Gregory is doing.*

She heard the words, but she was befuddled. Nothing made sense. *Who is talking to me?* She felt as if she were floating, and Gregory's perfect face and magnificent body flooded her senses. *Is this a dream?* His voice caressed her, telling her he loved her and wanted her. She felt his hands under her shirt, pulling her arms through it and then lifting her tank top over her head, stroking her body. His hands were at her waist, unzipping her pants as he kissed her mouth and neck. He seemed to be everywhere at once. She was falling through clouds of sensation.

Xander could stand it no longer. He spoke forcefully into her mind. *Elizabeth!* he cried. *Do not do this! I am pleading with you. Please, Elizabeth. Fight him.*

Elizabeth recognized that voice. "Xander?"

In response, Gregory covered her mouth with his, preventing her from speaking again.

Do you want me to help you, Elizabeth? I can if you will call for me. Say that you need me, Elizabeth. Say it. I will come to you. Fight him off. Obey my training commands. Ask for help.

Xander's voice filled her mind, and she turned her face from side to side, breaking the kiss. Gregory had always worn his black hair so that it covered his ears and most of his neck. As he moved his head in an effort to recapture her lips, his hair fell to the side, and Elizabeth saw a tattoo behind his ear. Though she could not see it clearly, it looked like three sixes intertwined. Her mind was not working as sharply as was normal for her, but Xander saw the tattoo in her thoughts, and everything fell into place. He suddenly knew Lucifer's plans for Gregory. He spoke forcefully into her mind. *Elizabeth, get away from him! Defend yourself, and call for me. Let me help you. Please.*

Elizabeth heard Xander and marshaled her energy, reacting in the way he had trained her. With all of her remaining strength, she focused her thoughts and brought her knee up into Gregory's groin at the same time that she pushed him away enough to force the heel of her palm up into his nose. Gregory cried out as blood spurted over her.

He doubled over in pain and rolled off the couch. "You will suffer for that, you slut," he growled with menace, holding his crotch.

At Gregory's threat, Michael drew his sword to defend his charge, but he was immediately attacked by Keir, Delano, and Cassandra, who had morphed into demonic form. Michael wielded his shield, blocking Cassandra on one side while he slashed at the other two guards, moving closer to the wall to protect his back.

Gregory struggled to his feet and loomed over the couch, his crimson eyes scorching her.

"Help me, Xander. Please, help me," Elizabeth said, slurring her words, unable to speak above a whisper. As Gregory drew back his fist, she covered her face with her hands, waiting for the blow.

Xander began to run as the thought formed in her mind, before the words left her mouth. He reached the locked front door, but did not stop to try the door knob. He instead leapt into the air and twisted his body, hitting the door with both feet. It buckled under the impact of his momentum, and Xander sprinted through the splintered hole. Gregory was in the motion of striking Elizabeth when Xander entered the room, vaulted the couch, and body slammed into his enemy, crashing both of them through the coffee table and to the floor.

Gabriel had unsheathed his sword and flown through the walls of the house as Xander ran. He engaged Delano, leaving Michael fighting Keir and Cassandra. Cassandra turned to her left to see if Gabriel was too close to her, and Michael seized the advantage, protecting his side with his shield while slicing her right arm and wing away. She roared in pain, collapsing to the floor and grabbing at her fallen sword with her left hand. Michael spun out of her reach and continued to slash at Keir.

Elizabeth uncovered her face when she heard the two men crash into the table. She was still disoriented and huddled into the corner of the couch, eyes wide with fright, hands clasped around her knees. Gregory was on the floor, and Xander straddled him as he pounded his fists into the demon's face. She whimpered, and Xander looked toward her. *I am frightening her with my anger.*

Xander knew that he could kill Gregory, and he wanted badly to do so, but he could not beat Gregory to death as Elizabeth watched, cowering. She was more important to him than the satisfaction he would derive from ridding the world of Gregory. *I will have another chance to fight the beast that is Gregory, but this is not the right time – not while Elizabeth watches.*

Xander stood over Gregory, his knuckles torn, wearing the fiend's blood, and spoke in a threatening voice, "I will not kill you in front of Elizabeth, Gregory, but do not try anything with her again. I promise you that the next time I have you down, I will not stop until you are dead."

Gregory, his face a battered mess and his eyes blazing red, quickly changed into demonic form and flew through the ceiling, followed by Delano and Keir. The demons were only too happy to flee, escaping Cassandra's fate. She had tried one last time to rise with her sword, and Michael had sliced her left arm from her body. The dark one had dissolved in a cloud of putrid smoke, leaving the present world for everlasting torment.

Elizabeth watched as Gregory disappeared before her eyes. *Is my mind playing tricks on me? Where did he go? And where is Cassandra?* She wrinkled her nose. *What's that awful smell?*

Michael and Gabriel came to stand on either side of Xander while he retrieved her bloody tank top and shirt from the floor and held them out toward her, averting his eyes, trying to give her some measure of privacy. When she saw her top in his hand, she looked down and saw that she was unclothed from the waist up except for her bra. Her humiliation was overwhelming, and she hid her face from him. *He is so disgusted that he cannot look at me. I cannot blame him.*

Hearing her thoughts, Xander knelt in front of her, put her clothes on the couch, and took her hands in his. "Let me help you, Elizabeth. This is not your fault. Gregory drugged you. Remember how the drink tasted salty? I have read of a date rape drug that has a slightly salty taste and causes a person to feel as if she were drunk."

She allowed him to put her hands through the arms of the top and pull it over her head. He then helped her with the shirt she had worn over it and zipped her pants for her. Her mind had not completely cleared, but she was more aware of her surroundings than she had been.

"My car is outside. Will you let me drive you home? I would let you take the car yourself, but you should not drive until you are fully alert. Please, Elizabeth? I promise not to bother you," asked Xander tenderly.

Elizabeth nodded and tried to stand, but nearly fell; Xander caught her and scooped her up in his arms, carrying her from Gregory's house to his car, Michael and Gabriel following. Still holding her, he opened the car door and placed her in the seat, hating to let her go but pulling the seatbelt across her and fastening it firmly.

Xander rounded the car quickly and got in, belting himself in and starting the car. She stared out the window, expressionless. He pushed the button for the CD player, and her piano music filled the car with beauty and peace. They drove the half hour without talking, as he had promised. Michael and Gabriel were quiet as well.

He pulled into her driveway and contemplated trying to talk to her, but one glance at the tears rolling silently down her cheeks told him that she was not ready for any sort of a discussion.

Xander got out, went around the car, and opened her door, leaning down to gaze at her face. "Are you able to walk yet?" he asked in a carefully modulated tone.

"I think I can if you will help me," she replied, looking at the ground, avoiding his eyes.

He reached across her, unbuckled her seatbelt, grabbed her purse from the floor where she had left it, and took her hand to help her. After she stood, he put her arm over his shoulder and half-carried her to the door.

"My key is in my purse," she said softly. "Do you mind getting it for me?"

Xander opened her bag and found the key, and then opened the front door. He helped her get inside the house, closed the door, and stood helplessly, not knowing what to do.

"Do you want to lie on the couch or go to your room?" he asked with concern, still supporting her.

"I want to get out of these bloody clothes so that Mom and Dad don't ask me about anything. Can you help me upstairs? I can probably handle it from there." Elizabeth still had not looked at his face.

Michael and Gabriel followed them as Xander carried her up the stairs. He took her to her room and stood by her while she leaned on her chest of drawers and pulled out pajama bottoms and a T shirt; then he helped her to the bathroom. Michael stood in the room, waiting for her, and Gabriel paused by the door.

"Elizabeth, I will be just outside the door if you need help."

"You wouldn't be seeing anything you haven't seen before, I suppose. You were my guardian angel," she said bitterly, finally meeting his eyes.

"I stopped watching you bathe when you were fourteen, Elizabeth. As soon as your body began to change, I could not invade your privacy any longer. Can we talk about this later?" he asked.

"I appreciate all your help today. I really do – but there isn't anything to talk about. You kept secrets from me, Xander – or is that really your name? I still love you, and I may always love you, but I can't trust you anymore." Her voice was flat.

"Elizabeth, please, let me explain. I will tell you everything. I was going to show you my true form when Gregory destroyed the ropes." His voice was soft and pleading.

"Gregory did something to the ropes? I should have known." She sighed. "I am so blind – so stupid." She paused, and then continued. "Has it occurred to you that you aren't the only one who's hurting? I've lost the only man I have ever loved, my perfect soulmate. I thought that we would always be together – that we were perfect for each other. You were my best friend." She stopped and leaned on the counter, looking at her hands. "I can't do this now. Please go. I'll be fine."

Xander heard the dismissal in her voice, and he turned and left the room, closing the door gently behind him. He leaned on the wall just outside the door, and then slid down to the floor, holding his face with his hands and praying as he listened to the water running for her shower. When he heard the water stop, he stood and listened to her thoughts. She was stuffing her bloody clothing into the trashcan, tying up the trash bag. *I will never wear these clothes again*, she thought. *I can't stand for them to touch me.*

Michael said, *You should go now, Xander. She needs to sleep.*

I will stay with her, answered Gabriel. *You go with Xander, Michael.*

Why? Michael asked.

Because I am the answer to Xander's prayer. Gabriel's voice was firm.

So be it, thought Michael as he and Gabriel exchanged places.

Michael and Xander went down to his car, while Elizabeth went to her room to sleep. She heard Xander's car engine start and looked out the window, watching him as he backed out of the driveway and out of her life. Her chest hurt, and the tears began to flow once more.

Miserable, she went to her bed, crawled under the covers, and sank into a dreamless sleep. After several hours, she opened her eyes to find that night had fallen but her room was glowing strangely.

"Elizabeth."

She turned her head toward the rich voice, and though she was dazzled by his appearance, she was at the same time afraid.

"Fear not." Gabriel spoke softly, smiling at her.

"Gabriel? Is that you?" She sat up, astounded.

He was garbed as an archangel in his flowing white robes, and the glory of the Lord shone around him. His golden hair flowed to his shoulders; he was stunning in his beauty – pure and holy.

"Yes, Elizabeth. I am Xander's brother, Gabriel." He smiled at her kindly.

"Are you *the* Gabriel, the archangel? The same Gabriel who appeared to Mary and Joseph?" Such a thought had not occurred to her before, but now it seemed to make sense.

He laughed. "I am. I deliver messages and make announcements for Jehovah-Elyon, and He has sent me to you this night."

"The Lord Most High sent you to talk to me?" she asked, amazed.

"Yes, Elizabeth. Your very name marks you for God. It can be translated 'I am God's daughter,' 'My God is an oath,' or 'God's promise.' You are very special, Elizabeth. Elohim has chosen you to do great works for Him. Are you willing to be His daughter in truth? The handmaiden and bondservant of the Lord?" Gabriel asked.

"I was angry at my Father today, and I am sorry for that. I am glad that He still wants me to be His daughter." She inclined her head in submission.

"You need to know that Xander was obedient to God, Elizabeth. He did what his Father asked him to do, and he has wanted to reveal the total truth to you for many months. He could not because it might have impacted your ministry this summer. All those thousands of people might not have come to

God had Xander done what he wanted to do and shown himself to you. What if you had reacted as you did today? He could not risk it. Can you honestly say that you would not have been angry had he told you earlier?" Gabriel's voice was gentle, but it demanded truth.

She thought a moment. "No, I cannot say that. I don't know how I would have reacted."

"Can you imagine what a burden this secret has been for him? Xander loves you beyond all reason. He thinks of your welfare constantly. I should know. I have been his guardian since he took human form in obedience to Jehovah's request."

"What request?" Her curiosity was piqued.

"God Almighty asked Xander, the Chief of Guardians to guard you, Elizabeth. Jehovah told Xander, whom you know as Xander Darcy, that it would require a great sacrifice on his part, but Xander wanted to serve his Master, to please Him in all things, so he accepted the assignment. We are not creatures of great emotion, but, in accordance with the Almighty's design, Xander fell in love with you. It changed him forever. He struggled with those feelings until Elohim assured him that it was His Will for him to love you, Elizabeth. In the last earth year, Xander was summoned before the throne. Jehovah asked Xander what he would desire above all things. Xander could have asked for wealth, power – anything. However, he asked to become human so that he could love you without sinning. He was willing to become mortal, to age and die, for you. Our Master was so pleased that He granted Xander a dual nature – fully human yet fully angel, the only one of his kind. God then told Xander that He wanted him to win your love and marry you so that you could serve Him together. Xander knew that God would not force you against your will; that he had to win your love as a human. He still willingly became human, not knowing whether or not you could ever love him. He became Alexander Darcy when he accepted the Son as his savior. The only sins he had ever committed were connected to you, Elizabeth. He was angry and jealous on your behalf. Apart from the love that is God Almighty, I have never seen a love as great as the love Xander has for you. Will his sacrifice be for nothing, Elizabeth? Will you nurse your anger and ruin both your lives? It is possible that instead of Lucifer successfully thwarting God's plans, you may be the instrument that does so."

Her shock at his speech registered on her face. She had no words as she pondered all that Gabriel had said.

Gabriel listened to her mind and waited patiently as she processed the information.

Finally, he broke the silence. "Do you love him?"

"You have read my thoughts, I am sure. You know that I love him with my whole heart. But how can I trust him again?" she asked.

"You need have no fears about Xander's trustworthiness. God has placed tremendous responsibilities on his shoulders. If God trusts him, why should you doubt him?" Gabriel asked.

"I have many questions. Will he be honest with me?"

"He greatly desires to be honest with you. He will answer all of your questions, if you will give him the chance to do so." Gabriel smiled at her, and it was glorious.

"Will you be there?"

"Michael and I are always with you and Xander now. I guard Xander, and Michael guards you. We exchanged places for tonight. Michael can be a bit intimidating. Our Master chose me to talk to you."

"Michael! He is *the* Michael, isn't he? The Captain of the Host?" She was astonished. Elizabeth had studied the Bible all of her life, and she believed every word of it; however, meeting anyone mentioned within its pages was supposed to be an event confined to the afterlife. Her mind reeled.

"Yes, you are correct. I think any further questions you have should be directed to Xander. Will you agree to talk to him?" Gabriel's face held the light of hope.

"Can I refuse?" she asked, raising an eyebrow. *Just how do you tell Gabriel 'no'?*

"The same way you tell Xander 'no.' I am no better or higher than he. You are certainly free to reject him. God never forces His will on anyone." Gabriel's tone was matter-of-fact, though he hoped that he had made Xander's case well enough that she would agree to meet with him.

Elizabeth hesitated only a moment. "I will talk to him tomorrow. I want all of my questions answered, however. Will you tell him that?"

"Xander is too far away for the two of us to communicate telepathically, but Michael is able to hear us as well as communicate with us at any distance. He has been listening to our conversation through my mind, and Xander has been hearing his mind. Xander will call you tomorrow morning."

"Tomorrow is Sunday. We won't be able to talk until after church. Will he come with me as usual?" Elizabeth's lively mind was fascinated by all she had learned.

"Do you wish for him to go to church with you?" asked Gabriel.

For the first time in more than twelve hours, Elizabeth smiled. "Yes. Tell him to come."

Gabriel inclined his head and disappeared.

Elizabeth lay back down and tried to sleep, but her mind was spinning.

"Gabriel? Are you still there?" she whispered.

A disembodied voice came from beside her bed. "Yes, Elizabeth. I am your guardian tonight. Now sleep."

She closed her eyes. *But I have so many questions.*

Just as she was drifting off to sleep, Elizabeth was sure that she heard a deep, soft chuckle and a soothing voice say, "That is no surprise. You will have your answers tomorrow. Sleep now."

The End of SoulFire

Continued in

Legacy: The Guardian Trilogy, Book 3

Available on Amazon in eBook and Print.

ABOUT THE AUTHOR

Robin Helm's books reflect her love of music, as well as her fascination with the paranormal and science fiction.

Published works include The Guardian Trilogy: *Guardian*, *SoulFire*, and *Legacy*), the Yours by Design series: *Accidentally Yours*, *Sincerely Yours*, and *Forever Yours* (Fitzwilliam Darcy switches places in time with his descendant, Will Darcy), and Understanding Elizabeth (Regency romance).

She contributed to *A Very Austen Christmas: Austen Anthologies, Book 1*, an anthology featuring like-minded authors, in 2017, and *A Very Austen Valentine: Austen Anthologies, Book 2* which was released on December 29, 2018.

New releases for 2019 include *More to Love*, a standalone historical sweet romance dealing with body image; *Lawfully Innocent*, a historical U.S. Marshal romance book in the Lawkeepers series; *Maestro*, a historical sweet romance featuring a brilliant musician and his student; and *A Very Austen Romance: Austen Anthologies, Book 3*.

She lives in sunny South Carolina where she teaches piano and adores her one husband, two married daughters, and three grandchildren.

For updates on new releases, follow Robin Helm on her Amazon Author page at https://www.amazon.com/Robin-Helm/e/B005MLFMTG/

SoulFire

Robin Helm recommends books by Wendi Sotis, Laura Hile, and Mandy Helm.

Our latest book -

A Very Austen Valentine: Austen Anthologies, Book 2

Six beloved authors deliver romantic Valentine novellas set in Jane Austen's Regency world. Robin Helm, Laura Hile, Wendi Sotis, and Barbara Cornthwaite, together with Susan Kaye and Mandy Cook, share variations of Pride and Prejudice, Persuasion, and Sense and Sensibility, featuring your favorite characters in sequels, adaptations, and spinoffs of Austen's adored novels.

Experience uplifting romance, laugh-out-loud humor, and poignant regret as these authors deftly tug on your heartstrings this Valentine's Day.

A Very Austen Valentine, the second book in the Austen Anthologies series, features six authors, all friends, who wished to share Austenesque variations, prequels, and sequels with their readers. Working together to produce the first book in the series (*A Very Austen Christmas*) was such an enjoyable experience, and the book was so well received, that we knew we had to do another one. Our four original authors invited two more to join us in the follow-up, and we plan to do at least five books in the series.

Most of our stories feature our own original characters, as well as the favorite characters of Austen. We strive to keep Austen's heroes and heroines within the confines she set for them herself. In other words, we do not have the characters act in ways she would not have written. The good guys remain good guys, and the bad guys remain bad guys. We also believe in happily-ever-afters. We want you to be happy at the end of each story.

All six of us are experienced writers with previously published books. I hope you enjoy this introduction to six authors, some of whom may be new to you. If you loved *Pride and Prejudice*, *Persuasion*, *Sense and Sensibility*, *Emma*, *Northanger Abbey*, or *Mansfield Park*, you will enjoy their books.

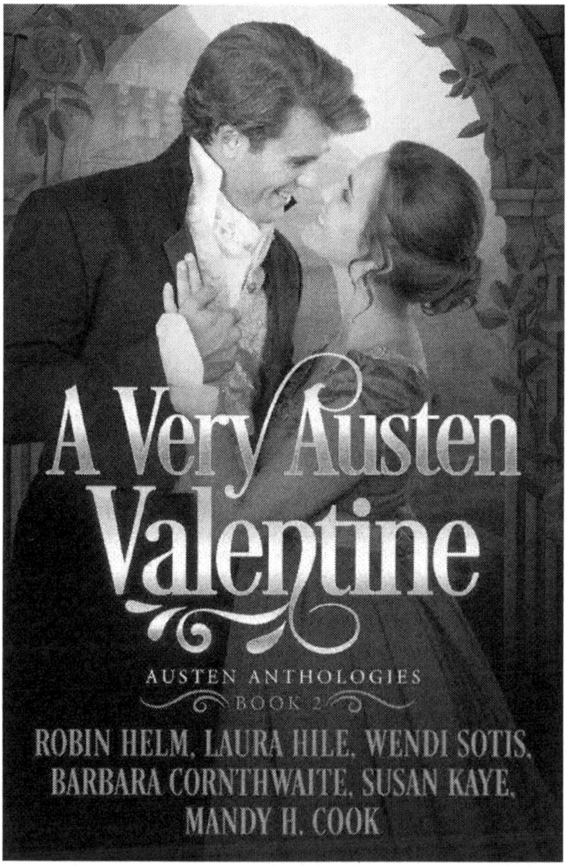
A Very Austen
Valentine
AUSTEN ANTHOLOGIES
BOOK 2
ROBIN HELM, LAURA HILE, WENDI SOTIS,
BARBARA CORNTHWAITE, SUSAN KAYE,
MANDY H. COOK

Made in the USA
Columbia, SC
19 March 2023